BEAUTIFUL
LITTLE
FURIES

LAUREL OSTERKAMP

Black Rose Writing | Texas

The author grants the final approval for this literary material.

First printing

This is a work of fiction. Names, characters, businesses, places, events, and incidents are either the products of the author's imagination or used in a fictitious manner. Any resemblance to actual persons, living or dead, or actual events is purely coincidental.

ISBN: 978-1-68513-339-9
PUBLISHED BY BLACK ROSE WRITING
www.blackrosewriting.com

Printed in the United States of America
Suggested Retail Price (SRP) $24.95

Beautiful Little Furies is printed in Bookman Old Style

*As a planet-friendly publisher, Black Rose Writing does its best to eliminate unnecessary waste to reduce paper usage and energy costs, while never compromising the reading experience. As a result, the final word count vs. page count may not meet common expectations.

To the staff and students, past and present,
at Columbia Heights High School.
It may not seem like it,
but this book is my love letter to you.

BEAUTIFUL
LITTLE
FURIES

Athena to the Furies: This is the life I offer,
It is yours to take.
Do great things.

The Furies to Athena: Your magic is working...I can feel the hate,
The fury slip away...

-Aeschylus, *Eumenides*

"I hope she'll be a fool—that's the best thing a girl can be in this world, a beautiful little fool."
-F. Scott Fitzgerald, *The Great Gatsby*

CHAPTER 1

February 2004

Tonight, I sort through my closet, pulling garments from their hangers. There's a woolen fisherman knit sweater I'd discovered in a thrift store years ago that was too scratchy to wear, a cheap faux-suede blazer from H&M that's always been too small, and an off-white tweed jumper with a barely noticeable coffee stain at its hem. I usually find joy in choosing my first-day-of-school outfit. But now, in the middle of the darkest Minnesota winter ever, I'm tempted to dive underneath the mountain of my past fashion missteps and suffocate, or at least hibernate, until my messy life has fixed itself.

But I don't.

I examine the contents of my tiny closet, recently made more vacuous since Vance moved out while I was still in the hospital. Looking through the options, I'm not inspired by any combination of my pullover sweaters, corduroy skirts, or low-ride khakis. Also, sorting is difficult because I have to be careful. Moving my head too quickly from side to side makes me dizzy.

I pivot carefully and see Baby Girl lounging on the queen bed that Vance and I used to share. She's doing that cute cat thing of licking her paw and then rubbing it behind her ear and along her cheek. I sit beside her and gently place my forehead on the mattress, letting it rest against the soft warmth of her luminous-orange belly.

"Oh, Baby Girl, I don't know if I'm ready for tomorrow." She barely responds to my murmuring. I'm pretty sure that, at best, Baby Girl only pretends to listen to me. Still, talking to her must be a step up from talking to myself. "The crash did a number on me. What if I can't handle going back?"

Baby Girl combines a yawn and a meow, probably saying, "Lady, we all have problems. Pipe down and let me nap."

I can take a hint. I don't lament my late-December-through-mid-January "break" when I was recovering from this miserable head injury, compounded by the disappearing act of my significant other, or that, even though I was riding shotgun, I don't remember the car accident that apparently was Vance's fault. However, I do remember waking up in the hospital, head pounding, wondering how I got there and why my best friend Olivia had this look on her face like the world was scheduled to end.

"Where's Vance?" I'd asked. "Is he okay?"

"Yeah," she'd rasped. "He escaped the accident with no life-threatening injuries. But he said he had to go."

I later learned that "go" meant dropping out of my life altogether. My beloved Vance only emailed explaining that he was staying with his parents because he needed "some space." He said he hoped I was okay and that he would be in touch when his "heart and head say it's time." I should be furious, but I'm not. It's like I've gone through my quota of extreme emotions for the past month, and now I need to process and figure out what the heck happened.

I hear my front door lock turn. My bestie Olivia has let herself in with the key she stole from Vance before he took off. "I'm so sorry," she'd said when I asked her about it. "But you shouldn't be all alone with a head injury, and I panicked, so I swiped this key. I know how independent you are, but you'll need someone to check in."

How could I be mad? I wouldn't have gotten through the last few weeks without her support. Now, Olivia walks through the entranceway, the sound of her footsteps announcing her presence.

"Hey," I call. "I'm in here."

Olivia knows that "in here" means the bedroom. She saunters in as I lie on the bed, petting Baby Girl. The cat's purrs are the loudest thing in the room. I have a fleece blanket wrapped around me, and I'm wearing Vance's old U of M sweatshirt with frayed cuffs and collar. I haven't washed it since the accident, and it still smells faintly of him.

I sit up to greet Olivia, who looks as gorgeous as always but in a way that seems effortless like she's from a Neutrogena commercial. Her hair is in its usual low ponytail, and it sways gently as she tosses her coat onto an armchair. She's wearing a forest green sweater with black leggings and black ankle boots, and her short nails look freshly filed and polished in a subtle light pink. I'd bet cash money she came from the nail salon, where she has a regular weekly appointment every Sunday at four. Olivia perches on the armchair's edge, her butt inches away from her discarded coat. She sighs and offers me a sympathetic smile.

I turn away from her and stare out the window at the darkening winter sky. It's a blank slate, like a child's painting, a smoky gray backdrop ripe for colorful brushstrokes.

"Are you ready to go back to work tomorrow?" she tenderly asks.

I adjust my position on the bed. The mattress is soft, and my body feels heavy and numb, like I have been drugged.

Rather than replying with a flat no, I try for an upbeat spin. "Well, I'm looking forward to seeing my students again."

"Hazy, do you think that going back is a good idea?"

My head feels swollen and heavy on top of my neck. I turn to look at Olivia. It is as if a lead blanket is draped over me, but when I look into my friend's eyes, I realize she can see through it. All of my problems are not lost on Olivia.

"I was out for two full weeks, not including winter break. Admin isn't giving me any more time off," I say.

She scrunches her brow irritably. "But you were in the hospital! You could have died! Don't they realize you need more time to regain your strength?"

I shrug. "I don't think they do."

Olivia rises from her chair but quickly sits again, only now she's next to me on the bed. She drapes her arm over my shoulder and gives me a tight side squeeze. "Screw them," she utters. "There's never been any humanity in human resources. That's the great irony, right? Or is it an oxymoron?"

I emit a sad little laugh. "I suppose it's both."

She laughs, too. "But I impressed you, right? My figurative language knowledge has improved, like 1000 percent since we've become friends."

"Only a math teacher could quantify something like figurative language knowledge."

"Yup! Don't forget it, Hazy."

"I won't." We sit my head on her shoulder, our hearts beating in tandem. What would I do without her?

After several moments, I break the silence. "Hey, will you help me pick an outfit for tomorrow?"

"I can. But..." She sighs, biting the side of her lip. "I worry that you're rushing it. I mean don't take this the wrong way, but are you even clear-headed enough to teach? What will you do when you can't remember your students' names, personalities, or what you've been studying all year? Have you figured out a plan?"

I can't hold it against Olivia for making such an assumption. It should follow that if I can't remember details about the accident and my relationship with Vance, other aspects of my life will also have blurred. But that's not the case. One doctor I saw immediately after the accident said our brains try to protect ourselves from trauma, which is why details associated with the trauma are fuzzy but other aspects of my life remain crystal clear.

"I don't need a strategy, Olivia. Seriously, I will be okay."

"Okay," she says, clearly not believing me. "But it's alright if you're *not* okay. Your students will survive without you for a few more days, even the ones in AP Lit."

About this, Olivia is wrong; she doesn't get it because she doesn't teach AP. In May, my AP Literature and Composition students will take a mega-hard test for which we need all year to prepare. And very few substitute teachers know how to enlighten high schoolers about the fine points of poetic devices, literary analysis, the impact of diction and dialect, or how any instance of symbolism can usually be boiled down to extended metaphor.

But more than that, most of my AP students come in disadvantaged. Maybe they are not native English speakers, perhaps they are immigrants, or maybe they are not familiar with all the vocab words or cultural references that the College Board assumes American high school students should know. Or perhaps my students hold after-school jobs or don't have a good place to study at home. It's often some combination of all those factors, but the result is the same: I must work my hardest for them, so they have the best possible chance of passing that test in the spring, getting a free college credit, and taking one step closer to a bright future.

I don't have the energy to explain that now. I close my eyes and use my thumb and index finger to rub them. "How are you, Olivia? I feel like, since the accident, we only ever talk about me."

"I'm fine. There's not much going on."

"Yeah? What about that blind date you went on a few weeks ago? Did that guy ever call you?"

She inspects her perfect nails and rubs at a nonexistent smudge. "No. And before you say anything, I know you're right. I will never again sleep with a guy on the first date."

Olivia has promised this several times before, but some people have a hard time sticking to their goals. "Oh well, I'm sure he just wasn't man enough to handle you."

"Yeah, but what guy is?" She keeps gazing at her nails, examining her manicurist's work. "Seriously, from now on, I won't allow more than a peck on the cheek before the third date. I've learned my lesson, and I'm tired of every guy I go out with either falling in love or acting like they've entered a witness relocation program."

I start to say something like I don't envy her being single, but then it hits me that I *am* single, so the words come out in a barely discernible grunt.

"Anyway," she shifts, "I think you should put in for a sub. I wouldn't say that if I hadn't just found you staring into space—"

Thank God Olivia didn't walk in on me talking to my cat. She would never let it go.

"I was petting Baby Girl!" I press down harder on her belly than I ought to. She emits a tiny meow.

Olivia sighs as if to say my words aren't worth responding to. "It's not even six yet. Some substitute will take the job."

I admit I felt sorry for myself a few moments ago, but Olivia's insistence snaps me out of my funk. "Give it a rest, Olivia! I'm going back to work tomorrow. I'm tired of moping around. Besides, I've got to figure out what happened with Vance and get our lives back on track, and the only way to do that is to return to school. So please stop being bossy and just be supportive, okay?"

There's a heavy pause, and then slowly, Olivia speaks. "Okay then. Be a bitch."

I don't have time to be offended because Olivia laughs in her trademark gravelly way a second later like she's channeling Al Pacino. Many months ago, we slung the b-word at each other for real in the only big fight of our friendship. Now, using the slur has become an inside joke.

"Please," I plead, after succumbing to laughter myself, "help pick out what to wear."

She stands from the bed and pulls me up. "Of course."

We go to my closet, and, as usual, Olivia makes the difficult choices easy.

To: VValby89@hotmail.com
From: H_Ford_AOGG@yahoo.com
Subject: New Strategy
Hi Vance,
Have you been eating a lot of your mom's cheesy broccoli soup? I hope so since, according to you, nobody equals

her soup-making prowess. Don't worry—I know you won't respond to my email, just like you haven't responded to most of my other emails. I do appreciate it when you occasionally confirm that you're still alive. Also, I believe that you want me to be okay. But I miss you, and I need to understand and process everything that's happened between us.

So, I'm going to focus on what I can remember. Maybe if I do, the rest of it, like what led up to the accident, will finally come back to me. I can't write you a super long email because my doctors say to limit screen time. But you can feel it, right? You can feel me remembering and revisiting our past. I hope so, and maybe then you'll come back to me. Then, we can move on and face the future . . .

Tomorrow, I return to school, and it's so strange that you won't be there. You've *always* been there. You and Olivia. Meeting you . . . even though it was two and a half years ago, it's still so crystal clear. I'm going to prove to you—and to myself—that there are tons of details that I can remember.

Feel me remember, Vance. And please, respond.

Love,

Hazel

CHAPTER 2

August 2001

We met during teacher orientation in the conference room at the district center. The chirpy woman who introduced herself as the head of Teaching and Learning did a sing-song into her microphone. "Okay, mingle and gather initials for your Bingo board! There are prizes for the winners!"

Things like "Lived in four different states" or "Graduated with a master's degree this year" or "Speaks a foreign language" were written into each box.

I groaned on the inside and headed to the back of the room to linger on the edges of the new-hire teacher cliques without being noticed. Dixon Heights water bottles, T-shirts, and lanyards were lined up, ready to be awarded to the winners.

A woman with a long, smooth ponytail walked up to me. She smelled like Aveda rosemary mint shampoo, and she wore her pale blue striped jersey dress with an elegance that most people could never manage. But something about her energy made me think she was a force to be reckoned with. "Here," she said, grabbing my Bingo card and, in exchange, inserting her card into my grasp. "Let's trade."

I looked over her card. She already had signatures for everything I could claim, like "Likes spicy food" and "Is an only child."

"I can't sign for anything that you don't already have signatures for," I said. "Sorry."

She shrugged. "No worries. Just initial whatever is blank. How about 'Knows sign language'?"

"But I don't know sign language."

"So? It's not like they're going to test you on it. Just put your initials down. I want one of those Dixon Heights T-shirts!"

Reluctantly, I initialed her card and handed it back. She gave me my card in return, with the letters "OD" scrawled across "Has lived in a foreign country."

"Thanks," I said. "Have you seriously lived in a foreign country?"

"Of course," she replied, flashing me a wild smile. "I wouldn't lie about something like that." Before I could figure out if she was serious, she charged away in search of more signatures.

Around thirty seconds later, you approached and uttered the first words you'd say to me. "Are you the one who knows sign language?"

"Umm . . ." I couldn't think or speak; you were too ridiculously good-looking for me to do anything but gawk.

"Olivia said you signed her card for that?"

"The gal with the throaty voice and ponytail?"

You nodded.

"Sure, why not." I reached for your Bingo card and initialed the sign language square.

"HF?" you asked.

"Hazel Ford," I stated.

"Cool name." Then you slipped my Bingo card from between my fingers, initialed a box, and handed it back to me. "VV" was written across "Has a tattoo."

"And I designed the tattoo myself." You raised the sleeve of your T-shirt to expose a lotus flower across your bicep.

"Wow." I felt myself blushing, which only made me blush harder.

Before I could think of anything else to say or ask your name, you strode off. Then, mercifully, several people called Bingo all at once, and we returned to our tables.

One of the Bingo callers was Olivia, and you two sat at the same table. The Teaching and Learning lady insisted on grilling everyone who had initialed Olivia's Bingo card, so when she got to "Knows sign language," the Teaching and Learning lady called out, "Who is HF?"

I tried to melt into the gray industrial carpet, but no telekinetic abilities surfaced. Damn it; they never did. "That's me," I said, raising my hand. "Hazel Ford."

"Fantastic!" the Teaching and Learning lady said. "Sign language will come in handy teaching kindergarten!"

I knew why she made that assumption. I'd come in at the last minute that morning and sat at the first spot I could find, which was at a table full of new kindergarten teachers who somehow already seemed to know each other.

"Actually, I'm teaching high school English."

"Okay!" the Teaching and Lady effused. "That's so exciting! So, can you show us some sign language?"

Her happy, expectant grin made my heart squeeze itself up into my throat, and I was paralyzed. Thankfully, Olivia saved me.

"She's shy," Olivia stated rather loudly. "Hazel? I don't mean to put you on the spot, but would you like to sit with the other new high school teachers?"

"Sure, thank you!"

I gathered my stuff, and the business of switching tables was distracting enough for the Teaching and Learning lady to move on to a new victim.

The contradiction struck me. Here I'd thought that day would be the start of my real adult life, one with a real grownup job and real responsibilities. Yet I felt more like a kid that day than I had in years. Thus far, my post-college existence was filled with student loan payments, a handful of failed relationships, working at coffee shops, and volunteering at the Playwrights' Center. I'd grown older, but I hadn't grown up.

It was time to become an adult.

After the Bingo winners were validated and prizes handed out, lunch was served. "Thanks for saving me," I said to Olivia.

She gave me a playful shrug. "It was the least I could do after putting you on the spot." She swung her new lanyard, though her smile had faltered when she got that prize rather than the coveted Dixon Heights T-shirt. "Besides," she continued, "you needed to sit with us before those kindergarten teachers got you singing Julie Andrews' songs or designing classroom decorations out of glitter and construction paper." Her face went slack for a moment, and then she chewed the bottom of her lip. "No disrespect to kindergarten teachers. I couldn't teach the little ones all day. I think you need to be the sort of person who embraces joy, and I'm way too cynical for that."

"Exactly," you said, and then you turned and introduced yourself to me. "I'm Vance, by the way."

"Hazel," I replied. Then, I wanted to smack myself, remembering that I'd already introduced myself to you.

"Yeah, I know. Nice to meet you, Hazel." Your smile was slow, and your eyes lingered on my gaze. You had the poutiest lips I'd ever seen on a male, and you flicked a wavy lock of hair off your forehead, revealing a set of eyelashes so thick they could sweep floors.

Make conversation, I told myself. *Pretend you're not already mooning over him.* "So, what will you teach?"

"AP Studio Art, Digital Art, and Sculpture."

"Wow," I replied. "That's a broad range!"

You shrugged, and when you said nothing, I figured I should fill the silence.

"I'm teaching English," I said. "I have AP Lit, plus a lot of English 11."

"Cool. Then we'll see each other at all the AP teacher meetings. I hear they're brutal." You gave me a wink to punctuate your statement.

Through herculean effort, I did not respond to your possible flirting. Because surely, if you were going to flirt, it would be with Olivia, who was clearly more extroverted and classically pretty than me. You were out of my league, even though I knew that, occasionally, guys dug my slightly mysterious vibe. And sure, I'd been blessed with a good metabolism and a small frame, a determined chin, and high cheekbones. Friends told me that not everyone could rock my coffee-colored pixie hairstyle, and I'd stopped wishing for blue or green eyes; dark brown suited me. However, growing up, my face was covered in freckles, making me feel ugly. By the time I met you, most of those freckles had faded away, except for the streak across my nose—you would later tell me those freckles made me so cool.

"What about you?" I asked, turning to Olivia. "What will you be teaching?"

"Algebra I and Algebra II." She shrugged. "Should be pretty easy. Besides," Olivia continued, "I graduated from high school here at Heights."

"Really?" I tried to keep the shock from my voice. "So, you grew up in Dixon Heights?"

"I bleed black and gold!" She laughed at her own hyperbole. "But I spent a couple of years after college doing disaster relief for Ameri-Corps, building houses for Habitat for Humanity, and mentoring disadvantaged kids, so I've done a lot of traveling. But now I'm ready to return to my roots!"

"Wow," I replied. "You must have had some amazing experiences."

She nodded sagely. "I did. But none of them were as wild as teaching high school. I've heard it can be crazy!"

"Exactly," you said, meeting eyes with Olivia. Had the two of you already formed a connection? "After college, I tried making it as an artist for years, and it was hard, but I've heard nothing compares to teaching."

I let my gaze shift back and forth. Olivia was probably a couple of years younger than me, like twenty-three or twenty-four, and I guessed you were a few years older, like in your early thirties. Nevertheless, you and Olivia would look good together.

You opened your boxed lunch and squeezed the little packet of mustard onto your turkey sandwich. "Where are you from, Hazel?"

"Kansas," I replied. "I came out here for college, and then I just stayed."

"Why?" Olivia asked. "I mean, Minnesota is so cold and far away from your family."

I shrugged. "I've always been artsy, so I wanted to be somewhere with lots of good theater."

That was mostly true, but as you later found out, the story had other layers.

"Kansas, huh?" said Olivia. "Don't worry. We'll spare you the Dorothy jokes."

"Thank you!" I replied.

Picking up your sandwich, you took a bite and narrowed your eyes at me. After setting it back down, you propped your elbows on the table and leaned forward. "So I get why you'd leave Kansas, but come on. You really just moved here without knowing anyone?"

I straightened my back and nodded. "Like lots of people do for college."

You furrowed your brows as if shocked. "But to become a teacher? That's bold."

Your gaze was so intense that I felt like I had done something wrong. But then you smiled, and your eyes sparkled with admiration. "But I like it; you must be an adventurous soul."

I tried to resist the warmth of your praise, but there was no hiding my delight. "Maybe a little," I said.

You threw me another smile, and Olivia slapped the table. "Well, here we all are," she exclaimed. "The beginning of our career. I have a feeling we're going to be great friends."

CHAPTER 3

The next morning, lots of my fellow teachers greet me as I enter the media center where the staff meeting will be held. "We've been thinking of you!" Jan, the orchestra teacher, takes my hand and squeezes it. "And we're so glad to see you back. How are you feeling?"

"Better. Thanks." I give Jan a warm smile as she leans in to hug me.

"Please let me know if there's anything I can do to help," she murmurs. "If you need to talk, I am here."

Jan is in her early sixties, and she enjoys public television and art museums, which Minneapolis has a lot of. She's got to be the nicest person on staff, and whenever I run into her in the mailroom or in the copy room, I give her a sincere, warm hello. Last year, Jan's husband of thirty years left her, and the divorce devastated Jan. Now, while I'm sure her intentions are good, I also know that misery loves company.

"Thanks, Jan. It helps, simply knowing that you're around. But I can't talk about any of it, not yet, and not at school."

"I understand."

There's this awkward moment where we're both trying to figure out if we should say something more. Then, Jan squeezes my shoulder again before she turns to talk to the teacher whose classroom is next door to her own, and I scan the room for members of the English department because I need to thank them for helping with substitute plans while I was away. I see Lucas, who is the head of the department and the only male English teacher.

He's in his early forties, has two kids whom his wife homeschools, and they grow their own vegetables in their backyard and even have a chicken coop. His family doesn't own a TV, which is something Lucas likes to work into most of the conversations we have at lunchtime, when all the English teachers sit around a wobbly conference table in the department's resource room, eating our Lean Cuisine while Lucas eats authentic grains. Surrounded by old class sets of books like *The Pearl*, *The Sun Also Rises*, and *Ulysses* (all of which were purchased decades ago and have since been abandoned in the state's push to include non-white male authors in the curriculum), we talk about what happened on *Orange County*, *American Idol*, or about George W Bush's latest gaffe, but Lucas tells us he wouldn't know anything about it because they don't own a TV.

Now, Lucas sits at a table in the corner of the media center, sorting through some papers. He looks the same as he did several weeks ago; his scraggly brown hair is pulled back in a ponytail, he's got a two-day growth beard, and he wears a wool sweater that looks so itchy I start scratching my arms just from glancing at it.

"Hey, Lucas," I say, sitting down next to him. "Thank you for helping me with sub plans while I was out."

"No problem, Hazel. Welcome back." His smile seems genuine; his voice is warm. "How are you?"

"I'm alright," I respond and hope I sound convincing. "How are you doing? What's been going on at school the last couple of weeks?"

He looks toward the ceiling as if in deep contemplation. "Oh, you know . . . same old stuff. They want us to do more curriculum writing and assessment alignment. I should have known better than to ask for more books."

My mind races with the implications of his words. "They" is the office of Teaching and Learning, and they hold our budget for things like books and other educational materials hostage. We are required to take a "deep look" into our lesson planning and essential questions or risk never seeing a dime. Do we represent the diversity that we're teaching? How do we target the kids who aren't learning the material? And how does our English department curriculum fit into the scope and sequence of the entire high school education?

Just the thought of having to sit in meetings and discuss all this with people who hide in offices rather than work with actual students in real classrooms makes me want to go home, climb into bed, and pull the covers over my head. But that's how I've felt ever since the accident.

"When is this curriculum writing and assessment alignment supposed to happen?" I ask Lucas.

"They want it done by next month."

"You can't be serious! How are we supposed to do that when our days are already filled with teaching, grading, and working with students?"

"Don't worry, Hazel. Nobody is expecting you to do it. I'll figure out a way to get it done."

I look at Lucas and see that, underneath his faux-professor demeanor, he's just as burnt out from jumping through bureaucratic hoops as I am. "What do you mean nobody is expecting me to do it? Shouldn't I help?"

A vertical line born of tension forms between his temples. "It's just . . . after the accident, and what led up to it . . . you know, probably it's better for you to sit out this round."

"I, um . . ." I resist the urge to rub my temples, to show that already my head hurts from stress. "Lucas, to be honest, there's a lot I don't remember about the accident and what led up to it."

"Oh." He smiles, but it's the type of smile an adult gives to a scared child. "I'm pretty sure Jim will talk to you, and he can explain better than me."

"Right." I feel the hairs on the back of my neck rise in dread. If Jim, the principal, told Lucas he'd be "talking" to me, that can't be good. I force out some bravado. "Whatever," I say. "You should cause a stir, Lucas. That's a great way to get out of curriculum writing."

Lucas rolls his eyes; it's subtle, but I sense his attitude. "Sure," he says, patting me on the arm. "I shouldn't have bothered you with any of it. We're all glad that you're okay and that you're back."

It's then that our principal, Jim, comes in, and the meeting starts.

I've never liked Monday morning meetings. But at least before, Vance and I would sit next to each other, side by side, sipping from our travel mugs of coffee while he tuned out, and I leaned forward, trying to pay attention. Jim's PowerPoint screen would glare brightly behind him, bullet point after bullet point of tedium.

"Good morning, staff," Jim says now, his voice officious. Jim is a tightly wound man who looks like he's in his late thirties but is probably a decade older. He goes for a run every day, even in the winter, and his energy seems recyclable, like it expands and multiplies upon its release. "First, I'd like to welcome back Hazel." He scans the room, trying to spot me, and when I give a subtle wave, he grins. "Hazel, we were all very worried about you, and we're so grateful to have you back. Please know that the entire staff is here for you and that we support you all the way."

I nod, sniffing back tears. "Thank you," I say, "that means a lot."

"Of course. And if you need anything, just let us know." Then, Jim looks away, clears his throat, and the color rises in his cheeks. "That said, I have an announcement. I am excited to introduce our long-term substitute art teacher. Please join me in welcoming Cyrus Gul." Jim's eyes search the room. "Cyrus, where are you?"

There's a moment before Cyrus stands, and my thoughts scramble to keep pace with my rapidly beating heart. How could Jim, with no warning or explanation, replace Vance with a long-term substitute? Nobody told me if Vance resigned, and I deserve to know.

But that's not even the worst part. I rake my fingers through my short hair as if I could massage my brain and erase the images of the Cyrus Gul I knew in college. Correction—I didn't just know him, I *knew* him, intimately. We shared one intense night before he transferred out of the class we had together. Cyrus pulled the ultimate disappearing act.

No, wait. Vance pulled the ultimate disappearing act. Next to him, Cyrus is an amateur. Still, in my twenty-eight years, I've accrued a grand total of six sexual partners, so precisely a third of them have vanished from my life with little or no explanation. Now, they will both have taught art at Dixon Heights Public High School.

Thy fate is the common fate of all; Into each life, some rain must fall. I recall Longfellow's words from "Rainy Day Ballad," a poem we studied in AP Lit this autumn. Most people see the poem as cheerful, but I see it as, "Yeah, fate exists, and we're all doomed." In other words, FML.

Suddenly, I realize that the moment when Jim asked Cyrus to stand has stretched out way too long. Is Cyrus a no-show?

Finally, from the back of the room, Cyrus rises like he wants to sink into the floor rather than stand upright. His tawny complexion and shaved head (he used to have silky black curls) gleam underneath the fluorescent lights, and he straightens his thick dark-rimmed glasses so that they sit straight on his friendly broad face.

But I know it's all a facade.

"Hello," he says. "I'm happy to be here. I mean . . . I hate the unfortunate circumstances and realize I have big shoes to fill."

Before I can think better, I break in. "Thank you, Cyrus. Vance would be happy that someone competent and caring is stepping into his classroom. And don't worry about the 'unfortunate circumstances.' I've heard from Vance, and he plans to return soon."

See, I can be the adult in the room, and if hard edges surround my words, it's not intentional, at least not entirely. So what if I'm lying about hearing from Vance?

"Thank you." Cyrus nods and looks like he wants to engage in a staring contest. But I know from experience that's his MO. Still, I squirm, wondering what I should do. After a moment, he sits down.

"Okay," Jim states, clearly uncomfortable. "I suppose we should get down to business." He turns on the projector, and a screen displays his Monday morning meeting notes. He gives us information about registration, parent-teacher conferences, and eighth-grade information night. It's a relief to think about mundane, tedious stuff, as if I'm replacing a migraine with a paper cut. However, Jim is notorious for running long, and as the clock inches closer to

8:00, then 8:05, and 8:10, I start to squirm. Class begins at 8:20, and I still need to organize the last-minute details of my morning lesson.

At 8:12, Jim finally wraps up with all our "business," and everyone prepares to go when Anton, the blowhard computer-technology teacher and teacher-union president, speaks up. "Jim, if I could just say one thing," he interjects, his voice booming.

Before I make a conscious decision to speak, I blurt out, "Oh, come on, Anton, not now. We need to get to our classrooms. This meeting has gone way too long."

I'm met with a room full of blank stares, and there's this shocked silence that lasts several seconds. Anton's mouth, which usually flaps from all the words coming out, now moves slowly. Anton is super tall, like 6′3″, and super blond and Nordic-looking. He wears the same combination of schleppy pants and gray sweatshirts every day and moves like someone who's always felt entitled to take up space. Now he looks down at me like I'm an ant he could step on. "Hazel . . ." It's as if he needs to remind himself of who I am. "If you need to leave, we all understand."

I should blush with embarrassment, stammer a little, and apologize. Young female teachers aren't allowed frustrated outbursts, and I've just broken a rule. But I don't want to be breezy and amiable, not now, not today. I stare him down, even though it's really Jim and not Anton who should be the subject of my ire.

But before I can get any more words out, Olivia steps up and intercedes. "Anton, class starts in seven minutes. We need to get going. How about you send us all an email?"

How is Olivia so good at asserting herself? What's perilous for me is a cakewalk for her.

Some teachers take their cue to leave. They pack up their stuff, rise from their chairs, and make their way out the door of the media center. I shift my weight, look Anton in the eye, and tell him, "Have a good day."

Then I walk off, out toward the media center's exit and up to my classroom. But I'm intercepted. Olivia approaches on my right. "That's got to be the first time Anton was ever at a loss for words," she whispers. "You just achieved the impossible dream."

"Right," I retort tightly. "Then why is my life such a nightmare?"

She grabs me by the wrist and peers into my eyes. "Are you okay, Hazy?"

"No." I look around, making sure no one is in earshot. Leaning in close, I whisper, "I know Cyrus Gul from college. He's, you know, the one I told you about, who transferred out of the class we had together after we'd hooked up . . ."

Her eyes widen. "*Seriously?* Wow. What are the chances?"

"I guess they weren't low enough. After all, he's a high school art teacher, apparently in need of a job."

"Yeah." She bites the bottom of her lip, thinking hard. "Hazy, did Vance really say that he plans to return?"

I nearly snort out my response. "Of course not." I'd kiss her on the forehead or hug her or something, but there's no time. I smile and wink so she'll know that nothing fazes me. Then, I rush past. I have students to teach.

CHAPTER 4

If you ever need proof that life goes on, spend a day in a high school classroom.

Like always, kids come in carrying their backpacks and boundless energy, still consumed with whatever drama went down via phone conversations last night. Or they're worried about their trig test third hour, which they didn't study for because they were too busy with sports, or work, or video games.

One student comes rushing up to me. Febe, with her gorgeous bottomless eyes, grins broadly but almost looks like she might cry. "Ms. Ford! I'm so happy you're back! We all missed you so much! *How are you!?*"

She speaks all in exclamation marks, yet it still seems genuine. I know teacher-student protocol says no physical contact, but I can't refuse the hug she captures me in. When she pulls away, the sleeve of her sweater has risen, and there are tiny thumbprint-sized bruises all along her wrist. She sees that I see and hastily pulls her sleeve back down. I look her in the eye and smile. "I'm good, happy to be back. But how are you, Febe? Is everything okay?"

She laughs breezily. "School is super hard this year, but otherwise, everything is perfect!"

"Really? Perfect sounds pretty great."

She relaxes her smile. "Okay, maybe things aren't exactly perfect."

I want to ask her what's wrong, but the bell rings, and she goes to her desk and sits. The rest of the students welcome me back, and none of them treat me like I might shatter if they look at me funny. They are all still caught inside their own minds and psyches, incapable of looking out from their personal whirling worlds. And I rejoice because finally, I can focus on something other than my own messed up life. I can think about them. I can think about literature. I can think about *The Great Gatsby*.

"I don't get why Nick doesn't just go back to the city," Febe states. She wears her hijab loosely around her head, pairing it with a fleece sweatshirt and jeans. "He's not that into Jordan, and both Daisy and Gatsby are using him. He ought to find new friends who won't get him into trouble."

"Nick has reasons to stay," I reply, "even if he doesn't know it. Plus, he lacks agency because he's an outsider, which can make him feel powerless."

Febe considers this, her face twisting in contemplation. "Wait. Nick is not an outsider. He's a white dude who can afford to live in West Egg. And he feels powerless? Sorry. I don't get that."

I shrug, worried I just said something insensitive. "Well, the meaning of power is open to interpretation. Everyone has their own understanding of it, and we all define it differently."

She squints at me. "How do you define 'power,' Ms. Ford? I want to know what you think."

Febe's eyes gaze up at me, one set among twenty-six others. These are the advanced students who care about class discussions and ideas, which means only about half of them have tuned out. So, roughly thirteen sets of eyes blink back at me; roughly thirteen teenagers wait for my reply.

"It doesn't matter what I think," I tell her.

"Yes, it does!" This comes from another student, Thomas, a beanpole of a kid with a wide smile and contagious laugh. "You're the teacher! You're supposed to tell us what you think."

"Nope. I'm supposed to tell you what I know, with the goal of getting you to think for yourself."

"We *do* think for ourselves, Ms. Ford!" Thomas insists, and several other students vocally concur.

If only that were true. But I've found that, while almost everyone believes that their mind is their own, few of us are immune to outside pressures telling us how to think. Still, these kids spend hours on homework every night with their AP Biology, AP Economics, AP Government, and AP Calculus. They already know way more than I do. What could be the harm?

I sigh, leaning my elbows against the heavy wooden podium that's been in my classroom since before I was born. "Okay," I launch in. "Power is the capacity to influence and control events, other people, or both. Some people use it for good, to make positive change, but bad people might use it to oppress those around them, or for material gain, or to further their own ambition. And the misuse of power can have devastating consequences."

Some students shift in their seats, murmuring to each other, trying to figure out if they agree. But I'm just impressed with myself that despite my muddled brain, I came up with something as coherent as I think that was.

"That's pretty dark, Ms. Ford," says Febe. She smiles like I've given her exactly what she wanted.

"It's only dark if the wrong people have power," I respond.

"Yeah, but it's like they say in *Spider-Man*," Thomas states. "'With great power comes great responsibility.' Mostly, it's irresponsible people who have all the power."

"Or," says Febe, "power makes people irresponsible, or at least hungry for more power."

"Okay, sure," I answer. "But then, how do you explain Nick? You say he has power, and I suppose as a white man with decent family connections, he does. But he doesn't seem hungry for more power, and he's the most responsible character in the novel."

Febe sighs. "*The Great Gatsby* is basically about reinvention, correct?"

"Correct," I reply, wondering where she is going with this.

"But it takes courage to reinvent yourself. And you can't change the past. Nick doesn't get that, and he thinks he's so honest, but he isn't even honest with himself. If he was, he'd realize that he has power, and he'd use it to change his own situation."

I contemplate her words for a moment before piecing it all together.

"So, you're saying that, before you can change your situation, you have to be honest with yourself?"

Febe gives me a knowing gaze and an exaggerated eye roll—her way of saying, "Duh!"—and I stifle a laugh. Her wise insights never cease to amaze me.

We debate back and forth a bit more, other kids chiming in, but never come to a hard and fast conclusion, and that's the beauty of literary analysis. There are no true right answers, but there often aren't entirely wrong answers either.

I tell them to read the next chapter and write three paragraphs identifying symbols and foreshadowing. That allows me time to go to my computer and glance over my slide presentation for next hour, which is on analogies using ACT vocab words. I have a standing desk where I keep my laptop, and below it and to the side is my real desk; light gray and elephantine, it must weigh around 500 pounds and is standard issue office desk furniture, built on an assembly line in the 1970s. In a fight, it could totally beat up any modern-day self-assembly office desk getting in its way.

I'm adjusting an animated transition on my PowerPoint slideshow when an email on my school account pops up. It's about kids dismissed early for a JV basketball game. No big deal, but it reminds me that I hadn't read my staff email since before the accident. Of course, I've checked it to see if Vance sent me anything, though I knew it was a long shot. If he was going to reach out, surely he'd call or text or use his personal email account. Still, I checked my email constantly but only by doing a search on his name. Now I must have hundreds of unopened, unread messages.

I hesitate for a moment, but then breathing deep and bracing myself, I click the little envelope icon at the bottom of my screen.

Sure enough, there are 208 unopened emails.

I scroll down. Most are to the entire staff: field trip notices, meeting reminders, and district business. Those, I delete without reading. There are also daily lists of which staff members are absent. I read a few, and my name is on each one, but Vance's is not. Instead, they just state that the Art position is absent again today.

I keep scrolling and scrolling, and then I find personal emails written and sent shortly after the accident. They're from students, parents, and community members, wishing me a speedy recovery. Of course, that's what they'll all say, right? Yet, I feel panicked, like I might find an angry message blaming me for what happened. Or worse, they'll help me remember something terrible, something I'm better off forgetting.

I scroll until I get to the bottom of my inbox, to the day of the accident, to hours before the crash. And then, I see what, in my gut, I knew I would find.

It's an unopened email from Vance's former student teacher, Annabelle. My stomach clenches. *I'm sorry*, it says. *But none of what they're saying is true. Please hear me out, and (I know it's a lot to ask) be on my side. You must remember what it's like to start out as a teacher. Everything will be ruined for me. Can we please talk?*

CHAPTER 5

I forward the email to Olivia with my own message included. *I found this in my inbox. What is she talking about? What were people saying?*

Olivia's response is slow; she must be instructing her class on equations, or maybe she's explaining how a negative times a negative equals a positive (something I still don't understand). But after twenty minutes, which feels like twenty hours, she emails back: *Don't know.*

Olivia's emails are always short; she doesn't share my preoccupation with writing in complete sentences. Still, I wish she'd gone into a little more detail. She could have expressed shock that I'd have an unopened email from Annabelle. I email back. *Is she still here at Dixon Heights?*

No, Olivia responds.

Why not? Was she forced out? I have a weird feeling about this. Should I email her back?

Do NOT contact her, Olivia writes, which is infuriating, but moments later, Olivia sends another email. *Annabelle was obsessed with Vance. She was NOT Vance's type. Don't worry about her. She lies.*

My insides lurch, and I feel a little sick. Olivia knows me too well. I can't help but be anxious, yet I don't have any time to spare. The bell buzzes, and my first-hour students filter out of the room. I rush to the restroom during passing time since it's my only chance for a break. I often contemplate what it would be like to work somewhere

where you can use the restroom whenever you want or take a lunch break without a timer ticking down.

My college writing course is next. This class has all the student leaders, and they will probably continue to lead after they leave school. As I walk back into the classroom, I'm scared I'll lose my composure if any of them are waiting to offer condolences. "Hi, Ms. Ford!" A trio of girls stands in the front of the room like they're the official welcome-back committee. It makes sense; a couple of these girls were in the homecoming court, and all three are on student council. "How *are* you? We missed you so much!"

They extend their arms as if to hug me. We're all ingrained with the strict no-touching code between teachers and students, and unlike with Febe, I resist the gesture. Their arms fall loosely to their sides. "I missed you all, too. And I'm okay, not great, but okay. It feels good to be back."

I'm sincere. I really missed them, yet after the adrenaline rush from first hour, my limbs feel heavy and the inside of my head is muddy, my thoughts slow. Mondays are always long, but today feels like light years before it will end. Several students have questions about their assignments while the substitute was here. They say she didn't explain what they were supposed to do or that she "lost" the work they'd turned in (which is the oldest excuse in the book). Other students figured they didn't have to do anything while I was gone, so now they have work they need to make up.

And yet, I survive the rest of the school day just fine. However, when the afternoon bell rings, it's merely a harbinger that the second part of my day, the will-you-be-around-after-school time, has begun.

Add to that, I am way behind on lesson planning and grading, and I have to do a marathon copy room session where I'll stand and grade quizzes while the machine chugs out 115 packets, enough for my three sections of eleventh graders. But the moment I'm about to head down to make those copies, my phone rings. It's Tamisha, the principal's secretary.

"Jim needs to see you in his office immediately," she states testily.

"I'll be right down," I say, wondering if Tamisha was supposed to have called me earlier in the day, and now she's blaming me for her having dropped the ball. Whatever. I may as well get this conversation over with.

When I get down to the main office, I walk past Tamisha with a wave and knock softly on Jim's door.

"Hi, Hazel," he says, without looking up from what he's reading. Jim taught before becoming principal, which must have been when he grew eyes on the top of his head. He gestures blindly toward the chair in front of his desk in a grand display of his power and tosses his reading material onto the desk and grabs a sheet of paper from a tray. I give him a moment before I sit down. When I do, it's quiet but not uncomfortable or tense. After a moment, he looks up at me.

"How have you been?" he asks bluntly, and I know he is trying to find something behind my response.

"I'm okay." And as I say it, I realize it's the truth.

He smiles again, and—maybe because of the kindness in his gaze—I smile back.

"Good, good," he says and nods. "HR wanted to be here for this meeting, but I felt, given the circumstances, it might be too overwhelming for you to see them right away, on your first day back, you know? It brings up too many feelings and emotions and stuff like that. I want you to know this is just a formality. I'm on your side, Hazel." His shoulder muscles coil up, and he seems to grow more intense. "You know me. I care about my teachers. After what happened, we need to move forward together and help each other get through it."

My mouth drops into what must be an O shape, my confusion sucking away any potential response.

Jim takes in my expression. "Do you have any questions?"

"Yes," I say slowly. "Sorry, my memory of the accident and what led up to it is sort of blurry. I guess it's a response to the trauma, but, umm . . . can you remind me what it is you're talking about? Did I do something wrong?"

Jim rubs his eyes, rapidly blinking when he's done. "There was an issue. Some parents complained about a cross-curriculum unit you and Vance assigned about the American Dream, that it was subversive and, well, that you were preaching anti-American sentiments." He looks down at his hands and taps his fingers against his desk. "In your case, it was more guilt by association. Except, you encouraged students to do a MySpace page for their assignment, which went against the district's internet policy." He looks back up at me and presses his lips together before continuing. "On the day of the accident, we disciplined you and Vance, saying a letter would go in your file. Vance was put on unpaid leave for an indeterminate amount of time."

"But . . ." I breathe in quick panicked bursts. "No, that can't be right. That unit was my idea. It was in connection to *The Great Gatsby*, which is all about the American Dream. Vance was just going along with what I wanted."

"Hazel." He says my name in a strong yet calm tone. "Vance and his student teacher, Annabelle, put together this example MySpace page that advocated for things like legalizing marijuana, government-funded abortions, and refuge for terrorists. It was all under the guise of freedom of expression, but when parents saw it, they threw a fit. And that wasn't even the worst part."

"What was the worst part?" My stomach revolts as I ask this, cramping so hard that it must be trying to reach up and clog my ears and prevent me from hearing Jim's response.

"Privacy laws prevent me from discussing it." He clears his throat as if in apology. "All I can say is, Annabelle was dismissed, Vance went on leave, and because, as you said, this American Dream project was your idea, you are receiving a disciplinary letter in your file. "

Jim slides the letter across his desk toward me. "Please read it, and if you agree with what it says, add your signature."

My stomach churns. "And if I don't agree?"

His eyebrows shoot up, and for the first time during this conversation, I sense Jim's disapproval. "If I were you, I'd agree, sign, and be done with it."

"What about Vance?"

Jim sighs. "Forgive me, Hazel. But if I were you, I'd also be done with Vance."

CHAPTER 6

I read the letter, which is a sterile account of parent complaints about the American Dream unit and how I went against the school's internet agreement in giving students the option to do a MySpace page. There is no mention of Vance or Annabelle. After taking a deep steadying breath, I clutch my Bic pen so tightly it nearly snaps and add my signature to the bottom.

When I get back to my classroom, I look at my email and reread the one from Annabelle. It would be a mistake to respond here at work. They've told us flat out that the district reserves the right to snoop through our messages and files. I forward Annabelle's email to my personal account. Then, I permanently delete it from my work account.

I groan to myself. "Oh my God, I have so much to do."

By the time I'm finished with all my lesson planning and copies, it's five thirty, and I've been at school for nearly eleven hours. I'm exhausted to the point of dizziness, yet I don't want to return to my empty house.

For as long as Vance and I were together, we set aside Monday evenings for work. We'd grade papers, hold meetings with students, and afterwards, treat ourselves to dinner at a nearby Middle Eastern restaurant owned by a family who was cycling each of their eight children through school at Dixon Heights. Over falafel and roasted lamb, Vance and I would plan our lessons for the week, bouncing ideas off each other and asking for advice on specific students or issues we had in the classroom. It made Mondays okay, having dinner to look forward to. Tonight, I'm not sure I can stomach even a cup of ramen.

But it's not like I'm going to spend the night at school. Besides, I want to see Baby Girl. So, I gather up my stuff: my purse, my bag of essays that I should start grading tonight but most likely won't, my copy of *The Great Gatsby* that I should reread tonight but probably won't, my travel coffee mug, and my huge puffy coat, which is a must for Minnesota winters.

I travel down two flights of stairs to the outside door nearest my car, that's in the staff parking lot on the side of the building. I got reasonably close to the building this morning, but sometimes I have to park across the street, which is like a punishment. It's unspoken among teachers that anyone who isn't here at least an hour before the first bell is a tad undedicated and therefore deserves a lousy parking spot.

"Oh, hello." Cyrus Gul, Vance's replacement, my nemesis, and whose art studio/classroom is directly three flights below mine in the school's basement, stands in the hallway, looking up at me and the landing I stand upon right as I'm about to exit into the cold dark evening.

"Hi." I'm not sure what else to say. Other than this morning's staff meeting, it's the first time Cyrus and I have spoken since that night we spent together, so long ago. And this moment is also the first time we've been alone since then. For years, I'd wanted to ask him questions, like, "What the hell happened?" But now that I finally have the opportunity, I've lost interest. Cyrus looks like he's on his way out. His coat is on, and he carries a large bag that's probably full of school related stuff. Because I know

I should say something, I stick with the benign. "I like your shaved head."

"Thank you." He clears his throat. "Umm . . . how was your first day back?"

"Okay." I descend the stairs and meet him by the outside door.

We nod in accidental unison. I guess we've made a silent mutual agreement not to acknowledge the ghost of our "almost" relationship. Clearly, he was never haunted by it the way I was for a while.

"Hey," he says, "I'm glad I ran into you. There's some stuff that belongs to Mr. Valby, still in his old classroom. I hear you two were—are—a couple, and I was wondering if you'd like to go through it. No rush, but I don't want to get rid of anything that might be important." His words flow out so casually, yet there's a certain weight to them as if he's adding some compassion, but not too much, because neither of us wants to get emotional or messy.

"Oh." I should say, "Thank you. How thoughtful. Yes, I will come down and go through his things just as soon as I can." But he's the invader that's taken over Vance's life, or at least his livelihood, and he's standing where Vance ought to be. "You know Vance is coming back, right? You're temporary here. So don't throw out anything that belongs to him."

He shifts his weight under my gaze, putting his hands into his back pockets. "Okay," he says. "But, umm . . ." Cyrus shakes his head. "Never mind."

"No. What were you going to say?"

"Nothing. I won't throw away anything, okay?"

"Thanks," I struggle out.

He squints at me. "Hey, you don't look too good. Are you alright?"

I feel myself sway a little, and I swallow roughly. "Fine." I push open the outside doors, and the burst of frigid air shocks me back to my senses.

"You're okay to drive home?"

In truth, I feel unsteady and spacey, but I will not admit that, so I answer, "Yeah, of course."

"Okay . . . Well, drive safe."

I nod, not wanting to prolong our conversation in the unforgiving winter air that's like diving into a cold bath. But at least I feel less feverish. And then, I remember that I'm annoyed. "Thanks, Cyrus. I really appreciate your concern."

He hears my sarcasm; I know he does. "Hazel . . . I had no idea you worked here. I hope that our being in the same building isn't a problem."

My face turns hot in the dark frosty night. "You and me, in the same building? No problem at all. I mean, years ago, it would have been 'a problem', back when I was devastated that you disappeared or that you'd 'forgotten' to mention that you were engaged. But now, I have a million other things to worry about. You're barely a blip on my radar."

He smiles with half of his face like we're sharing a joke. "Right. I figured." Cyrus tilts his head back, looking up at the night sky, which is full of stars. "God, what chaos, right?" He laughs and looks back at me. "It's good to see you, Hazel, but I'm sorry about the circumstances."

"You're sorry about the circumstances?"

"Yes."

"Seriously? Cyrus, the circumstances have nothing to do with you. If you want to apologize to me, at least pick something relevant."

Cyrus laughs again, though I clearly was not joking. "Right. See you tomorrow." He walks toward his car, which is parked further away than mine. His movement spurs me to action, and I move toward my own vehicle. I climb in, turn on the ignition, and let it warm up for maybe ten seconds before I drive off, taking the fifteen-minute drive to the little house that I call home.

It's a bungalow in the northernmost corner of Minneapolis, right by a huge parkway and an easy commute to school. As soon as I get inside, I head straight to our bedroom, where I collapse onto the bed with my coat and shoes still on. Baby Girl hops up and starts grooming me at my hairline, purring all the while.

"Hi," I rasp. "I missed you. Did you miss me?"

She headbutts me in response, so I scratch behind her ears, giving her what she wants.

I'm so feverish and exhausted; it's like I'm drunk. I close my eyes to see and remember Vance's face, which is too beautiful to be real. I love his dark eyebrows and high cheekbones and the way his lower lip is, like, twice the size of his upper lip, which is also pretty plump.

"I miss you," I say, and I let Baby Girl think I was talking to her and not to my phantom boyfriend. Then, because I know I won't get an answer, I add, "But what happened with Annabelle?"

To: AnnaGRRLL9999@yahoo.com
From: H_Ford_AOGG@hotmail.com
Hi Annabelle,

It's Hazel. I just now saw the email you sent on the day before Vance and I were in the accident. I'm not sure if you're aware, but I got a head injury, and there's a lot I don't remember about what went down. Plus, Vance left me. I hear you were dismissed from your student teaching position early. Let me know if you still want to talk.

I'll wait for your response.
Hazel

To: VValby89@yahoo.com
From: H_Ford_AOGG@hotmail.com
Subject: My first day back
Dear Vance,

I got through my first day back wearing that sweater your mom got me for Christmas a year ago. Do you remember? It's a cardigan with red and blue piping. I asked Olivia to help me decide what to wear, and when she looked through my closet, she found that sweater. "Why don't you ever wear this?" she'd asked.

Unable to come up with a good response, I simply put it on. My feelings towards your mother are so convoluted; while I'm sure this entire ordeal is painful for her, it's still messed up that nobody will tell me what's happening. I imagine everyone who knows of our situation laughing at my expense. *God, Hazel is such a fool. If she can't figure out why Vance left, she deserves to suffer.*

Honestly, though, today was easier than staying at home has been. I've had worse days. Today I knew what was coming, at least sort of. Well, I didn't expect the stuff about the letter in my file, or what Jim said about you, or seeing Cyrus again (I'll tell you all about him some other time), or the email from Annabelle. So, actually, I guess a lot of it was unexpected. But I knew that I'd be doing it all without you.

I found an unopened email from Annabelle that she had written on the day of the accident. She asked me to be on her side. She asked me to remember what it was like to start out as a teacher—as if I could forget.

And yet, even though that was a crazy, difficult time, it was also the best time of my life because I was getting to know you, because I was falling in love with you.

Feel me remember, Vance. And please come back to me.

Love,

Hazel

CHAPTER 7

September 2001

We'd been teaching for only one week when, on Tuesday during second hour, I overheard students talking.

"Maybe the planes hit the towers by accident."

"Don't be stupid. They did it on purpose."

I was handing out a worksheet on chapter two of *Animal Farm*. "What are you talking about?" I asked.

They pivoted in their desk chairs and looked at me. "Haven't you heard, Ms. Ford? Two planes flew into the Twin Towers in New York City."

My heart flip-flopped, but I pushed the sensation away. "That's terrible," I said. "I hope everyone is okay."

And that was all the thought I allowed for this grave nugget of news, at least for the moment. Surely, Jim would make an announcement over the intercom if there'd been a national emergency. Meanwhile, I was just finding my groove, trying to establish a routine and learn the names of all my students.

We spent the class discussing how the animals' song of revolution, "Beasts of England," compares to other protest songs and I had them make predictions for which animals would prosper under their collective rule and which might suffer. The kids seemed distracted, and more than once, I had to implore them to focus, but I thought little of it. When the bell rang and they filed out, I was already sitting at my desk, organizing a stack of assignments, grateful for a chance to breathe. It was third hour, and I had prep. So did Olivia, and I wasn't surprised to see her stroll into my room, though her expression was pinched and troubled.

"Hey, what's up?" I asked.

She raised both eyebrows. "Haven't you heard?"

I thought for a moment, trying to reference what she could mean, and the conversation between my students at the beginning of the hour pushed its way back into my consciousness. "You mean, the thing about the plane crash?"

"Yeah," she replied breathlessly, but there was an edge to her voice. "It wasn't just a plane crash. Two planes crashed into the Twin Towers, and they, like, collapsed. It was on purpose, done by terrorists. And they're saying there was another plane headed for the Pentagon, but it went down in a field in Pennsylvania."

"Oh my God."

I turned toward my computer, an antiquated laptop that was way too heavy to carry anywhere. "How do you open the internet on this thing again?"

"Click on the globe icon."

"Right."

I clicked and went to CNN's website, where I found horrific images and headlines: "Apparent Terrorist Attacks Hit NYC, DC, and the Pentagon."

"I had no idea," I said to Olivia. "I mean I heard some students talking, but I didn't realize how serious it was. And I made the class discuss *Animal Farm*. I even yelled at them to focus!"

Olivia pressed her lips together, looked off toward the window, and shook her head. "It's not your fault. They should have made an announcement. I guess they didn't want to cause a panic."

"What kind of panic?"

"Like, that other cities could be attacked. I guess people in Chicago are freaking out and racing home. But Governor Ventura said we should all stay calm and keep kids in school."

"Olivia, how do you know all this?"

"I went down to the office when I heard something was up, and I said we need to know what's going on. So they wheeled a bunch of TVs into the gym. Come on; I'll show you."

Marveling at Olivia's chutzpah—she made demands of the front office on her very first week—I followed her downstairs and was surprised to see that a crowd of students and staff were sitting in the bleachers, watching one of several TVs that had been wheeled in on carts, all turned to CNN.

Here and there, students joked or horse played, oblivious to the gravity of the situation and simply happy for an excuse to miss class. But most sat in reverent horror.

And then I saw you, sitting alone, pale and stricken. You gave me a half-hearted wave like you'd been waiting for me.

Olivia and I climbed the bleachers and sat next to you.

"Can you believe this?" you asked.

"No. I wasn't even aware it happened until Olivia came and told me."

That's when you took a deep breath, your ribcage rose and fell, and then you subtly pointed to a group of ninth-grade girls sitting a few rows down. Their hijabs brushed against each other as they huddled like delicate Aspen trees that find strength when joined together.

"I can't imagine what it's like for them," you murmured. "They must be especially terrified."

"I hope we bomb the shit out of the Middle East," Olivia loudly declared. "We should just take out the entire region."

I knew she didn't mean that. People say crazy things when they're scared, and on that day, fear hung in the air like poisonous gas. And yet, we all needed to be careful. "Olivia," I whispered, "they can hear you."

One girl who sat on the edge of her group turned and looked directly at us. She had huge eyes, dark and soulful, and when those eyes met mine, she offered me a sad, knowing smile. What if she thought it was me who'd said we should bomb the Middle East?

"Excuse me," I said to you and Olivia.

I rose and moved down to the group of girls, sitting by the one who'd smiled at me. "Hey," I said. "What's your name?"

"Febe."

"Nice to meet you, Febe. I'm Ms. Ford. Do you mind if I sit with you?"

"Sure."

We sat in companionable silence, watching CNN. I was so focused on seeing the clip of the planes flying into the towers, over and over, and on the new ticker tape thing at the bottom of the screen, scrolling updated headlines, and on how Febe and her friends were coping, that it was several minutes before I realized that you and Olivia had moved down as well. Together, we formed a thin layer of security for these girls in this new menacing world.

And the world is menacing, isn't it?

CHAPTER 8

On Annabelle's first day, when she came to his classroom after school so they could do their initial conference, and they'd met as two adults, as near equals, she still felt like a little girl in his presence.

"You probably don't remember me, Mr. Valby," Annabelle said to him. They both sat upon stools around one of the high, wide tables. Years ago, she'd listened to one of his lectures at a similarly shaped table when she'd done a summer camp for gifted kids, and he'd taught at the camp. She'd been fifteen, just old enough to swoon in his presence, and she'd prayed he would come and gaze over her shoulder and offer his thoughts on her sketching. Although Annabelle had sent him her resume and cover letter as part of the application to be his student teacher, she didn't dare believe that he'd look closely at it or that he'd remember her.

"Are you kidding?" He laughed, and adorably, his cheeks grew pink. Mr. Valby had always embarrassed so easily. Is it possible for someone so beautiful to be so self-conscious? "Come on, Annabelle," he now insisted. "With all that time you spent painting in my room after camp was over, working on your projects, how could you possibly think I wouldn't remember you?"

She glanced down, resisting the urge to reach for his hand. "Sorry, Mr. Valby," she said.

"No apology necessary," he told her, "and you can call me Vance now."

She imagined her heart pole vaulting inside her chest, feeling it might just break through her ribcage in a burst of joy and nerves. Over and over, for the last seven years, she'd dreamt about the moment when he'd see her as something other than a forgettable schoolgirl.

Annabelle had graduated from Dixon Heights in 1998, three years before Mr. Valby had started teaching there. But her sister had had Mr. Valby for a teacher, and when Annabelle saw him again at parent-teacher conferences, she was in love. She'd also been in love with art, with painting, for as long as she could remember. Yet, it wasn't until she saw Mr. Valby for the second time that it all clicked into place; she was meant to be an art teacher.

It wasn't just because she wanted to be with him. Sure, simply put, he was beautiful, Godlike, and if she'd been asked to create an image of the "perfect male," he would have been it. His silky-looking shiny dark hair, his amazingly deep eyes, his mouth that was obviously built for kissing . . . Plus, he had a tattoo of a lotus flower on his bicep, which she could see peeking out beneath the rim of this T-shirt. Glancing at it felt deliciously forbidden.

And when he spoke, it was like he was talking intimately to each student in the room, making them all feel like he *saw* them, like they mattered.

What Annabelle felt for him was more than infatuation. He saw the beauty in the world, and he taught others to see it too and to express that beauty, to recreate it in their own way. That made her love him, but she also wanted to emulate him.

That was why Annabelle had chosen the U of M in the first place; she knew they had an arrangement with Dixon Heights, that student teachers from the university came there all the time. Now, here she was, standing next to him. Sure, he was still her mentor, but she was over twenty-one now and so close to being out in the world as a real adult, and their relationship was more like colleagues, like they could go out for a beer after school and that wouldn't be illegal or even scandalous. Well, maybe it would be a bit scandalous, but so what? That would be part of the fun.

Annabelle knew she was attractive. She'd had boyfriends, and she'd had flings, and she'd never doubted her ability to lure in whomever she wanted if the time was right. And now, the time was right.

"Okay, Vance," she answered him. "I am so excited we'll be working together. It's like a dream come true for me."

He smiled, and—*oh my gosh*—was he blushing more deeply? Annabelle gazed deep into his eyes, and their gazes locked. They had a connection already. Of that, she was sure.

"Me too," Vance stated. "Let's get started."

CHAPTER 9

By all rights, Vance belonged to her. She deserved his love and Hazel didn't; it was as simple as that. But poor Vance was so confused and couldn't see the truth. When she saw how he looked at Hazel with love and how his expression softened whenever Hazel was around, instead of getting mad, her competitive spirit kicked in. It's not like he and Hazel were married, and Hazel neither understood nor appreciated Vance Valby, not how she did.

She wasn't used to coming in second, but so be it. At least she wasn't dead last.

"I have a favor to ask," she told him at lunchtime. Hazel wasn't around.

"Sure. What?"

She sighed and tried to sound shaky. It was better if he thought she was nervous. "My best friend has this dining table set and chairs that she's looking to get rid of. It's super cool, linoleum, like from a fifties' diner. I can have it for free, but I need to get it from her. Would you be willing to drive me in your truck to get it?"

Vance barely blinked. "Where does your friend live?"

"Northfield."

"That's, like, over an hour away."

She swallowed roughly. "I know. Never mind. I shouldn't have asked."

He tapped her lightly on the wrist, and her skin burned at his touch. "No, I didn't mean it that way. I can drive you. It's not a problem."

She suppressed a smile. Vance loved to feel needed; that much was obvious.

"Thank you so much."

All the way down and all the way back, they talked about him. She asked all the right questions, about his art, about his students, about his dreams. When he carried the table and chairs to his truck, she complimented him on his strength. Once they were back on the road, she praised him for his driving skills.

By the end of the evening, when he carried the table and chairs into her dining room, she said, "Thank you so much. I owe you dinner. I'll cook, and we can sit and eat at my new table."

They both looked at the table, pearly green and glowing under the ceiling lights, and the chairs, with their diamond-shaped holes in the middle of the back support; they were like vintage emeralds, old but holding the promise of something shiny and new.

"I'd love to have dinner with you at this table," said Vance.

"Tomorrow night?" she asked.

"Yes." He paused, thinking. "Hazel has something going on tomorrow night, so that's perfect."

"So, there's no need to mention it to her?"

"Right," he said. "Let's keep this between us."

That's exactly how she wanted it.

CHAPTER 10

My Tuesday morning commute is quiet without Vance, like a sore throat that muffles your voice. When I arrive at school, I park and trek to the building, and the January wind is every bit as punishing as it was the day before.

Ever since the accident, I've been working through my brain fog so I can figure out a plan to get Vance back. I wanted us to both get tenure at the end of the year so we could fully commit to each other and settle into the life we dreamt about. But maybe I'm on the wrong track. I could still get back together with Vance, but then we could move somewhere warm and turn a new page. Recently, I'd read an article about how states like Hawaii, California, and Arizona all face teacher shortages. And sure, that same article explained *why* they had teacher shortages: terrible working conditions, pay that doesn't match the state's cost of living and school systems that are antiquated and unjust. But even if we got the worst paying jobs at the worst school in the state of Hawaii, we'd be warm and near a beach, and we'd have gotten away from this Annabelle-MySpace-American-Dream scandal that's dragging us both down.

Yet, something keeps me here, and it isn't just the student loans I have to pay off. And it's not just Vance. I'm tied to this place in a way that I don't yet know how to define.

I reach my classroom, which is at the top of two and a half flights of stairs. Outside my classroom door waits

Febe, still bundled in her coat and carrying what looks like a supremely heavy backpack. "Good morning, Febe. How are you?"

"I'm okay. But, Ms. Ford, I need to talk to you."

She follows me into my room and stands, shifting her weight, while I take off my coat and store it, along with my purse, in the locked cabinet where I keep all my personal stuff. It smells like PineSol in here, which means they cleaned last night. Sometimes, the janitors are short staffed, and they don't always get to each room.

Febe is full of urgency, so I say, "What do you need to talk to me about?"

I'm expecting her to ask me for a letter of recommendation or possibly for an extension on an essay assignment. So, I'm not prepared for the words that come out of her mouth. "I'm looking for a staff sponsor to start an art and literature blog."

"What?" I don't really need her to repeat it, so I just shake my head like my ears are filled with water, and then I change my question. "Why?"

She takes a deep breath. "It's second semester of my junior year, and I haven't done much to distinguish myself. I need to get into this summer program at Princeton if I want any chance of getting accepted there full-time for college, but it's important to show them that I'm not just a good student. I've got to do something big."

"Right. But why an art blog?"

Febe's dark eyes grow round and glistening. "Because we don't have one! Ms. Ford, there are so many talented artists and writers at this school who need a venue. This magazine would be for the entire student population. You know, anyone who wants to submit something could, and it would be so cool. Our friends and family could read it, and that would be great, but other people could see it, too, and we could show off how talented the students at Dixon Heights are."

My first thought is, *Vance will love this idea! We can work on it together, and it will be like old times!* Then it's like, *Oh yeah, Vance left you, and you were just planning your escape from this school,* and the realization punches me so hard that I take a moment to catch my breath. "I don't know, Febe. I'm probably not the best person to work on this with you."

"I think you're perfect."

Tears rush to my eyes, and I blink them away. I realize she means I'm the perfect staff person to sponsor her blog, not that I'm literally perfect, but still . . . I guess I'm more desperate for some kind words than I'd realized.

"Thank you, Febe. I really appreciate that. But what I mean is, I'm sort of in trouble with the school administration for incorrect internet use, so if you're looking to do something that will create positive buzz, I'm not the teacher you want."

Her face falls. "Oh no. I didn't realize you'd gotten in trouble, too, Ms. Ford."

Surprised, I stutter out my response. "What . . . what are you talking about?"

"Mr. Valby and the MySpace page? I heard that's why he didn't come back and why Ms. Gomez didn't finish her student teaching here."

"How did you hear all that, Febe?"

She rubs the edges of her hijab, which is a lovely royal blue, absently between her fingers. "Everyone was talking about it. Only a few people saw it before the school took it down, but the damage was done. They're saying a student faked the page, to hurt Mr. Valby."

"Are you serious?" I lean against my desk. "Who's the student? And why would anyone want to hurt Mr. Valby?"

"I don't know." Her voice is hard, and her gaze darts around as she answers, landing on my shelves stuffed full of old dusty books. I know she's lying.

"Febe." I use my gravest, strictest teacher voice. "If you know something, you need to tell me. This is an incredibly serious situation. You understand that, right? Reputations and careers are destroyed over stuff like this."

She gasps. "It wasn't me, Ms. Ford! I swear! I wouldn't do something like that!"

I place my hand on Febe's back. She's near tears and bordering on hyperventilation. "Calm down. I wasn't saying it was you. I just need to know what you know."

"I don't know anything!"

"Okay," I tell her, letting her off the hook for now. I believe Febe when she says that it wasn't her. Whether she knows who did it . . . Well, it's a lot to ask of a kid to rat out a peer. Maybe this sort of thing requires delicacy. If I want to find out who this student is and thus clear Vance's name, I'll need to gain Febe's trust. Working on the blog together is the perfect way to do that, even if I could get in more trouble for incorrect internet use. "So, given that I'm persona non grata right now, are you sure you want me to work on the blog?"

"I don't know what 'persona non grata' means, but, Ms. Ford, yes! You know all about artsy stuff, and everyone says that you care about the students. Don't you want to give them a voice?"

Her compliment, however sideways and manipulative, still lodges right into the softest spot of my heart. "Fine," I concede. "I'll work with you on the writing part of the blog, but I can't promise for how long. And you'll need to find someone else who knows about the design and the visual arts portion."

Febe does a little jump, clapping her hands together in glee. "Yes, thank you, Ms. Ford. And don't worry; I already talked to Mr. Gul. Did you know he's Iranian, like me? And he knows a ton about both web design and art, and he said he'd love to work with us."

More of my first-hour students come in, and Febe rushes to talk to them and announce her exciting plans for the art blog. I start organizing my desk like I'm trying to organize my sorry, messy life.

But it's no use. I've just signed up to work on a project with Cyrus Gul.

CHAPTER 11

By Friday morning, I am so ready for a day off. Recovering from this head injury is exhausting. All week, I've made minor adjustments, and I've felt like a foreigner in England or Australia, somewhere where they speak English, but I still don't understand the slang or know my way around. I've had to change my teaching style to accommodate my newly sluggish mind, and I've needed to plan for enough time to gather my thoughts and explain the material to my students. There were even new physical limitations like I can't stand for as long as before the accident. And I'm just constantly tired.

But while I'm happy to have made it through my first week back, the prospect of the weekend haunts me, and I mean in a scary, non-Casper-the-friendly-ghost type of way. I need something to occupy me, some sort of plan where I'll interact with a real person so I don't become a crazy cat lady and talk Baby Girl's ear off.

During lunch on Friday, Olivia pops into my room, which she almost never does because we only get twenty-five minutes to eat, and there's usually a line at the microwave. Plus, the math department is several hallways away from the English department. She carries a container of yogurt and a plastic spoon, and says, "Hi, stranger."

"Hey, what's up?" I smile, not masking my surprise at seeing her.

"Not much. TGIF, right?" She plops down in a student desk directly across from my teacher desk. "I feel like I haven't talked to you all week. I'm such a bad friend for not checking in on you."

I wave her off. "Please. I'm fine. And I know how busy you are."

"Yeah, but still . . . How've you been doing?"

Grasping my water bottle, I take a swig as if to fortify myself, before asking Olivia the questions that have been simmering in my mind. "I'm okay," I rasp, "but do you know anything about Vance, Annabelle, and a MySpace page? I heard that's why he left."

Olivia rolls her eyes. "I mean the students are murmuring about it, but you can't trust anything they say."

"Okay, but what have they been saying?"

"That they posted porn on the American Dream MySpace example assignment, as, like, a statement against the over-sexualization of pop culture."

"What? That doesn't even make any sense."

"I know, right?" Olivia peels the foil off her yogurt container and dips in her spoon.

"I heard a student who had it out for Vance actually posted the page."

"Probably."

Olivia seems breezy and unconcerned with the issue. I decide not to tell her that I emailed Annabelle, who has not gotten back to me yet.

"What are your plans this weekend?" Olivia asks as she stirs her yogurt.

I shrug. "I thought I'd lie on my couch with Baby Girl and alternate between grading essays, watching bad television, and wallowing in self-pity."

"Well, that sounds fun, but I have a better idea." Olivia's cheeks pinken, and her throaty voice sounds pitchy. It's like she's nervous, but Olivia is rarely nervous.

"I'm doing a girls' weekend with my church group. It's a cabin retreat in Wisconsin. You should totally come."

Hell no, I shouldn't come. But how do I let Olivia down without hurting her feelings?

"Gosh, Olivia, I appreciate the offer. But I don't think I'm up for something like that. More than anything, I need rest."

She puts her yogurt spoon into her mouth, swallows, and then her lips spread into this line that's neither a smile nor a frown. Maybe it's both. "You can rest at the retreat. Everyone who's going is really chill, and we're all about drinking wine, going for hikes—which you don't have to go on if you don't want to—and sure, we'll talk about how spirituality impacts our lives, but I promise, no one will try to shove Christ down your throat."

I laugh. "You mean I won't have to gag on Jesus?"

Olivia laughs, too. "Exactly."

"But, Olivia, you know I'm not into organized religion. You'd understand if you'd had to go to bible study in Topeka, Kansas, like my parents made me."

"I do understand, Hazy." Her voice is soft. "And I know your experience growing up with religion is different from mine. But nobody should have to experience what you're going through right now, not without some spiritual guidance. I'm just being honest here—you're not coping as well as you think you are."

"Oh no, you're totally wrong. I don't think I'm coping well at all."

She doesn't crack a smile, and instead, her eyes pool with concern. "Nobody in your position would! You're in denial, but you need to face your grief and find a way to heal. And I want to help you with that."

"Olivia . . ."

"It's not like we're going to chant or do anything crazy. The ladies who will be there are super cool, and they know all about you, and they're ready to give you love and support."

I know her heart is in the right place, but Olivia will never understand why I can't buy into God and Christianity. She is such a believer that just my use of the term "buy in" would probably set her off. I struggle for the right words, anything that might make her accept that my answer is no, but then I am saved, perhaps by divine intervention. Febe comes into my room.

"Ms. Ford, I have three more students interested in working on our blog! And Mr. Gul says he can come in on Saturday morning but that you'd need to be there too because he doesn't have keys yet."

Of course he doesn't. Our school is notorious for stuff like that, not giving keys, email accounts, or copy room access to new staff because of papers that need processing and everything takes way too long. I feel sorry for him despite myself. He must have to stand outside when he gets to school and wait, shivering in the cold, until somebody with a prox card approaches, to let him in.

But I digress. I would kiss Febe for saving me just now, but that would be weird. "Sure," I tell her, perhaps a touch too enthusiastically. "I reserved time for this weekend since you and I had already talked about it. What time are you thinking?"

"8:00 a.m."

I choke just a little. "Why so early?"

"Most of us who are interested have a Key Club event at noon."

Key Club is a service organization attracting all the students, mostly girls, who genuinely want to make the world a better place. Olivia barks out a fake sort of laugh. "I thought Key Club was for the good kids."

Febe hadn't noticed Olivia was in the room until now, and her mouth drops open.

Olivia laughs again. "I'm kidding, of course!"

But Febe seems unconvinced, and the air drips with awkwardness. "We're planning to shovel driveways for senior citizens who live alone."

"That sounds important," I state. "8:00 a.m. it is. I'll bring donuts."

I turn to Olivia as Febe exits my room. "I really appreciate the invitation, Olivia. But I can't make it. Sorry."

Olivia scrunches up her face. "Wait a sec. Didn't Febe say something about Mr. Gul? Isn't that—"

"Yeah," I break in. "It's Cyrus, Vance's replacement. He agreed to help with the blog. Febe asked him before she asked me."

Olivia widens her eyes. "Have you lost your mind? What about that stuff you told me, that the two of you have a history?"

I let my chest rise and fall. "Yeah," I concede. "When I agreed to work on the blog, I didn't realize Cyrus was working on it, too. So that part should be . . . interesting. But you know Febe is one of my favorite students. And I think she has information that will exonerate Vance."

Olivia's face tightens; her lips pull back. "What do you mean?"

"Like I said, apparently, a student did the MySpace page in Vance's name. But Febe isn't ready to squeal yet, so I need to gain her trust."

Olivia waves her yogurt spoon at me. "Fine. You're off the hook for the retreat. But don't blame me if things get weird with Cyrus Gul. It's like your life is already pretty messed up, and now you're just trying to make it worse."

To: VValby89@yahoo.com
From: H_Ford_AOGG@hotmail.com
Subject: Do you think about me?
Hi Vance,

I tell myself there's no way you would post porn, that you could not be that self-destructive and stupid. But then, why did you take off? You must feel some combination of guilt, embarrassment, and shame unless it's all about the accident. Did you leave because you blame yourself?

Your silence is so unfair. It's so cruel.

I feel the lack of you constantly. I tell myself that I will survive, that there was a time before we were together when I functioned at school without you by my side. But it wasn't for long.

Can you feel me, remembering?

Love,

Hazel

CHAPTER 12

October 2001

That first year, for all of September, I felt like something had forced me underwater for long stretches of time. Occasionally I could come up to the surface and gasp for breath, but then I'd be forced down again, trying to teach, grade, and plan lessons, all during the biggest national tragedy for generations.

In October, it was my birthday, and my mom sent me a $50 gift certificate to Target. I could have used it on groceries or household items, and that was my plan, but when I walked into the store, I was immediately drawn to this super cute sleeveless sweater dress they had on display, with brown, pink, and light blue zigzag knitting. It had been so long since I'd had new clothes, and though I worried it might be too clingy and skimpy for work, I figured if I wore it over thick tights and a turtleneck, I'd be fine. So, I splurged.

It was the following Monday when I wore my new dress, and I strode into the copy room. There you were, standing at the copy machine, reading something on a sheet of paper while the copier spat out more into the output tray. "Morning, Vance," I said. "How was your weekend?"

"Great. You?" you asked without looking up.

"It was good. I celebrated my birthday."

That got your attention. "Oh yeah?" Now you looked up at me, and your eyes widened when you took me in, standing there in my new sweater dress. "Happy birthday," you said huskily. "How old are you?"

"Twenty-six."

Your laugh wrapped me in warmth as you said, "Such a baby." But the way you looked at me felt like you thought I was anything but a baby. "I should buy you a drink as a belated celebration."

"Sure. When?"

I knew that when someone offered to buy you a drink, you're not supposed to immediately pin them down to a time. But all at once, I desperately wanted to go for a drink with you, and I knew it had to be just the two of us.

"Today?" You flicked the hair off your forehead, blinking at me as you spoke.

"Yes."

The copier finished your job at that moment, and the sudden silence was deafening. You turned and retrieved your stack of papers. "Alright. I'll swing by your room after school."

"Great. Have a great day." I cringed, noticing I'd used great twice in the same breath, but you didn't seem bothered by it.

I spent the day wondering if you'd actually show or if you'd conveniently "forget" or say that "something came up," but ten minutes after the bell rang, you were standing in the doorway of my room, holding a large piece of cardstock, your fingertips framing its edges. "The paint hasn't quite dried," you said. "My prep wasn't until sixth hour, and I only started painting this an hour ago."

On the cardstock you'd painted me, wearing my new outfit, the zigzags of my dress bleeding into each other as the paint wasn't quite dry. You had painted a crown upon my head, and I held a bouquet of flowers. Behind me, balloons floated toward the sky.

I took a sharp breath, moved to near speechlessness. "Vance . . . I . . ."

"Happy Birthday, Hazel."

Hearing your voice made my knees go weak, and I knew then that I was beyond smitten. "Thank you so much, Vance. This is . . . amazing."

We went for that drink and took a seat at a corner table, and the conversation bounced between us like sparks— covering everything from our favorite bands to which *Harry Potter* characters we identified with.

After an hour or so, you said, "I'm starving. Should we order food?"

I said yes. Over dinner, I couldn't take my eyes off you. Eventually, when we moved outside to the parking lot, time seemed to stop. My heart raced as we stood underneath a sprinkle of stars that lit up the night sky.

Suddenly, you pressed your lips against mine, and your kiss was a bolt of electricity that ignited my entire body. I felt your embrace wrap around me, pulling me closer to you as if we would never be separated again.

The kiss seemed to last an eternity, yet it ended all too soon. We both stepped back with flushed cheeks and widened eyes. "Was that okay?" You asked.

I only had to grin in response. We were two worlds colliding at that moment and we just stared at each other for what felt like hours, taking in every detail from the curve of our faces to how our hands fit together.

CHAPTER 13

Saturday morning is a sunny and brittle sort of cold, like glistening, hardened sugar. Before I get to school, I stop at Heights Bakery and pick up a box of a dozen glazed donuts. Usually, I prefer my donuts with chocolate frosting and sprinkles, but this bakery has the most amazing glazed donuts ever, and when they're fresh out of the oven, it's like biting into bliss.

I park right by the school building, and when I walk in, ten minutes before Febe and her crew are due to arrive, I hear a familiar voice coming from Vance's classroom—I mean Cyrus Gul's classroom. The voice is musical and female and sad; I realize in an instant that it belongs to Madeline Valby, Vance's mother.

Awkwardly clutching my gigantic box of donuts, I follow the sounds, which are mixed with murmurings from—I'm assuming—Cyrus Gul. When I reach the doorway to his classroom, I blurt out, "Hello," and they both turn toward me like they've been caught doing something criminal. Madeline wears a long cashmere coat over jeans and a sweatshirt, her hair pulled back into a loose ponytail. It's a disarming look like she's part college girl, part mature sophisticate. She opens her mouth to speak, but there are several moments before any sound comes out. "Hello, Hazel. How are you?" With a voice like a public radio announcer, she sounds not unkind but soft, measured, and unflappable.

I kick into fight-or-flight gear as my feet tingle with the urge to run, and my hands, were they free, would be clenched into fists. I'd never punch Madeline, but that doesn't mean I don't have the urge to. Through a thick throat, I manage a civilized, "Fine."

"I'm so glad," she answers, sniffing. "I'm here to clean out Vance's classroom. He asked me to pack up some of his things."

I'm sent spinning. I back up about a foot so I can lean against one of the school's painted concrete walls where I won't have to meet Cyrus's gaze. "Oh. When did Vance tell you he's for sure not coming back?"

Madeline arches an eyebrow. "Hazel, like I've told you several times, I can't get in the middle of you and Vance. I assure you that Vance is safe and well, but he needs to decide when he wants to contact you."

"Right." A cold lump of something—shame, anger, resentment—lodges further down my throat, making it hard to speak. "The thing is, I heard that what happened with the MySpace page wasn't his fault. And it's not like he was fired. Vance has the chance to clear his name."

Madeline grips the edges of her coat, using it like a shield. "I won't get involved, Hazel. I'm just here doing what Vance asked me to do."

"Of course," I say. "Umm . . . would you like me to help?"

She shakes her head. "No, no. Don't worry about it. You're busy recovering from the accident and returning to school. And Cyrus tells me you're starting an art blog? That's so ambitious of you."

Is she being condescending to me? Confused, I look at Cyrus who raises his eyebrows and gives me a flat lipped smile before speaking. "Madeline was curious why I'm here on a Saturday, so I explained about our new project."

Madeline takes off her coat and pushes up her sleeves. "Well, if you don't mind, I'd like to get this over with." She speaks to Cyrus. "You'll be upstairs? I can show you my boxes when I'm done so we can be sure I have taken nothing that belongs to you or to the school."

"That sounds good." Cyrus moves toward me. "Shall we go upstairs to your classroom? That's where I told Febe to meet us."

"Yeah, alright."

Something in my chest deflates like it's a heavy red kickball that's too roughed up to bounce again. I begin the trek up to my classroom, still holding on to the box of donuts, but if a moment ago their smell was all sugar and dough and goodness, now it's just grease, and it's making me nauseous. When we arrive at my classroom door, I hand the box to Cyrus. "Here, take this, please."

He complies, and I fish in my oversized purse for my keys.

"Sorry about that," he states flippantly, like he's done nothing more benign than brushing his shoulder against me as we pass in the hallway.

"Why?" I snap. "You did nothing wrong. You don't owe me anything." My hands pass over tubes of lip balm, my house and car keys, a comb, hairpins, and even a small bottle of lotion, but my classroom keys remain elusive. "You offered to let me come down to your classroom and go through Vance's stuff, and my response was pretty bitchy, so honestly, I don't see how you have anything to apologize for."

Cyrus nods. "Yeah, sure, but . . ."

"*Where the hell are my keys?*"

He clears his throat. "Did you try your coat pocket?"

I want to bang my head against the wall, but instead, I reach inside my left coat pocket, where of course, I find my classroom keys. I unlock my door, we go in, and Cyrus places the box of donuts down on a student desk while I take off my coat and shove my purse into the large drawer at the bottom of my large teacher desk.

"Speaking of keys," I say tersely, "I thought you didn't have any. How did you get in?"

"They finally issued me a set yesterday afternoon," Cyrus replies.

"Oh."

There's a long tense moment that I know I should fill somehow, but I don't have the drive.

"Hey, I know that what just happened down there wasn't my fault," Cyrus states, and it takes a beat for my brain to catch up, to remember where we'd left the conversation mere moments ago. "But it is seriously messed up that Vance took off while you were in the hospital, and now his mom is cleaning up his mess? And neither of them seems worried about how you're doing, which is . . ." He shakes his head to complete his thought. "I thought my relationships and family dynamics were screwed up, but they have nothing on yours."

"Thanks?" I offer.

Cyrus raises an eyebrow in response. "I only apologized because I understand what you're going through. I get it: the guilt, the awkwardness, the misplaced anger. I know how much it all sucks."

"Really?" I put my hands on my hips, only so I don't start wagging my finger in his face. "I seriously doubt that. Unless you suffered a head injury, lost the love of your life, and can't remember most of how it all happened, I doubt that you 'get it'."

If Cyrus is intimidated by my intensity, he doesn't show it. "Sure," he replies, nodding in this sideways indifferent sort of way. "But I got married and divorced before I turned twenty-five, and my parents pretty much disowned me, so I at least sort of 'get it'."

I look at him quizzically. "Seriously?"

He nods. "I could go into the whole sad story, but we'd run out of time before the kids get here. And if I remember correctly, you hate cliffhangers."

Wow. He went there and referenced something from the epic conversation that we'd had on our epic night. It was so many years ago, and now we stand awkwardly in my classroom on a chilly Saturday morning when the heat vents are programmed to run at half their normal rate.

"I don't know what you mean," I state, and then I shiver at the lie.

I move some desks out of their rows and into a circle so, once the kids are here, we can do a group discourse sort of thing as we begin the creation of our blog.

"Okay," Cyrus says softly. "I don't want to spill my guts or anything, except I have no excuse for how I treated you. But I hope you can forgive me."

"Don't worry about it. You're like minor league compared to the bullshit Vance has recently pulled."

I look up from the desk I've just moved to see Cyrus staring, his eyes squinted and his mouth a straight line, strangely resembling the face of the Hulk on the comic book T-shirt he wears underneath his cardigan. He doesn't look angry, though, just surprised, and he quickly snaps his jaw shut and gives me another tight-lipped smile. "Got it," he murmurs, and then he busies himself by pulling more desks into the circle I'm creating.

"We probably don't need that many desks," I say. "I don't think too many kids will show up."

He stops. "Oh. Okay. Should I pull these back?"

I shrug, and then something in me releases. "Hey, why don't we just acknowledge that we're at cross purposes? I want to exonerate Vance and get him back here so he can have tenure. But then you'd be out of a job. And I'm sure you're not thrilled that we're working together. You'd probably like it if I just went away."

He lifts his head and interlocks his fingers, cracking his knuckles before turning back to one desk he just moved, perhaps examining the scrawling that some disgruntled student left behind. "How about this? Let's just not worry about what the other one is thinking, okay?"

I force a smile. "Okay."

He's a strange one, this Cyrus Gul. But then again, lately, I'm not exactly normal. "I guess we've both supplied our fair share of awkward this morning, huh?"

He grins. "Can I have one of these donuts, or are they just for the kids?"

"No, no, help yourself."

For a moment, Cyrus is consumed with peeling the tiny piece of tape that is holding the large flimsy white box of donuts shut. I worry the whole thing will topple down from the desk it is perched upon and the donuts will roll out between the gaps, landing on the not-so-sanitary gray carpet where I've seen the occasional mouse venture out during my prep time, scrounging for crumbs of untoasted Pop-Tarts or Doritos that my students left behind. But then I focus on Cyrus's thick fingers, and the memory of those fingers brushing my skin and my lips and running through my hair . . . I must turn bright red as heat rushes through me.

Cyrus successfully lifts the box's lid, and he pulls out one perfect round donut, all golden and gooey and waiting to be enjoyed. He takes a bite.

"Yum! So delicious. There's nothing as good as fresh-baked glazed donuts. You're having one, right?" He narrows his eyes as he takes in my appearance. "Are you okay?"

"Yeah. I think I'm just hungry."

It's true that, even in my fit of desire, my stomach growls at the sight and smell of those donuts, whereas moments ago, it had turned just at their smell.

I take one from the box and bite, grateful that I'm able to compose myself.

All at once, Febe's gleeful voice comes from behind. "Ms. Ford, you remembered the donuts!" She bounces into the room. "Thank you so much! You would not believe how hungry I am! We have, like, *no* food at the house, and I have been running on empty! Can I have two?"

Again, Febe speaks purely in exclamation points, and if what she said is true about having no food, I don't know how she's so full of beans. But the energy she brings into the room is like the heater kicking on, creating a warmth that makes my muscles relax. "Yes, of course," I tell her.

The other students, representing a variety of nationalities and skin tones, also come in, eat donuts, and chat about their mornings. This is what I love about Heights; the diversity and the community feel are always there, always an issue, and yet never one as well. We're like a microcosm of how society ought to work.

"Okay, so some of us have to be at Key Club in a little while, so I think we should get started," Febe says. Leave it to her to be the taskmaster. We sit in the desks that I'd pulled into a circle, and she goes through what needs to be done: setting up the blog (which will be Cyrus's domain), the literary content (my domain), the artistic content (Cyrus), and the supervisor officially in charge of it all (me). But it's the students who will do most of the work; they know how to do everything and have lots of great ideas.

"I'm thinking we should go edgy," says Febe. "This should give voice to people who haven't been listened to before. And if people want to publish anonymously, then they should get to."

"Um, maybe . . ." I tap my pencil against my notebook. "But what are you thinking we might publish that people wouldn't want to attach their names to?"

She shrugs in nonchalance, and I wonder if she's faking it. How can she be so blasé? "You know, like if they're being abused, or if they have an unpopular opinion about something—that sort of thing."

"I don't know." Cyrus squints and twists his mouth in doubt. "Shouldn't you check with the principal first? He might have a problem with that."

Scoffing, Febe responds. "The whole point of doing an arts blog is to challenge people, to make them think, to change their hearts and minds!"

"Yeah," he answers, "but we still need to be careful."

"I disagree!" Febe leans forward, intense. "Mr. Gul, I know you understand that, ever since 9/11, people are going to be upset with us, no matter what we say or do. So, we may as well say and do things that matter. Right?"

He opens his mouth to respond, but no words come out. Febe laughs. "Don't worry, Mr. Gul. You won't get the blame for any of it. That will fall on me or on Ms. Ford, and you have *ten-year*, right?"

"You mean tenure, and no, not yet. But that's not the point. We need to be careful. Causing a huge stir won't help any of us." Yet as soon as I say this, I realize I'm wrong and that Febe knows it. If her arts blog gets everyone talking out of controversy, she'll be in the center of the storm, and the attention she reaps could be exactly what she needs to catch the eye of several college admissions boards. "We will not be reckless, Febe. I won't allow it."

"I know." She widens her eyes and presses her lips together, seeming sincere. "I'm not asking you to be reckless, Ms. Ford, just brave. Let's publish stuff that is real, that people care about, and that could get them talking or even change how they think about things . . . Couldn't we be brave about that?"

I pause, considering, feeling my heart rate increase. This is hardly the time to be brave when Vance has been exiled over a fake social media post. Why would I set myself up for more? Yet, if we could give voice to the unseen and unheard or to those who endure racism and/or prejudice, well, that *is* a reason to be brave.

Plus, the more I get Febe to see me as an ally, the more likely she will give me information that will clear Vance's name.

"Alright, Febe," I respond. "We'll be 'brave', and I won't go to Principal Thomas for approval. But I get final say over everything that goes in, and I alone will have access to the login info."

Febe manages to jump up and down while staying seated at her desk. She claps, and her eyes dance with joy. "Yay! Thank you, Ms. Ford!"

What have I just agreed to?

CHAPTER 14

"And are you still experiencing headaches?"

Dr. Arney, who has been my GP since I moved to Minneapolis, shines her mini flashlight into my eyes. I am fully clothed but sit on the exam table so she can test my reflexes, see if my pupils are dilated, and listen to my heart rate.

"Sometimes."

She turns off the little flashlight and steps back, meeting my gaze. "I see. Have you been resting, or are you back at work?"

"I'm back at work," I say guiltily, feeling like I'm letting her down. "But it's been several weeks since the accident. You said to rest for around ten days, which I did. I didn't even read or look at a screen which was hard to do. At a certain point, you need to return to your life."

Dr. Arney nods. She's tall, a little dorky, and around my age. With her unpolished air and awkward laugh, she's the sort of woman who used to be the sort of girl I would have been friends with back in high school. That is why I trust her. "I understand," she says. "But the accident affected you both physically and emotionally, and you can't recover in one sense unless you recover in both."

"I'm not sure what that means."

She sighs, not in exasperation but in what appears to be nerves. "I'm going to refer you to a psychiatrist. After the trauma you and your brain have been through, anyone would need some extra help processing."

She sounds almost exactly like Olivia, even though she's pushing psychiatry rather than spirituality. "I don't know, Dr. Arney. I've never been one for therapy."

"Then don't think of it that way."

"How should I think of it, then?"

"Like an extension of your treatment after an extremely traumatic accident. A psychiatrist can also monitor the physical effects that the accident had on you."

Sure, except that sort of care is for the wealthy. Working-class people like me must figure out a way to just move on. "Do you think my insurance will pay for it?"

She smiles grimly. "That's why I'm giving you this referral. Depending on your insurance plan, they'll have to pay for at least some of it."

I take the referral because it's easier than arguing. After all, accepting this slip of paper is not a signed contract stating that I'll show up for therapy. And while I'm sure she's right and that I could benefit from talking to someone, I don't know if I'm that interested in what will help me. Right now, I'm more about immediate gratification and denial.

After my appointment, which happened first thing on Monday morning, I drive to school. Olivia, who has first-hour prep, had agreed to cover my AP Lit class, and I arrive about halfway through the period. My little class full of well-behaved honor students quietly reads *The Great Gatsby*, and Olivia appears to be grading some math worksheets.

"Hey, I'm here," I whisper to Olivia, although my students have noticed my entrance and looked up from their reading. "Thanks so much."

"No problem," she says and, in a fairly loud whisper, asks, "How'd your appointment go?"

"It was fine." Now is not the time to tell her about the psychiatric referral, not with two dozen teenagers eavesdropping on our conversation. "I'll tell you more later."

She wrinkles her brow. "But you're okay, right?"

"Yeah, great. I'm recovering like a champ."

"Sure, but I've heard it can take a while to rebound from a head injury. I know you pride yourself on being self-sufficient, but if you're still struggling, I hope you'll say so."

I glance around the room. Febe, Thomas, and several other students are unabashedly listening in. "I seriously am fine. Thanks again, Olivia." I make to usher her out of my classroom, but she doesn't budge.

"Hey, did you see Mary's outfit?" Olivia loves to make fun of Mary, the dinosaur of a media specialist at Dixon Heights High. Everyone, staff and students alike, is fascinated by her pinkish hair and bright red lipstick that always bleeds onto her teeth. She's like an accident you can't look away from. "Today, she's wearing this long black blazer that seriously goes down past her knees. She looks like she should teach at Hogwarts."

Despite myself, I giggle, even though I realize the students will probably repeat what they've heard. They're like vultures when teachers throw shade at each other.

Olivia looks around and finally notices the teenaged eyes focused on her, focused on both of us. "Okay," she states at her regular volume. "I'll let you get to explaining *The Great Gatsby*. I know they have lots of questions, and even though that was my favorite book in high school, I'm sure I never understood all its metaphors and symbolism."

"Bye, Ms. Davis. See you third hour!" one of my students calls out.

"That's right," Olivia answers in her usual throaty voice. "Today's lesson is going to be so great. We're adding and subtracting polynomials in a tarsia puzzle."

I have no concept of what that means, but my students must because several of them *ooh* and *ah*.

Olivia waves goodbye, and after the door shuts behind her, the girl who has her class third hour says, "I love Ms. Davis. She is so much fun."

"Yeah, she really is, isn't she?" I say.

"Are you two, like, best friends?" Febe asks.

"I suppose," I answer. "We started teaching the same year, and we've always been close." *Except for that huge fight we had*, I silently add.

"That's weird," Thomas says.

I do a double-take. "Why is it weird? Adults still need besties."

He laughs. "I know, but that's not what I meant. You and Ms. Davis seem really different, like with how you see the world or how you think about things."

"Huh." I don't have a response to that, probably because he makes a valid point. After all, Olivia's energy and drive pull me to her. She's not like me—that's true—but her essence is so strong that it overcomes our distinct personalities and approaches to life. "Okay then. You all had questions about *The Great Gatsby*?"

"I do," Febe asserts herself instantly, just like always. "Can you explain the whole illusion versus reality thing that's going on? What is real, and what isn't? And how is it possible that none of the characters truly know each other, let alone themselves? Was that all on purpose?"

Other students chime in. "Is Gatsby stupid?" "Is Daisy a whore?" "What's with the green light?" "Why does Nick settle for being an audience member of his own life?"

"These are excellent questions," I say. "Let's take them one at a time." I clear my throat. "Regarding the theme of illusion versus reality, I think Fitzgerald is saying that reality is subjective and that we all must find our truth. That coincides with knowing yourself, knowing others, and taking an active role in the events that transpire around you. Does that make sense?"

"Not even a little," Febe answers.

I sigh. I can't blame her for not understanding my explanation since I am not sure I understand it myself. At any rate, I haven't lived it myself.

Later, when the bell rings, Febe approaches me.

"Ms. Ford, you're not going to believe it," she says without preamble.

"What?"

"We've already gotten like dozens of submissions. I only posted on message boards about the art blog yesterday, but so many people have already sent me stuff. Some of it is good too."

"Great."

"Yeah, so the best one, I'm emailing to you. And before you read it, let me just say I really think we should publish it. This voice needs to be heard."

"Okay . . ." I glance at her. "Is there something about it I won't like?"

She shrugs. "Probably. But just read it. Then talk to me after."

I don't read the submission that Febe sends me until after the school day is over. But once I get to it, I can't tear my eyes away. Sure, the writing is poetic and wise beyond a teenager's years. But that's not what gets me. It's the story: a strong family bond with strict morals and expectations, the anticipation of sacrifice and complicity, the "betrayal" the young woman commits by lying and going to a party rather than to a friend's house to study.

At the party, she drinks, has fun, and even takes off her hijab, attracting the attention of a star basketball player. He isn't referred to by name, but it has to be Brady Burns, the guy who might just get Dixon Heights to State this year.

"Your hair is so pretty," he slurs, reaching to touch her lush long dark waves.

They stand close to each other, talking about nothing until he leads her to a vacant bedroom. She's drunk enough not to worry, to not have alarm bells go off in her head, at least not until he's kissing her, groping her, and ignoring her pleas to slow down.

Soon she's pushing him away, but he's 6'5" and broad and probably weighs twice as much as she does. It takes no time: a hand over her mouth, another hand down her pants, a shifting and yanking of clothes, and he's assault-ing her. Everything she valued and everything she knew shatters. It only takes a few seconds, but the reverbera-tions will last forever.

So will the silence that comes afterward.

Because who can she tell? There isn't a single person who wouldn't blame her for what happened.

When I'm done reading, I lean back in my office chair and rub my brow with the palm of my hand and let out a heavy sigh. Brady Burns is a legend in this school. He's barely passing most of his classes, and even then, if he didn't both cheat and have a mother who calls teachers and yells until they give him better grades, he probably would have dropped out. But Brady is too valuable a com-modity to our basketball team (the one area where our school shines at a state level) for us to let him fall through the cracks. I'd heard rumors before that he's "not a good guy" but never anything about a specific incident or a specific girl, never anything with a name.

Then again, this piece doesn't have a name. But does it need one?

The weight on my heart is an anvil, and suddenly my breath comes out short and raspy. How is it that girls can be abused and nobody does anything, and nobody cares? Well, I must do something. I must care, because if I let this go unredressed, I may as well have blood on my hands.

Tomorrow I will arrive at school early. Tomorrow I will be here to greet Febe when she gets here, and I will ask her: "Did you write this?" Please, God, let her say no, and please, God, let me believe her.

I pack up my stuff, shrug my coat on, lock up my classroom, and head out. There's a light on down the hall. Lucas, the English department head, is still working. I peek my head into his classroom. "Hey, there," I say to him. "Burning the midnight oil?"

He looks up from his computer. "Yeah. More curriculum alignment."

Ah, yes, the "aligning" of our courses—making sure that they have similar goals, follow the same state standards, and assess the students fairly and with the same amount of rigor—is what Lucas referred to on my first morning back. I still think it's a total headache and sort of meaningless to put it all on paper. Yet, it's not fair that Lucas should have to do it all by himself.

"Lucas, everyone in the English department can help."

He scowls. "I don't want to bother the rest of the department with it."

"That's nice of you, but I think we should all be in on this."

I've long suspected that Lucas takes on the job of English department head because he wants the modicum of power and control that comes with it. If he aligns the curriculum by himself, then he alone gets to decide what the curriculum will be. And I understand this strategy. I often prefer working alone than by committee, and I hate compromising, which is precisely why I don't want Lucas making all the decisions for the courses I teach.

My subtext isn't lost on Lucas. He sighs, and a frown sets in more deeply around his mouth, reaching up to his eyes. "Hazel, you need to be aware of what's coming. Teaching and Learning demands we update the curriculum and include more nonfiction and historical documents, and the fiction we cover needs to be by diverse authors."

I shrug. "Okay. We already do that for English 11."

"But not for AP Lit."

"Yes, we do. Not the historical documents, but we read plenty of diverse authors, like Zora Neale Hurston, Richard Wright, and Sandra Cisneros."

"You also read Fitzgerald and lots of other dead white guys. However diverse you think the syllabus is, you need to take it up a notch."

I take a steadying breath and try not to get angry. "Come on, Lucas. The College Board decides what we should read in AP Lit. I follow it, and I do a course audit. You know that."

Lucas shakes his head. "The college board leaves it very loose, what you study. You can do any variety of world lit from the ancient Greeks on up."

"Yeah, but we're supposed to do an equal distribution of British and American fiction and poetry. And nonfiction is irrelevant. Don't get me wrong; I'm all for adopting a reading list with authors that reflect our student population. But I think there's merit to covering at least a couple of old school classics, like *The Great Gatsby*."

"Maybe. But since you got that letter in your file, you need to watch your step. If you think they're not paying attention, then you're wrong." Lucas looks back at his computer screen and types—a subtle yet clear dismissal.

Anger bubbles inside me. Sure, he pretends to be on my side by issuing this warning, but I can't help but wonder if Lucas is angling to wrest AP Lit away from me. As the only male in the English department, and as the department chair, he has way more power than I do. I bet he's sitting there in his itchy wool sweater, his stringy hair tied back in a ponytail, thinking about going home to eat farro and tofu with his family, and they'll enjoy an evening where they don't talk about news or pop culture since they don't have a TV. Probably, after the kids go to bed, he'll reread something by Chinua Achebe or Toni Morrison and come up with lesson plans for AP Lit.

"We'll continue this conversation tomorrow," I say, with more confidence than I feel. That makes two conversations to dread, two conversations that I will think about when my alarm goes off. *Oh yeah, today I need to talk to Febe, and then I need to talk to Lucas* . . . and in the early morning pitch black of my bedroom, I will rise from my empty bed and face the day alone, wondering why I don't pull a Jay Gatsby and reinvent myself and start somewhere new.

Then, I remember what Febe said during class on my first day back: *"It takes courage to reinvent yourself. And you can't change the past."*

Later, when I'm home, there's an email from Vance in my inbox. It's only the third time he's emailed since the accident, and the jolt I experience when I see he's contacted me is more powerful than an espresso shot.

To: H_Ford_AOGG@hotmail.com
From: VValby89@yahoo.com
Subject: I can't
Hazel,
I will always love you, and that's why I'm answering your last email, even though I can't handle thinking about what happened between us right now. There's too much you don't understand, and I don't have it in me to explain, not yet. I'm sorry. Please take care of yourself, focus on getting well, and don't worry about me.
Yours,
Vance.

First, I want to scream and cry, but I don't. Next, I'm tempted to analyze his diction and tone, starting with "I will always love you" and ending with "Yours, Vance," but before I fall down that rabbit hole, I email him back.

To: VValby89@yahoo.com
From: H_Ford_AOGG@hotmail.com
Subject: Re: I can't
Hi Vance.
You want me to focus on getting well? Then I have to keep emailing you. I need you to know how I feel and what I'm thinking and doing. If I give up the last bit of our connection, then I'm truly lost. So here it goes . . .
Even though you and I both got in trouble for using MySpace, I'm working on a blog with Febe. She showed me this heartbreaking piece that I think she wrote herself, and I must help her. But now Lucas is trying to push me out

of teaching AP, and he said that Teaching and Learning is watching me, waiting for me to mess up again.

Oh, and I saw your mom at school. Did she tell you, or am I so unimportant that I no longer merit a mention? If I sound bitter and needy, that's on purpose. Not so long ago, you were there for me, ready to swoop in and pull a Prince Charming without being asked. Please, do that now.

Love,

Hazel

CHAPTER 15

April 2002

You, Olivia, and I made it through a series of firsts: our first parent-teacher conferences, our first time submitting semester grades, our first time chaperoning a high school dance. Then, second semester came, and during a staff meeting, the superintendent announced that the school district was going through some major budget cuts. Sure enough, in April, all of us non-tenured teachers got "pink-slipped," meaning we'd been laid off. Even though they said we'd likely get hired back, I took the news hard. At lunch, both you and Olivia saw I was upset.

"Are you okay, Hazy?" Olivia asked.

I nodded even though I wasn't okay. My situation differed from hers; math teachers were always in high demand, whereas English teachers were a dime a dozen.

"What do you think, Vance?" Olivia turned toward you. "I don't think Hazy is okay. She doesn't *look* okay, does she?"

You shrugged, and I let out a sigh that came out like a groan. "I can already hear my dad gloating." Doing my best impersonation of him, I used a gruff voice. "'Come on, Hazel, you said schools in Minnesota are well funded. Now your district can't even afford, what, thirty thousand a year to keep you? Did you pick a bad district, or are you just a bad teacher?'"

Olivia's mouth dropped open. "Would your dad really say something so awful?"

He'd probably just think it, but I, with my English-teacher inference superpower, would hear the silent criticism loud and clear. Shrugging, I answered simply, "He might."

Olivia held out her hand. "Give me your phone. I'll call your dad right now and tell him to be more supportive. You are an amazing teacher, and he should be proud to have you as a daughter."

Sometimes, Olivia could shock me with her fiercely loyal protectiveness. "I, um . . ." I stuttered, unable to find the right words.

She used her outstretched hand to punch me playfully in the shoulder. "Don't worry, Hazy. I won't seriously call your dad. But we need to lift your spirits." She twisted her mouth in contemplation. "I know! We'll go lingerie shopping. Let's buy real pink slips to celebrate the paper ones we got handed today."

It was Friday, and often we'd go out after work to kick off the weekend. "But what about me?" you asked. "I want to celebrate, too."

"Don't worry, Vance," Olivia responded. "You can meet us for drinks later."

You agreed, and after school, Olivia and I went to Victoria's Secret at Rosewood Mall where she and I both picked out pink satin slips with spaghetti straps, but otherwise, they were different. Olivia's slip was short, low cut, and bright pink, and mine was pale, knee-length, and gathered directly under the bust, flaring out slightly in soft folds that fell to the bottom of my thighs.

When we left the store, a couple of guys followed us out. They both looked like dudes who lived in their parents' basements and who had never seen a naked woman in real life. Their bodies were pale and doughy, and their faces were wide with weak chins and little eyes. And yes, they were creepy, but I figured they were harmless. We were in a busy mall, and they were barely within spitting distance of Olivia and me.

But that wasn't how Olivia saw it. "These pervs need to back off," she said to me as we walked.

"They're probably just headed in the same direction as we are," I replied.

"They better not be!" Olivia's voice was deliberately loud. We passed a Bath and Body Works and turned past Macys, and they kept following us. Olivia stopped abruptly and spun around.

"What do you think you're doing?" she demanded.

One of them, the taller of the two, smiled menacingly.

"We were just admiring your lingerie," he said.

Olivia's eyes grew flinty. "You need to leave now," she said firmly.

The other one stepped forward, his face contorted with anger. "We don't need your permission to walk around here!" he said, his voice thick.

Olivia's eyes widened, and her hands balled into fists at her sides. She was about to lose it. Before I could stop her, she grabbed her purse and pulled out a can of mace that she had stashed inside. She brandished the can in front of them, shaking it for added effect.

"You two better back off," she growled, "or you're going to get a face full of mace." The two guys both looked like they might pee their pants.

The taller guy opened his mouth as if to say something else, but Olivia didn't give him a chance. "I will not tell you again! I will spray you with mace if I have to! Get out of here or clsc!"

Passersby in the mall hurried past us, not wanting to get involved, and mall security was nowhere near.

The guys stepped back quickly and walked away, casting nervous glances over their shoulders as they moved further down the mall. Olivia watched them go with a satisfied smile before turning to me. "See? That's how it's done!"

I didn't know if I should be impressed or terrified. "Let's go," I said. "After that, I could use a drink." We went to The Cheesecake Factory where we splurged once again, this time on sugary cocktails and avocado eggrolls. I texted, and you came to meet us.

"Olivia's a badass," I said as soon as you sat down.

"Tell me something I don't already know," you responded. "But what was her latest badass move?"

I started to relay the story, but Olivia broke in. "Let me tell him, Hazy. You're getting all the details wrong."

Olivia described what happened, but in her version, the guys were muscular and they had verbally threatened us as well as invaded our space. In reality, they'd always been at least four feet away.

"To Olivia," you said, raising your glass. "I hope I never get on the wrong side of you."

We toasted Olivia's bravery, and then we pivoted to school gossip. Usually, that was Olivia's favorite topic, but after a while, she started to deflate.

"Do you think we'll really get hired back?" Olivia asked as she stared into her Cosmo. Perhaps she was crashing after the adrenaline rush from before.

You arched an eyebrow. "I think so. When Jim called me down, he was all, 'Let me know right away if you decide to look for another job. We don't want to lose you.'"

Olivia looked up from her drink. "Really? He didn't say that to me. I think Jim hates me."

"Why would Jim hate you?" I asked Olivia. "You're a good teacher, and you teach math, which is way more in demand than English. If any of us don't get hired back, it will be me."

Amidst the noise and bustle of The Cheesecake Factory, you scrutinized me, tilting your head so a lock of your waves brushed the top of your cheek. "You could be right," you said slowly as if measuring your words. "English teachers are undervalued. We need to make you less expendable."

I bit my lower lip, stung and unsure how to respond. We'd been sleeping together for months, and it was hard keeping our relationship a secret, especially from Olivia. Were you hiding your feelings, were you trying to be casual, or did you honestly believe that I was "expendable"?

"Vance, that's so mean," Olivia said. But there was a hint of joy in her voice, as if she were happy that it was me and not her who was the object of your pity and concern.

You widened your eyes like a little boy, suddenly aware you'd said something wrong. "No, no. I wasn't trying to be mean. I just want to help." You placed your hand upon mine. "It's not too late, you know. You could still make a splash."

"How?" I asked, unsure if I really wanted the answer.

You chewed the side of your mouth, a tick that on most people is slightly awkward, but on you, with your pillowy lips, was sort of erotic. "I don't know. Help the students write a play?" Your eyes lit up. "Yes! That's what you should do, and they could perform it at a local theater company! Just think of the PR!" Your voice squeaked slightly in excitement, and I couldn't help but find you endearing, even though I wasn't ready to buy what you were selling.

"Yeah, but Vance, there's no way. It's too late in the year, and how do we get a theater company to agree?"

You shook your head dismissively. "Leave that to me. I have connections."

You seemed to know everyone who was anyone in the Minneapolis arts community, and I'm sure there were several local theater companies you could contact for a favor. But more importantly, once a plan was a seed in your mind, it grew into an uncontrollable vine.

We finished our drinks and appetizers, and you insisted on walking us to our cars. "Just in case those guys hung around," you said. We got to Olivia's car first.

"Thanks, Vance," she said.

Olivia gave you a tight hug, and in a fit of jealousy, I saw something—a connection, mutual attraction?—between the two of you. But Olivia got into her car and drove off, and you turned to me in The Cheesecake Factory's parking lot and said, "So, are you going to model that new pink slip for me?"

I must have had a strange expression on my face, because you said, "What's wrong?"

"Nothing, except sometimes I wonder why you chose me and not Olivia. She's so charismatic and pretty."

"Are you drunk?" Vance laughed. "Come on, Hazel. Olivia's great, but she's way too much work. I need to be with someone more subtle."

"You like me because I'm subtle?"

You reached for me, wrapping your arms around my waist. "That's one reason. But there are so, so many others." Planting kisses along my neck, you paused and said, "Do you need me to tell you what they are?"

I gripped your shoulders and pressed my forehead to yours. "I kinda do."

"You're smart, you're unique, and you have layers. I *love* your layers."

I was so easily convinced. "Let's go to my place," I said.

Back at my apartment, I showed you my new pink slip, only to have you deftly slide it off my body. Afterward, we lay in bed, you stroked my skin with your artist's hands, and then you started talking as if we'd never left the subject of the play you'd decided I'd produce. "You'll hand-select a few students and help them write a play, and I'll get my art kids to design the scenery, and my friend Buck's theater company will foot the bill for the whole thing, and it can be performed in their space on an off night. The PR will be incredible."

I didn't share your confidence that it would all come off without a hitch. Still, on Monday, I asked the other English teachers to recommend their most creative students, and soon I had a list of several talented kids from each grade. Febe was on the list. Since I only taught upperclassmen, it would be the first time I'd work with her.

On Tuesday afternoon, Febe came into my room, her pink hijab sailing behind her. She was like a fresh breeze bursting into a sauna.

"Ms. Ford, are we seriously getting to write our own play?"

"Yeah," I responded. "Do you have any ideas?"

"Totally! Have you ever read *The Oresteia*, by Aeschylus?"

I wrinkled my brow in surprise. "Umm, maybe? There are so many Greek tragedies, sometimes I get them confused."

Her mouth dropped open. "I can't believe you're not familiar with it, Ms. Ford! It's a whole trilogy of plays with major characters from mythology. And it is so, so good!" Excited, she waved her hands as she spoke. "Agamemnon returns from war, and his wife Clytemnestra is mad because he'd raped her and sacrificed their daughter to win the war, so she murders him in the bathtub. But then, his son Orestes is all, 'Apollo wants me to kill you, Mom', and he murders Clytemnestra, and then the last play is about Orestes's trial."

"Wow, Febe, I'm impressed with your knowledge of this stuff."

She let out an embarrassed little laugh. "Well, we had the mythology unit in English 9, and I really got into it, but I guess I'm also sort of a reading geek."

"Yeah, me too," I replied.

She nodded, her face serious, determined to finish her thoughts. "But, Ms. Ford, we could do a modern-day version! Updated, you know? In the last play of the trilogy, there are these three furies who want to condemn Orestes, but they're just dismissed by Apollo who is all, 'Females shouldn't have any power.' We could totally relate it to the world today and how strong females are labeled and condemned whenever they get angry!"

I loved her enthusiasm. "Febe, will you propose your ideas to the whole group when we have our first meeting on Thursday?"

"Sure! And don't worry, Ms. Ford; I'm good at convincing people. This idea is going to take off!"

Febe was right. Turned out she's just as good as you are at making things happen. Our play was incredible, super artsy, and with a strong feminist message, it generated lots of positive PR.

And you were right. Shortly after that, I was hired back.

CHAPTER 16

This morning, there's a shift. I get up when my alarm goes off, and I get ready for school without struggling over silly choices, like what to wear or what to pack for lunch. I pet Baby Girl and promise her we'll have more snuggles this evening. And while Vance's absence is still like an icepick to my heart, I'm more consumed with what lies ahead than with what has already passed.

But Febe isn't at school, and Lucas doesn't emerge from his classroom, and whenever I go to find him, he's busy teaching or talking with students. By 3:05 p.m., I have a terrible headache, and I want to go home. I am still recovering from a head injury, after all, but I worry about what Lucas might plan or talk to Teaching and Learning about while I'm not here. Still, my need to lie down in a dark quiet room is overpowering, so I give in.

On my way out, I spot Cyrus in the corridor outside his classroom. His lips part into a pleased smile when he sees me, and he adjusts his Buddy Holly-style glasses up over the bridge of his nose. I can't help but admire the way he moves with such strength and grace. Reminding myself not to be attracted to him, I begrudgingly, silently acknowledge that he's sexier than his nerd persona would suggest. "Do you have a minute? There's something I should show you."

I want to say no but can't, not without sounding totally rude. "Um, okay."

I follow him into the art room, which should feel sur-
real—Vance is still here even though he's noticeably,
painfully absent—but I don't have the energy to feel much
of anything right now. As Cyrus leads me to the back, I
notice new posters decorating the walls. Besides the student work that hangs everywhere, there are mounted
prints by Warhol and by other pop artists, brightly colored
collages with mixed media, and actual comic book prints,
images of Marvel superheroes saving the day.

Okay then. Cyrus Gul is a geek.

Cyrus and I reach the very back of the studio space
where canvases are stacked like dominoes against the far
wall. Cyrus picks up one that is at the front of the stack
and shows it to me. "I asked the students if they knew who
painted this, thinking it was by a student, but they said it
was Mr. Valby's." Cyrus clears his throat. "They said he'd
painted it in class as a demonstration."

I look at the painting. It's a portrait of a beautiful
woman with long dark hair, huge brown eyes lined by
thick lashes, and pouty lips. She's stunning, and so is the
painting, and just looking at it feels like freezer burn in my
blood. Because some part of my memory comes flooding
back and I recognize her instantly.

"Do you know if she's a student here?" Cyrus asks.

"It's Annabelle. She was Vance's student teacher."

"Oh, well, that makes sense." Cyrus shifts his weight,
and his gaze moves across the room like he's looking for
something. "I wasn't sure what to do with it, and um . . ."

I turn away from the painting and force his eyes to meet
mine. Cyrus wears a pained expression. "You were scared
to show this to me, weren't you?"

"Scared?" He offers a soft burst of laughter. "Why would
you think that?"

"You're an artist, so it's easy for you to read another artist's attitude toward his subject. And this . . ." I gesture toward the painting. "I mean it's so obvious, isn't it? Vance was totally infatuated. Maybe he hadn't slept with her yet, but he clearly wanted to."

I expect Cyrus to shuffle more, to deflect, or to turn this into an awkward joke. But it's like his center of gravity is pulled down as his chin tilts up, his gaze turning confident.

"I'm sorry, Hazel." His words come out like a strong and warm balm. "I wasn't trying to upset you. I just didn't know what I should do with it."

I'm at a loss for words. Cyrus blinks at me and then looks down at the painting he holds.

I take a deep breath. "No, I'm sorry. I didn't mean to accuse you. I guess I'm just emotionally unstable right now."

He cocks his head, half smiling and creasing his brow. "You don't seem emotionally unstable to me. You're stunned and confused, and you're recovering from major trauma. There's a difference."

Cyrus says this softly, his shaved head gleaming copper in the fluorescent lights of the classroom. It's almost like he has a halo. And his eyes are a surprising shade of hazel. With his dark complexion, you'd expect them to be brown. I flashback to when those hazel eyes had peered into mine, to when I was sure he knew some truth about me I couldn't display, not to just anyone.

But it had all been a lie.

I won't find him endearing. I refuse to notice that, despite being tall and broad and potentially imposing, right now, his demeanor seems kind and studious. With that constant worn cardigan over rotating graphic T-shirts and his thick-rimmed glasses, he gives off the vibe of a mellow intellectual. And that could all be a lie too.

"Thanks," I say curtly. "I appreciate the empathy. But I'm not confused."

"It's just that . . ." Cyrus lets his voice trail off for a moment. "Don't you have a head injury? I mean how could you *not* be confused?"

I search for a response, but words are elusive inside my murky mind, which, I suppose, proves Cyrus's point. My answer comes out in a sigh as I let my shoulders slump. "I don't care what you do with that stupid painting. Just keep it out of my sight."

"We could burn it if it would make you feel better."

"Ha. I'm beyond feeling better at this point." I pause. "Anyway, thanks? I guess I'll see you tomorrow."

"Yeah, sounds good."

"Okay then. Bye." I walk toward the door of his classroom, wondering if he'll follow me out.

He doesn't.

CHAPTER 17

Getting close to Vance was almost too easy for Annabelle. Whenever she asked him something, he never hesitated to answer, even when the questions were about his personal life or the ambitions he'd put on hold. It took little to get him to admit that he needed someone who understood and supported him 100 percent. They spoke for hours about art and education, but then Vance would suddenly start talking about himself and seeking her praise. In the same breath though, he'd turn around and ask her about her own dreams and hang onto her every word to try and find ways to help her make them come true. Maybe he had a hero complex, or maybe he was just a genuinely nice guy.

It was her idea for him to paint her, but he was enthusiastic from the start. They'd been planning a unit on portraits, and Annabelle suggested he model the techniques for the students with her as his subject. Vance began by sketching her, and then he worked tirelessly, trying to shade and highlight and capture "her essence" with color and shadow. Sometimes she would model for him after school when no one was around, but other times Vance would have her sit and he would work on her portrait in front of the students, explaining his process as he went.

Annabelle could only imagine what his students, especially the young girls who were in love with Vance, thought of that.

On the day he finished her portrait, Annabelle said they should celebrate. They drove to an out-of-the-way bar and nestled in a back table, out of sight from prying eyes. They talked for hours, savoring each other's company and getting lost in their time together. It was as if no one existed beyond them.

When it was time to go home, Vance escorted her to her car and pulled her close, his hands burning against her skin from the desire that had slowly built throughout the evening. He kissed her longingly, passionately - a forbidden kiss that threatened to undo them both.

"I shouldn't have done that," he said in a low whisper.

Annabelle stepped back, understanding why it had to be this way. "Because of Hazel."

Vance nodded slowly. "Yes, that's part of it." His voice filled with sadness and regret. "But even if she wasn't in the equation, this still wouldn't be appropriate." He looked away. "If anyone found out we both could be in big trouble."

Annabelle wanted nothing more than for him to take her in his arms again but she nodded in agreement instead. "Okay. We'll keep it on the down low."

"Thank you," he whispered, stroking her hair behind her ear. "God," he whispered, "you are so beautiful."

She didn't respond. Annabelle, who had never been a fool, wasn't about to become one now.

CHAPTER 18

The first time happened on a Thursday. She'd been out that day, not able to teach owing to a nasty case of food poisoning.

"What's up?" he'd texted. "Where are you? Are you okay?"

She texted back. "I had some bad tuna salad. Stomach cramps. You don't want to know."

He didn't respond, and she figured she'd grossed him out. Guys could be so squeamish. But at five thirty, there was a knock on her door. She opened it to find Vance, adorable in his thin sweater hoodie and worn dress pants, holding a container of chicken broth, bagels, and a DVD of *The Ring*.

"I come bearing gifts," he said. "How are you feeling?"

"Better," she said, ushering him inside. "The stomach pain went away about an hour ago."

"Cool," he said. "Let's eat and watch a movie."

"I thought you hated scary movies."

He'd already moved toward her linoleum table, lining up the contents of what he brought into a neat row.

"Yeah, but you don't. I can be strong if you promise to hold me during the scary parts."

"Okay," she said. She didn't ask him about Hazel or how he was free to come to her this evening. "But you realize that most of the movie is scary?"

"Yeah," he said, his voice raspy, coming close enough to her that she could smell his musky scent.

They sat on her couch, sipping reheated chicken broth from mugs and chewing on toasted, buttered sesame bagels. By the time that creepy girl from *The Ring* climbed out of the screen, they were done eating, and Vance dove into her lap.

It was like they'd been together a thousand times already. His lips effortlessly found hers, and they automatically knew each other's rhythms. When he came, melting into a pool of pleasure as his chest heaved and collapsed on top of her, she'd never felt more alive, more necessary.

"This is only the beginning," she tenderly whispered into his ear.

He didn't disagree.

CHAPTER 19

I stand at my kitchen sink, rinsing a pile of dishes and putting them into the dishwasher, when Baby Girl comes up to me, meowing and brushing against my legs.

"What's the matter?"

She responds with a wistful meow.

"Is your food dish empty?"

She meows again as if she understands. But with the amount I talk to her, she ought to have an honorary degree in human communication. I shake my head. "I'm sorry, Baby Girl. Did I forget to feed you?"

She beckons me toward her food dish, and I turn off the sink and follow her into the little hallway by the back entrance where her food, water, and litter box are kept. Sure enough, her food dish needs refilling, and I scoop out kibbles from the nearly empty bag.

"I need to buy you more soon, don't I?"

Baby Girl is unconcerned with this question. Instead, she eats and purrs with the vigor of a much younger, healthier cat.

I look at the bag of cat food, which Vance would buy in large quantities from the animal shelter where we'd volunteered and found Baby Girl. I'll have to make a special trip, and while I'm there, I may as well get cat litter and some of those special cat treats she likes. The bag of litter is right by my foot, but Vance kept the treats in a drawer in our bedroom because he used to lure Baby Girl in there to get her to snuggle in all our comforters.

I do not know what brand the cat treats are, so I go look for the container now. Once in the bedroom, I pause, trying to remember which drawer he kept them in, and I go for the top drawer on the right of his dresser, feeling nervous. I haven't wanted to go through his things.

Vance came to our house while I was in the hospital, got his art supplies, and cleared his stuff from the closet. But this old dresser was left uninterrupted. Vance found it at a garage sale, sanded it, and repainted it to mirror the landscape in a Degas nature scene, the colors soft and blending into a pastel spectrum that lights up the room. He kept little in it, except for some underwear, socks, and T-shirts because that's about all the dresser has room to hold.

I pull open the top right drawer and, taking in a sharp breath, prepare myself to be rocked by some heavy emotion. All I find are boxer shorts. They're just boxer shorts, and they don't make me cry or laugh or melt or anything. I feel around, but no container of cat treats lurks beneath these boxers, so I close the top right drawer and move to the left.

In the top left drawer sit some neatly rolled socks, all identical in that they're black and the type that you buy in a large bag at Target. In between two sets of socks sits the bag of cat treats. Success! I turn to find Baby Girl, thinking I'll give her a treat right now, but then I think again, turning back toward the dresser.

Baby Girl meows mournfully. "You are so good at guilt trips," I tell her. "But I may as well get it over with—opening the other drawers. Then, I promise, it's treat time."

In the right middle drawer, I find a bunch of folded white T-shirts. I feel around underneath them, and there's nothing. The middle left drawer holds the old paint-splattered shirts he wore while working on his projects. The bottom right drawer has two sweaters he never wore, gifts from his mom that were expensive, and that he did not like but felt too guilty to get rid of. None of these drawers holds anything troubling.

"What am I so scared of?" I look to Baby Girl for an answer, and she gives me her most solemn expression. "You're right. I'm being silly. There's only one more drawer to go." I pull open the bottom left drawer, holding my breath. Inside I find some wool gloves and the Irish knit scarf Vance bought when he studied abroad his junior year of college. This scarf is his favorite. I pull it out and press it to my face, trying to absorb his scent, his essence, or both. But when I pull the scarf away, something sticks to my cheek. I pick whatever it is off and hold it up so I can see.

It's a long dark hair.

Vance's hair wasn't this long, and I've had the same pixie cut for years. But Annabelle? In that portrait Vance painted, her hair was long and dark.

Oh my God.

Like a criminal who wants to hide the evidence, I shove the scarf back in its drawer, flick the hair away so it's now underneath Vance's dresser, and then I climb into bed, literally hiding my head underneath the covers.

Baby Girl jumps onto the bed, meowing and kneading the blanket that covers my head.

"Okay, okay. You're right. A promise is a promise."

I rise from the bed and give Baby Girl her promised treats. She purrs as she eats them, then, when she's finished, looks at me with knowing eyes.

"What?" I demand. "Have I been an idiot this whole time? I never thought I'd be the sort of woman who wouldn't know her man was cheating."

In response, she plops down on the floor and starts grooming herself everywhere, including her unmentionables. I give Baby Girl some privacy and climb back into bed.

I fall into a deep sleep, the type where my dreams are disorientating, but I can't remember any of the details except for one: Vance said he wanted to get back together, and I told him no. I guess my subconscious realizes the benefits of solitude. However, in the night, Baby Girl curls up into a ball on top of Vance's old pillow, her presence a soothing, companionable relief.

The next morning, I wake even though I hadn't set my alarm; apparently, my body clock is trained for 5:30 a.m. on the dot. I rub the sleep from my eyes, stretch in bed, and then sit up. It's time to start the day, revelations about my relationship be damned.

I barely have time to shower and brew coffee, and I must push all my angst aside as I have an early morning meeting with a student, her mom, and the student's case manager. It's an IEP meeting, short for *Individual Educational Plan*, where a special ed student gets feedback about how they're doing in class. The case manager is also a special ed teacher meant to advocate for the student and ensure that she's receiving adequate accommodations in the classroom.

When I walk into the meeting room, I realize there's a translator. Her presence is necessary because the student's mom only speaks Spanish. The mom looks like she could be in high school herself, but probably she's in her early thirties. So, she's not much older than me. I don't think of myself as being old enough to have a teenage child, yet technically, I am.

I sit in a chair at the big conference room table, wishing I had brought my coffee mug with me. The general ed teachers go around and describe how Sonia, the student in question, is doing in their class, giving rave reviews for Sonia's performance in both math and music.

Then it's my turn. "Sonia has a D minus in English 11, mostly because she hasn't turned in her literary analysis essay. If she needs more time or help, I'm happy to give it to her, but she does need to get that essay in."

Then the mother starts talking, directing her words only to Sonia, which the translator then speaks for us.

"You can say how you feel, Sonia. Tell them you don't like this teacher. You told me she doesn't help you and you are lost in her class. If you want to change teachers, you can, but you have to tell them how you feel and that you don't like her."

Sonia says nothing; she just sits with her head down, teary-eyed and sniffling. The mom talks to her daughter again. "You need to say something, Sonia. This is your chance to speak up about the teacher you do not like."

"Hold on," I interject. I try to make eye contact with both Sonia and her mom, but neither will meet my gaze. "I have to say this is hard to hear. But this is not about my feelings; it's about Sonia. I had no idea . . ." My voice cracks as it trails off. I take a steadying breath, knowing I should not let my bruised ego stand in the way of helping Sonia pass English. "Sonia," I say, trying to make direct eye contact though she evades me. "You never said you were frustrated, or that you needed help. If you have questions, you need to let me know."

Mr. Fischer and the dean of students chime in, making half-hearted pitches in my defense, saying things like Sonia needs to advocate for herself, and English 11 is a difficult class, and it's different from the resource English class she was used to last year where there were two teachers and fewer students so one-on-one attention was more possible. But they don't defend my reputation as a good teacher who cares about her students, and the passive betrayal chafes me.

Sonia continues to cry, and now the mother is crying, too. "You have to make an effort," she says to Sonia, and the translator continues to articulate her words for us. "You think I like going to my job where I am the only person who doesn't speak English? You think I am treated well there? I am not, but I do it for you, to give you a better life, so now you are in this situation you do not like, and you have to do this for me."

My heart twists knowing that I'm not helping them. They both see me as the villain here, and well, it makes me wonder if maybe I am.

"Okay," Mr. Fischer finally says, "I think we should move on from talking about this class. Can we agree that Sonia will do a better job of asking Ms. Ford for help, and Ms. Ford will be sure to check in with Sonia daily to see if she has questions?"

"Sure," I reply, and Sonia nods.

Mr. Fischer and the dean of students thank me for coming, and I get up to go. This has to be an all-new low for morning meetings that start my day. With a sigh, I check my box in the mailroom, and then I head toward my classroom, walking past students shrugging off their coats and shoving them into their lockers, many of them crying out to their friends with teenager-type theatrics. Meanwhile, I'm trying to shake off what just happened.

When I get up to my hallway, Febe is waiting outside my door. "Febe," I exclaim, "how are you? I missed you yesterday." I unlock my classroom, and we both step inside.

She shrugs, her energy diminished, and her general vibe is "Don't mess with me." "Is everything okay?" I ask.

"Yeah, of course," she answers, and she heads to her desk where she sits and immediately puts her head down on the flat surface and covers it with her arms.

I refuse to be deterred and step up to her. "I read the submissions you sent me. Most of them are quite good, and I think we have a lot to work with. But the one that was your favorite, that one we need to talk about."

Febe doesn't move; there's no lifting of her head, no eye contact, no vocal cue to even acknowledge that she heard me. I don't know why she's acting like this, and most likely, it isn't personal, but she's freezing me out. On a normal day, I'd probably let it go, assume she's having a rough morning, and give her space. But right now, her iciness and the hurt from minutes before combine, and my emotions get the better of me.

"You could respond, Febe. I think you owe me that much."

Again, there's no sound, no movement, but I don't back away. "Febe!" I simultaneously raise my voice and force some laughter, trying to sound like I'm joking, but I'm sure it comes off as desperation. "Can you act like a human being and answer me?"

Slowly she lifts her head. "Not right now, Ms. Ford. Leave me alone."

Her eyes, which are red and watery, speak volumes. Instantly, my irritation morphs into concern. I sit at the desk next to her and put a tentative hand on her shoulder. She immediately shrugs it off. "Febe," I say softly, "what's wrong?"

Now her words come out strong and harsh, even though her head is again buried and she speaks into her desk. "I said *not right now!*"

I recoil, my cheeks burning. Other students enter the class, and I bolt up from the student desk where I sit as if they'd caught me in the act of something forbidden. "Good morning," I murmur, but they don't hear me. They're too immersed in their own conversation, something about pep band and whether they'll ride on the team bus to the away basketball game tonight.

Minutes later, the morning bell rings, and I take attendance and begin class. We start with poetry analysis: "Invictus" by William Ernest Henley. It's very relevant to the character of Jay Gatsby, and every semester the students always love it, especially the last two lines: "I am the captain of my fate, I am the master of my soul."

Febe keeps her head down for the entire lesson as I explain how the poet suffered through a childhood illness but came out of it still believing he controlled his own destiny. All my other students agree with him, which is unsurprising because teenagers love to believe they can conquer the world if they simply make the right choices and stay committed to their own personal cause.

"So, the poet is like Gatsby, right?" Thomas, who is always chatty and engaged, asks this. "He believes in reinvention and that it's possible to overcome hardship and create a new identity and a new life."

"Right." I'm answering Thomas, but my eyes are on Febe; the top of her head is still buried in her arms and resting upon her desk. "Overcoming hardship and reinvention are definitely connecting themes. But is reinvention necessary after tragedy? Is it wise? Shouldn't we incorporate our experiences, learn from them, and figure out a way to move on?"

Thomas laughs. "Are you asking for a friend, Ms. Ford?"

I'm sure he was just trying to be funny, to lighten the mood, but his question embarrasses me.

I murmur something incoherent, resume talking about the lesson, and get through the rest of the hour. When the bell rings, Febe finally lifts her head from her desk, but she walks out without so much as a word or even a glance in my direction.

I try not to dwell on it, though, as I have the rest of my classes to teach and get through.

By the end of the day, I'm thinking there's no way I can tough this out; it's too hard. Screw incorporating my experiences, learning from them, and moving on. I'm ready to run off and reinvent myself somewhere new, somewhere warm, somewhere I can be someone else, with or without Vance.

But I will have to figure out how to do that later. Today, I'll simply cut out of here and not stick around to grade papers, plan lessons, and/or be available if any students pop by for after-school help.

Problem is, I'm not sure where I want to go. Home? No thank you; I'll just start wallowing again. The gym? Since the accident, I haven't been able to summon the energy to work out, even though I'd probably feel better once I got going. Shopping? I suppose some retail therapy might help, except I could see it going the other direction. I might feel more useless and depressed surrounded by all the false promises at the mall, that buying this sweater/jacket/lip balm will change my world and fix my problems.

Weary, I hang my head in my hands and collapse my arms onto my teacher's desk, not unlike the pose Febe assumed all during first hour. Perhaps she was on to something. Sitting this way, cocooned in my own darkness, kind of helps.

"Ahem," I hear a male clearing his throat, and I raise my head to see who it is.

Cyrus.

He's stands in the open doorway of my classroom, his head tilted to the side, gazing at me with concern. "Hey . . ." he says as our eyes meet. "Is this a bad time?"

I rub my eyes. My sense of defeat is so strong it drowns out any embarrassment I should most likely feel. "No, no. Come in. What's up?"

Cyrus steps in toward my desk. "Not much. I was just wondering when you'd like to publish the first issue of *Burnt Moon*?"

That's the name the kids came up with for our art blog. They thought it sounded catchy and edgy, plus, it would be easy to use our school colors of black and gold on the homepage.

When I don't respond right away, Cyrus continues talking. "Pretty much everything is ready to go on our end. Now we just need to post the submissions. I can show you and Febe how to do that whenever you want."

"Febe!" I growl her name as I stare straight ahead. I must seem unbalanced.

"Is something wrong?"

"Yes!" my head snaps toward Cyrus. "Febe came to class this morning clearly upset, and I was worried about her. Then, she snapped at me when I asked her what's wrong. She kept her head down for the entire hour, and she rushed out the second class was over. So, I do not know what's up or if she's ever going to talk to me again."

Cyrus nods as if to confirm he understands. "That's rough. But I'm sure it wasn't about you. She's probably just going through something, and she needed a little space."

I squeeze my eyes shut. After reading that piece, I hate to imagine just what Febe might be going through. "Right, except, lately, I've been thinking that I suck as a teacher—no, not just as a teacher, but as a human being."

"Wow." Cyrus scratches his head. "I guess you're in a dark place right now."

"You mean, other than the dark place I was already in where every guy who I get close to takes off without an explanation?"

"Sure." He shrugs. "I mean I was just thinking it might be seasonal depression or the mid-week doldrums, but yeah, all that."

I gaze at him, furrowing my brow, unsure if he's joking or maybe he's just too oblivious to understand I was in-cluding him in the guys "I get close to."

When I don't respond, he breaks into an apologetic grin. "Come on; let me take you for a drink."

"On a Wednesday?"

"Exactly." His smile reaches his eyes, which are warm, and while his words are decisive, his voice is gentle. "Let's go."

It's sort of a relief to be told what to do, especially since a moment ago I was immobilized by indecision. "Alright." I push my hands against my desk, rise from my office chair, and move toward my cabinet where my purse and coat are stored. Day drinking on a Wednesday afternoon might be exactly what I need. As for hanging out with Cyrus, that's a little iffy, but at this point, what have I got to lose?

CHAPTER 20

We head to a pizza restaurant fifteen minutes away from Dixon Heights. The place has string lights hanging from the ceiling, exposed brick walls, and large unopened cans of crushed tomatoes on the tables, used to raise the pizza platters and preserve space for plates and utensils. The air smells like garlic and rising dough, and instantly, I feel at home. We find a table, and Cyrus sits across from me. It's refreshing because there's no concerned look in his eye, and he's not about to give me advice like I should find God, get therapy, move on, or some combination of the three.

I almost relax, almost let myself enjoy this moment, but then I remember: *Vance*. True, he abandoned me. And yes, it's likely he was cheating on me with Annabelle. But he is still my boyfriend, and now I'm here with Cyrus whom I kind of fell in love with during our one-night stand and who nearly broke me a little. Afterwards, I had a string of disposable relationships with forgettable guys, and it wasn't until Vance came along that I could exorcize Cyrus from my heart. So, for many reasons, I must proceed with caution.

I say the most generic thing I can think of. "I like this place. Do you come here a lot?"

Cyrus smiles lopsidedly, peering at me like we share a secret. How is he still so handsome? Is it because he's bathed in an orangey low light? He wears those thick glasses and comic book T-shirts, and I tell myself that maybe he used to be my type but not since I met Vance.

"I used to work here," he answers. "Around a year ago."

"As a waiter?"

"No, as a chef. I made pizzas."

"That's impressive."

"Yeah." He fiddles with the crushed red pepper canister, twirling it a bit. "I learned on the job. The staff was always really cool to me."

"Do any of them still work here?"

"I'm not sure. Sometimes I still hang out with friends I made here, but they've all moved on to other jobs, too. And once I started teaching, I kind of stopped socializing, and people who aren't educators don't get it. They don't know how busy and exhausted you are, like, all the time."

"Yeah, I know what you mean." I laugh self-consciously. "It's why I became so attached to Vance and Olivia. We all understood what the other was going through."

Cyrus nods. "You started teaching together, the three of you?"

"Yeah, almost three years ago now. What about you?"

"I had to quit school for a while," he says. "After I moved to California, things got complicated. It's a long story, but it took me a while to finish my teaching degree and get certified."

Everything about Cyrus' manner—his clipped tone, his hunched shoulders, his clenched jaw—screams that he doesn't want to give me any details, even though that might exonerate him for ghosting me so many years ago. But I have no desire to press him.

"Is this long-term sub position your first teaching job?"

"I taught for a few years out in California as a specialist who traveled around to different elementary schools. But I wanted to get to know my students and really challenge them, and I couldn't do that in the job I had. So, after my divorce, I moved here even though I had to do some coursework to get my license and teach secondary in Minnesota."

I sip from my wine glass and peer at him. "Why did you move from California back to Minnesota? Wouldn't it have been easier to stay?"

"You ask a lot of questions, don't you?"

I'd worry Cyrus is annoyed with me, but his eyes are warm and twinkly and his tone is light. "Sorry. I'm just curious."

"Yes, it would've been easier to stay in California. But I needed a change."

Do his cheeks look slightly pink? It's hard to tell with his dark skin. "Understood," I state. "If you don't feel like talking about it, that's cool."

"I'll give you the CliffNotes version, okay?"

"Sure."

His chest heaves up and down. "I married the girl my parents wanted me to marry. It wasn't an arranged marriage or anything—my family isn't like that—but she's the daughter of my dad's best friend, and it was always just expected, you know?" I nod in agreement, and he continues, "The idea was always that once I finished school in Minnesota, I'd move back to California, and Leila and I would marry and start a family. She was great, like a little sister, but we didn't love each other like that, even though we tried. Eventually, she started having an affair with the man she actually loved, and when I confronted her, she said we should get a divorce. But she begged me not to tell our families about her affair. She wanted to say our breakup was mutual, and since I wanted out, too, I agreed, even though I knew my parents would disown me."

"Wow." I regard him, so straightforward and strong, meeting my gaze. "I am so sorry that happened to you, Cyrus. That's awful."

"Thanks." He shrugs. "It was pretty bad, but I got through it. I mean it wasn't the first time I'd had to start over. I was a kid when the Iranian revolution happened, and my parents moved us to California, and I had no idea what I was in for, how people would just assume that my family and I were violent radicals. And with Leila, I felt like everyone assumed the worst about me all over again."

I grapple with my response, not wanting to minimize what he's gone through or falsely presume to understand. "Are your parents still in California?"

"Yeah. My divorce isn't the only reason we fell out. I don't really follow the five pillars of Islam, and they think that my moving back here means I've abandoned my culture. But there is a strong Iranian community in Minneapolis, even though it's one of the most segregated cities in the U.S."

"Oh." My cheeks grow warm. I've heard how segregated Minneapolis really is, and I know there has been racial tension here, but I figured that was true everywhere. "Do you feel like it's worse here than it was in California?"

"I don't know. Everyone here is supposed to be so nice, and it's true that they *act* nice, but often I can't tell if it's genuine. You know?"

"Sure. But it's different for me, with my white privilege and all." I get hot all over. Did I seriously just mention my white privilege? How stupid. I was trying to sound self-aware, but it came out awkward, just like other missteps I've made with Cyrus. I stumble past the regrettable moment and ask, "How do you like working at Heights?"

"It's fine."

"Just fine?"

Cyrus's mouth twists a little as he tries to form his response. "I'm grateful to finally have a full-time job teaching secondary art, even if it's only temporary until Vance returns. And the kids are great. But I'm still trying to acclimate myself to the community. It can feel sort of insular, you know?"

"Of course." I sip more wine, hyper-aware that, if I succeed in bringing Vance back, Cyrus will lose what he's worked so hard to attain.

I change the subject. "Did you know Olivia graduated from Heights around ten years ago? And she's not the only Heights alum on the teaching staff. It's such a strange little community, with Minneapolis literally only two miles away. Meanwhile, all these diverse groups are moving in, so the demographics have exploded in the last decade . . ." I trail off and shrug. "I'm from Kansas, which is nothing compared to being from Iran, yet it took me a while to adjust. Sometimes I feel like I am still trying."

"But now you're one of them. Will you be a 'lifer'?"

Cyrus is leaning toward me with this quiet intensity, his eyes darker now but still warm, like he deeply cares about what I'll say next. Flashes of our night together years ago play behind my eyes: Cyrus, peering at me in that same way, saying, "You should follow your dreams, Hazel." Everything about him, what he said and how he felt, was like warm caramel, and I could have melted right into him.

Oh, wait. I did and look at how that turned out.

I shake off the memory. "I don't know. When I first started teaching, I thought I'd move on after a few years and do something else, and then I settled in and figured I would stay until retirement, but now, after the accident, and Vance, and the week I've had, I don't know what I want anymore."

"Yeah," says Cyrus softly. "I get that."

I roll my eyes toward the ceiling, needing a break from the intensity we share. "I've had fantasies about getting a teaching job in Hawaii or becoming a working playwright. But they're just that—fantasies—and I doubt they'll come to anything."

Cyrus shrugs. "They won't if you dismiss them so easily. But why couldn't you do either of those things?"

I sigh, still not looking at him. "I've heard horror stories about the public schools in Hawaii, that they're worse than anything you could imagine here. And very few playwrights make enough to live off of." I shake my head. "It's not going to happen."

"But you could try—"

"No," I cut him off. "I'd have no chance. I'm just not that talented."

Cyrus tightens his lips together, and then slowly opens them before answering. "Oh, come on, who told you that? You're plenty talented."

"Thanks for the vote of confidence." I trace the rim of my nearly empty wineglass with my finger. "But you barely know me."

"Not true," he states, his voice low. His fingers grip the edge of the table like he might pull it toward him. "I do know you, and I remember what a talented writer you are. You are rare and gifted. And shame on you for listening to anyone who says otherwise."

My mouth drops open as a deep hot flush envelopes my entire body. Luckily, I'm saved from having to respond when my phone vibrates with a text. It's from Olivia. *I'm at your house. Where are you?*

I rub my forehead, confused. Had Olivia and I made plans, or did she just show up at my house even though I'd told her she doesn't need to keep stopping by?

Cyrus must take in my expression because he asks, "Is everything okay?"

"Yeah," I reply. "But I have to go. Sorry."

He smiles. "No worries. I'm glad we did this."

"Yeah, me too." I don't know what else to say, so I add, "Let's do it again soon."

I drive home, trying to gather my thoughts. When I walk in through my front door, Olivia is sitting on my couch. "Where were you?" she asks.

"I was shopping," I state flatly. "I'd had a hard day and thought some retail therapy might help."

Her eyebrows shoot up. "You should have told me. I heard that Kohl's is having a huge sale. So, what'd you buy?"

"Nothing. I couldn't find anything that I liked."

Olivia scowls like she knows I'm lying. But there's no way I'm telling her that I went out with Cyrus. No matter what, it will come out wrong. "We hadn't made plans, had we?"

She widens her eyes in shock. "Umm, Hazy, do you seriously not remember?"

"Remember what?"

"This morning, in the mailroom, I said, 'Will you be around later this afternoon? I'll stop by and we can catch up?' And you said sure."

I rub my head as if that could trigger my memory. "I . . . umm . . ."

"Oh, Hazy. It's okay. You've had a lot on your plate."

"Gosh. I had an IEP meeting this morning, and I was upset afterwards, so I must have been on another planet when I saw you in the mailroom." But would I have completely blocked out our interaction? It seems unlikely, but I suppose it's possible.

I press my lips together to keep the word "Sorry" from slipping out. I did nothing wrong.

"So, what's up?' I say instead.

Olivia stands. "I have something for you." She hands me a small cloth bag that seems to hold a heavy object. "I've been thinking about it, and I'll feel a lot better with you alone in this house, if I give you this."

I take it and reach into the cloth bag to find a pistol, small and shiny and weighing what feels like a thousand pounds.

"Olivia, no. I can't take this."

"Yes, you can. I know you like being passive, but you're a single woman living by herself. You have a target on your back."

"That's not true. I don't *like* being passive, and there's no target on my back."

She shakes her head and crosses her arms over her chest. "Yes, there is. You just don't realize it. Look, I'm sorry I said you're passive; I realize that not everyone is as hot headed as me." She beams like she's proud to call herself such a thing. "You're my best friend, Hazy. I want you to be safe."

"But that's just it, Olivia. I know nothing about guns. Even if I wasn't still recovering from a head injury, I couldn't use this thing."

She sighs. "It's not hard. Total idiots use guns every day. I'll teach you. Come on."

"I don't know. Is it even legal for me to borrow it without filling out some form or something?"

Olivia shrugs. "Are you planning on holding up a convenience store or a bank? Are you going to carry it around in your purse?"

"Of course not."

"Then it's fine."

At that moment, Baby Girl walks up to me, rubbing herself against my legs and meow-purring.

"Hi, Baby Girl." Olivia kneels and scratches behind my cat's ears, which Baby Girl is totally into. Olivia looks up at me. "Do you think she misses Vance?"

"Yeah." Suddenly, I'm sniffing back tears. Olivia notices and stands. "Oh no, I'm sorry. I didn't mean to upset you."

I squeeze my eyes shut and massage them. "It's okay," I croak. "I'm just emotional. Long day and all that."

She uses her flat palm to rub my back. "Do you want to talk about it?"

"That's okay. You've already heard my sad, sad story several times."

"Okay, then how about we eat some Mac & Cheese? There's nothing that cheese and carbs won't cure."

"Sounds great. I think I have a box in my pantry."

We move toward the kitchen. I'm still holding the gun. "Here, take this."

She does. "Hey, I know. If you don't want the gun, we should take a self-defense class together or something. Then we can really toughen up."

"But you're already tough."

"True, but there's no harm in growing tougher." She sits down at my kitchen table while I root around for the blue and yellow *Kraft* box. "I can't believe you don't know how to use a gun. My dad taught me when I was twelve."

"I never wanted to learn."

"Okay, but will you at least let me teach you the basics?"

Resigned, I sigh. "Fine. You can show me how the gun works. But I'm not taking any practice shots."

To: VValby89@yahoo.com
From: H_Ford_AOGG@hotmail.com
Dear Vance,

Today was long and mostly bad. And then Olivia dropped by, which she does all the time, and I know she comes on strong because she cares, but sometimes I'm not sure how to respond to her. I can't go into it in an email. Let me just say, you never know when the Department of Homeland Security is reading in.

Also, you left your favorite scarf here. It's beautiful, but a magnet for hair and lint, right?

I think I'll return to a simpler time. Even though it hurts to revisit our relationship, I don't know how to stop.

Love?

Hazel

CHAPTER 21

September 2002

You came into my room at 3:05 p.m. on Friday. It was the end of the first week of our second year teaching. "A bunch of people are doing happy hour at La Casita," you said. "Wanna go?"

I hesitated. I was still nostalgic about summer, which had been ideal. Taking long walks around Lake Harriet, we'd meander through the rose gardens or venture out onto the docks and imagine what it would be like to own a sailboat that gently rocked in the lapping waves. Occasionally, we'd wander into Uptown and eat sushi with an expensive cocktail that we couldn't afford. More likely, we'd walk home, make grilled cheese, and watch something on broadcast TV, and then we'd make love with the windows open but with the blinds drawn, letting the breeze cool us as we would lie in your unairconditioned apartment. Now you were standing before me more like a stranger than the familiar Vance I'd become accustomed to.

"I don't know," I replied. "You want to do a group thing?"

"Well, yeah. We didn't see most of these people all summer."

"I know. It's only . . ."

"What?"

"Nothing. I'm just tired, and I've been looking forward to Friday afternoon all week."

That part was true. Friday came with the promise of sleeping in. And there was the prospect of Saturday: one full free day before Sunday when we'd do laundry and plan the coming week's lessons and call our families and grade any students' assignments we hadn't finished during the week.

On that Friday, I'd missed you. I missed having the time and energy to linger over dinner, to go for our evening walk when we'd peer into the windows of the several-hundred-thousand-dollar homes in a neighborhood where we could barely afford to rent, to start making out when we got bored while playing Scrabble, which wasn't often since I'm quite competitive and I play to win. But you claimed that my English-teacher vocab words were a turn-on.

The part about me being tired was also true. What I didn't say was that keeping our relationship a secret was especially exhausting.

Yet, I turned to you, answering your question about happy hour, giving the response I knew you wanted. "Okay, let's go to La Casita."

We headed out and sat on stools around high tables, eating nachos from the free appetizer bar, joking with Olivia and other young teachers. Then, I managed to kick off my low-heeled Skechers pumps and discreetly ran my toes along your ankle and up the cuff of your pants.

It didn't take long.

"That's it for me." You stood and tossed a twenty on the table. We'd agreed ahead of time that you'd go first and that I'd wait a few minutes before following so people wouldn't think we were leaving together.

We went back to your place and had sex on your lumpy queen mattress, which you'd bought from a married friend who'd upgraded to a king. When we were done, you walked into your kitchen and retrieved a pint of Ben & Jerry's Chunky Monkey.

You offered me your spoon. "Want some?"

"No thanks."

Your smile collapsed. "Really? Come on. It's so good."

You came toward the bed, waving the spoon like it was an airplane, and my mouth was the landing pad.

"I don't like bananas."

You were sitting beside me on the bed, and you leaned back. "Seriously? How could I not know that?"

"I don't know . . . but you can't expect to know every-thing about me."

You shrugged. "But I want to know everything about you. How about Half Baked? You like chocolate chip cookie dough and brownie batter, right?"

I nodded. "I love them both." We leaned toward each other and kissed. "And I love you," I murmured before the words could be restrained.

You cocked your head. I was a puzzle that needed fig-uring out. "We should go public with our relationship," you breathed. "I'm tired of keeping us a secret, especially at school."

I was overjoyed, so much so that I barely noticed that you hadn't said, "I love you, too."

Barely.

CHAPTER 22

The next morning Olivia's words still echo in my mind. *"There's a target on your back."* As I enter the media center for the staff meeting, my gaze darts around the room, and each face suddenly seems sinister. Someone here must have information about Vance and the MySpace scandal. Someone here doesn't want to tell me what really happened. Someone here is keeping secrets; I'm sure of it.

Jim begins his PowerPoint presentation on his policy of calling home to parents of failing students, but Dana, a former-lawyer-turned-sociology teacher, speaks up. "I don't have extra prep time to do that," she asserts. Jim grasps for an argument but can't find one; he knows he won't win this debate. "We're doing this for the kids," he sighs.

Aaron, last year's teacher of the year, offers an alternative. "Maybe we could do email blasts instead?"

Jim fumbles for an answer, while Michelle and Chris, two social studies teachers, quirk an eyebrow and almost simultaneously scribble down notes and snicker. Jim's face flushes as he takes in their collective confidence. It's obvious he's intimidated by their "evil genius" way of running the school. "Email blasts will be fine," he says quickly, before moving on to the breakfast controversy. Should we let students who arrive late bring their breakfast trays to class? Some of them won't be able to eat any other way, but officially, we don't allow food in the classroom. People go back and forth, but the staff never comes to a conclusion.

I look around the media center and see that, behind me, Cyrus stands with a fellow art teacher, Liza. They must have come in shortly after I did and decided against sitting. I subtly wave to them, and while it's Cyrus I'm happy to see, it's Liza whom I'm more interested in talking to.

When the meeting lets out, I approach as they gather their stuff: coats, bags, and travel mugs with coffee. They both must have gotten here late enough that they couldn't stop in their classroom to drop all that off. "Hey, you two," I say, "tough morning commute?"

Liza laughs breathily. "It's my fault. Cyrus gave me a ride this morning because Arthur needed the car. It was so sweet of Cyrus to pick me up, and yet I slowed him down because I was running late." She looks at Cyrus. "I'm so sorry."

Cyrus shrugs. "It's really no big deal." The three of us head toward the media center doors, but once we exit them, Cyrus veers left, toward his classroom, while Liza veers right toward the main office, probably so she can check her mailbox. When Cyrus realizes we're going in different directions, his eyes meet mine, and even under the harsh fluorescent lights of the hallway, they're warm. "Have a good morning," he says, and with a smile, he heads off.

"Thanks again," Liza calls, and she waves. Before her arm returns to her side, she tucks one of her thick wavy silver locks behind her ear. She keeps it long, below her shoulders. Combine that with her flowy bohemian tunics and a small sparkly stud in her nose—well, Liza rocks a look that few fiftyish women could get away with.

"Liza," I say, "I hope you don't mind, but there's something I've been meaning to ask you."

As we walk toward the office, the hallways are loud, with students converging in the entryway, socializing and waiting until the last minute to go to their lockers and then to class. I must speak loudly, or Liza won't hear me. Problem is, I don't want others to hear me.

"Sure," Liza responds breezily. Her lanyard with her keys, ID, and a Che Guevara pin sways as she walks. "How are you doing, sweetness? I've been meaning to ask."

"I'm okay." We reach the office, and the moment we step inside, the noisy bustle of the hallway ceases. She and I step into the mailroom where a couple of other teachers check their boxes, but they leave almost as soon as we enter. "Liza, my memory of events leading up to the accident is still fuzzy, and I'm trying to put things together. Um . . . as head of the art department, what can you tell me about what went down with Vance and Annabelle?"

Liza looks at me sideways. "Do you mean with the MySpace American Dream project?"

"Yeah." My response is tentative, nearly questioning like I'm not sure what I want to know. "Jim called me down, said I had a letter in my file because of it, but Vance was put on temporary leave, and Annabelle wasn't allowed to finish her student teaching assignment. For privacy reasons, he wouldn't go into detail about the two of them, and Vance won't respond to texts, calls, or emails."

Liza looks around, making sure no one is approaching. Nobody is, nevertheless, she speaks softly. "You know that Vance and Annabelle assigned students an electronic collage about what the American Dream means to them. You must since it included a written component that was connected to your class."

"Right." I rub at my throat, feeling anxious. I recite what Jim told me. "We didn't get permission to use a social media site like MySpace, which went against the school's internet policy, hence the letter in my file."

"Yes."

"But why was the punishment so much worse for Annabelle and Vance?"

"Oh, Hazel," Liza says with a sigh. "I shouldn't be the one to tell you. And I never saw it because it was taken down almost immediately."

"You mean the MySpace example Vance supposedly put up? Because I heard he was framed, that a student put it up as a prank."

"I'm sure that's true. But it's not really the point."

"Why not?"

Liza presses her lips together, breathes deeply through her nose, and reaches out, grasping my elbow. "Because the rumor is, the fake project example includes a photo of Vance and Annabelle having sex in his classroom."

I step back, nearly stumbling into the mailboxes. A science teacher comes in, senses the tension in the room, quickly checks her mailbox, and exits. Liza raises both hands, as if in anticipation of having to subdue me. "Hazel, honey, look." Her usual accommodating tone adopts a firm edge. "We don't know if the rumors are true."

"But . . ." I take a deep, fortifying breath, "they might be."

"Yes, but if there really were pictures like that, Vance would have been fired on the spot, not just put on temporary leave."

"Have you talked to him?"

She shakes her head no. "Sorry." Looking at the clock, she says, "I've got to go. Class starts soon, and I still need to set up."

"Okay. Thanks, Liza."

She squeezes my shoulder on her way out, and I'm left alone, feeling the aftershocks of my own personal earthquake. I swallow, and my throat feels like it's made of sandpaper. Can I even make it through the day?

But once I'm walking through the hallway toward my classroom, I discover that I'm not falling apart. I'm thinking about next hour's lesson and how we'll discuss examples of paradox in *The Great Gatsby*. I'll tell them that, when Jordan Baker said she likes Gatsby's large parties because they're so intimate, that is an example of an absurd statement that, after inspection, also proves to be true—just like it's possible that a photo of Vance and Annabelle having sex in his classroom isn't *really* a picture of them having sex, and Vance does still love me.

But I won't use that second example.

God, I need more information. These uncertainties are driving me crazy. And the truth is, I know exactly whom I should ask about what went on between Vance and Annabelle and, for that matter, what went on between Vance and me leading up to the accident—Olivia. She must know but probably has some reason for not telling me yet. Is she protecting me from the truth? Or is it something less innocent? Last year, when Olivia and I had our big fight, it was about Vance. She'd told me he was out of my league and that, eventually, he'd lose interest. Perhaps she feels bad about being proven right.

When I get up to my classroom, Febe is waiting outside my door. She isn't covering her face with her hood or burying her head in a book or even averting my gaze. She looks right at me, her expression open and direct. "Hello, Ms. Ford," she says. "How are you today?"

"I'm okay," I tell her. "How are you? Hopefully better than yesterday."

Febe shrugs as we enter my classroom. "Yesterday, I was below the line, but now I'm back on it or maybe even above."

"Huh?"

She laughs. "Last fall in Health Class, we had this motivational speaker come in, and he told us all that we'd have 'below the line' days and 'above the line' days. I guess 'the line' is like a metaphor for our equilibrium or something, and if we're in a bad mood or tired or not feeling well, then we're below the line."

"Right. That makes sense."

"Yeah, I suppose it would. Haven't you been below the line a lot lately, Ms. Ford?"

If there had been even the faintest hint of snippiness in her tone, I'd be offended by the question. Yet, she sounded more concerned than anything. That's not the way it's supposed to be. I'm the teacher, the adult who should look after my teenage student, but I respond without thinking. "Well, sure. I'm recovering from brain trauma, my memory sucks, and my boyfriend dumped me, so yeah, I'd say that recently I've mostly been below the line."

Febe's mouth drops open while her eyes narrow. She looks like she's about to say something but bites her lip.

"What?" I demand.

"You . . . you can't remember what happened?"

"About the accident?" I curl my toes inside my boots. This conversation is way too personal for a teacher to have with her student.

Febe must understand my apprehensive silence because she doesn't press me. Instead, she uses a gentle tone and says, "Ms. Ford, I'm sorry. I mean . . ." She inhales sharply, and her words come out in a rush. "It was all over school, the fight you had with Mr. Valby on the day before holiday break. You were the one to dump him."

My ears start ringing. Other students enter my classroom, laughing and talking about something I can't decipher. Febe stares at me, her eyes pooling with concern. "It's okay," she says softly. "When something bad happens, we all want to remember things differently, like they were better than they actually were."

"No," I utter, not recognizing my own voice. "No. You're wrong. I wouldn't have argued with him publicly like that."

"Okay. I'm wrong about stuff all the time. What do I know?" Her question-mark-tinged laughter sounds tinny.

"I need to get class started."

I turn away from her and force my confusion out from the forefront of my brain. I can't think about my life right now, and whether I'm delusional, so I'll turn to Jay Gatsby who is likely the most famous self-deluded character in modern fiction.

We discuss paradox, and then I assign my students some silent reading and a written reflection, and when the bell rings, they file out, just like any other day. Febe approaches my desk.

"Ms. Ford, I'm so sorry. I shouldn't have said what I said."

"No worries," I tell her. "Either you're right, and you're braver than all my adult friends and family for telling me, or you're wrong, in which case, no harm done."

"So, you really don't remember?"

"No. I guess I don't."

"Ms. Ford, I hope you don't mind me giving you some advice. I don't want to overstep."

"That's okay." I pause for a second, inhaling, and it feels like the first time I have breathed in hours. "I'm curious. Tell me your advice."

She looks at me, tilting her chin. "I've had crappy stuff happen that wasn't my fault, but I still blamed myself. I've also done things I regret, but usually, I don't take responsibility for it. And in the end, I beat myself up and do everything wrong, and it's easy for me to start hating myself. You know?"

"Oh, Febe."

She holds up a hand. "I'm not telling you this so you can worry about me. I'm fine, at least most of the time. I'm telling you all this so you know that when I say, 'Don't hate yourself', I understand what it's like to fall into that trap, and it's not worth it."

"Ms. Ford?" Another student has approached my desk, and I turn to her. "I need my missing assignments from when I was sick," she says.

"Hold on," I tell her, and I turn back so I can respond to Febe.

But she's already gone.

CHAPTER 23

Annabelle came to realize that she'd never thought past the initial phases of her relationship with Vance. Was it enough for her to sneak around, to flirt with the idea of something more? Or did she want the whole deal—walking down the aisle, buying a house, having babies, and growing old together?

She was only twenty-two, and even though her mother had been her age when she got married, she felt way too young to think about "forever." Being with Vance had felt like something she should do, an item to cross off her post-adolescence bucket list, so she could enter adulthood knowing she'd been slightly wild and highly desired.

"Hazel is acting weird," Vance told her one morning. They were drinking coffee and setting out the art materials for first hour—plastic containers of oil pastels and cardstock—and he mentioned this so casually like he was stating the weather report.

Annabelle wasn't sure she wanted to pursue this conversation, but the temptation to ask for details was strong. "Weird, how?"

"She freaked out about holiday plans." He took a long sip of his coffee, making a slurping sound that Annabelle found grating.

"Have you told her that you're moving out yet?"

Vance's face registered shock, like she'd pinched him hard for no reason at all.

"No. Why would I? I never said that I was."

"Yes, you did. I remember."

Annabelle suppressed a laugh as he looked at her, doubt in his eyes. Of course he said no such thing, but it shouldn't be so easy to mess with him.

"I really don't think that I did," he said, shrugging. "Well, whatever. We're pretty much broken up now."

"What do you mean 'pretty much'?"

"We live like we're roommates. I can't even remember the last time we had sex."

Annabelle kept her voice light. "I see. Maybe she should be the one to leave? You could kick her out."

"I can't. She owns the house. I've been paying her rent the whole time."

"Oh." Annabelle regarded him in his black long-sleeved T-shirt and jeans, his wavy hair hanging down against his forehead, his rosy mouth forming its resting pout. "Why?"

"It was my idea. Hazel wanted to buy a house, but I guess something inside me knew we wouldn't last and that it would be a mistake to sign a mortgage together. It had seemed smart at the time, but now, if I want to end it with her, then I'm out of a place to live."

"You could always stay with your parents."

Vance laughed. "No way. My commute would be over an hour each way, and besides, I'd go crazy living with my mom and dad again. And my dad is allergic to cats, and I can't leave Baby Girl."

"Oh." She searched for something else to say but couldn't find anything.

Was this her cue to offer to let him stay with her? She already had a roommate, and besides, Vance had been the one to insist that they keep things between them a secret.

"Well," she continued, "I'm sure you don't make a ton with your teaching salary, but you should be able to find something nice, a one-bedroom apartment somewhere. Maybe you could rent a studio in the warehouse district and live there, too. I've heard that a lot of artists do that."

Vance frowned, and he answered in a flat sort of voice. "Yeah, maybe."

CHAPTER 24

"When are you going to tell Hazel about you and me?"

Vance sighed and stared up at the ceiling. He lay in her bed, flat on his back, his skin warm and dewy—she should savor this moment of intimacy, and instantly, she regretted nagging him.

But his answer surprised her. "Soon," he said. "Once the holidays are over."

"Seriously?"

He reached over and grasped her hand, bringing it to his mouth and pressing his lips against her palm. "Yes. I'll tell her it's over, that I'm moving out, that I'm in love with you. Then we'll deal with the shitstorm at school together."

Vance gazed expectantly into her eyes. Was she supposed to squeal with joy?

"What?" he demanded.

"It's going to be so much worse for me; you know that, right?"

"No. I'm the one who will have betrayed Hazel. Everyone will hate me."

"Maybe, for a day or two. But then you'll be forgiven because, you know, 'Boys will be boys.' But I'll be the cold, calculating homewrecker who's breaking all the rules."

Vance sat up and looked down at her, his face twisted in skepticism. "Come on. We're living in the twenty-first century. Don't tell me those stupid double standards still exist."

She rolled away from him, her gaze now fixed on the wall. "Fine. I won't tell you that."

There was a long, profound pause, and she felt like she could hear his thoughts, his railing against how unfair she was being. Then, in a careful tone that he surely thought was an example of diplomatic restraint, he said, "Okay. What do you want? Should I stay with Hazel?"

Tired of being naked, she rose and moved toward the bathroom, picking up her discarded clothes from the floor along the way. "I can't tell you what to do, Vance, and I won't tell you what I want, not until you're clear on what you want."

CHAPTER 25

A major winter storm is in the forecast, up to a foot of snow overnight and blowing snow afterward. Everybody is hoping for a snow day tomorrow, but we'll see. Years ago, the kids enrolled in our district mostly lived within walking distance. So on days when every other school in the area was closed, we remained open, the kids begrudgingly trekking in on perilous roads.

But last year, the Twin Cities' temperatures plummeted into the negative teens, with wind chills at around –40. Yet every school in the area remained open, and this poor girl, a student in the Saint Paul district, had to wait at the city bus stop for hours. She ended up getting a bad case of frostbite. Fearing litigation, Saint Paul created a broad policy and guidelines for when they'd close owing to weather, and other schools followed suit. Dixon Heights hadn't had a snow day or a cold day, not once, in over five years. Then, suddenly, we had three in a row. That was in January, the first winter Vance and I were in our new house.

I sit in my living room, remembering. But I don't email Vance. This time, I don't want him to know what I'm thinking. This time, I don't want him to feel me remember.

"I heard that, if you go outside and throw hot water into the air, it will evaporate immediately and turn into an icy mist."

We were lying in bed, post-coital, listening to the wind rattle the windows. "Are you sure you want to do that?" Vance asked. "I'm not stepping foot outside. I think it's better if you stay here with me. Let me keep you safe and warm."

I snuggled more deeply into his arms, relishing the feel of him drawing lazy circles on my back. "Are you doodling, or are you writing something?"

"Writing something?" He scoffed as his finger made a long, deliberate arc from my left shoulder blade down toward the small vertebrae of my spine. "That's your department. I'm drawing your face."

"You're drawing my face onto my back?"

"Yes."

I tilted up my chin and lifted my eyes so I could see where Vance focused his gaze. He was staring at the window, which was completely frosted over with a hard mist. "But you're not even looking at my face."

Vance stroked my hair with his left hand and kissed the top of my head. "It doesn't matter. I have your face memorized. Your face is painted on the back of my eyelids."

I sat up. Was he for real? I studied *his* face, looking for a sign that he was sincere or that he was full of crap. Vance felt my scrutiny and chuckled softly. "What? You don't believe me?"

I shrugged. He was so beautiful, lying in that bed, his skin like pale warm honey, his two-day beard growth giving him this slightly unfamiliar scruffiness. And the way his ribcage rose and fell, so slender and sinewy, I wanted to burrow into his arms and let my head sink into his chest, and then somehow, I would be absorbed into his heart.

But I just shrugged.

Vance sat up and cupped my face in his hand. "I think about you all the time, Hazel. I love you."

Tears sprang to my eyes. "I love you, too." I turned my face away, suddenly needing levity, and sprang from the bed. Picking up my discarded clothes from the floor, I got dressed, pulling on leggings and a flannel shirt. But I needed to go to my dresser to find a pair of thick wool socks.

"Are you going out?" Vance asked, watching me intently.

"Yes, and so are you." I went to him, tugging on his arm, but he was too heavy for me to pull up. "I'm going to boil some water and then go outside and toss it in the air. And if you really love me, you'll join me out there."

Vance groaned and put his head underneath his pillow. I left the bedroom and went into the kitchen to boil water. "Vance, come on!" I yelled after a few minutes. "The water is nearly done!"

Only quiet came from the bedroom, and I'd figured he'd fallen asleep. My big pot, which I usually use for cooking pasta, was full of boiling water. I'd put on my coat, hat, and gloves and was trying to figure out the best way to lift the pot without spilling the water, knowing I would then need to open the backdoor. Suddenly, Vance, fully dressed and ready to step outside, appeared next to me. "I'll get that," he said, referring to the pot. "You get the door."

I gave him my warmest smile as we ventured out, however briefly, into the arctic weather. The day was bright and sunny, as the coldest days in Minnesota often are. Once we stepped outside, it took mere seconds for my eyelashes and my nose hairs to freeze, and my limbs felt like they were full of liquid nitrogen. We stood on our patio, Vance clutching the pot of boiling water with gloved hands. He turned to me, his hood pulled up, his face pink from the cold. "What do I do? Where do I throw it?"

I pointed in the wind's direction. "That way," I said as I shivered, "so the hot water doesn't get thrown back into your face."

We stood with the wind at our backs. "Okay, are you ready? Here I go!"

Vance tossed the entire pot of water into the air, and like magic, it evaporated into a beautiful silver mist, sprinkling down like fairy dust.

I gasped. "Have you ever seen anything so beautiful?"

"Yes, I have." His voice was soft, nearly a whisper, and I could feel his eyes on me.

When I turned toward Vance, I found him down on one knee. His gloved hand grasped my mittened one. "Hazel Anne Ford, will you marry me?"

I gulped back some strange combination of tears and joy and nodded vigorously. "Yes! Of course!" I leaped into his arms, and we embraced, still shaking with cold as we drew our lips together. I pulled back. "But we need to go inside before you kiss me, because if we kiss out here, I'm afraid our lips will freeze together."

And that was our magical fairy-tale moment. At least, that's how I remember it happening.

But did it?

Since Febe gently broke it to me that I am delusional, I have been combing through my memories, trying to distinguish between what was real and what wasn't. I'm tempted to call Olivia and confess my situation, tell her that I'm doubting not just my relationship with Vance, but my sanity as well. But it's too humiliating to admit that I don't remember if Vance proposed, and she would be all over me if I admitted such a thing, insisting I get therapy and then shepherding me to church as well.

It makes me wonder. Why hasn't she, or any other staff member at Heights, mentioned this "very public fight" where I broke up with Vance? Do they see me as a sleep-walker and think it's too dangerous to wake me up?

As if on cue, my phone dings with a text from Olivia. *I have a good feeling about tomorrow. You heard it here first. Snow Day!*

I don't respond. A day off tomorrow would be great; I could sleep in and wear my pajamas all day. But, I'd be stuck here with nothing but struggling memories of my failed relationship with Vance to contend with. It's easier to live in denial if you have something else to occupy your mind.

Shortly after 9:00 p.m., we receive the call that school is, in fact, canceled. Olivia texts me again, but instead of responding to her, I text Cyrus whose phone number I got the other day when we went out after school.

Your first snow day! Excited?

Yes! he texts back. *Do you have plans tomorrow?*

Yup. I'll be shoveling out my car & my sidewalk & front step.

I could do all that for you & then we could bake brownies.

It's so sweet and innocent. I can't guard myself against his charm. I type in my address.

He texts back a thumbs-up—no ETA or any words at all confirming that he'll come. I guess it will be a surprise.

The next morning, I sleep in. When I wake up, I do some stretches and change into yoga pants and an old Kansas State Capitol sweatshirt that I inherited from my dad years ago. Thankfully, I didn't bring home any essays to grade. Now I have an excuse to sit around and watch *Real World* reruns, eat toast and drink coffee, and feel snug at home for the first time in a while.

Shortly after eleven, there's a knock at my door. I open it to find Cyrus, and tiny corners of joy edge into my already content state. Then I'm instantly swimming in panic. I'm still a train wreck, and it's way too soon to let Cyrus Gul make me happy, especially before I've resolved things with Vance. "You made it," I say, trying not to betray my rollercoaster of emotions. "I wasn't sure that you would. How are the roads?"

"Terrible," he replies, still standing on my stoop, not coming in. "But digging out my car was the worst part. Do you want me to do yours while I'm still covered in snow?"

"You really don't have to do that."

He grins. "I don't mind. I enjoy feeling useful. Where's your shovel?"

"Seriously?"

He nods emphatically, so I get him my shovel. While he works, I cook. My pantry is pretty bare, but I find some cheese, butter, and thick-cut sandwich bread. And there's a can of tomato soup, so it's perfect. We'll have grilled cheese and tomato soup, which is fantastic snow-day food. And after lunch, we can bake brownies.

As I prepare lunch, and Cyrus is out shoveling, my phone rings. Olivia's ringtone—it's such a familiar sound. Before I can think twice, I pick up. Answering Olivia's call is like muscle memory.

"Hi!" she says, her voice filled with so much cheer that it almost sounds suspicious. "I'm just checking on you, making sure you're okay."

"Why wouldn't I be?"

"Well, you didn't text me back last night, and I don't know . . . I worry about you in that house all by yourself."

"So you've said." My gaze shifts to Cyrus shoveling my driveway out of the kindness of his heart. Is he just being nice, or does he have an ulterior motive?

"Maybe you should move back home," Olivia says suddenly, snapping my attention back to her.

"Are you crazy?" I exclaim. "I worked way too hard to leave Topeka to move back there."

"Okay . . ." her voice is tinged with disappointment. "It was just an idea." But then she adopts a more determined tone. "Look, Hazy, I hate to say it, but you'll never move on as long as you hold on to the fantasy of that house and the so-called perfect life you had with Vance."

A rush of anger surges through me. How dare she? "I realize that life with Vance was not perfect," I spit out. "And I get that he's not coming back to me."

I gulp. Is that true? I've been clinging to the idea that Vance and I would reunite somehow, but perhaps I am ready to let go.

"Hazy . . ." Her voice is soft. "When I said that you're holding on to a fantasy, I meant about the past, not the future." She pauses for a few moments before continuing. "Okay, I don't know what you know or what you remember, but this is a conversation we should have in person. I'll come over, okay?"

My emotions are a chaotic blend of confusion, anger, and hurt. She thinks she knows me and my life better than I do. And the worst part is, she probably does.

Through the window, I see that Cyrus has finished shoveling, and he's about to head inside. "No, not okay. Stay where you are. Do not come over." Now my words are forceful, rude little bullets, the type that would fit inside that gun she lent me. "Olivia, thanks for calling, but I have to go."

"Why? Do you have somewhere to be?"

"Bye!" I hang up.

She calls back immediately, but I reject the call right as Cyrus steps through my back door.

"Okay," he says brightly. "You should be able to get out tomorrow, assuming we have school."

"Thank you so much! I made you lunch. I hope you like grilled cheese and tomato soup."

Cyrus shakes the snow off his head, arms, and legs and removes his coat, gloves, and boots, creating a puddle on the little mat I have by my back door. His glasses fog as he steps further inside.

"That's perfect snow-day food," he says.

"That's what I thought!"

He looks toward my living room. "Can we eat by your fireplace and have, like, a living room picnic?"

"Umm, sure. Why not?" He's referring to my gas fireplace. After I moved in, I splurged on getting it converted since it wasn't usable for traditional fires. I travel the short distance from the kitchen to the living room, find the fireplace remote, and press the button. Flames instantly jump to life.

"Cool!" Cyrus has followed me in here, and he stands gazing at the dancing flames.

"Yeah, Vance said I was crazy, spending so much money to have it installed, but it's been worth every penny. One reason I moved to Minnesota was so I could feel warm and cozy on cold winter days." Chuckling self-consciously, I gesture to my bookcase, which holds all my favorite classics. "I grew up reading *Little Women* and *Anne of Green Gables* where the characters always gathered around the fire, drinking tea and telling stories, and it seemed so romantic. I wanted a life like that."

"So you bought a charming bungalow with a fireplace and found a job that's all about telling stories?"

I laugh. "Not in that order, but yeah, I suppose so."

"It makes total sense to me. I can't believe Vance didn't understand."

I shrug, feeling how close Cyrus stands to me, wondering if I should step away but not wanting to. Softly, I say, "I heard that I broke up with Vance right before the accident."

"But you don't know for sure?" Cyrus asks simply.

I skip a breath, my voice coming out shaky. "No, but there are rumors and signs that he and Annabelle were messing around. So, it would make sense. I wish I could remember."

Thankfully, Cyrus doesn't offer some platitude telling me it's okay, and breakups and trauma are hard, and blah, blah, blah. He says nothing. He does, however, place his hand on my shoulder, giving it a squeeze. I look into his eyes, and we silently share an understanding about mistakes and the uncertainty that comes with loving someone or something.

"I should get lunch together," I say, and his hand drifts from my shoulder.

"I brought brownie mix," he answers. "After we're done eating, we can bake."

"That sounds perfect."

And it is perfect, even if I'm not sure that I want it to be.

CHAPTER 26

Cyrus and I spend the afternoon eating and chatting by the fire, baking brownies, and discussing plans for the art blog. "I didn't mean to make you work today," Cyrus tells me after I get out my computer so he can show me the changes he and the students put in place.

"This hardly qualifies as work, and I want to see." We're sitting on the floor, surrounded by couch cushions, almost like kids who've made a living room fort. I stretch my legs and curl my toes, wishing this day could extend into a week, that I could delay leaving the warm safety of this moment and emerging back into the cold reality of my life.

Cyrus types and, seconds later, hands me the laptop. Brightly painted across the top of the screen is "Burnt Moon" in loopy lettering, the school colors softly muted yet chosen with purpose. Below are photos taken by the students, all based on the topic "A Day in the Life at Dixon Heights." Shots of locker doors, a tray of unappetizing lunch food, feet in loafers that obviously belong to a teacher standing at the head of a classroom, and a clock whose hands have stopped three minutes before afternoon bell time. Those images are expected. Others, not so much—unidentifiable students smoking in the restroom, a label of a water bottle with scrawled notes used to cheat on a test, and another of two kids sharing a kiss in a secluded corner down the hallway by the pool. "These photos are super cool," I say. "But how were they taken in secret, without the subjects knowing?"

"They used the tiny cameras that the digital arts students can check out. Didn't Vance tell you about them? I heard the district spent a lot of money."

I swallow, and it feels like acid. "So, any kid with one of these cameras could take a photo without a flash or a clicking sound?"

"Sometimes there's a flash, but only if they turn it on."

"I see."

Cyrus exhales. "I know what you're worried about. You think Jim will freak out, say that we're violating privacy laws and depicting the school in a bad light, and once the community sees it, there will be pushback. I thought of that, too."

He's wrong. I'm not worried about Jim's reaction, though I should be. No, until now, I told myself there was no logical way a student could take a picture of Vance having sex in his classroom, but apparently, there is.

When I don't respond, Cyrus continues, "I wasn't sure how honest and edgy we wanted to be and how much creative license to grant the kids. I mean a few years ago, when I was fresh out of school, I was sure I'd never be one of 'those teachers,' you know, the kind that play it safe and keep their heads in the sand about what teenagers are really like. But then, there's such a thing as job security . . ."

"Right." I snap myself back to the present. "But we've already decided that I'll be the one to take the fall. If Jim doesn't like our blog, I'll say that you only helped set it up, and all the content decisions were mine and mine alone."

Cyrus tilts his head to the side. "You feel safe doing that when you're up for tenure?"

"Not at all." I sigh. "But I'm already in hot water, so why not take a risk when it matters? It's what Febe wants, and to be honest, I think I want it, too. Lately, I've realized that life is short."

"Sure." Cyrus leans back against the couch cushions that prop him up, the glow of the fire lighting up one side of his face, the reflection of the flames bouncing off his glasses. "Except, some things are worth the risk, and some aren't."

I shrug. "But how do you know the difference?"

He pushes up the sleeves of his V-neck sweater, and it doesn't escape me how muscular his arms are. "I don't know. I guess we just need to ask ourselves questions. Like, does our little art blog need to be so inflammatory?"

At that moment, Baby Girl, who'd been sleeping on the couch, hops down, announcing her presence with a thud and a "mrwrrr." She saunters over and starts brushing against Cyrus. He pets her, and she instantly purrs.

"This is Baby Girl," I say. "I didn't name her myself. One day, Vance and I volunteered at the Humane Society, and she was there, and we instantly fell in love. We had to take her home, even though she was fourteen years old with cancer."

The smile falls from Cyrus's face, and he looks at me in shock. "She has cancer?"

"That's what they said, but apparently, it's under control, and she could live another six years, which is already super old for a cat, even without cancer. I have some pretty hefty vet bills. But she's the sweetest cat in the world, and I'll love her for however long she has left."

Cyrus goes back to petting her. "Hi, Baby Girl. You are a sweetie, aren't you?"

She bumps her head against his hand in response.

"She likes you," I say.

He chuckles. "I think you have the right idea, loving her for however long you have together. I mean we never know how long any of us has. Nothing is forever."

True. But some things should be at least semi-permanent.

I take a deep bracing breath. "Cyrus, you may not believe me, but I'm on your side, and I only want to help you keep your job at Dixon Heights."

His eyes, raised and surprised, meet mine. "I believe you. But why do you say that?"

"Because, in answer to your question about how inflammatory our blog needs to be, probably more inflammatory than you'd like."

I describe the written piece, the one I'm sure is by Febe though she didn't sign her name to it, the one that describes the sexual assault by this guy who has to be Brady Burns, Dixon Height's star basketball player.

Cyrus sighs, winces, and rubs his forehead like he's in pain. "Oh, man. That's terrible. Guys like Brady Burns . . ." Cyrus lets the thought just hang there, unfinished, but I can sense his anger and imagine the words he doesn't say.

"You'd publish the story without knowing for sure who wrote it?" Cyrus asks.

"Yeah, I think I will." Cyrus gives me a blank stare, and it demands a response. "I get that it will cause a stir."

"That's an understatement," says Cyrus. "Look, I don't like Brady Burns, and I don't doubt that he could be dangerous, but if you publish this story, when he can't defend himself against his accuser, you could have an uprising on your hands."

"Well, he's not mentioned by name, though everyone will know it's him. I'm much more worried about protecting the girl who wrote it than I am about protecting Brady Burns."

Cyrus looks down, pressing his lips together.

I continue. "The blog was Febe's idea, and posting that story is what she *needs* me to do. And I am determined to help Febe however I can, however she'll let me." I pause, giving him a chance to contradict me, but he stays silent. After a couple of moments, I ask, "Can you show me how to load content onto the blog so I can publish it?"

"Yes," Cyrus answers with resolve. He leans forward slightly as if he might kiss me, and I feel a rush of heat and a spark of panic and desire. But the moment dissipates, and then it's gone, leaving no kiss in its wake.

"Hand me your laptop," he tells me, "and I'll walk you through what to do."

Cyrus takes me through the steps, but I don't load what's supposedly Febe's piece in his presence. I wait until after he goes home. He hugs me as he leaves, and the feel of his arms around me, of how perfect his warm broad chest feels against my cheek, is reassuring. It also brings a whoosh of anxiety, so I tell myself I'm shaking from nerves and not the residual effect of my body pressed into his.

I'm shaking because it's risky and dangerous, loading this piece that's probably by Febe that, once seen, could explode into a mass of accusations and controversy— which is why I only load the content and don't hit publish.

For that, I wait until the next day, after school. I told Febe when I saw her that morning to come to my room as soon as the afternoon bell rang. I've already loaded the blog onto my computer so she can see it the moment she arrives.

"It's ready to go," I tell her. "And I think it looks great. But I want you to be sure. I want you to be the one to publish it."

Today, Febe's hijab is black and draped loosely around her head. It makes her already huge brown eyes look even more like dark bottomless pools. Or perhaps her eyes look so big because they're filled with fear and excitement. She peers at my computer screen and sucks in a breath.

"Oh, Ms. Ford," she exclaims. "It's perfect, isn't it?"

Her story, titled "Don't Hate Yourself; Hate Him," is front and center.

"Yes, it's perfect. Are you ready for the world to know?"

She looks at me, smiles, and blinks away what I think are happy tears. "Let's do it," she says.

I gesture toward my keyboard. "You do the honors."

Febe doesn't need me to tell her how to publish the blog. She already knows, and when her finger hits the enter key, it's with finality; it's with a sense of purpose.

"Done."

I want to hug her, and even though I know that teacher-student contact isn't supposed to happen, the moment is too emotional to just skip over. I hold her to me, shocked at how underneath her clothes she feels like no flesh and all bones.

"Thank you, Ms. Ford," she says.

"Don't thank me yet. Wait until we see how people react. We may have just done something really foolish."

Febe laughs. "I hope we did. We'll be beautiful little fools, just like Daisy Buchanan said. 'A beautiful little fool is the best thing a girl in this world can be.'"

"Daisy Buchanan was a fictional, self-serving, superficial alcoholic."

Febe shrugs. "So? She had Gatsby and Tom fighting over her."

"Still," I insist, "we can aspire for more."

"True." Febe swipes at a tear. "I can be more than obedient, and more than passive, and more than silent." She nods firmly as if agreeing with her statement. "And you,

Ms. Ford, all you have to do is go back to being who you were before."

"Do you mean before the accident?"

"No, I mean before you came here and before you knew Mr. Valby."

"I, umm . . ." I grasp for a response, finding nothing. "Why would you say that, Febe?"

"Sorry." She steps away from my desk, picking up her backpack and preparing to leave. "I wasn't trying to insult you. I say stupid things all the time, stuff I should just keep to myself."

"I'm not insulted," I tell her, and it's the truth. "I just don't understand what you meant."

"I don't know . . ." Febe shifts her weight as she places her backpack's straps around her shoulders. "Never mind. I should go."

She shuffles out. I look back at my computer screen, again at the title splayed across the blog's front page: "Don't Hate Yourself; Hate Him."

I'm left wondering: who is the teacher here, and who is the student?

CHAPTER 27

November 1998

I was late for class, *Teaching in an Urban Setting.* My alarm didn't go off and I overslept, but there was nobody to blame but myself. I stumbled in ten minutes late, and Cyrus had already begun presenting his project on cultural stereotypes in popular culture. He showed a clip of *Aladdin* and was in the middle of explaining how the song lyrics and the stereotypical "Arab" features on the film's villains (as opposed to Aladdin who looked like Tom Cruise) all perpetuated negativity around Arab culture.

I was bustling around in my seat, pawing through my backpack to retrieve my notebook and pen, struggling to wrest my arms from the sleeves of my heavy coat, and pretending not to be embarrassed by my late, awkward entrance. Just in case people weren't already convinced, I interjected without even raising my hand. "Look at the source, though."

Cyrus, who had never once smiled at me since the semester began, squinted at me now. "Excuse me? Are you defending Disney?"

"Not at all. I'm talking about the original source, the literary work *Arabian Nights*. It was written centuries ago, when Middle Eastern culture did not value literature. The premise shows a clear disregard for women. Scheherazade's tale is seen as a victory because she survives. Yet, there are no consequences for the murderous king."

Cyrus tilted his head, waiting for me to continue. When I didn't, he asked, "What's your point?"

I realized I didn't have one. Unfortunately, I was all bluster, trying to look smart and irreverent to make up for my tardiness. I'd taken his critique of Disney's racism and made it about me, or at least about my own agenda. Opening my mouth, I started to apologize, but he cut me off, "If you're done criticizing my cultural heritage, I'd like to continue."

I swallowed roughly and felt my cheeks burn. "Sorry," I muttered, mortified.

After that, I avoided Cyrus Gul at all costs. When it was my turn to present my project, which was on the lack of female protagonists in children's literature, like Dr. Seuss, I prayed Cyrus wouldn't treat me the way I'd treated him.

He didn't. He sat with his eyes closed, his head tilted back, pretending to sleep. But the moment I was done, he snapped back to life.

It was a slap in the face.

***

The black box theater housed around one hundred audience members, and unsurprisingly, only half the seats were full. My play, *Debbie and Jane*, was part of Hamline's student-directed series where the budget was low and the production values non-existent. If I wasn't friends with people in the theater department, *Debbie and Jane* wouldn't have been produced.

I sat alone, springs in the aging chair pressing against my back. All my friends were either involved in the production, unwilling to go out on a cold November Wednesday evening, or had graduated on time last year. There I was, a fifth-year senior, taking my time with my double major and student-teaching assignment.

Alternating between leafing through the program, which had been thrown together at Kinkos only hours before, and gazing at the "set," which was nothing but a few folding chairs and a table and stool that sat upon a raised platform, I squashed down the butterflies in my stomach.

Moments before the play began, Cyrus entered the theater and looked for a seat. He didn't notice me right away, and I prayed he wouldn't notice me at all, but no. The seats stretched out into a horseshoe, and Cyrus sat almost directly across from me. Right before the lights dimmed, his gaze met mine.

I gave a perfunctory little wave. He responded with a barely perceptible nod. Thank God there wouldn't be an intermission. Maybe I could escape without Cyrus realizing that I was the playwright.

Debby and Jane began, and what I once thought was evidence of my clever irreverence now seemed like proof that I was a silly, foolish girl. My play was inspired by a Bible story I'd heard and read at Sunday school. Deborah is a prophet called upon by God to get men to go to battle. She orchestrates it all, and the warriors kill almost everyone they're supposed to, except the main enemy guy. It's Jael, one warrior's wife, who gets that done when she invites him in for refreshments, waits until he falls asleep, and stabs him in the heart.

I set the play in the present-day late-1990s corporate world. Debby is an IT wiz who understands what must be done to prepare for the year 2000, but first, her bosses don't believe her, and then they don't trust her. But Jane, a trophy wife and a courageous receptionist, goes into the computer system and prevents a digital apocalypse.

I think the audience laughed at all the right spots, and their applause at the end seemed genuine, but I was too preoccupied with the expression on Cyrus's face to know for sure. He stared at the stage intensely, like he was trying to memorize the lines as they were spoken. He never cracked a smile or leaned back in his seat. As soon as the lights dimmed and then came back up for curtain call, Cyrus bolted, navigating the aisle of still-sitting, clapping people, exiting through the theater doors and out into the night.

"That was rude," I whispered to myself.

****

That evening, I went with the cast and crew for drinks at a bar near campus. Immediately I spotted Cyrus there with some friends. *Screw it*, I told myself. *I'll just ignore him. I'm not letting Cyrus Gul ruin my night.* But after a couple of rounds of liquid courage, I decided to approach him. He'd been playing darts, but the game had just ended, and he was sort of standing alone.

"Good game," I said. "You're talented at darts."

"Hello, Hazel." His hazel eyes projected no warmth, and neither did his voice. But he took me in as I stood there in front of him, wearing my wide-legged pants and cropped sweater. I wished I'd taken more care in choosing my outfit that night.

I sighed. "You hate me, don't you?"

"No." It was one simple syllable, but somehow, said in his guileless, velvety voice, it held volumes.

I looked straight into his eyes, trying to assess if he was lying. "Okay. But you hated my play."

"Not at all. I thought it was clever."

Was he for real? Well, at least he didn't say it was "fun" or "cute."

"Thanks." I took a deep fortifying breath. "I'm sorry about that time when I interrupted your presentation. I wasn't trying to insult your culture. I just . . . felt bad for being late, so like an idiot, I made it worse by showing off."

Finally, he cracked a smile. "I'd forgotten about that."

"Liar. Ever since it happened, you won't even look at me."

His mouth dropped open. "You think I won't look at you because I'm pissed over something you said in class?"

"Well, isn't that it?"

"No." Now he broke my gaze and looked down at his sneakers, worn navy blue Adidas with scruffy white stripes. "I don't want to be rude and stare. So, I try not to look at you too much."

A burst of cold air came as the bar door opened, and a large group of people entered, loud and unruly. They ambled past us, one of them bumping my side, making me nearly fall into Cyrus's arms. Luckily, I caught myself in time. "I don't understand," I said, straightening up, trying to use a jokey tone. "Why would you stare at me? Is there something weird about how I look?"

"Of course not." His chest heaved up and down as he looked around the room at anything but me. "I think you're really pretty, okay? That's why I try not to stare."

"Oh." My breath hitched in my chest. I wanted to touch him, to cradle his cheek in my hand and stare into his eyes and tell him all my secrets. I wanted to hear every story from his childhood. Instead, I took a swig from my bottle of Leinenkugel's, which had grown warm. Standing close to him, the bustle of the bar was like static, messing with the signals I sent and perhaps received from Cyrus. But his sandalwood scent filled my nostrils, and suddenly I acknowledged what I'd known all along. I found Cyrus Gul, with his nerdy dark thick-rimmed glasses, slow smile, and silky black curls, achingly attractive. There was something so Clark Kentish about him, the way he carried himself with modesty, probably hiding both the physique and the heart of a superhero.

"Thank you. But why'd you rush out of the play without saying hello?"

Cyrus gestures behind him to his friends. "I'd made plans to meet up with them, and I was running late."

I raised my eyebrows, smiled at him, and silently urged him to smile back. "You care that much about punctuality when you're meeting friends at a bar?"

He shrugged. "I was already over an hour late."

"Then why did you go to the play in the first place?"

He stared into my eyes, his gaze smoldering. "I wasn't planning to. I was on my way to the bar, saw the poster advertising the play you wrote, and well . . . I was curious."

"I'm flattered."

There was a long pause, and I could feel the silent friction crackling between us.

He smiled. "Do you have any more questions, Hazel?"

Hearing him say my name did something to me. "Just one." I leaned in and brazenly planted a soft discreet kiss at the base of his neck. "Will you walk me home?"

"Okay," he murmured breathily.

We retrieved our coats and walked out of the bar, shifting from unnaturally warm air heavy with the dampness of people and beer to a brisk, clear star-filled night.

"I'm this way." I led him toward campus where my apartment sat on the edge, near the dorms.

He looked straight ahead, walking like he just happened to be next to me but we weren't together. Our breathing and footsteps were the only sounds in the quiet evening, and he kept a solid pace.

"I really did like your play," he said. "How'd you get the idea for it?"

"My parents used to make me go to Sunday school when I was a kid, so I learned all these Bible stories. And whenever anyone talks about Y2K, it's like the potential problems will be Biblical. So, my imagination just sort of took off."

He laughed. "I know nothing about Bible stories. Actually, I know nothing about the Bible, period."

I playfully shoved my shoulder into his. "Trust me; you're not missing out."

"Oh no? You're not a fan of the Bible?"

I almost slipped on a patch of ice, and Cyrus reached out to steady me. With his arms around me, I flushed hot, despite the arctic air. "Thanks." Then, remembering his question, I said, "There are some really beautiful parts of the Bible. But growing up, my parents were pretty strict in their beliefs, and I don't know . . . I felt boxed in. I could never accept that all the other religions were absolutely wrong and that ours was right."

"What about now?"

His hand still lingered on the small of my back, making me flush with desire. "Nothing's changed."

"Do you still feel boxed in?"

I thought for a moment. "Like, just in general? I suppose. I guess that's why I'm a double major; education and creative writing." I sighed, my chest heavy. "Can I tell you a secret?"

"Sure," he said softly.

"Sometimes, I don't know what I want, and then, it's not like I'm making bad choices. I just don't make any choices at all."

"Yeah, me too."

I stop, gazing at him. "Really?"

"Yeah. There's the path of least resistance, and there's going after what you want. Too often, I take the easy way out."

"You seem like such a strong person, though." He didn't respond, but we had reached the entrance of my building. "Here's where I live."

He walked me up to the front.

"Thanks for walking me home. And by the way, I really am sorry about how I acted during your presentation. That's not how I usually am."

The corners of Cyrus's mouth inched up, and his eyes gleamed. "How are you, usually?"

I shrugged. "I wish I knew. I'm still waiting to find out."

He smiled. "So, it's like a cliffhanger?"

"Maybe, but I hate cliffhangers. They're a cheap, dramatic device. Any writer worth her salt will resolve all the plot points."

"Well, I already know that you're an amazing writer, so I bet you'll figure out the rest real soon." It was like he stared right into the darkest part of me and turned on the light. "You should follow your dreams, Hazel. Figure out who you are and go after what you want."

I must have been emboldened by the beers I'd drunk that night and the invigorating cold air. "What about going after *who* I want? Do you recommend that too?"

He looked at me for a long moment, and then, he leaned in and kissed me, and as his mouth met mine, his warmth soothed and excited me all at once.

I pulled away. "Would you like to come in?"

"Yes," he husked.

I led him inside.

***

It was the most passionate night of my entire life. As soon as we made it inside, we had urgent sex, tugging at each other's clothing, aggressively kissing, and gasping as if we'd been punched when really it was all pure pleasure.

Cyrus was gone before I woke up the next morning. That Monday, he wasn't in class. When, after two weeks, he was still absent, I feared the worst. Was he ill? Did he have a family emergency? At the end of class one day, I finally summoned the courage to approach the girl he'd always sat next to. She was still at her desk, and I leaned against the one he used to occupy. "Hey," I said, aware this would be the first thing I'd ever said to her, "is Cyrus okay? Do you know why he hasn't been in class?"

"He's fine," the friend said curtly. "He just transferred to Cal State so he could get married and be with his family in California. I'm surprised you didn't know."

Stunned, I reached for a response, stammering as my words came out. "Oh . . . Umm, so . . . he got married?"

The friend stood and grabbed her tote bag. "Yeah," she said, the word coming out in breathy indignation. "He'd been engaged for a while."

She walked past me, out of class, and into the late morning December sun.

I rushed back home, resigned to skipping my next class, so I could release hot tears full of shame and resentment into my pillow. How had I gotten everything so completely wrong? I'd practically thrown myself at a man with a fiancé. He probably planned to finish the semester here, but our encounter must have freaked him out so badly that he had no choice but to run.

Still, he could have told me.

He could have said goodbye.

***

My student teaching assignment began the first of February, bringing with it long nights of lesson planning and essay grading and longer days of navigating the halls of a high school as an adult, as a pseudo-authority figure. Five times a day, I'd stand in front of a room of thirty bored teenagers, ones who refused to read when called upon or who assumed I was easy prey. They would compete over who would be the first to make me cry.

But I loved the energy that crackled inside a public high school's walls, and I connected with the kids who shared my passion for reading. We'd discuss the library books they carried around, like *Speak* or *The Perks of Being a Wallflower.* Some girls saw me as a big sister type and would pass me notes at the end of class. I could see myself teaching full time and, through the years, finding more and more kids to care about, more and more kids in whose success stories I could play a part.

Then, on a Tuesday in late April, two teenagers from Columbine High School killed twelve of their classmates, a teacher, and themselves, all in the space of twenty minutes. It had happened hundreds of miles away, yet, it may as well have been next door. I knew how to explain metaphors and parallel sentence structure, but I couldn't tell these kids how to feel safe in a world that grew more dangerous by the minute.

And I didn't know how to feel safe myself.

Student teaching ended, and my controversial "you're ruining your life"—according to my parents—internship at the Playwrights' Center began, where I could take classes for free, where I coordinated the reading series, and where I was encouraged to develop and workshop my writing, receiving tough-love feedback that made me more determined to create the next Tony-winning phenomenon.

I worked at a coffee shop, connecting with the starving creative types who also brewed espresso to supplement their income. I prayed the tip jar would be full. I had a series of deadbeat boyfriends and questionable roommates. I felt alive in a bohemian sort of way but was directionless. When my bank account balance was too depressing to contemplate, I signed up to work as a substitute teacher, thinking at least I'd make decent money. After a couple of months, I landed a long-term substitute position, and the principal at that school liked me enough to recommend me for a full-time position at a nearby district, Dixon Heights, which was hiring.

I never forgot Cyrus's words of advice: "Figure out who you are, and go after what you want." I'd accomplished the second half anyway, but the first half? Febe was right. Once I met Vance, I quit figuring out who I was.

Perhaps that's unfair. I'm a teacher. That should be enough.

CHAPTER 28

February 2004

I haven't seen Cyrus all day, not in the hallways on the way to my office, nor in the copy room, nor outside his classroom when I run down to the bathroom. True, I haven't sought him out, but he hasn't sought me out, either. Is he avoiding me?

No. I won't worry about that right now. There are too many pressing concerns demanding my attention. I should sit at my desk and grade essays, which is what I do, but it's hard to focus. I'm curious who may be looking at the art blog. There's a way to track how many views we get and who is visiting the site. Unfortunately, I need Cyrus to show me that.

"Hazy, we need to talk. I know you're mad at me, and I want to make things right."

As Olivia enters my classroom, she swishes her ponytail. It's her form of bravado. She's also squeezing both her thumbs, her index fingers wrapped so tightly it looks as if her circulation is threatened. That's what she does when she's nervous and seeing her like this breaks my guard a little.

I quickly close out the literary magazine's webpage so that all that's left on my screen is a file about my students' essays on isolation in literature. My eyes scan the line, "The internal journey happens when the protagonist travels to the center of his/her own soul, discovering essential universal truths about identity and humanity by first revealing their own truth."

I sigh, letting my eyes venture from my computer screen to Olivia's face. "Okay, Olivia, I guess we're doing this now. Here's the thing: I know that you've been lying to me, and you've been letting me lie to myself. Why didn't you tell me that I broke up with Vance in this 'really public fight' on the day before holiday break?"

Olivia's fingers straighten and flex as she plops into a student desk. "Who told you that?"

"Febe."

She bites her bottom lip as if she fears the words that might escape. "And you believe Febe?" she asks gently.

"I do. She wouldn't lie."

"Okay." Olivia nods solemnly. "It's just . . . I heard she's been getting into trouble this year."

"So? Are you saying that Febe was lying, and that I *didn't* actually argue and publicly break up with Vance?"

"No, but . . ." Her voice trails off.

"What?"

With a deep breath, Olivia completes her thought. "On the day of the accident, you told me that you didn't trust Febe. I'd asked you to explain, but you were too upset to go into detail."

I want to process this but can't. "Walk me through what happened that day." She doesn't respond, so I flatly add, "Please."

Olivia looks down at the desk where she sits. Every second she waits before answering feels like a tedious dream where, no matter how hard I try, I can't complete a simple task.

"Well," she finally says a tad defensively, "you and Vance were called out for that American Dream project on MySpace, and then these rumors flew that he'd posted porn."

"You mean that he'd posted a picture of him and Annabelle having sex."

"Right." Olivia shudders as if she's in pain. "But why would he post something like that? He wouldn't. The picture was photoshopped to look like him and Annabelle, I'm sure. And there's no doubt that a student with a vendetta posted it . . ." Olivia pauses, and I get the sense that she's bracing herself. "In fact, I heard that it might have been Febe."

"What?" A sudden chill spreads into my core. "No." I almost start hyperventilating but keep my breathing even. "Did I say that? Is that why I thought I shouldn't trust her?"

"Well, you never said it outright, but that's what I assumed." She looks at me, cocking her head in sympathy. "I know how important Febe is to you. So try to remember that it's just a rumor, Hazy. The whole thing is a twisted, drama-packed mess, and I told you that when it all went down. You were so upset, though. I tried to stop you, but you ran down to his classroom when you knew he had prep, and I guess you started arguing, and students heard you yell, 'We're done!' Later you told me that you meant you both were done professionally here at school, and I was like, 'Make a show of strength.' I convinced you to go with me to the holiday party that night, but well, we know how that ended. And then I felt like it was all my fault, like I convinced you to go to the party when you'd just wanted to go home, and you left with him in the middle of an argument, and then there was the accident." She breaks off, needing to take a deep breath. "I'm sorry I didn't tell you. I just didn't know how."

Funny—of everything that Olivia just said, the only part I find truly shocking and disturbing is that Febe might be involved.

"That's okay," I mutter. "None of it was your fault."

"I was worried about you, Hazy." She reaches out and grabs my shoulder. "You have every reason to be furious with Vance, both for what happened before the accident and how he's freezing you out now. I don't think anyone blames you for breaking up with him."

"Wait, what?" I lean toward her. "I thought you said I didn't break up with him at school."

"Right. You broke up with him at the party, right before you got into the car and drove home. So, that's the other reason I didn't tell you. I didn't want you to blame yourself for what happened, like if he hadn't been so upset, the accident wouldn't have happened."

My brain is on overload, to where I can literally feel my synapses buzzing. "This is a lot to take in," I say. "*Was* the accident my fault?" I look at her beseechingly, tears pooling in my eyes.

"I don't think so," Olivia says.

"But you don't know for sure."

"I wasn't there, Hazy." She sighs. "I am so, so, sorry."

"Alright." I resolutely square my shoulders. "Tell me what else you know."

To: VValby89@yahoo.com
From: H_Ford_AOGG@hotmail.com
Subject: Olivia
Dear Vance,

I finally confronted Olivia today. I told her I needed to know her version of what went down before the accident. She accused me of being angry with her, and I couldn't deny it. Of course I was angry. She's been keeping me from the truth, but not anymore.

She said I broke off our engagement at the Christmas party, that I accused you of sleeping with Annabelle, that we were still fighting as we got into our car to drive home and everybody assumed that our argument led to the

accident, that, because of everything that happened between us, nobody is surprised that you've "disappeared."

I suppose I believe her because I've always trusted
Olivia. Well, I've always trusted her, except for when it
comes to you. Do you remember, Vance? Do you ever think
about it now?

Take Care.

Hazel

CHAPTER 29

September 2002

After you and I decided to go public with our relationship, I knew Olivia needed to find out about us first, and I also knew I must be the one to tell her. "She will not take it well," you had warned me.

"What makes you think so?" I'd asked.

"Because we've kept it from her for too long. She'll freak out because nobody likes being lied to."

"We didn't exactly lie."

"We withheld the truth, and you know that's the same thing."

"Well," I'd responded, "all the more reason to come clean now." You were always so nonchalant, and now you just shrugged. I took that as a signal of your approval. So, on the Monday after the Friday when I'd said "I love you" and you'd answered with "I'm tired of keeping our relationship a secret," I found Olivia after school, straightening up her classroom. She never seemed to have much grading to do, but she always had some student group or meeting in her room, and after they left, Olivia, ever the neat freak, couldn't rest until the desks were aligned and all the surfaces were wiped down.

"How was your Mathletes meeting?" I asked as I walked in.

"Great!" Olivia looked up from the desk she was scrubbing, a washcloth in one hand, a bottle of 409 in the other. "We have some really sharp minds this year. We could go all the way to State."

I sat at a desk that had already been wiped. "Do you always clean every desk at the end of the day?"

"Of course," she answered. "The janitors won't do it. And do you know how many germs and bacteria circulate around the place? Thinking about it makes me nauseous. But just watch, Hazy. You all will get sick this winter, over and over, and I guarantee you, I'll stay healthy."

"Because you clean off your desks?"

"That, and I don't use the bathrooms here, and I don't get my flu shot. I swear flu shots are a government conspiracy to weaken our immune systems."

We'd already debated the validity of flu shots, but arguing about stuff like that reminded me of things my parents would say. As for public restrooms, I knew Olivia was near-phobic and hated using them, so she'd trained her bladder to last for hours. Meanwhile, I feared my students secretly mocking me for always running to the staff bathroom every passing time because all the coffee and water I drank would run right through me. It couldn't be helped, but sometimes I envied Olivia's resolve.

"Yeah, time will tell," I answered, regarding Olivia's prediction about the flu. "Look, there's something I need to talk to you about."

Olivia momentarily stopped scrubbing the desk she was working on and looked up. "That sounds scary. People never tell you they have to 'talk to you about something' unless it's bad news."

"No, no. It's not like that. Actually, it's really pretty great."

"Okay . . ." Olivia sat at the desk across from me, peering into my eyes. "Don't keep me in suspense, then. What is it?"

I let a self-conscious laugh escape. "I'm in love with Vance."

Olivia smirked. "You think this is news? I could have told you that a long time ago. I'm glad you're finally admitting it yourself, Hazy, but be careful. That 'nice guy' schtick he has going is a façade. Vance is totally capable of breaking your heart."

Her response made me skip a beat. Olivia had this uncanny ability to voice my unspoken thoughts. Often, this felt liberating, but not now. Now, I had to keep the upper hand in this conversation. "No, what I'm trying to say is that we're in love with each other."

Olivia's smirk only intensified and was now accompanied by an arched eyebrow. "Has he told you that?"

I felt heat rush to my cheeks. "Not in so many words, but it was Vance's idea to go public with our relationship. I think that means a lot, that he wants everyone to know we're together."

"Right." Olivia sighed like she was speaking to a child, like she was burdened with breaking the news that there is no Santa Claus. "Tell me, Hazy, how long have you been in a," she used air quotes for the next word, "'relationship'?"

"Around eight months." I straightened my spine and forced my shoulders back. This was not how I envisioned the conversation going. Sure, I figured Olivia would be annoyed that I'd kept my romance with you from her for so long, but I hadn't pictured her disbelief or her dismissal. "It's real, Olivia. You can ask Vance. He's just as into me as I am into him."

"How do you know?"

"Because, like I said, it was his idea to go public."

"Yeah, but whose idea was it to keep your relationship private in the first place? And before you say, 'It was both of us', think back, really hard. Did Vance sort of suggest or imply that it would be better to keep it all on the down low, letting you believe it's what you wanted? Because that's exactly how guys like him operate."

I bolted up from my desk. "Thanks for the support, Olivia. But you don't know what you're talking about."

"I'm sorry, Hazy, but I just don't want to see you get hurt."

"Yeah, well, you're hurting me right now."

"Oh, come on; lighten up."

She rolled her eyes, which only intensified my ire. "It's like I'm some big joke to you. Or you think I'm so naïve that you need to protect me from Vance *and* from myself. But I'm not that person."

Olivia's face hardened, and her voice dropped an octave. "Hazel, I'm only saying this because I'm your friend, and real friends are honest with each other. Vance is not the commitment type. Maybe he'll stay with you for a little while, but eventually, he'll either leave, cheat, or both. If you were smart, you'd end it now, while you can be the one to walk away."

"You're jealous."

"No." Olivia raised her eyebrows, as if daring me to contradict her. "I mean Vance is cute and all, but he's too metrosexual for me. I like my men to be tough, hockey-playing, deer-hunting types. That's the only way they could keep up with me." She let out a steely laugh. "Besides, if anyone here is jealous, it's you."

I crossed my arms over my chest. "Why would I be jealous of you?"

"Because," she said carefully, "I'm strong. I don't fall for players like Vance, and if I did, I'd destroy them before I'd let them take advantage of me. But you're not that way."

"Okay. Now you're just being a bitch." In my whole life, I'd never called anyone that, not unless I was joking. "Don't talk to me again unless you've come to apologize."

I stormed off, proud that I'd stood up for myself, yet shaking with self-doubt. What if Olivia was right about everything? What if I was the one who'd eventually have to apologize?

CHAPTER **30**

In the morning, I wake from a restless sleep, hungry because I'd forgotten to eat last night. I still have two days
left of my work week, and even though I feel like Sisyphus
pushing the boulder up a hill, I know I need to see it
through. I'm not expecting anything more than a typical
Thursday, but when I get to school, I realize that was naïve. The message light on my classroom phone blinks
bright red, casting an ominous glow before I turn on the
overhead lights.

When I play the message, my chest knots up. Jim, the
principal, has called me. That never happens. Usually, he
emails. If a phone call is necessary, it's always his secretary, Tamisha, who makes it. Not this time. "Hazel, we
need to talk. Come see me now, and I mean *now.*"

The message is time-stamped from twenty minutes ago.
That's not good. Jim rarely gets to school early, but he's
very critical of anyone who arrives after him. I'm on the
late side today. In fact, first hour starts in twenty minutes.
My tardiness will only make things worse.

I hurry down to Jim's office.

Of course, he's not there. "Um, Tamisha?" I interrupt
her handing a folder to one of today's subs and explaining
how to take attendance. "Sorry. Jim called, said he wanted
to see me right away this morning. Do you know where he
is?"

She scowls. "He probably thought you would be here sooner." She picks up her radio and speaks into it. "Jim, do you copy?"

There's a moment of static as my stomach flips and churns. Then I hear Jim's voice. "Copy."

Tamisha gives me the stink eye as she speaks back into her radio. "Hazel is here to see you."

"I'll be right there," I hear Jim respond.

Tamisha tells me to wait in his office, so I enter the space that is twice as big as most of the classrooms in this school, with a conference table, desk, and framed photos by the district's PR person, catching the students looking wholesome, happy, and diverse at games and graduation. I'm staring at one photo, the crowd at the state basketball tournament from two years ago, girls with gold and black face paint on, waving signs to cheer for the team. The first girl wears a hijab, the second has rows of tightly braided hair, and the third's golden locks fall into waves that rival a Disney princess. Two of the girls were in my English 11 class, and I'm trying to remember their names. Then Jim walks in.

"Good morning, Hazel," Jim says brusquely, and instantly I know that this morning is anything but good. "How are you?"

He doesn't make eye contact as he asks me that question, making it clear he doesn't really care about my answer. "Okay," I venture. "How are you?"

"Me? I'm fine. I feel bad that I haven't been able to check in with you sooner after you returned from medical leave, the accident and all."

Now Jim looks at me. Everything about him is colored tan—his skin, his slicked-back hair, his shirt and tie—even his eyes are a light brown, bordering on tan. It's disarming, all that monochromaticity. "Is that why you wanted to see me, to check in?"

"No." Jim's nostrils flare as he takes a breath through tightened lips. "I saw the art blog—what is it, *Burning Moon*?"

"*Burnt Moon*," I correct, "but I may like *Burning Moon* better." I smile weakly. Jim's eyes do not soften.

"What the hell were you thinking, Hazel? You didn't run this by me first! You didn't even mention it! Don't I deserve a heads-up before you pull something like that?"

"I'm sorry," I say before I realize I've said it. Sitting up straight, I try to project a non-groveling sort of reticence while also communicating strength. "I didn't mean to put you in a bad spot. The students came to me, eager to have their voices heard, and I thought it would be better *not* to tell you about it because that way, if people in the community or in the district office were upset, you could honestly claim you were blindsided by the whole thing."

Jim shakes his head. "Hazel, pardon my French, but that's the stupidest dang thing I've ever heard!"

I almost ask him what part of his statement qualifies as "French"—stupid, dang? But now's not the time. Anyway, Jim isn't done.

"You have no right to make decisions like that. Don't you realize that everything about this school is ultimately a reflection of my leadership? That's how the community sees it, and if I didn't know this blog was getting published, that's just as bad as if I'd known and okayed it."

He pauses, apparently waiting for me to respond.

"Again," I tell him, "I didn't mean to put you in an awkward position. It was about the kids. I was trying to help them."

"Yeah, well, your 'help' is incredibly harmful. Community members are very upset, wondering what sort of school they're sending their kids to, what sort of school their tax dollars are supporting. And then there's the piece about the girl and the guy who is obviously Brady Burns. We're going to address that."

"What do you mean 'address'?" I ask.

"We're going to need the name of the girl so we can get her the help she needs."

"You make it sound like she's the one with the problem, like she needs therapy or counseling or restorative justice. She's the victim in this situation, Jim."

"No. If she were the victim, she wouldn't be broadcasting her situation to the entire community, implicating others without attaching her name to her accusations. That's taking things too far."

I swallow roughly, trying to keep my cool. "Well, I can't help you. I don't even know who the author is. She submitted anonymously."

"Then we have a problem." Jim scowls. "Let me be clear, Hazel. I think you're full of crap. I believe you know who wrote the piece. And if you're smart, you'll tell me."

Something inside me hardens, like my spine is morphing into steel. "And if I don't?"

Jim glares at me. "You're up for tenure this year, and you already have a letter in your file. But let's say I keep you on. I could still make your life miserable. I could take away all those precious advanced classes you like teaching. Lucas has been gunning to teach AP anyway."

"I knew it!" I cry. "I've totally been getting that vibe from him. But, Jim, he doesn't understand that we need to follow a classic College Board-approved curriculum."

Jim's face goes from tan to orangey. "I don't care! I will give Lucas your schedule, and I will switch things around so you're teaching remedial English 9, or better yet, I will transfer you down to the middle school."

I gasp. "You'd do that after all I've put into this job?"

"Frankly, Hazel, the fact that you call it 'a job' really troubles me. I don't go to work every day; I go to school. My heart is in this for the good of the kids, but I'm starting to believe that you're in this for you."

I've heard variations on this stump speech from Jim several times already. Yet, it's never been weaponized against me, not until now. Stunned, I struggle to form my reply, but then it magically flows out of me. "Why? Because I want to protect the identity of a vulnerable young woman, or because I donated my time to start an art blog to give silent students a voice, or because I enjoy spending extra hours grading essays and developing challenging lessons for Advanced Placement?"

"Nice job of twisting things, Hazel. This isn't about any of what you just said. This is about your ego. Tell me who wrote the piece, or face the middle school or, better yet, unemployment."

I pause, realizing this is one of those moments where the decision I make will alter the course of my entire life. But I don't pause for too long because, really, the choice is obvious.

"Sorry, Jim. Truly, I have no desire to hurt you or the school, this place I have loved for years. But clearly, with everything that's happened recently, it's time for me to go. You'll have my written resignation by Monday."

The warning bell for first hour rings. I stand.

"I'd better get going. I still plan to finish out the school year, and I don't want to keep my students waiting."

For once, Jim appears to be speechless, and he lets me go, the ring of the warning bell still echoing in my ears.

CHAPTER 31

I have become adept at keeping my cool despite all the crazy emotions and confusion that roil through me. Instead of letting on that I just quit my job, I teach like it's a normal day. In AP English, we debate whether Tom and Daisy are cruelly careless or carelessly cruel. In my college writing class, we're onto the morality unit, and today's lesson is about the trolley problem: should you change course and consciously kill one person to avoid inadvertently killing five? The answer seems easy at first, but like most puzzles, it becomes more complex the more you think about it. Few things in life are clear, and increasingly I believe that our intentions, whether good or bad, alter the outcome of any given situation. Jim must agree, or he wouldn't have threatened my job after accusing me of feeding my ego.

Maybe he's right. Maybe I became a teacher for all the wrong reasons. And now that I've lost almost everything that I thought I had, I ought to take stock and look to the future. But I'm like one of those boats Nick describes in *The Great Gatsby*, beating against the current but pulled relentlessly back into the past.

To: H_Ford_AOGG@hotmail.com
From: VValby89@yahoo.com
Dear Hazel,
Wanted you to know that I've been reading your emails. You've always been a natural writer. If I could send you a painting of all my thoughts and feelings, I would, but I

can't. For now, I'll just say that you have nothing to apologize for. None of what happened was your fault.

Take care of yourself.

Love always,

Vance

I should have known better than to check my personal
email at school. Of course, Vance chooses today to reach
out. Before I can think better of it, I respond.

To: VValby89@yahoo.com
From: H_Ford_AOGG@hotmail.com
Subject: I just quit my job
Dear Vance,

I'm writing this email from school. It's my prep time,
and that it's from my personal and not my school account
is the one concession I'm making to giving a rat's ass.

So, yeah, I told Jim that I'm done at the end of the year.
I could give you all the details, but I'm more interested in
remembering how I got to this point. It all comes back to
you and to Olivia.

You said I've always been a natural writer? Well, this
time, I'm going to write out the full memory that I'm combing through at the moment. Hope you don't have anywhere
to be.

After our fight, Olivia and I weren't friends for nearly a
year. Meanwhile, you and I rarely spent a night apart, and
we almost always drove to and from work together. We
both hated the amount of money we threw away every
month on our exorbitant rents, and that winter, mortgage
rates were at an all-time low. "Now is the perfect time to
buy," I said.

That led to what was probably the sweetest phase of our relationship when we'd spend weekends going from open house to open house, looking at starter homes in North Minneapolis and in first-ring suburbs like Robbinsdale and Brooklyn Center.

"I've never seen this parkway before. Have you?" I asked you one Sunday afternoon when we pulled up to a tiny little house for sale along Victory Memorial Parkway. I was amazed by the huge stretch of grass and trees with separate paths for bikes and pedestrians that led directly into Theo Wirth Park, which I'd also never heard of but learned was the largest park in Minneapolis, with a public golf course, a lake with a beach and play area, a bird sanctuary/wildflower garden, and even a quaking bog. The house we were there to see sat right on the parkway and was within walking distance of Theo Wirth Park's entrance.

"You would think I'd have seen it before," you answered, "since I've lived in this city my entire life. But it's not ringing any bells."

I didn't remind you that you hadn't actually lived in Minneapolis your whole life, that you'd grown up in Chanhassen, which was like the most outer-ring privileged-person-living-in-a-bubble sort of suburb there was.

We walked the steps up to the open house. The home for sale was built in the 1920s: a charming little bungalow with a steep rickety staircase, a second floor where you had to be under 5'5" to stand up straight, close to zero closet space, and an unfinished basement that smelled of mildew. The flier advertised the house as 950 square feet, in a prime location, and renovated with an artist's touch. It's true that the paint, hardwood floors, and light fixtures were done beautifully, and the kitchen had what looked like the original wood cabinets, newly refurbished and gleaming golden brown.

"It's probably too small," I said to you. What I didn't say was that it would be a terrible house in which to raise children, and I knew I shouldn't even have thought in that direction, yet what was the point of home shopping without keeping the future in mind?

You shrugged. "It's not too small for a single person. This could be the perfect home for you." You wandered off as you spoke, heading toward the three-season porch with rustic hardwood floors and a high vaulted ceiling, from which hung an industrial farmhouse chandelier where a nest of wire wove around otherwise exposed bulbs, creating this shabby-chic French farmhouse feel that made me want to move in instantly.

Still . . . "But I'm not a single person, am I?"

You laughed. "I didn't mean it like that."

"Like what?"

"Like you're on your own in this. What if you bought it, I paid you rent, and in a few years, you could make a ton selling it, and then we'd buy something together that's bigger and more practical?"

My head was swimming. "So, if I buy this house, you'll give up your apartment and live here with me?"

You flicked the hair off your forehead and smiled down at me. "Sure."

Visions of our potential life together burst into my mind: lazy autumn Sundays with you painting on our three-season porch/studio while I reread *Pride and Prejudice* and planned my lessons for the following week; taking evening strolls in the parkway with you, hand in hand, admiring the orange skies at sunset; hosting Friday night happy hours here with wine and beer, cheese and crackers, while trying not to act too smug at our luck, that you and I have each other, and we live together in this adorable quietly elegant home in this hidden gem part of the city.

"Okay," I said, not caring about caution or reason; they were inconvenient concepts meant to slow us down. "I'll ask the real estate agent if they're expecting any offers."

They were, and the real estate agent assured me that this place would go quickly. Suddenly, I was sure I couldn't live without this house, that I had to share this imagined life with you in this exact spot. I was so consumed with getting the house that I didn't question your logic; I just wanted what was slightly out of reach, and in the end, I got it.

The day after my house signing, I ran into Olivia in the copy room. I was in such a good mood that I forgot to act awkward and tense around her and just said, "Hey, how are you?"

She was clutching a workbook in one hand and a bunch of tissues in the other. Her eyes seemed glassy, and when she spoke, she sounded nasally and like it hurt to talk. "Okay." She gestured toward the copier, "Do you have a lot to do?"

"No. You sound terrible. Are you sick?"

Olivia rolled her eyes. "Obviously. And I don't need any snarky comments, okay? I don't have the flu, and everybody gets a cold from time to time, no matter how much they clean and use hand sanitizer."

"Sure. I mean I wasn't going to tease you or anything. Maybe you should call in tomorrow and get some rest." I stepped to the side as the copier spat out the last few pages of the job I'd put in. "I'm done. The copier is all yours."

Olivia wordlessly stepped up and started pressing the touch screen on the copier, selecting her preferences for the worksheets she needed, a scowl on her face as she did so. "I hope you feel better," I said as I turned to walk away.

But Olivia's voice stopped me. "I heard you bought a house."

"Yeah." I checked myself, not wanting to seem too eager. "Just signed the paperwork yesterday."

"Congratulations," Olivia replied. "Vance was talking about it yesterday. He said it's really cool and that he's moving in with you."

"Yeah." Internally, I cringed, expecting Olivia to ask why Vance didn't buy the house with me. But she offered me a smile.

"Good for you, Hazy. I guess you're getting everything you wanted, after all."

If her statement seemed like a backward sort of compliment, I would take it as what I wanted: a peace offering.

"Thank you," I replied. "I hope you'll come over and see the house as soon as we're all moved in. I can't wait to show it off."

"That would be great."

I smiled back at her, and we left it at that.

So, thanks for the email, but when will I hear from you again? I deserved more than having you as a renter, and I hate that Olivia was right. Now I know she was just being nice when she'd said I'd gotten everything I wanted. Now, everything I wanted is gone.

Hazel

CHAPTER 32

I'm feeling something entirely unfamiliar: an urgent need to return home and see my parents.

It's Thursday afternoon, and if I call in sick for Friday, I'll give myself a three-day weekend. What have I got to lose?

As soon as the afternoon bell rings, I rush to Olivia's room. "Hey!" She shifts nervously when she sees me standing in her doorway. "What's up?"

"All sorts of things," I confess, "but I'll have to tell you about it all later. I'm calling in tomorrow because I need to drive down to see my parents. Would you do me a huge favor and check in on Baby Girl in the afternoon?"

"Of course," Olivia answers. "When will you be back?"

"Sunday. But if the trip goes longer, I'll let you know."

Unexpectedly, Olivia approaches me and captures me in a fierce hug. "Take all the time you need, Hazy. Me and Baby Girl will be just fine."

I'm not sure how long I should keep hugging her before it's okay to pull away. "Thanks, Olivia. You are a good friend."

When I get home from school, I stop only to pet Baby Girl goodbye, fill her food dish and water bowl, change her litter box, and load up my car with an overnight bag and some snacks for the road. Then I head off down 35W South, toward Iowa, and ultimately to Kansas. The conversation I must have with my parents will best be done in person.

I've made this trip around a dozen times since I moved to Minneapolis, and the landscape, other than with the seasons, does not change. Prairies sprawl on either side of the freeway, littered with billboards advertising outlet malls and fast-food restaurants. I stop outside of Des Moines for the night at a Super 8 Hotel next to a Taco Bell, so I grab some fast food and watch TV while I eat.

At around 10:00 p.m., it occurs to me that maybe I should call my parents and tell them I'm coming home for the weekend.

I worry it's too late in the evening to call Mom and Dad's landline and wake them. So, I text my mother, aware that the chances she'll see my text and know how to respond are slim. Even though my dad works in IT in so many ways, it's like he and my mom never entered the twenty-first century.

But I text her, nonetheless, letting her know to expect me at around noon tomorrow. The next day I rise early and drive from Des Moines, through southern Iowa, and into Kansas, which I still think of as my home state.

Growing up, I thought there couldn't be anywhere more boring. Smack dab in the middle of the country, it has none of the charm of the South, the rustic nature of the North, the excitement of the West, nor the sophistication of the East. Kansas is like a slice of Velveeta cheese that, through a combination of too many parts, loses all its flavor. For too long, I thought that meant I was flavorless as well, that I couldn't be interesting simply because of where I grew up. And maybe I'm not interesting. But Velveeta isn't always bad. And to be fair, neither is Kansas.

I'm feeling nostalgic as I drive into Topeka and enter my old Westboro neighborhood where the red and white-trimmed home I grew up in is located. In summer and fall, there's great shade from all the trees in the yard, and we even have a veranda where I spent many hours reading my favorite books as a kid: all the classics like *Little Women, Anne of Green Gables,* and a hot find from Washburn University Library's annual book sale, an old textbook called *Treasury of the Theater.*

I would sit on that veranda reading that dusty tomb of a book published in the 1950s, learning about authors like Thornton Wilder, Tennessee Williams, and Lillian Hellman. That was when I first decided to become a playwright, but I left that dream behind somewhere between getting my teaching degree and becoming an artist's girlfriend. Vance was the talented, special one, and if either of us were to flake off and try to make a living without a steady job, it would be him. My job was to make sure things stayed steady and predictable.

I park in front of my childhood home, so bright and vivid, standing out in the gray winter landscape. My mom's car is in the driveway, so that's a good sign, even if she didn't text back. I walk the path from my car to the front door, careful not to slip on the ice. Here, the afternoon sun will melt snow that's quick to ice over on the pavement come nightfall.

I knock briefly, mostly to warn them I'm here. Then, I turn the doorknob, walking in. "Hello? Mom? Dad? I'm home."

My mother enters from the kitchen. She looks pretty much the same as the last time I saw her. I suppose her dark wavy hair has become increasingly sprinkled with gray, but that's most likely because she's gone longer without dying it. She still wears glasses that are too big for her face, and she has on her favorite mock turtleneck sweater, bright red with black zigzag lining the bottom hem and her sleeves. I've always thought it looks just a little too much like Charlie Brown.

"Hazel," she says warmly. "Here you are. How are you, honey?" She comes close, extending her arms and capturing me in a loose hug. "If I'd known you were coming, I would have gone shopping and gotten stuff to make chicken carbonara."

"That's alright, Mom. It was sort of last minute, coming down. You don't need to go to any trouble for me."

"Okay . . ." Her eyes search my face, looking for a sign of something. Perhaps she wants evidence that I'm okay, so she peers into my eyes, and I shoot back the sanest look I can muster.

"I just needed to come home. Everything's been so crazy lately, and I'm frustrated that I can't remember stuff, so I thought talking to you and Dad would help."

"Sure." She smiles, and we stand there awkwardly. Truth is, this hasn't really been my home for a while, so I kind of feel like I need her to invite me to sit down, make myself comfortable, or go to the kitchen to grab something to drink.

She must sense that.

"Why don't you take your bag upstairs and relax a little after your drive? Your father is at work, and he won't be home for a few hours . . . But we can all talk over dinner."

"Thanks, Mom."

I take my bag and travel upstairs to what used to be my bedroom but is now both a guest room and my mom's puzzle room. One side of the room has a double bed and a dresser, but the rest of it is filled with a large table where her current puzzle project is laid out. It looks like she's about halfway done with it, images of vintage flowers coming together. The puzzles that she's most proud of are framed and mounted on the walls: a Norman Rockwell painting, the Japanese masterpiece "The Great Wave," and a photo of a bunch of pastel-frosted donuts, among others. They're all over one thousand pieces; mom never bothers with less because then, she says, there's no challenge.

When I was younger, Mom tried to get me interested in doing puzzles with her, but it never appealed to me. There was no room for imagination, and puzzles were so unforgiving, with each piece only fitting into one specific spot. Plus, I never understood her desire to put something back together that shouldn't have been cut apart in the first place, and in my cruel teenage years, I told her that puzzles were unimaginative, pointless, and a waste of time. I guess it's all a metaphor for how I just don't get her, which itself is ironic since Mom has never understood how I view the world through metaphors and other types of literary devices.

Later, after I've had time to "relax" upstairs—code for me to stay out of the way while Mom went to the store, got ingredients for dinner, and cooked—and after Dad got home from work, we sit down for dinner.

"Mom, thanks for going to the trouble of making chicken carbonara. It looks and smells delicious."

"Well, hopefully, it will taste delicious, too." She laughs self-deprecatingly.

Dad takes a bite. "It does!" He chews, speaks, and smiles at the same time, and Mom and I beam back at him, each of us doing our part to contribute to the forced gaiety. I don't want the mood to deflate too soon, so I eat, compliment Mom on the food, and ask them both questions about how they've been. They tell me about work, the neighbors, and the TV shows they're watching, and for a while, everything is pleasant.

Yet, it nags at me. I'm their only daughter. I've just suffered a major accident and trauma. Why don't they ask me how I'm doing? Why didn't they come up to Minneapolis to help me through the ordeal?

I place my fork down on the side of my plate and let my eyes travel back and forth between both their faces. "So, I need to talk to you guys about something."

They must hear the gravity in my words because I see a look pass between them, like, "Oh no, here we go . . ." and I cringe on the inside. But I forge on. "It's just that there's so much about what happened with Vance, both with the accident and before, that I don't remember or that I must remember wrong. I need you guys to help me put the pieces back together." Like one of Mom's puzzles, only the puzzle is me.

My mother's expression is compassionate, her voice soft. "Of course, we want to help you however we can, Hazel, but I doubt there's much we can do. You told us not to come."

"I did?"

"Commanded is more like it," Dad responds. "I can't believe you don't remember. We were all set to drive up there, but you got on the phone, sobbing and yelling, telling us to stay away."

"We didn't take it personally," Mom says reassuringly. "We knew you weren't yourself, and you'd just been through something terrible. And we almost drove up anyway. But your father and I prayed on it, and we decided God's love would see you through this difficult time and that we should respect your wishes."

"Oh." I stare down at my plate, at the chunks of chicken and cheese in sauce, so good yet suddenly unappetizing.

"I'm sorry. I honestly don't remember yelling at you guys not to come, and I have no idea why I did that."

"Well, it didn't surprise me too much," Dad responds. "You haven't wanted our help in a while. And it's not like we see each other all that often."

"Right." Now I'm fighting tears. Swallowing a lump in my throat, I say, "This is really embarrassing, but I have to ask. Did I ever tell you two that Vance and I were getting married?"

Mom and Dad pass a look between them again, hesitant yet solemn. "You mentioned it," Mom tells us. "But there was never a date set or anything. You said that at some point you would go to city hall and make things official but that you would not have a ceremony."

"Huh." That doesn't exactly ring any bells, yet it sounds about right. "And did I ever tell you the engagement was off?"

Dad shakes his head. "No. Why? Were you two having problems?"

"I think so. Like I said, I'm having trouble remembering. So, you're sure I said nothing else to you two about Vance and me?"

"Hazel, sweetheart, you just didn't talk to us about your relationship with him. You knew we didn't approve, so you kept all that to yourself."

"But . . ." I look back and forth between them, peering into their eyes. "We never really talked about *why* you didn't approve. Was it because Vance and I lived together without being married or because he came from a liberal artsy family?"

"Neither," my dad says gruffly. "We didn't approve because he wasn't near good enough for you, and he didn't treat you right. Stringing you along like that, mooching off you in the house *you* bought, never agreeing to drive down here with you for a visit. The two or three times we drove up and met him, he acted like he was doing us a favor, letting us take him out for dinner."

That much I remember. A year ago, Mom and Dad drove up to visit on a weekend in October when every school in Minnesota was off for our annual education conference. Teachers always get those days off even though conference attendance isn't mandatory, so I took Mom and Dad around the city. We went to a regional park with a waterfall and to the sculpture garden at the Walker where the famous Spoonbridge and Cherry sculpture, for which Minneapolis is known, sits. Vance had opted out of the daytime activities, but he joined us for dinner, meeting us at a brick-oven pizza restaurant. He'd rolled his eyes when Mom and Dad wanted to stick with traditional pepperoni instead of trying the spicy Korean kimchi pizza. I knew Dad could sense Vance's disdain, but he'd said nothing about it, at least not directly.

Instead, Dad egged Vance on, talking about how the federal government was too big and that we needed to rethink how we fund education and the arts.

"I don't know how you handle having them as parents," Vance had said later. "It's like they disregard everything that is important to you. And you're nothing like either of them. Please, tell me you were adopted."

I'd laughed, but his words nudged some bitterness buttons inside me. It was okay for me to dismiss my parents, but Vance was not yet allowed.

Now the bitterness I feel is more than just a nudge. I'm swallowing back bile that has nothing to do with Mom's chicken carbonara.

198 BEAUTIFUL LITTLE FURIES

"Mom, Dad, I'm sorry that Vance acted like he was better than you. That wasn't okay."

"We didn't care about that," Mom says. "We only cared that he acted like he was better than *you*. But it isn't just him. It's your whole life up there, working at a school where they don't appreciate you, in a profession where you're underpaid, and living in a city that's unsafe and overpriced."

"And all the time, you're acting like it's some tremendous honor, being with Vance, and being an English teacher when you're treated like dirt, when you could have had so much more," Dad adds.

Okay. Now I remember why I don't visit my parents very often. I forget about moments like this, and that has nothing to do with a head injury. It's selective amnesia, a determined state of denial, a feeble hope that someday my parents will understand me.

"Well," I respond, "you'll be happy to know that I quit my job. I'm finishing out the school year, but I won't be back in the fall. And I'll probably sell my house and move from Minneapolis, but past that, I don't know where I'll go or what I'll do."

"You can always stay here," Mom says. Her voice is calm, and if she's at all surprised by what I just said, she doesn't let on.

Dad laughs. "Staying here is the last thing Hazel would do."

I laugh, too. Might as well call a spade a spade.

But I say, "Thanks, Mom, and thanks again for dinner. It really is delicious."

Suddenly, my appetite has returned. I may as well enjoy the meal.

CHAPTER 33

I spend most of the day on Saturday with my parents, and I even help my mom with her current puzzle. I can tell she's trying hard with me, like how she gushes every time I fit two pieces together or when she holds her tongue after I accidentally hoard the piece she needs for a crucial block of purple flowers. Before I leave in the late afternoon, my mother hugs me close.

"I meant what I said," she whispers in my ear. "You can stay here if you need to, sweetheart. Sometimes it's okay to take a step back before you move forward."

"Thanks, Mom." I squeeze her hard, making this the longest, tightest hug we've had in a while. But I don't say I'll stay with her and Dad because I know I can't. Whatever my next step will be, it won't be back to Topeka. I worked too hard to leave.

On my drive home, my phone buzzes several times, but I ignore it. Well, I ignore it to the extent that I don't answer. But I glance down at my phone and see it's Oliva calling. By the time I reach my hotel for the night, I have three phone calls from her.

"I can't believe you published that lit mag and then just took off! I bet you have no idea what's happened. The fallout will be huge. Call me!" Her message makes me think she hasn't heard that I quit. Then her second message plays. "Hazy, why haven't you called me back? I'm trying to help you. Call me!" But her third message is practically screechy. "Okay. I mean it. You need to call me. You're missing the biggest thing to happen in Heights in, like, forever, and you were the start of it all. Call me, seriously, like right now."

She'd left that message ninety minutes ago. I am curious about this shocking news Olivia has but in no mood to be chastised. Still, curiosity wins, and stretching out on the polyester bedspread atop the hotel room queen bed, I call her, staring at the ceiling while my cell phone rings.

Surprisingly, it takes Olivia several seconds to pick up, and when she speaks, her voice holds none of the urgency it had in her messages. "Hi, Hazy. Are you back?"

"Not yet," I answer. "I'm outside of Des Moines, staying over in a hotel. I couldn't pick up when you called because I was on the highway. But how's Baby Girl? Have you had time to check on her?"

"Yes, of course. I said I would, didn't I? I went over both yesterday and today, refilled her food and water, and scratched behind her ears like you said I should."

"Thank you."

There's silence, and I know Olivia is waiting for me to ask about the messages she left. Tentatively, I ask, "So, what's going on?"

"Well, it's a huge mess. I can't believe you missed it!"

"What? Just tell me." I take a deep breath, wondering how much of whatever happened relates to me. I'm already preparing a massive cringe.

"Okay, so people were responding to *Burnt Moon*. Everybody was talking about it, wondering how it got past Jim and the district and whether you'll get fired."

"Uh-huh." I'm not ready to disclose anything, so I just wait for her to continue.

Olivia pauses, but when she realizes I'm staying silent, she lets out a little huff. "Anyway, a ton of people were wondering which student wrote that piece about Brady Burns, if it was real, that sort of thing."

"What do you mean 'if it was real'? Why would anyone make something like that up?"

"Obviously for attention."

"But the piece was anonymous. That makes no sense!"

"Actually, it does if you think about it. I'm not saying that it was made up, but the girl who wrote it could get a huge kick out of watching people speculate and get nervous about more accusations coming out. Some people are really twisted. And Brady Burns says it never happened."

"Well, of course he says that. But the piece is not made up." I can hear how hard my voice sounds.

"Fine, fine. But there was an article in the *Star Tribune* about the whole big controversy, and Greg Turner, who sits on the school board, commented online about the article, saying all this racist stuff. Like Muslim girls are liars, and nobody would want to molest one of them anyway, and they wash their feet in the toilets, and he can prove it—just come to the school and see all the puddles in the girls' bathrooms."

Hearing that, I'm so angry that I forget to breathe for a moment, blood rushing to my brain like it's going to explode. When I permit myself to gasp for breath, words come out in an indignant rush. "Are you kidding me? A school board member posted that garbage? That's obscene. He should be fired and run out of town!"

"I know." Olivia keeps her voice calm to juxtapose my aggression. "Everybody at school agrees, even the administration and the other school board members. But Greg Turner is not apologizing, and here's the thing, Hazy . . . He demands that the author come forward. He says that Brady Burns is a victim in all this and that the only way we can confirm that it wasn't made up is to hear from the author herself."

"But that's just distracting from the issue! Greg Turner is a racist, and he needs to be called out."

"True, but the problem is, there are two issues here. Greg Turner's racism is only one of them."

"What's the other issue?" I demand, already knowing what she'll say and feeling myself crouch into a verbal fighting stance, ready to argue back.

"Obviously, the other issue is this piece you published. People in the community are really upset. You're ruining a student's reputation, and if it's not true I mean . . . Hazy, are you 100 percent sure the story wasn't made up?"

I open my mouth to respond vociferously, but no words come out. Suddenly, I am clobbered by fists of doubt. What if I did just ruin an innocent boy's reputation? Sure, Brady's name was never mentioned, but that makes no difference if everyone just assumes it was him. Febe wouldn't make that up, would she? But Febe never even confirmed that she wrote the dang thing, not definitively. And if she was looking to cause a stir and, in the process, hopefully, attract the attention of some Ivy League schools, then she's well on her way as the editor and creator of *Burnt Moon.*

And if she has a history of lying, like with that MySpace page . . .

No. I can't think that way. My job is to defend and protect her—end of story.

"Of course I'm sure," I state. "I will be home tomorrow afternoon, and I'll deal with this more then. But if anyone is going down over this, it's Greg Turner and not the poor anonymous writer who showed more courage than scum like Turner will ever have."

"Right," says Olivia, sounding unconvinced. "Just get home soon, okay? I have a feeling that things are going to get worse before they get better. Hazy, we're in for a long haul."

To: VValby89@yahoo.com
From: H_Ford_AOGG@hotmail.com
Subject: My parents
Dear Vance,
I'm in Iowa at the moment, driving back from Topeka. Even though school is crazy right now, I had to drop everything to go see my parents. You should be able to understand the desire to just up and go, right?

I asked them why they never liked you, and they said it was because you didn't treat me well. At first, I was surprised, but then I got to thinking, and it makes sense.

Because of our fight last spring. Do you remember?
Hazel

CHAPTER 34

April 2004

"So, don't go."

That was your response when I said that I didn't want to visit my parents that summer.

"I have to."

"No, you don't. Just tell them you don't have time. Tell them you have too much prep work, what with *No Child Left Behind* and curriculum writing."

"They won't understand, and their feelings will be hurt. No. I'll get a trip out of the way at the beginning of the summer before Topeka is sweltering."

We were in our kitchen. I was making soup from a grocery store rotisserie chicken and small chunks of refrigerated biscuit dough, which this recipe on the internet said would cook into dumplings, but as I made the soup, I worried that I should have baked the dumplings in the oven first.

You were throwing together a salad from one of those bags that come with little packets of dressing and croutons, adding chopped vegetables to enhance it. "Whatever you say. Have fun."

Turning up the heat on the stove up to high, willing the chicken broth to boil so the biscuit dough wouldn't be raw, I stared at my pot of soup as I responded. "Would you go with me?"

"Pass," you said. "You know I'm traveling with my family in June."

How could I forget? Your entire family was doing an Italian bike tour; I was not invited. I bit my bottom lip hard enough that it stung. "Okay. I guess I didn't realize the trip was for the entire month. What if I go over the Fourth? Would you come with me then?"

"Hazel, come on. We've been over this. You have nothing in common with your parents, so why should I travel down to Topeka for July Fourth to see them?"

"To support me."

"I'm supporting you by telling you not to go."

"Yeah, but I can't just give up on our relationship completely."

"Look, do what you want," you said. "It's no big deal to me when you decide to go down."

I turned. You were oblivious, casually chopping a carrot up into little orange bits and scooping them into the bowl of lettuce. "Why doesn't it matter to you, Vance?"

"Huh?" You looked up from your knife and vegetable board, your brow knit in confusion. "I'm trying to be flexible. I would have thought you'd appreciate that."

"*Okay.*" I drew out the syllables, trying to understand. "You won't travel with me for the Fourth. You don't care if I stick around so we can celebrate together. What exactly am I supposed to appreciate?"

"Man, never mind." You dropped your knife and cutting board in the sink and stalked off, clearly now uninterested in your salad and in me.

You always acted like a big baby whenever we argued, which wasn't very often, because I would usually give in before any conflict grew too serious. This time was no different. But Olivia's warning from months ago still rang in my ears. *"Vance is not the commitment type . . . Eventually, he'll leave, cheat, or both."*

"I'm sorry," I said as soon as I found you in the living room, angrily flipping through channels on the TV and clutching the remote like it was a weapon. "I didn't mean to upset you, and I don't want to fight."

"Then don't say things to upset me."

"I just said I was sorry."

You sighed and flipped off the TV, and then you looked up at me, standing over you. "I think you should spend the Fourth with your family. It's the right thing to do."

I winced like you'd pinched me, but I buried the pain. "And what about you?"

You shrugged. "It doesn't matter. You know I'm going to that midsummer artists' retreat up in Bemidji."

This was new devastating information. "Umm, no. What artists' retreat?"

"I told you about it. I know I did."

I shook my head. You were messing with your hair, which I'd learned was your tell. You were lying. But were you lying about going to the retreat, or were you lying about having told me? I widened my eyes, silently demanding that you explain.

And you did. "There's a little art center right by the lake. Area artists come to celebrate the solstice, and they stay through the Fourth, working on their craft and sharing ideas. It's going to be amazing."

"You didn't tell me that, Vance. I'd remember if you had."

"Well, maybe I figured it didn't matter since you always have your own plans anyway."

"Right. So now we're not spending the entire first half of summer together. Is that right?"

You leaned back against the couch, slumping your shoulders against the cushions, pressing your fingers against your brow as if you had a headache. "I see you every day, Hazel. Would a break be so bad?"

Your words hit me so hard that I gasped in pain. Turning on my heel, I rushed back into the kitchen where a simmering pot of chicken and dumpling soup greeted me. I needed to act fast as it had boiled over, like pale lava erupting from a volcano. I grabbed an oven mitt, removed the pot from the burner, and turned the stove off. As the bubbling soup retreated into its pot, I peered at it. The bulbous, glistening opaque mess now reminded me of white vomit, and if I ate it, that's how it would come back up. I dumped the entire pot into the sink.

You heard the clattering and came into the kitchen.

"What are you doing?" you cried in shock.

"Getting rid of the soup."

"But—*why?*"

"Because it looks disgusting, and I've lost my appetite."

"Yeah, but why did you dump it in the sink? We don't have a garbage disposal."

I turned, enraged. "You think I don't know that we don't have a garbage disposal, Vance? I'm actually pretty good at figuring things like that out. I get that we don't have a garbage disposal, I get that you're sick of me, and I get that, even though we're supposedly engaged, you don't want to spend any time off with me or my family over summer break. So fine, you win; you don't have to, and now you can go fuck off!"

Your mouth dropped open, and you stood silent for a moment. After that, you went to the sink, got out a garbage bag from underneath it, and used it like a giant glove, scooping up all the contents of my soup that was too thick to run down the drain. You said nothing, neither words of

anger nor anything that resembled an olive branch. Instead, you silently cleaned up my mess.

I went to our bedroom and laid my head down on my
pillow and cried.

Later, you came in and got down on the bed, spooning
me. I was too weak to resist. You nuzzled my ear. "I love
you, Hazel. You know I love you."

You kept saying it over and over, and eventually, I accepted it as an apology, melting in your embrace, and we
came together physically, if not emotionally, for you denied
none of the allegations I'd hurled at you.

And you never said you were sorry.

CHAPTER 35

On Sunday, when I pull up to my house, I'm almost surprised that nothing has changed. It looks the same, and so does the street where I live. I was half expecting to see a mob waiting outside, but all I find are some squirrels and a neighbor chipping at the ice buildup on his backyard patio. Once I'm inside, it's more of the same. My house looks exactly as I'd left it. There's laundry that needs folding, and I should really wipe down the bathroom, but there's no evidence of a crisis other than Baby Girl glaring at me and letting out one long tortured meow as a reproach for my absence.

Perhaps I should check my school email.

I can access it on my personal computer, which is sitting on the table in my living room, silently mocking me, daring me to come over and assess the damage. With a sigh, I give in. May as well rip off the Band-Aid now.

I scroll through my inbox. There are a few emails from supposedly "concerned" parents, but irate is probably a better description. How dare I subject their kids to garbage stories that are left unsigned? I should be fired. I compose an email back to the tune of "don't worry because I already quit," but sending that won't help Febe. Helping her comes first, so I delete my response before sending it. Whatever I do or say, it should be with Febe's interests in mind.

I'm surprised she hasn't emailed. Is she too freaked out to contact me? Or does she just not care?

But Cyrus emailed. It was from Friday, urgent words to the tune of *"Talk to me!"* He must not have realized I wasn't at school when he sent that, so I text him an apology. He responds immediately. *Are you okay? What's going on?*

Long story. I'll tell you the whole thing in person ASAP.

His response takes a while. Perhaps he's laboring over the right words. Perhaps he put his phone down to go to the bathroom. Finally, a new text pops up. *I'm coming over. We should talk about it now.*

Twenty minutes later, Cyrus is in my living room.

"You could have warned me," he says. The edge of irritation in his voice invades the armor I've erected over the last few days—no, weeks—no, months. My tear ducts spring to attention, but I refuse to cry. That would just insult us both. Cyrus deserves a straightforward, unemotional explanation and apology. It's just that I don't know if I can handle him being mad at me. I need Cyrus to be on my side, even if everyone else abandons me.

"You're right," I state, "and I am so sorry. Everything happened all at once, and I selfishly only thought of myself."

"Tell me what happened," he says.

I describe my disastrous conversation with Jim, and my truth-seeking mission to see my parents, and how I learned about the controversy at school from Olivia. I don't mention the seeds of doubt that she'd planted in my mind over Febe, because I can't verbalize it, not yet. But I tell Cyrus everything else, and he listens, apparently without judgment.

When I'm done, he rubs his face like he's tired at the end of a long hard day. "Wow. You have a lot going on right now."

"Yeah, I do." I contemplate this man sitting in my living room. He must have his own agenda. Everybody does. "But aren't you more worried about how this all is going to affect you?"

I didn't mean to sound snappish, but I must have because Cyrus's mouth drops open, and then it sets into a firm line. His eyes narrow as well, and it looks like he's debating how to respond.

"Sorry," I say. "That came out wrong. I just mean that it's only natural you would worry about yourself. After all, the last thing you need is me and all my drama."

"I'm sure you're right." Now, he rubs his forehead, an action that seems to relax his entire face. "But what if I want you and all your drama?"

I let out a puff of air, looking down at my hands resting in my lap. That way, I don't have to look at his hazel eyes, which stare at me with such intensity behind his thick-rimmed glasses.

"That doesn't sound too healthy." I stand and cross to the window, looking out, trying to create as much distance between him and me as possible in my tiny living room. "And it's not like we got off to a good start all those years ago."

"True. But the heart wants what it wants."

"Come on, Cyrus." I laugh humorlessly. "Now's your chance. Run. Say you had nothing to do with the art blog, that we were never friends, and forget all about me. I won't blame you if you do."

He stands and comes toward me. "I tried that once before. It didn't work."

"Didn't it? I mean you got married."

"And then I got divorced."

"Okay. I'm sorry your marriage didn't work out. But you took off without an explanation or a goodbye, and if you hadn't started working at Heights, I'm sure I would never have seen you again."

Cyrus sighs. "The thing is, Hazel, I was already engaged when we had that class together. My parents wouldn't stop pressuring me to move out to California and marry Leila. I kept putting them all off, but then after what happened with you and me, well, I felt so guilty that I just fled."

I let out an abrupt laugh. "I seem to have that effect on guys, making them flee from guilt."

"Hazel . . ." He's standing within inches of me, close enough for me to take in his cedarwood scent. "I don't know what happened with Vance, but I know you deserve better. You deserve better than him or me."

"Okay." I'm trying to be brave, to ignore how my heart is deflating like a punctured balloon. "Just so we're clear, one-night stands are not something I often do. And it meant something to me, and even if it made you flee the state, I'm not sorry it happened."

"I'm not sorry either." His words come out strangled. "So, I should go."

"I understand."

Yet, a moment passes, and he makes no move to leave my house. Instead, after a heavy, weighted silence, he speaks in a loud whisper.

"Here's the thing . . . I think about you all the time because, well, you're interesting, and you're beautiful and real, and even though your life is messy, you still care about what other people are going through, like Febe. You worry more about her than you do yourself, and I think that's so . . ." he struggles for the right word and settles on "cool."

I laugh, this time with a bit of warmth. "Thank you." I turn away from the window, facing him. "But to be honest, I think I worry about Febe because it's easier than trying to solve my own problems."

"I get that. But I still think you're . . ." His hand lunges toward me like he wants an embrace, but it sails through the air before landing at his side. "I think you're incredible."

Nobody has ever said that to me, and even though I know suddenly that I've been waiting my whole life to hear it, I can form no response. I just stare at Cyrus, my mouth hanging open. Then I'm aware of his mouth, and how I'd like our mouths, our lips, to be pressed together. So, I lean in and kiss him.

He tilts back, and at first, I'm scared he's rejecting me, but no, he just needs to take off his glasses. Then he kisses me back enthusiastically. It's like I'm using a muscle I'd forgotten I had. This closeness, this feel of him, and the way his arms are so strong around me but his lips are so soft . . . I could melt right into him, and then I'd forget everything that's ever gone horribly wrong. I'd do that because, God, he smells like cedar and he tastes like cream and I could totally live forever in this moment, but we're interrupted by a knocking on my door.

Cyrus pulls away. "Are you expecting someone?"

"Yes and no," I sigh. "It's got to be Olivia. And we're lucky she knocked instead of just letting herself in."

I go to answer the door, and sure enough, there stands Olivia.

"Hey," she says, "I see there's a car pulled up in front of your house. Do you have company? I thought you'd call as soon as you were back so I could come over and we'd figure this whole mess out."

She walks past me and into my living room where she encounters Cyrus, his cheeks pink underneath his olive skin.

"Oh, hello," she says. "Cyrus, right?"

"Yes."

When he doesn't say her name, she assumes it's because he doesn't remember it, and she laughs. "I'm Olivia. It's a big job, trying to learn the names of all the students and staff."

"Right," he replies, and it comes out in a self-conscious chuckle.

"Cyrus is here because of *Burnt Moon*," I interject, trying to negate some of the awkwardness and Olivia's suspicions. "Remember, I told you he's in charge of the art side and the technology. But," I add quickly, seeing Olivia narrow her eyes, "he had nothing to do with posting the piece about Brady Burns. That was all me."

"So, you're here figuring out a strategy?" Olivia asks.

"Something like that," says Cyrus.

"Well, I'm glad I stopped by. I can tell you both what you need to do. You must convince Febe to confess she wrote the piece. It's the only way to subvert the damage."

"We don't know that Febe wrote it, though," I say.

"Of course you do, Hazy. And believe me, Febe is not as innocent as she seems. I caught her cheating on a math test recently. And there's been other stuff too, stuff that makes me think I can't trust her."

"Like what, the MySpace rumors? Because I don't believe she'd do something like that."

"Maybe, but I also saw her bullying this friend of hers, Najah. The two of them had a big falling out, and when I asked Najah if she was okay, she started crying and told me she never wanted to sit next to Febe again."

"Okay," I sigh. "But that's just student drama. I'm sure there are two sides to the story."

Olivia presses her lips together, as if considering what to say next. "Okay. Look, I didn't want to have to remind you, because I know you're sensitive about your memory, but before the accident, you told me you were worried that Febe had a huge crush on Vance."

"*What?*" I put my hands on my hips. "Come on. I don't buy it."

"No really, Hazy."

"Okay, suppose you're right," I tell her. "Half the girls in school had a crush on Vance."

"True," responds Olivia, "but the difference is that Febe can be so intense, just like how she's being intense with you now. She latches on and doesn't relent, and back in December, you were worried what she might do."

Suddenly, the image of that long dark hair stuck on Vance's scarf pops into my mind. Underneath her hijab, Febe's hair is probably long and dark.

My stomach takes a nosedive, and my face must turn white, because Olivia says, "Look, Vance would never mess around with a student. If anything happened between them, it was one-sided, for sure. I'm only telling you now so you'll know who you're dealing with."

I open my mouth to respond, but no words come out.

"I should go," Cyrus says suddenly. His eyes dart to Olivia. "It was nice to officially meet you." Then he looks at me. "I'll see you tomorrow?"

"Yeah, of course. I'll walk you out."

He holds up his hand in a stop gesture. "It's cool. I can find my way." Cyrus smiles and walks toward my door, and I find him impossible to read.

"Bye," I call out. "Thanks, Cyrus."

"Anything for a friend," he replies, and then he walks away.

"What were you thanking him for?" Olivia asks.

"I don't know," I say truthfully. "I guess, just being cool about all the controversy with *Burnt Moon*. If it were me, I'd be pissed."

"Yeah, but after what you told me about him? I'm surprised you're even on speaking terms."

Suddenly, I'm exhausted. "I can't explain it right now, Olivia. It's just too complicated."

Inspecting me, her face shows her concern. "Are you okay, Hazy?"

"Just tired."

"No, you're upset."

I shrug. "Shouldn't I be?"

Olivia comes over to me and, draping her arm over my shoulders, leads me to my couch. "Talk to Febe tomorrow. She clearly adores you. And even though she obviously has some issues, she's still a sweet girl. You can figure this out."

I nod. "Okay. Thanks, Olivia."

"Hey, what do you say we order a pizza and watch movies? We can just veg for a while and not think about anything too difficult."

"Don't you have your weekly manicure?"

She shrugs. "I can miss one time. Come on, what do you say? How about pepperoni?"

Honestly, a movie and pizza sound perfect. "Sure. But we're not watching anything scary this time. I want something that will make me laugh."

CHAPTER 36

Monday morning comes with temperatures slightly above freezing. A warm front with highs in the mid-forties is moving in, and it feels almost like Minnesota's version of spring. Roads and sidewalks will be covered in brownish slush, despite that, I'll take some balmy winter temps.

Febe is, thankfully, waiting outside my classroom when I get to school. I was worried she might pull another disappearing act, but I guess not. I was also worried she'd be freaked out and maybe even despondent, but that's also a no. When she sees me, she practically jumps up and down in glee. "Can you believe it? It's like the entire world has read *Burnt Moon*! And we've caused such controversy!"

"Yeah, so maybe you don't want to shout about it?"

If Febe is surprised by my snappishness, she doesn't let it faze her. Her smile is wide as she responds. "I never thought it would take off like this. And I can't believe the *Star Tribune* covered it!"

I've unlocked my classroom, and I'm taking off my coat. Febe puts her heavy backpack by her desk and, unburdened, bounces on the tips of her feet.

I take a deep breath. "Yeah. Look, Febe, we need to talk."

She cocks her head and peers at me. "About what?"

"I have some questions I need to ask you. Can you meet me after school?"

"Ask me now." Febe states this simply, and she stands before me, guileless. Her confidence is disarming, and for a moment, I forget all my doubts about her.

She takes my silence as acquiescence. "Don't worry, Ms. Ford. Everyone is really pumped about the walkout; that's what they'll remember about today."

My heart skips a beat. "What walkout?"

"It's gonna be off the chain. At eight thirty, the entire school is walking out to protest that racist school board member."

"According to whom?"

Febe shrugs. "I may have had something to do with organizing it."

"Of course you did."

Febe and I both turn sharply to see who'd said that. Olivia stands in my doorway. "So, you've heard about the protest?" she says to me.

"The walkout, you mean? Febe only just mentioned it." I pull at my sleeves, chilly since the heaters haven't kicked on yet.

Olivia's response is tense. "No. It's not a walkout; it's a protest. Or I guess you could call it a counter protest."

"Oh, that," Febe says dismissively. "It's not a big deal." She turns to me. "Some of the school's white dudes are mad. They think I wrote the sex abuse column, and I lied, and I'm trying to get people riled up, and I'm a radical feminist, and blah, blah, blah. A few of them plan to go down to the gym and make some noise while the rest of us walk out."

"It's not just white male students, Febe." Olivia scowls, looking how she must when she's disciplining a class of naughty ninth graders. "Some African American and even some Muslim students are joining, and some females will be there, too. This really is *not good.*"

"Trust me," Febe replies, "more people will walk out in protest than will go down to yell in the gym."

"Yeah," I say to Febe, "that doesn't make me feel any better." I turn to Olivia. "Does Jim know about it?"

"I don't know."

"We should go tell him. Come on." I motion to Olivia, ignoring the look of betrayal passing over Febe's face. "Please don't stir up any more trouble. I'll be back soon."

"Fine," Febe huffs, but I don't entirely believe her.

Olivia and I keep a brisk pace, walking side by side and dodging groups of students on our way down to see Jim. Talking to him is not high on my list of things I wanted to do this morning, but I figure it's my professional responsibility to at least warn him about what I know. I glance at Olivia's face; it's all twisted and pink.

"Are you okay?" I ask.

"Sure. I'm just wondering: when are you going to talk to that girl about what she's doing to our school?"

That girl? "You mean Febe?"

"Of course! She can't just come in, write a few flowery sentences, and destroy our school community. But that's what she's doing, and it's really not right."

I take a second to respond, trying to stay calm. "Okay, let's say for a second that she wrote it. That means that she was sexually assaulted, which would be horrible anyway, but when you take her culture and beliefs into account, it's even more devastating. So how is this her fault?"

Olivia's head whips around, her ponytail snapping back and forth as she takes in the students in the hallway. There is definitely a higher pitch to the hallways this morning. Thankfully, we're nearing Jim's office. "Oh my God. You're such an honest person that you can't tell when other people are lying. I'm sorry, Hazy, but you need to accept that she made the whole thing up."

"Really?" We're standing outside Jim's office now. I cross my arms over my chest. "And why would anyone lie about sexual assault?"

She plants both feet in front of her in a defiant stance. "I don't know. But it happens. Some girls are needy and messed up, and they'll do anything, say anything, or hurt anyone just to feel better about themselves. I'll admit that, and it doesn't mean I'm not a feminist or that I've entered the dark side."

"Actually, it sort of does." I shake my head, trying to reconcile the Olivia from last night, whom I sat with eating pizza and laughing over *School of Rock*, with the borderline hostile person in front of me. "Wow. I thought I knew you."

"Come on! You're lost in your own liberal world and trying to be different from your parents. You never took the time to get to know me. If you did, you'd only see your own biases reflected back."

It's like I've been slapped. My short rapid breaths do little to soothe my simmering rage and sense of betrayal. How could Olivia say such things, and why can't I form a decent response? My mouth hangs open, trying to find words to match the moment, but Olivia speaks before I do.

"Are you going into Jim's office or not?" Olivia demands, glancing down at my hand, which is on the doorknob.

I turn and open the door, and together—though we're hardly a team at this moment—we enter Jim's office.

Tamisha is at her desk, talking on the phone and to the students and substitute teachers who stand in front of her simultaneously. The usual morning hustle is no less intense than it ought to be, but there's also no sign that two major student protests are about to take place.

"Tamisha!" Olivia barks, way more assertive than I could ever be. I'd stand there, politely waiting for dozens of stretched-out minutes until I could naturally gain her attention. "Where's Jim? We have something urgent to tell him."

"He's outside greeting the kids as they get off the bus."

"The buses are just getting here?" I turn toward the windows as if I needed confirmation. "They're late."

Tamisha shrugs. "What else is new?"

"Come on." Olivia motions for me to follow her, and I hate that I'm letting her lead but whatever. We go out into the chilly morning, clouds of bus exhaust wafting together with the students' breaths as they rush from the curb where they were dropped off to the front entrance of the school. Jim stands on the sidewalk, gloveless and hatless, but he does at least have on a coat, which is more than you can say for Olivia and me.

He stands, shouting, "Good morning! Happy Monday! Let's make this a great week!" Jim high-fives students as they walk by, sharing jokes with a couple of them, and he's laughing a little too loud. I'd think he's overcompensating for whatever tension he either knows about or senses, but Jim always laughs a little too loud.

Olivia leads the charge and marches right up to him and doesn't care that he's in the middle of interacting with a student. "Jim, we have a situation on our hands. You need to hear about it."

Jim doesn't look at or acknowledge that he heard Olivia. "Keep it real, buddy," he says, giving the kid a fist bump. Once the kid has passed, Jim turns to Olivia. "Good morning, Olivia." He notices me standing behind her and scowls. "Good morning, Hazel." Now, his voice is as cold as the 36° air we're shivering in.

"Jim, we've heard directly from students that there are going to be two protests today." Olivia doesn't wait for Jim to respond before continuing. "One is mostly the Muslim kids, led by Febe, in response to Greg Turner's comments. The other is the rest of the kids because they're angry about Febe's allegations, and they're not walking out. They're just heading down to the gym."

"Hold on." Already, I feel my pulse quicken. "You're totally mischaracterizing everything. I don't think it's just the Muslim kids versus everyone else."

"That's not what I said!" Olivia interjects.

"And we still don't know who wrote that piece. You can't just assume that it's Febe."

"She's the one who published it, and she isn't saying otherwise," Olivia counters. "You *know* it was Febe. *Everyone* knows it was Febe! What we don't know is if she was telling the truth."

"Great!" I cry. "Doubt the woman. Everyone always does."

"She's not a woman. She's a girl and an untrustworthy one at that. Frankly, Hazy, I doubt your judgment in getting so close to her and publishing her story."

"Stop calling me Hazy!"

"Ladies!" Jim cuts us off. His gaze had been vaulting back and forth, tracking our argument like it was a tennis match, but now he steps back and addresses us both at once. "It's inappropriate to argue where students can hear you, and I don't have time for this! If there's seriously going to be two walkouts today, I need you to tell me everything you know, *now*. Come on; we're going inside."

Dutifully, we follow Jim into his office where we describe what we've heard about the students' protest plans for this morning. Although I know Jim is definitely Team

Olivia and totally uninterested in supporting me, I get that we have a common interest in keeping the students safe.

"I'm sending out an entire staff email now, and we'll do an announcement to make sure that teachers check it." Jim can be efficient when he wants to be, and he briskly types his email. "Teachers will bring their first hours down to the gym, and we'll let the students air their grievances in a supervised environment. Got it?"

"What if some students still try to walk out?" I ask.

"I don't think they will because they'll be disoriented by the change of plans. But if they try to walk out, let them go. We're not blocking them." He hits Send on his computer, then stands. "Now go back to your classrooms and get ready to bring your students down to the gym. Tell any teachers you see on your way back up the same thing. I'm getting on the intercom now."

Olivia and I both take that as our cue to leave. I bolt up first and charge out before she can follow and chide me more than she already has. Most of the time, Olivia and I have enough in common that I can forget about some of the stark differences between us. I remember that, ultimately, we're good friends who have each other's backs. Most of the time, I remember that.

But not today.

CHAPTER 37

Jim makes the announcement for teachers to check their emails, and I hear his voice as I rush through the halls, getting back to my classroom just in time to organize the kids and bring them down to the gym. When I see Febe, a mix of anger and desperation stirs inside me. I've got to protect her, but can I trust her? I just don't know.

She eyes me suspiciously, as well. "What did you tell Principal Thomas?"

"I'm not divulging the details of our conversation."

"Seriously?" She grimaces and shakes her head. "I thought you were on our side, Ms. Ford! But you're going to sabotage our walkout, aren't you?"

"This isn't a game, Febe!"

Febe's jaw sets with tension. "You don't have to tell me that! Half the school is coming after me for lying about Brady Burns, and the other half says I'm a race traitor trying to act white."

I pause. What did Febe just admit to? "Wait. Febe, what do you mean?"

She rolls her eyes and launches into an explanation that I hadn't meant to ask for. "If I just hung out with other Muslims and acted quiet and humble, I wouldn't have brought attention to myself, and none of this would have happened. That's what some people think. But everybody believes I should just keep my mouth shut and act like a beautiful little fool. That's not going to happen."

The bell rings.

I look around at my students, all sitting at their desks, leaning forward with a sense of expectation. They must have heard the rumblings, or, if nothing else, they could feel the electricity in the air. "Good morning," I say. "I need you all to head down quietly to the gym. We're having an all-school meeting."

"Should we bring our stuff?" one student asks.

"Does this mean we're not having that Gatsby quiz?" asks another.

"Do not bring your stuff," I tell them. "We'll be back. But I don't know if it will be in time for the quiz."

Everyone gets up, and we join the hoard of other students in the hallway, all filing down to the gym. I'm sure my directive of "heading down quietly" was a waste of breath. The entire student body is riled up by the prospect of something different and unexpected.

I spin back to close my classroom door and catch Febe still seated at her desk, her slight frame cloaked in an oversized coat, her backpack hefted onto her back. "Febe, come on. We have to go to the gym."

She rises slowly, and her eyes scorch with betrayal. "Not a chance," she snarls, her words like darts puncturing my skin. "I can't believe you'd even do this to me, Ms. Ford. How could you set me up for a crash? When you know all about crashes!"

My chest tightens under the weight of her words as I try to defend myself. "I . . . I had no other choice," I stammer, taken aback by the sheer force of her accusation. "It's my job as a teacher—"

"What about your job as a human being?"

Her words strike me like a ton of bricks, and I struggle to catch my breath. "Come down with us to the gym right now."

"No way! I'm leaving, and you can't stop me," she growls with determination. "You think you know me and what I'm capable of? You don't even know yourself, so drop it and leave me alone!" She spins away from me, nearly throwing herself into the throng of students streaming toward the gymnasium.

And with that, she bolts off, attempting to push her way through the frenzied crowd, desperate to make a break for the outside doors. I try to follow, but I'm stopped by the assistant principal who rigidly stands between me and my goal.

"We need you down in the gym, Ms. Ford," he commands, all but trapping me with his gaze.

"But Febe has run off. I need to make sure she's alright!" I plead as my worry and frustration boil over.

"No, you need to let her go. It's not our place to physically restrain students."

"I said nothing about restraining her! She's really upset, and I'm worried about her!" I cry out in desperation, my voice breaking from the sheer anxiety of it all.

"Ms. Ford, this is not a request. It is a command. Get down to the gym, now!" His voice thunders in my ears, and I'm about to speak up and defend myself when a sharp pain sears through my head like a hot knife.

Surprised, I double over as a kaleidoscope of colors swirls before my eyes, and dizziness takes over until I'm on the brink of unconsciousness. My mouth opens, but no words come out as I try to explain myself.

"My head," I let out a feeble whisper as numerous students and staff still mill around us, until one of them is Cyrus.

"Hazel, are you alright?" He steadies me with an arm around my shoulder, but before I can properly respond, darkness envelopes me as my world fades away.

***

When I come to, I realize I'm in the nurses' office. Glennis, the school nurse, peers over me. She's always had a bit of facial hair, and it's the first thing I notice when I open my eyes. Then, like always when I face Glennis's fuzzy mustache, I worry she'll think I'm staring, so I look away. My eye movement must catch her attention. "Oh good, you're awake. How are you feeling?"

"Like somebody bashed me in the head."

"You should go to the doctor, then," Glennis responds. "Because you didn't hit your head, not that I know of. You passed out from something going on inside you."

"But what about when I fell? Didn't I hit my head then?"

"No. Cyrus said he caught you in time."

"Cyrus?" I say his name like I don't remember who he is, but, despite everything, I can still feel his arms around me.

"Yes. He carried you down here, and he was going to stay by your side, but they wanted all hands on deck for the protest in the gym."

I wince. Many concerns compete within me. First, there's Febe. She must think I didn't care enough to go after her, and now I'm not even at the protest. Who will be there to defend her? But those thoughts are crowded out by how much my head hurts and the constant stream of questions running through my mind: Why is this happening now? What does it mean? And what will everyone think of Cyrus carrying me down to the nurses' office? I know how quickly rumors can spread.

"Is there someone you can call to take you to the doctor?" Glennis asks.

I think for a moment. All my friends work here. None of my family lives in the area. Wow, I guess that makes me sort of pathetic.

"No," I reply. "I guess I'll just have to wait until the school day is over. Then, maybe Olivia can take me." But Olivia and I are in a fight. "Or maybe I could take a taxi."

"There's no one who could come pick you up and take you in now? I don't think you should wait. It's not healthy."

"I'll take her."

I struggle to sit up to see who said that. Her voice is familiar, but I need to see her face to place her. When I do, my stomach drops.

It's Annabelle.

CHAPTER 38

Turns out, Annabelle was at school this morning to get some papers signed about her failed student teaching assignment. Vance should have been the one to sign along the dotted line, but since he's MIA, the task fell on an administrator. As everyone in the office was consumed with today's protest, Annabelle fruitlessly waited in the hallway of the main office, which is within spitting distance of the nurses' office. She heard Glennis insist I needed a ride to the doctor, and since Annabelle had nowhere else to be, here we are.

Now I'm sitting in the passenger seat of her two-door Kia, unsure of how to act or what to say. If there are etiquette rules for when your ex/missing fiancé's new lover drives you to urgent care, I'm not aware of them. Of course, there are many questions I could ask; I don't even know where to start. The pain in my head only makes it more difficult.

We've been sitting in silence for several minutes when I say, "It's nice of you to drive me. I'm not sure that many people in the same situation would."

"I'm happy to help," Annabelle replies. "I've been wanting a chance to talk to you. So, this works out for both of us."

"Oh." I choose my words carefully, like they're delicate, breakable things. "Then, why didn't you email me back?"

She sighs. "I wrote you, like, a dozen emails. I just couldn't make myself hit Send. It's going to sound stupid, but I have a low-key anxiety attack every time I even think about reaching out. It's all just too much, you know?"

"Yeah. I get it." I hesitate, afraid of how she'll answer. "Have you heard from Vance?"

"No. You?"

"No. He's staying with his parents, and I've talked to his mom a couple of times, but she doesn't 'want to get involved'."

"Hmm..." Annabelle sounds like I've just confirmed some suspicion of hers.

"Yeah," I continue as if I'm responding to a question. "Vance took off right after the accident; he cleared out his stuff from our house while I was still in the hospital. I called him. I texted him. But now I'm just sending him emails, trying to figure out what the heck happened."

"You mean you don't know?" She gives me a sideways look, taking her eyes off the road for a moment. "Do you have, like, amnesia from hitting your head so hard?"

"Pretty much." I exhale, letting my shoulders rise and then fall. "Mostly about what happened on the day of the accident and immediately after."

"Oh. Wow. So, you don't remember your argument with Vance about the MySpace page?" Annabelle white-knuckles the steering wheel while she asks, revealing how tense this conversation must be for her.

"Just glimpses, plus what people told me."

"And what did people tell you?"

The way she asks, it's like I'm the one who needs to justify my behavior. But if it will get me some answers, I'll comply. "People told me that an unknown disgruntled student posted a MySpace page in Vance's name, and it had a picture of you two having sex in his classroom."

"That's not what happened. Vance and I never had sex. I swear."

"Oh." I look out the window at all the grayish grimy snow and the overcast, sooty sky. Other than that, there's not much to see. But I remain turned away from Annabelle. "The thing is, I don't know what to believe."

"Look, I don't claim to be a genius or anything. I've made plenty of stupid mistakes in my life. But having sex with my mentor teacher in his classroom during school hours? Nobody is that dumb."

"Then explain the photo."

"I never saw the photo. But there's such a thing as photoshop."

"Okay. Why would a student go to that much trouble?"

"I don't know!" Annabelle snaps. "Maybe it was some girl who was crushing on Vance, who felt rejected when he wasn't into her, and she wanted to get back at him and me. I know a lot of students thought we were involved. Or maybe it was just a kid who liked to stir the pot and create trouble. There are plenty of people like that in the world."

That is true. But what about the hair on Vance's scarf? I shudder as I ask myself this.

Looking at her now, I see that she's so pretty with her long glossy hair and her hourglass figure. I guess there's no mystery over what Vance saw in her. "Do you have anyone specific in mind, someone who would do such a thing?"

Annabelle pulls into the clinic's lot, speaking as she finds a place to park. "That Iranian girl, Febe. She was always staring daggers at me."

I skip a breath, and then my exhale is raspy. "Come again?"

She turns the ignition off and faces me. "Hazel, I'm sorry I don't have more answers for you. But please know, ever since the accident, I haven't been able to live with myself. I feel so guilty."

Good God. I didn't think there was a way to make my headache worse, but this conversation is doing just that. "Right, but what about Febe? Do you think she had a crush on Vance? If that's true, and you and Vance weren't involved, why would she try to sabotage you?"

She bats her eyes and purses her lips as if she might flirt her way out of this conversation. Then, her chest collapses a little, like she's ready to come clean. "Early on, when Vance and I had first started working together, I was into him, and I flirted a lot, even during class. He didn't discourage it. In fact, he'd tell me all this personal stuff when we talked before or after school, like how the two of you were having problems. Then he painted me, and I was sure that meant we were in love. I would make eyes at him in front of the students, and I'm sure they could sense our chemistry."

"I see." I breathe in and out, letting her words seep in with the rise and fall of my chest. "And then what happened?"

"Then, somebody posted that MySpace page. Nobody believed I had nothing to do with it, and I was dismissed on the spot. My student teaching assignment ended, I had to drop out of college, and all my time and student loans were a colossal waste. Now, I have nowhere to go."

"That's too bad." I'm sure that I should say more, but for the life of me, I can't think of anything.

Her oversized eyes burn into mine. "You can help. Vouch for me, say that it wasn't me in the photo, that there is no way that Vance and I were involved."

Fresh pain shoots through my head. "The thing is, I'm in trouble at school, too, and between clearing my name and then possibly Vance's, I don't know if I can help you."

Annabelle sniffs and widens her eyes, letting a tear escape. Swallowing roughly, she says, "I want to be an art teacher. I don't want to be a disappointment to my parents. I can't let what happened ruin my whole life."

Inwardly, I sigh. It should not be my job to reassure Annabelle. So, I simply say, "I can't make any promises, but I'll see what I can do."

A thick silence ensues as I'm torn between thanking her, feeling bad for her, and hating her. Strangely, none of those options seem to fit. "Take care of yourself, Annabelle." I reach for the door handle, but I stop before I get out. "Hey, just out of curiosity, how did you find out about the party and the accident?"

Annabelle tilts her chin, regaining a bit of the composure she'd had minutes ago. "It was Olivia. She called two days after it happened and told me everything."

CHAPTER 39

At urgent care, they give me a CT scan, and then I sit and wait for a long while until a doctor I don't know comes in to go over the results.

"Your scan looks fairly clear," she says. "I see you had some swelling after your accident in December, but the swelling has gone down, and now I'm not seeing any red flags."

"That's good, right?"

The doctor looks at me, clearly concerned. "You came in today because your head hurt?"

"Yes," I respond. "It hurt so much that I passed out, and that's never happened before."

She nods. "Did anything upset you right before you passed out?"

"Why?" I ask her, surprised.

"Sometimes, after we experience a trauma that is too much for our brains to process, something else occurs that will trigger those unprocessed parts of the brain, and it feels like we're living the traumatic event all over again."

"Oh." I chuckle a little like I'm trying to turn this whole thing into a joke. "Well, that would make sense because my morning totally sucked." The doctor's expression doesn't yield with a smile or a softening around her eyes, so I switch gears. "What do you mean about trauma and the unprocessed parts of our brain? Could that cause me to forget stuff?"

"Of course. There are different components to our memory system, but when something is so upsetting that your brain feels the need to protect you from remembering the event, parts of your autobiographical memory and/or working memory can stop functioning correctly."

"Oh. Do you think it's possible to block out something you deeply regret? Like if you made something terrible happen, could you just *forget* about it entirely, including other events that may have led up to it?"

The doctor narrows her eyes, glancing at my face before she gazes down and flips through my chart. "Hazel, I see your GP wrote you a referral for a psychotherapist. Have you made an appointment?"

"No, not yet."

"I strongly urge you to make one. I can't answer your questions. Clearly, you need someone to help you process and understand the physical and emotional trauma you've experienced. Until that happens, I expect you'll experience episodes like the one you had today more frequently."

In other words, I'm a head case.

I receive a new referral for a psychotherapist and a prescription for something stronger than Advil for when these headaches come on, and I have it filled at the pharmacy attached to the Urgent Care. I don't take any, though, because it's supposed to make me loopy.

I take a taxi back to school where my car is parked. Once there, I'm afraid to go in, lest I suffer another "trigger event" and spur another "episode." I look at the school building, this place to which I've devoted so much of myself. Now it's full of monsters, and the biggest, scariest monster I might discover here is myself.

I'm walking toward my car, hoping nobody notices me in the parking lot, hoping I can make a clean getaway, seeing as how it's only a little past noon and there are still three hours of the school day left. Since it's lunch hour, people are out and about, even though students are not supposed to leave since we have a closed campus for lunch.

Then, I hear someone weeping. I turn and find Sonia, my student from the IEP meeting last week, wiping her eyes and banging on an outside door. "Por favor!" she shouts. "De'jame entrar!"

"Sonia, what's wrong?"

Sonia turns, and when she sees it's me addressing her, her face grows even more anguished. "Nothing, Ms. Ford."

"Obviously, that's not true. Tell me what's going on."

Sonia scrubs away her tears and, apparently realizing that she has nothing to lose, concedes. "They said anyone who left during the protest would be suspended. But my little sister threw up at school and my mom needed me to bring her home, so I slipped out when everyone was yelling. And my friends said they would wait by the outside door to let me back in, but then they laughed and ran off like it was a game, but it's not! I can't get suspended; my mom will be so mad!"

I sigh and reach inside my purse for my electronic key card. "Okay, I'll fix it so that you won't get in trouble. Just come with me." When I hold my card against the blinking box next to the door, it beeps and lets us in, and then I usher Sonia down to the office. "Let me do the talking, okay?"

Sonia, still tearful, simply nods. Once inside the office, we go straight toward Tamisha's desk. "Hi, Tamisha," I say. "Sonia is with me. She's in my English 11 class this hour, and we're headed up there right now, but can you look and see if she's been marked absent for any other classes today?"

Tamisha scrutinizes me. "I thought you were out for the rest of the day."

"Yeah, well, I feel better, and I am returning to teach." That is only partially true; my head still hurts like getting your fingernails pulled off, but now, somehow, I am determined to be in my classroom with my students. In fact, it feels like my life depends upon it. "First, I need you to clear any of Sonia's unexcused absences. She had a family emergency earlier."

Tamisha purses her lips and gives me a subtle eye roll. "Her mother would need to call that in."

All the day's tension presses on me, and when I speak, I'm surprised at how forceful I sound, even to my own ears. "Her mother only speaks Spanish and finds calling into school very intimidating. So, Tamisha, you will take my word for it, you will believe in me and my professional judgment, and you will excuse Sonia."

"Really?" Tamisha laughs. "You're falling back on your 'professional judgment' today? Seems like bad timing to me."

Something inside me snaps. "I don't give a rat's ass what it 'seems like to you', Tamisha, and I won't let Sonia be punished for something that isn't her fault. You want to punish me, fine, but leave her out of it." I bang my fist on her desk, raising my voice, letting my intensity pour out. "Unless you want me to scream at the top of my lungs, you will go into that computer, and you will hit whatever button you need to hit, and you will excuse her!"

We stare at each other for a moment, but magically, Tamisha blinks first. She speaks to Sonia. "What's your last name, sweetheart?"

"Martinez."

Tamisha clicks on her keyboard, and after a moment, she smiles at Sonia. "Okay, you're set to go." Then she glares at me, and if a look could cause internal bleeding, I'd probably be passing out all over again. It's no wonder Tamisha can survive in her job here; she has a hide that's thicker than a rhinoceros' and nerves like iron. "This isn't over," she whispers.

I pretend like I don't hear. "Let's go, Sonia."

Wordlessly, we leave the office and walk upstairs to my classroom. Probably a minute goes by, and then Sonia murmurs softly, "Thank you, Ms. Ford."

"You don't have to thank me, Sonia. The way I see it, I owe you."

"Why?"

"Because if what you said at the IEP meeting is true, I haven't been teaching you well enough, and it's time I make things right. We'll consider this a first step, okay?"

"Okay."

We're nearly to my classroom. I stop and face her. "Hey, I know you had to leave to pick up your sister, but can you tell me anything about what happened at the protest this morning?"

Sonia furrows her brow. "It was pretty crazy. Half the school was yelling 'Free Brady Burns' like he was put in prison or something, and then other people were yelling 'Greg Turner must resign', but I don't even know who Greg Turner is."

"He's the school board member who wrote racist stuff about Muslim girls."

"Oh." Sonia presses her mouth into a line like she's afraid to say what she's thinking.

"Did anything else happen, Sonia?"

She shrugs, her face relaxing. "I don't know that much about the whole thing, but some Muslim girls were upset, and they stood in a group, and then people started swearing at them."

"Seriously?"

"Yeah, but then I had to slip out to get my sister, so I don't know what happened after that."

"Right." We resume our walk toward my classroom. "Sonia, do you remember if Febe Rashidi was in that group of Muslim girls?"

Sonia shakes her head. "I don't know Febe, but I heard people talking about her."

"What were they saying?"

We stop again, but this time it's Sonia who halts our path. "Ms. Ford, people are mad, and sometimes they say stuff they don't mean, ya know?"

"Okay . . . but what were they saying about Febe?"

Sonia's shoulders slump, and she looks around the hallway, perhaps to make sure nobody is around to overhear. "I can't give you names of who said it, but, Ms. Ford, some guys said they were going to hurt Febe, like really mess her up and rape her for real."

CHAPTER 40

As soon as the afternoon bell rings, I head down to find Cyrus in the art room. When I walk in, he is leaning over a canvas, pointing to it, and conferring with a student. Cyrus murmurs something about lines and shading, and the student, his brow furrowed, nods in what looks like reluctant agreement. It takes me a moment, but then I realize it's Brady Burns.

There's a knocking in my brain as many recriminations come sprinting to my lips. I want to yell at him to stay away from Febe and that, if he hurts her again, I will make his life a living hell. But I'm not stupid, and I know my lashing out would only turn the temperature up in an already sweltering situation.

"Hi," I say. It comes out a little strangled, but Cyrus lifts his gaze to meet mine, and a broad smile spreads across his face.

"Hi!" He steps toward me and then halts like it's dangerous to get too close. "You're back! You're okay, then?"

Brady stands with his arms crossed over his chest, witnessing our interaction, his eyes blinking with questions. I clear my throat, attempting to sound officious. "I'm fine. Thanks for your help this morning; it was kind of you."

Cyrus' face turns vulnerable as he takes in my tone. "You're welcome. I'm just glad you're alright."

"Yeah, I'll be fine. But I need to talk to you."

"Okay . . ." Cyrus looks at Brady. "Can we finish this later, Brady?"

"Sure." Brady smiles benevolently at Cyrus but glares at me before he strolls off.

"What's going on?" Cyrus asks once Brady is out of earshot.

I look after Brady, gesturing to the door he just walked out of. "What was that about?"

Cyrus scowls. "Brady is in my painting class, and he had questions about his project. I have to treat him like I'd treat any other student and help him."

"Right." I walk around to see Brady's work. I don't know what to expect, and I find what looks like a portrait of an angry Pacman, sporting shades, a mohawk, and a goatee, glowering, with a blood-red background shining behind him. Sure, it's benign, yet it gives me the creeps. "What do you think of his painting?" I ask Cyrus.

"Well, I suppose it's fairly creative, but I wouldn't hang it in my living room."

I laugh. Vance says that the "I wouldn't hang it in my living room" line is the common man's standard art critique and that it displays cultural ignorance. But now I can admit to myself, Vance could be pretty pretentious. "Yeah, me neither."

"Anyway," Cyrus states, "tell me about what happened after I took you down to the health office. Did you go to the doctor?"

"Yes. I'm fine. They ran some scans and told me the pain is both literally and figuratively all in my head. They urged me to get therapy."

Cyrus' eyebrows shoot up. "That's it?"

"I got some pain medication that's slightly more powerful than ibuprofen. But yeah, that's about it."

"Are you going to make an appointment with a therapist?"

I wave him off. "I don't know, and I can't think about that right now. I'm too worried about Febe. There are rumors circulating that guys in this school are so mad that they plan to rape her for real."

Cyrus's face twists in disgust. "That's awful."

"I know. Maybe it's not true, but what if it is? Febe ran off before the protest because she was furious, thinking I'd betrayed her, that I'd set her up. I was running after her when I passed out, so she got away. But now I'm so worried, and Cyrus, I need your help. We need to go look for her, and what if her family only speaks Farsi? Do you speak Farsi?"

Cyrus looks like he's having trouble keeping up. "Yeah. I'm fluent. But . . ." he scratches at his temple, "what's the plan? We drive to her house, tell her parents what's going on, and then what? Couldn't that just make everything worse?"

"I don't know. Maybe we don't tell her parents everything. Maybe we just say we're looking for her for some other reason, and they'll help us find her, and then we can work everything else out."

"Hazel." Cyrus rubs his forehead with the heel of his right hand. "I'm not going to drive you all over town, looking for Febe and acting as your interpreter. That's crazy."

I immediately go on the defensive. "I wasn't asking you to 'drive me all over town', and you'd only have one conversation with her parents. It's not crazy; it's the right thing to do!"

Cyrus sighs. "You should be home, resting. You need to take better care of yourself."

"Yeah, well, I'm taking care of myself just fine, and I don't need your protection!"

But I can't deny that I sort of want Cyrus to protect me. I can recall the sweet relief of being caught by him this morning, and now I have this powerful urge to cry against his shoulder. But I can't transition so soon from letting one man call the shots to letting a different man call the shots. That *would* make me crazy.

"Look," I say, "never mind. I promised I wouldn't involve you in any drama, and now it's unfair of me to ask this of you. I'll figure it out on my own."

He takes only a moment to respond, and his chest caves. "No, Hazel. I'll do it. Do you have her parents' address?"

"Yeah. I looked it up earlier. They live about a mile away."

"Okay." Cyrus pushes up his glasses as they'd slid down his nose a bit. The gesture reminds me of an undercover superhero posing as a regular guy right before he transforms into the powerhouse that is his true self. "Let's go," he says.

On the short drive over to Febe's house, Cyrus tells me about what went down at the morning's protest, and it pretty much lines up with Sonia's version of events. "There was so much going on, too many issues and too many people upset over different things. Jim tried to give equal voice to everyone, but I think the Muslim students' legitimate complaint about that awful school board member got lost over all the controversy with Brady Burns. Some kids were all 'expel him now', and others said that everyone involved with *Burnt Moon* should be sued for libel."

"Well, at least they know what libel is," I say. "I guess the journalism teacher is doing a good job."

"Yeah." Cyrus lets out a little chuckle, but there's no joy in it. "I get that Jim was in an impossible situation, and by having joint protests in the gym, he at least kept things contained. It could have been so much worse, but the kids are still divided and all riled up."

"I'm just so worried about what those boys want to do to Febe."

"So, what do we do about it?" Cyrus asks, as he stares grimly ahead.

"We start by finding her." I point at the upcoming intersection in the residential neighborhood we drive through. "I think you turn here."

Cyrus turns and drives slowly down the block of run-down houses with battered siding, sagging roofs, and unkept yards. We pull up to 8915 Harrison, the house listed as Febe's address. "Are you sure this is it?" Cyrus asks. "This can't be right."

Unfortunately, though, it is. I'd checked and double-checked the address before writing it down, and there's no other home it could be—all boarded up, with a "Foreclosed" sign posted in the yard.

Stunned and defeated, we drive back toward school. "Now what?" I ask, though I don't expect Cyrus to have an answer.

"What about the school social worker?" Cyrus asks. "Wouldn't she know if Febe and her family are homeless?"

"She might, but unfortunately, several of our Heights students are homeless, and the school doesn't always realize it. But maybe the family just moved. It's possible, right?"

Cyrus nods, though he seems unconvinced. I think about Febe's behavior these last few weeks: how up and down she's been, how she's often at school early, how she devoured those donuts, how skinny and desperate she's become. And I know the truth—Febe is in far more danger than I'd dared to realize.

My phone rings. It's Jim. I want to ignore the call, but I pick up on the first ring. "Hi, Jim. How are you?"

"I'm fine. Actually, I'm calling to find out how you are doing. Tamisha says you returned to school after lunch today."

"That's right."

"I'm sure you understand there are liability issues here. I've already told Tamisha to put in for a sub for you tomorrow."

"What?" Panic rises in my throat. If I'm not at school, how will I protect Febe? "You can't do that. I'm fine."

"Honestly, Hazel, there are multiple reasons why I can put you on enforced leave, and you passing out this morning is only one of them. We'll have a meeting tomorrow and go over everything. If you'd like to have a union rep with you, then that's your prerogative."

His abrupt goodbye is a sure sign: if I need a teacher's union rep to accompany me to tomorrow's meeting, then things are serious. I tell Cyrus about it.

"Don't go to that meeting without a union rep," Cyrus says when I'm done relaying the conversation with Jim.

"Right." I rub my temple. Man, this has been the longest worst day ever. "The only problem is, our union rep isn't exactly an effective advocate. He tends to set people off."

"Who is he?"

"Anton Higgins. He teaches computer science."

Cyrus laughs. "Wait, isn't he the guy you yelled at, at the end of the staff meeting on my first morning at school?"

"Correct. And now I need to ask for his help."

To: VValby89@yahoo.com
From: H_Ford_AOGG@hotmail.com
Subject: Worst Day Ever
Dear Vance,

I passed out at school today. And Annabelle drove me to the hospital.

Want to know what's really crazy? That wasn't even the worst part of my day.

I blame you for all of it. If you'd been here, if you'd stuck around after the accident, or if you at least responded to my emails, none of it would have happened. Now everything is a mess, and I don't know whom to believe.

Was Annabelle telling me the truth when she said that you never had sex with her? Should I feel bad for Annabelle? Should I help her?

It's hard to fathom when Febe so obviously needs me. When I think back to the beginning of the year, it's both tragic and inevitable that things worked out this way.

I should have known. I should have seen where we were headed. I should have believed Febe when she tried to warn me. Do you remember the open house?

-Hazel

CHAPTER 41

September 2003

"Ms. Ford, can you believe it? I'm finally a junior. I feel like I've been waiting my entire life to be in AP Lit, but now my time has come!"

Febe stood before me on the evening of the fall open house. It was the dawn of a new school year: Febe's junior year and my tenure year. The stakes were high.

But this moment felt light. "Congratulations!" I looked over her shoulder, though she obviously stood alone, no parental figures lurking in the doorway. "Are you here on your own?"

"Yes," she replied simply, and I didn't question it. It was not uncommon for my more determined students to attend the open house or parent/teacher conferences alone, especially if they came from a home where English wasn't the first language. And I already knew Febe was not just determined, but also super intelligent and intellectually curious as well.

"So," she inquired, leaning against a desk, "what are we going to read this year?"

"Well, our units will be thematic. We're going to start with the theme of isolation, and we'll read *Oedipus*. You'll like that since it's a Greek tragedy. We'll also do some poetry, and short stories like *Yellow Wallpaper*, which will transition us to our next unit, which is focused on women's place in society."

"Seriously? That's so cool!"

"Yeah, we'll do *House on Mango Street* and *Their Eyes Were Watching God*. After that, we'll cover the tragic hero, and we'll read *Native Son* and *The Great Gatsby*."

Febe's eyes widened more and more with each title I listed. Most students, even the advanced ones, would gasp at the amount of reading they'd be required to do, but not Febe.

"I've always wanted to read *The Great Gatsby*!"

"Great! Now's your chance."

The evening was winding down, and I glanced at the clock: seven twenty-five. Open house ended at seven thirty, but the last thing I wanted was to make Febe feel unwelcome. She could stay for as long as she wanted. Although, outside, heavy storm clouds loomed, and through the open windows, damp, thick warm air breezed in.

"How was your summer?"

"It was okay," answered Febe.

She explained how she'd had her first job bagging groceries and that it was alright except for when the customers were racist, but most people were nice. We were chatting about the possibility of starting a school literary blog when you popped your head into my classroom.

"Hey," you said, "you just about done?"

"Yeah. I've just been talking to Febe."

You smiled. "Of course. I remember Febe. You did great work in Painting class last year."

"Really?" Febe nearly gushed. "Thanks so much, Mr. Valby. I have Digital Arts with you this year."

"Oh yeah? That's great. I should introduce you to Ms. Gomez."

You stepped back, revealing the young woman who stood behind you. She was gorgeous, with long thick dark hair, olive skin, and an hourglass figure. I couldn't imagine any warm-blooded heterosexual male *not* being attracted to her.

"Ms. Gomez will student teach with me this year."

"Cool," said Febe, "nice to meet you."

"Nice to meet you too," she replied.

"Hello," I choked out, "I'm Hazel." And then, to my horror, I added, "Vance's girlfriend."

"Hi," she said. "I'm Annabelle."

At that moment, lightning flashed, and thunder clapped, calling our attention to the window. But I kept my focus on Annabelle. Her face went blank, but then it arranged itself into a pleasant smile. "Vance said that the two of you work together. That must be so nice."

"Oh, yeah. It's great." I tried to smile back at her convincingly. "Vance hadn't mentioned that he'd have a student teacher this fall. I thought you had to be tenured for that."

She shrugged. "It was last minute," she said. "My original post fell through."

Heavy rain pinged against the windows, some drops making it inside.

"Annabelle is at the U," you interjected. "Since my old professor runs her program, he called me in a panic, asking if I could take Annabelle on."

"Right. Of course." I nodded a little too emphatically. "I'm so glad that worked out for you."

There was a too-long pause where no one could think of anything to say.

"Well," you said to me, "I think I'll walk Annabelle out. Meet you down by the front entrance? I'll bring the car around so you can stay dry."

"Sure. Thanks."

"Nice meeting you both," Annabelle said to Febe and me.

We waved goodbye. Once they were clearly out of ear-shot, Febe turned to me. "She seems nice. But I'd be careful if I were you, Ms. Ford."

I played dumb. "I don't know what you mean, Febe."

She shook her head. "Yeah, you do. That was like some major foreshadowing there, with the storm starting just as Mr. Valby introduced Ms. Gomez."

I chuckled, though I didn't really find anything funny. "If that was foreshadowing, it was a very clumsy and obvious attempt."

"Okay, then how about it's an example of dramatic irony, like the 'reader'," she used air quotes, "knows before you do that this student teacher is trouble?"

Febe was too smart for me. She sensed everything that was about to go wrong with my life. And Febe would bear witness to it all. I am desperate to find her, to help her, and to discover what else she knows and what she alone understands.

CHAPTER 42

She relived every moment that occurred between her and Vance, trying to figure which points in time had significance. What if they all did? What if none of them did?

She could not answer these questions, but she knew she missed him. It was almost like time not spent with Vance was time wasted.

It was late afternoon, and of course, Vance was still working in that art classroom he loved. She'd had a meeting but was entirely confident she'd be able to find him afterward. "Hey," she said softly, knocking against the doorframe so as not to startle him as he looked like he was deep in thought over a painting.

When he looked up and saw her, Vance smiled. "Hey yourself," he drawled, as if there was no tension, no awkwardness. "What's up?"

Such an innocuous question, yet there were a million ways to answer it. She could say something stupid, like "The sky." Or she could be clever and say, "Thanks to you, my anxiety level," but she went for simple and honest. "I've been feeling sad all day."

He frowned. "Why?"

"Why do you think?"

"Because of me?"

"Because of us." She knew that what she was about to do was wrong, but there was nothing for it. What was the point of being strong if you couldn't be happy? "This is insane."

"I agree." He stood, navigated his way around the easels and art tables, and then he was in her personal bubble, and her heartbeat throbbed in her ears. "We can't go on like this," he whispered, his breath so close it danced on her skin.

"What do we do?"

"Just trust me, okay?" He stepped around her, closed the door to his classroom, switched off the lights, and then took her hand, leading her to the art supply closet, a large walk-in space full of shelves lined with bottles of paint and reams of paper. It was a tight fit, the two of them standing in there, but they were so close that it worked.

Then, his mouth was on hers, and he kissed her like he wanted to lap her up. His hands reached underneath her sweater, underneath her bra, and his touch became urgent, almost territorial. They grasped at each other, releasing buttons, pulling down pants, until finally, the two of them were joined together, and she found him, there in her arms, belonging to her and to her alone.

It would all have been so perfect, except she heard something, a clicking sound. Then she saw, from the corner of her eye, someone scurrying.

That someone was wearing a hijab.

CHAPTER 43

The next morning, Anton, Jim, the head of HR, and I meet in Jim's office. Jim runs through a litany of "issues" he is worried about. "You passed out while you were responsible for students," he says. "And Tamisha says you threatened her upon returning to school. By the way, you owe her an apology."

"Okay. I feel bad about how I spoke to Tamisha and I'm happy to apologize for that. But I didn't threaten *her*. I just threatened to scream if she didn't mark Sonia's absences as excused. I was helping a student."

"That's just it, Hazel. You're so wrapped up in protecting certain kids, I fear you'll wind up hurting both them and yourself."

"Come on." Scoffing, I look at Anton who, for once in his life, seems to have nothing to say. He sits silently, taking notes and not speaking up for me.

"You published *Burnt Moon* without consulting with me, you won't confirm who implicated Brady Burns of assault, you yelled at Tamisha, and you threatened to resign for next year, although we've yet to receive your letter of resignation. All this points to instability, and that doesn't include the American Dream MySpace fiasco or the head injury and post-traumatic stress you still suffer from."

"You can't blame me for something involving Vance, and you can't diagnose me!"

Leslie, the head of HR, speaks in a soft mousy voice that matches her appearance. "Perhaps not, but we are worried about your mental health and, thus, your ability to teach right now. Which is why we are placing you on two weeks' paid leave so that you can get some rest and some counseling and come back to us recuperated."

"During this time, you are not allowed on school grounds," Jim states. "And we will have a readmittance conference before you return. In the meantime, we insist you see a therapist and provide proof that you've done so."

I'm speechless. Anton, however, speaks for me. "We'll accept those terms on one condition. There will be no letter in her permanent file, nothing that states Hazel's mental health is the reason for her enforced paid leave."

Jim and Leslie share a look, Leslie nods, and Jim says, "Fine. Your leave starts now, Hazel. Leslie will walk you to your car."

I speak to Anton. "How could you accept those terms? I never said I agreed."

Anton spreads his arms in surrender. "Hazel, they have too much against you. You're lucky the leave is paid and that you won't have a marred record. Now go home, enjoy your time off, and get ready to come back stronger than ever."

I'm not even allowed a trip up to my classroom to gather my things. Instead, Leslie escorts me to my car, insisting I don't need any of my teaching materials. "You need to take this time for recovery," she says. "Planning lessons or grading essays should be the last thing on your mind!"

"But my students will suffer."

"Your students will be fine. We'll take care of them. Focus on yourself and on getting well."

Part of me appreciates this spin on my "enforced paid leave," that they're worried about my well-being. It's not so much that I'm a menace to the school, but a menace to myself. Yet, I still feel like a criminal, being escorted to my car, and I can only pray that nobody will notice the spectacle or that rumors won't fly.

When I get home, the first thing I do is text Cyrus. *Sorry again to involve you in all this, but I'm not allowed anywhere near school for two weeks. Please watch out for Febe and protect her as best you can. You're the only one I can ask!*

Cyrus texts back when it's passing time between first and second hour. *I'll do my best. Call you later.*

Really, I can't expect more than that. He's already going above and beyond. Yet I'm so frustrated, I could scream.

So, I do.

Even though I live alone, I don't want to scare the neighbors, so I bury my face in my bedroom pillow and let it all out: the anger, the fear, the frustration. They're all released in a torrent of yelling, swear words, and tears. After a while, I grow tired, and I roll over, and I look at the ceiling and lie in the bed Vance and I used to share. I turn my head toward his side, realizing that I still keep strictly to my side. I'd thought maybe I was over him, but then why don't I sleep in the middle of the mattress?

With a deep breath, I rise and look for the referral I got the other day, the one for a psychotherapist. I call Jennifer Dengel, a licensed professional clinical counselor, and request her soonest appointment. Two days later—days that are marked by a couple of phone conversations with Cyrus where he tells me Febe has not been at school and he's heard no rumblings about her in the hallways—I sit in her office, a pretty space with brick walls, white-curtained southern-exposure windows, and brightly painted abstract art hung in frames. Dr. Dengel is also pretty. She couldn't be more than a few years older than me, with long blonde hair, high cheekbones, and wide blue eyes. "Tell me about what brings you here today," she says. She sits in an armchair, her legs crossed. I'm across from her in another armchair that I chose upon entering. It's wide and cushy, lined with denim.

"I have to get therapy, or they won't let me return to work," I say. "I'm a teacher, and one of my students is in trouble, but I can't help her until I supposedly help myself."

Dr. Dengel nods. "Why do you think your school believes you'd benefit from therapy?"

"Oh, that's easy. Right before Christmas, I was in a car accident with another teacher, who I guess was my fiancé, but I may have broken up with him, and I'm pretty sure he was cheating on me with his student teacher. He took off while I was still in the hospital recovering from a head injury. He's staying with his parents, and I haven't heard from him, even though I send him imploring emails where I try to piece everything back together." I scratch my head. "And I guess my behavior at school has been sort of erratic."

Dr. Dengel raises an eyebrow. "Wow," she says, keeping her voice even and her tone soft. "You have a lot to process. How have you handled it?"

I consider her question. "Well . . . to be honest, I can't say that I've handled it at all, and now I have headaches, and I even passed out the other day, right before there was this student protest that the administration blames me for. And I've had a temper. I quit my job, and I yelled at the school secretary, so . . ." I shrug and sigh simultaneously, "I guess I can't fault them for thinking I need therapy, especially since my doctor agrees. But it's frustrating."

"Sure." If Dr. Dengel is surprised by anything I've said, she betrays nothing. "Let's talk about the accident. You were injured, but your partner was okay?"

"That's right. Vance—he and I were together for a couple of years, and we were briefly engaged. I'm trying to piece together what happened in the weeks leading up to the accident. Is it strange that I can't remember something so important? Does it mean I'm going crazy?"

"Not at all. It's a defense. However, I think our first step will be to tap into those memories so you can find closure and forgive yourself."

I'm struck as if she'd dumped ice on my chest. "What do you mean? Why do I need to forgive myself?"

"Hazel . . ." Dr. Dengel taps her pen against her notepad, contemplating her next statement. "It sounds like there were some cracks both in your relationship and in your professional life, that perhaps you've made some mistakes or choices you regret. Everything came to a head on the night of the accident, and your brain is protecting itself by blocking the painful memories. Yet, you won't heal from that pain until you remember. So, to begin, tell me a good memory with Vance before he left. Try to pick something that was fairly recent and describe it to me."

My head begins to hurt. I squeeze my eyes shut, feeling tears form. I picture Vance's face, those pouty lips, those expansive eyes. It takes me a moment to access a memory, and when I do, I realize it's from early December.

I open my eyes, look at Dr. Dengel, and with a shaky voice, tell her all about it.

CHAPTER 44

It was a Sunday evening in early December. Vance was stretched out in bed, his long body beautiful and luminescent in the blueish evening light. Before Baby Girl hopped onto the bed, we'd been doing some post-coital spooning, talking about what we should make for dinner and about the lessons we'd planned for the upcoming week. I told him that I was about to start *The Great Gatsby* in AP Lit, and Vance, who loves the Jazz Age, seemed intrigued.

I nudged him with my foot, trying to get his attention. "Hey, maybe we could do some cross curriculum."

He scrunched up his face in skepticism. "What sort of cross curriculum?"

"Like, you could do an art déco unit?"

He shook his head. "My students aren't ready for specific stylistic stuff like that."

"Well, what about something thematic, then? You could go simple and do it on self-invention and the American Dream."

Vance pondered this, chewing on the bottom of his lip while scratching the bottom of Baby Girl's chin. "Wasn't the whole point of *Great Gatsby* that he's a phony and the American Dream doesn't really exist?"

"Sort of. Everyone has selfish ulterior motives, and they all value flash over substance, and nobody tells the truth, not even to themselves."

"So it's all just a scam?"

Sitting up, I wrapped myself in a blanket, partly because I was cold and partly because I had trouble discussing work-related stuff while naked. "Well, that's the question my students will hopefully answer by the end of the unit. Like, do our dreams guide us or condemn us? And do only the powerful have the agency to make their dreams come true?"

"Sounds interesting," said Vance. He sat up, rolled his head around, and I could hear a soft popping from his neck. "And you're thinking I'll assign my class to do visual representations of their version of the American Dream?"

"Yeah, what it means to them. That would be cool. I know we share a lot of students, and it would get them examining the themes and their feelings in connection with the American Dream. It might inspire some really cool work."

Vance kissed my neck. "Would that assignment make you happy?"

"Yes."

He lifted his face to mine and kissed my nose and then my ear and then, softly, my lips. "Then I'm all in. Let's eat dinner, and you can tell me more about the novel. It's been forever since I read it."

I threw my arms around him, squeezing him tight. "Thank you!"

We threw on some sweatpants and T-shirts made soft from too many wash cycles. We cooked up an enormous pot of pasta and opened a bottle of wine. Then, we spent the evening secure and happy in our love.

It wasn't until later that Vance strolled off into the other room to make a phone call. After around forty minutes of hearing him laugh and banter, he finally hung up and sat next to me on the living room couch.

"Who were you talking to?"

"Annabelle. I had to tell her about the American Dream unit ASAP so we could start brainstorming lesson plans."

Vance looked at me in uneasy anticipation, like he was waiting for me to explode. I wouldn't give him the satisfaction.

"What'd she think of the idea?"

"She liked it."

"Cool."

Vance stood. "I think I'll take a shower before bed."

He walked toward the bedroom, and I remained still. Whatever happy spell we'd been under was broken.

CHAPTER 45

Vance's arrogance was enough to make her blood boil. She'd let him twist her around his little finger for too long, and it was time to take control. First, she must convince him she didn't care—even though, deep down, she ached for Vance like a wound that refused to heal. This needed to change, because everyone knew the person who cared less was the one in power. When he found her in the copy room on Monday morning, excitement bubbled up inside her as she realized what she must do.

"How's it going?" he asked, stepping close to her. The door leading out to the hallway was open, and students and staff roamed noisily by, a few of them looking in to where she and Vance stood. She noticed Vance carried some papers that needed copying, so this was a necessary visit upstairs. Still, he treated her so intimately.

"I'm okay," she said in response to his question. "You?"

He shrugged. "Too much is going on lately. I can't keep my head straight."

She gave him a playful punch on the shoulder. "Then I guess you'd better try a little harder, huh?" She turned away from his sad expression, pivoting back toward the mammoth machine that spat out papers in a clunky rhythm. She needed to create distance so he wouldn't start insisting that she give him another chance, or to let him stay with her, or that it was her he had loved all this time.

"Hey," he mumbled. "Come here for a second." Vance tilted his head toward the corner of the room where they'd be out of sight. Against her better judgment, she followed.

"What?" she asked in a loud whisper. "I'm kind of busy this morning."

His response was also hushed. He grasped her arm, tilting his head down so that their foreheads nearly met. "I just want you to know that I'm going to make things right between us. I promise, okay?"

She'd heard this before. "What about Hazel?"

His smile oozed warmth as if it could offset the cold reality of his words. "It's complicated. You know that. But you also know how I feel about you."

What she knew was that "complicated" meant he still had feelings for Hazel. Suddenly she was savagely angry, like to the level that she must do some physical damage. She grabbed the stack of papers Vance held, tearing them from his arms, not caring if her fingernails scratched him in the process. Then she ripped the papers in twos, fours, eights, and shoved them into the recycling bin.

As physical destruction went, it wasn't the most satisfying type, but it would have to do.

Before he could respond, before he could do anything but stand there, stunned, she gracefully removed her own stack of papers from the output tray, turned on her heel, and walked back into the hallway. First hour started in thirteen minutes, after all.

She was still open to a future with Vance but not unless he learned his lesson first. Vance needed to understand who he was dealing with, that she wouldn't put up with any other women in his life and that he owed her a big apology. In fact, he owed her a lot more.

And she refused to give him what he wanted until he gave her what she deserved.

CHAPTER 46

Anger, jealousy, and even a lust for vengeance: they're all emotions people often experience at the end of a relationship. Dr. Dengel tells me this. "But you could never work through it all," she says. "You were robbed of that opportunity when Vance suddenly left."

We discuss this, and I try to remember more details about what happened between Vance and me. Still, I come up blank, except for one thing. "It's funny. I keep thinking about this ancient Greek play, *Eumenides*, because in it, there are these three furies, and they each represent either anger, jealousy, or vengeance. And two years ago, when things were still good between Vance and me, he helped me put together a student production where they wrote and performed their own version of the play."

"Really?" Dr. Dengel crosses and uncrosses her legs. "What about that do you find funny?"

"Umm . . . I don't mean funny as in 'ha-ha' funny, but like, it's a coincidence?"

"Are you asking me if it's a coincidence?"

"No. I'm saying it is a coincidence because that was one time when I really felt like Vance was on my side."

"How so, Hazel?"

I look up at the ceiling, but inside my mind, I see Vance, remembering him at his most beautiful in the gloaming spring light. "He worried about me losing my job, so he pulled some strings and helped me do this last-minute project with our students at a friend's theater."

"And was it his idea to do something about the Furies?"

"Huh?" Abruptly my vision tilts back down to Dr. Dengel and her office. "No. Actually, it was Febe's."

"Who is Febe?"

"A student. She's this brilliant, troubled girl who . . ." I let my voice trail off, unsure how to finish.

Dr. Dengel cocks an eyebrow at me. "Yes?" she asks.

"She's way ahead of her time," I state. "Sometimes she reminds me of myself, but I think that's just wishful thinking. She's way more talented than I'll ever be."

"You don't think you're talented?"

I shrug. "I don't know. But before I became a teacher, I wanted to be a playwright."

Dr. Dengel contemplates this, furrowing her brow before she speaks. "You have powerful feelings about this play and how it connects to Febe and Vance." Dr. Dengel gives a quick smile. "Let's make an assignment out of this. As a teacher, I'm sure you can handle homework. I want you to reread *Eumenides*, and then write your own adaptation of it, unlike the one that you wrote with Febe previously. Make it as original as possible. Doing this might help awaken some of those emotions or ideas which you have been suppressing."

Ever the vigilant student, I do as directed. Honestly, it's a relief to have something to work on. I page through the original text, remembering that Orestes murders his own mother. However, before she croaks, she's able to get out some dying words, cursing her son and prompting the three Furies—anger, jealousy, and vengeance—to drive Orestes mad.

I decide that my modern-day retelling of the play will be set in a courtroom, and the three Furies are all lawyers who each have their own personal grudge against Orestes, aka Vance. I'll be "Hannah," the Fury for anger, and Annabelle will be "Angela," the Fury for jealousy. I'm not sure why but it feels natural to model the Fury for vengeance off Olivia, so I name her Liz and give her a throaty voice and a ponytail.

Vance/Orestes is a slick litigator, feeding the three females in his orbit the same lines, telling them he loves them and, in the very next breath, lying to their faces. But then he gets caught, and Angela, Liz, and Hannah put him on trial.

The problem is, in Aeschylus's original play, Orestes gets off because Athena convinces the Furies to become good and to use their power for something other than vengeance. "This is the life I offer. It is yours to take," she tells them. "Do great things."

After a lot of persuading, they agree and tell her, "Your magic is working. I can feel the fury, the hate slipping away . . ."

But how do I translate that into an empowering message?

I sit at my computer, having lost track of time, as the sky darkens and my stomach growls. I'm wrestling with that line, feeling like it's not quite right, when I get a text from Cyrus.

How are you?

I text back without thinking. *Okay. Wanna come over?*

Sure, he responds. *I still have stuff to do at school. In a while?*

Of course, whenever, I text, feigning nonchalance.

Two hours later, Cyrus is here in my living room, and it feels so good, too good.

"Thanks for inviting me over," he says, shortly after he has taken off his coat and settled onto my living room couch. I have the fireplace turned on, and he looks at the flames. "There's so much to talk about, and it's better to do it in person."

I sit on the couch next to him, leaving the middle cushion between us. "Cyrus, look. I owe you big time, and if you need me to back off, I will. I just really appreciate all you've done for me and that you're looking out for Febe."

Cyrus' smile is gentle, and so is his voice. "I've been looking out for Febe because I'm worried about her. I'd do it even if you hadn't asked me to."

I nod, feeling my breath catch in my throat and my pulse quickening. "So, what have you found out? Has she been back to school?"

"She came yesterday and today."

"Did you talk to her?"

"Yeah." Cyrus shifts, his face now partially in shadows. "At least I tried to. I pulled her aside, and I was about to ask her how she was doing and if she and her family were okay, but right then, Brady Burns came up and demanded that I talk to him."

"Seriously? What did you do?"

"I tried to make him go away and wait until I was done talking to Febe. But she ran off."

I sigh and stand, needing to pace. "He's trying to intimidate her, and it's working."

"Yeah, probably."

"What do you mean 'probably'?"

Cyrus's chest rises and falls. "Brady stayed after class to talk about his painting. But then, he started talking about Febe instead. He was like, 'I saw you talking to her, Mr. Gul. You know I'm innocent, right? I didn't do anything to her.' Then he launched into his side of the story."

I put my hands on my hips in a defiant, questioning stance. "And do you believe him?"

Cyrus stands and comes toward me. "I don't know what to believe, Hazel. Febe never admitted to writing that story about Brady. But I'll do everything I can to make things right for her, and if you let me, I'll do the same for you."

With a jolt, I'm reminded of Vance and of what I'd discussed today with Dr. Dengel. I wince, and Cyrus notices.

"What? What's wrong?"

"Nothing," I say. "It's just—my therapist thinks I feel guilty about Vance and the accident, and that's why I'm blocking stuff out. So, in other words, I'm too dangerous to care about."

Cyrus brushes my arm with his finger. "I'll be the judge of that."

I can't think of a decent response, so I stop thinking altogether, and I wrap my arms around his shoulders. He smells heavenly, probably some combination of cologne and breath mints, but I'm intoxicated. At first, he simply stands there, immobile, before his body melts a little, and he holds me. Then, slowly, his lips caress mine, and when I place my hand against the bare skin on the back of his neck, I can feel it; we both fill with desire. Still, I pull away.

"We should stop."

Cyrus pulls away, too, but he uses his thumb to brush the freckles over my cheekbones. "I love your freckles," he murmurs, and then he softly taps the side of my nose. "Especially this one, right here."

"It's actually a tiny mole."

"Yeah, it's so cool. I keep thinking it's a stud like you had your nose pierced." He leans in, kisses that spot, and then his lips are warm and sweet against my cheek.

"Stop," I whisper.

He does stop, and now there's enough space between us that I see him frown.

"Are you sure about this?" I ask.

"No." His voice is husky, and I can feel his heart pounding through his chest. "But . . . God . . . I want to."

"Cyrus—"

He presses his finger against my lips, his eyes hungry for an answer. "I need to know one thing. It'll hurt me now but I'd rather you be honest than lie, and devastate me later."

I breathe, in and out, in and out. "Okay . . . what do you need to know?"

His voice quavers as he asks, "Am I just a stand-in for Vance?"

I shudder. A cocktail of laughter and tears escapes. "No. You stand in for no one. And even though my life is completely crazy, here you are, so strong, so honest, so amazing. I've always felt that way, even when I hated you for leaving without saying goodbye." I feel his pulse through his skin, beating where I rest my hands on his chest, and my fingers travel down to the waistband of his jeans. "Now you're back, and I'm torn. Should I take your hand and run away with you, or should I leave you be, so I don't cause any more damage?"

He gives me a wry smile. "If we ran away together, where would we go?"

"Wherever you want."

He kisses me again. Wow. Cyrus is a really good kisser. "How about Portugal?" He murmurs, his lips brushing my chin. "There's this cave that's only accessible by water that I've always wanted to see."

"Consider it done." Gingerly, I take his glasses and drop them to the side table, and I move closer to him until our faces are mere inches apart, barely touching but connected by some powerful force, stemming from both security and passion. Our kiss is filled with emotion—distress and desperation melting away into desire and devotion—as we move together without thought until we find ourselves in my bedroom, surrounded by moonlight spilling through the window and highlighting our connection as one body and one mind.

Nothing else matters—only us.

CHAPTER 47

Early the next morning, a light kiss is planted on my cheek. I open my eyes and murmur, "Do you need to go? I'll walk you out."

"No, no," Cyrus says. "Go back to sleep. I'll call you later."

I snuggle under my sheets and comforter, back to enjoying the best sleep I've had in months. When I finally wake again, daylight streams through the blinds and the clock says it's after nine, which for me, a consummate early riser, is like a normal person sleeping until noon.

I stretch, make my way toward my kitchen, and brew a pot of coffee. Lost in thought about how good it felt being with Cyrus last night, I'm startled by a buzz. I look for my phone, find it, and realize that it is not my phone making noise. Further inspection causes me to find Cyrus' phone, slid between two of my couch cushions.

There's a voicemail.

Now I'm awake. What if it's important? I'd hate to cause any sort of distress, or even inconvenience, to Cyrus. He's done so much for me; surely, I could do one little thing for him and drop his phone off at school.

"During your leave, you are not allowed on school grounds." I recall Jim's words. In fact, they ring in my ears, and I know that, if I was smart, I'd heed his warning. However, Cyrus needs his phone.

I get dressed, brush my teeth, and prepare to go. It's not until I'm on the road, steering my car toward Dixon

Heights High School, that I admit it to myself: I'm not risking my job and my reputation to bring Cyrus his phone. I'm doing it because there's a chance that I could find Febe, that I could talk to her and make sure she's okay. And if she's not okay? I could tell her that I'll support her however I can.

It's almost the end of first hour when I get to school. Febe would be in my classroom right now, so I know where to find her. I also know that Olivia has prep. Recklessly, I call Olivia, praying that she'll pick up.

She does.

"Hi," she says simply, her voice cold. We haven't spoken since the morning of the protest, the morning of our fight. I have yet to ask her why she'd called Annabelle after the accident, but I'll save that for another day.

"I know you're still mad at me, Olivia. But will you do me a favor? I'm outside the school, at door five. Can you come down and let me in?"

"Don't you have your keycard?"

"Yeah, but I can't use it. The school can scan that info so they know who's been coming and going, and I'm not allowed back on school grounds until a week from Monday."

"So . . . what? You're going to sneak in, wearing a disguise or something? Have you gone crazy?"

"Please, Olivia!" I can hear the desperation in my voice. "First hour is almost over, and I need to find Febe. I'm begging you."

Olivia hangs up, and I don't know if that means she's on her way or if she's telling me to buzz off. I stand outside the door, the February wind cutting through me, and then, two minutes later, she's there, opening the door for me.

"You're a Godsend, Olivia. Thank you so much."

"So, when I'm useful, when I serve a purpose, then I'm a Godsend? What am I the rest of the time?"

Heat rushes to my face. For all her shortcomings, Olivia has been there for me during tragedy and turmoil. She hasn't accused me of taking her for granted, not exactly, but she wouldn't be out of line if she did.

"I'm sorry," I say, hoping I sound as genuine as I feel. "I don't appreciate you enough, and I haven't been open with you. That will change; I promise. There's just so much going on right now, but once I get it figured out, I swear that you and I will get back on track."

Olivia blinks twice like she has something in her eye. But after a couple of moments, she relents, and a smile warms her face. "Alright. I hold you to that, Hazy."

"Good. I hope you do." I smile back, and then I rush off so I can get to my classroom as the bell rings. That way, I can catch Febe on her way out. But Olivia stops me by grabbing my arm.

"Wait," she hisses. "There's something you need to know."

"Not now. Later, okay?"

Olivia's grip tightens, her fingers pressed into my arm. "No. You need to hear this. Now! Brady Burns is innocent. He didn't do anything to Febe. She made it all up."

"There's no way of proving that!"

"Yes, there is! The article she wrote—it said the incident happened at a party in November, but Brady was sick with mono during that time." Olivia's face has grown flushed, and her voice is urgently high. "I'm telling you; Febe was lying!"

"Olivia, honestly, right now, I don't care if she *was* lying. Maybe she made a mistake, but even so, she needs help." I yank my arm away and rush off right as the bell rings, ending first hour. Students emerge from class-rooms, and it's like a switch has been flipped, from relative quiet to noisy chaos. I keep my head down, practically jumping up the stairs, hoping I can keep from being no-ticed and that I can reach Febe in time.

I get to the top floor, to where my classroom is, in rec-ord time. A skinny figure wearing a hijab exits, her back to me. I sprint toward her. "Febe!" I cry. She turns, and thank God, it's her.

"Ms. Ford? What are you doing here? I thought you'd been banned from the building."

"Only sort of. But I had to find out if you were okay."

She looks at me like I'm deranged, like I'm making a huge deal out of nothing. "I'm fine. You should go. I don't want you losing your job over me."

"It's a little late to worry about that." I look around and notice the scornful, suspicious eyes of students and teach-ers alike. Lucas stands outside his classroom further down the hall, frowning and staring daggers at me.

What a jerk. I bet he's about to call the office and tattle.

"Look," I say to Febe, leaning in so only she can hear me. "I know you're in trouble, Febe. I'm just not sure how bad it is. But I can help. Meet me at Perkins at three thirty, okay?"

"I don't know if I can."

"Figure it out." I look into her eyes, channeling all the authority I've ever had, trying to impress upon her the ur-gency of this situation. "I'm on your side, Febe. Please, just trust me one more time and meet me later, okay?"

"There's stuff, Ms. Ford, that if you knew, you wouldn't be on my side."

The edges of my heart break open a little. "You think I haven't heard the rumors?" I soften my voice. "None of it matters. At least it doesn't matter to me. What matters is getting you out of trouble. So, Perkins, three thirty?"

She gives me such an abrupt nod that I'm not completely sure she's actually agreed to anything. "I have to get to class." And then she's gone.

The warning bell chimes, letting students know they have only two more minutes to get to class on time. I should hightail it out of here. But I haven't achieved my original purpose in coming here, which was, of course, to bring Cyrus his phone. I pull it out of my coat pocket; there are now five missed notifications.

Oh, what the heck. It's not like Jim won't eventually find out I've been here. I turn back toward the stairs and push on to find Cyrus.

When I get to his classroom, it seems there is no one coming in or out of it. Cyrus must have second-hour prep. I peek in, and he's sitting at his desk all the way in the back. "Hey," I call out softly.

Cyrus looks up, his face instantly invaded by shock. "Hazel! What are you doing here?"

"You left your phone at my place last night." I come toward him, holding his phone in my outstretched hand. "Someone's been trying to get a hold of you, and I thought it might be important."

He takes his phone and looks at it. "It was my sister."

"I hope everything is okay."

Cyrus shakes his head. "It was probably nothing. She calls a lot, and if I don't call her back right away, she keeps trying every twenty minutes until I respond." He laughs a little like we're sharing a joke, and then his face turns serious. "You shouldn't have risked coming here just to give me my phone."

"Don't worry. It was an excuse to find Febe. But I'll go."

"Can I call you later?"

"Of course." I give him a smile, and he returns it. I'm warm all over. "I hope you do."

Now, finally, I'm on my way out. I walk out of Cyrus' classroom, make my way to the outside door, and I'm about to push it open to find some fresh, cold freedom, but I'm stopped. "Hazel!" I hear someone shout.

I turn around to see Jim coming toward me.

CHAPTER 48

Jim insists I come with him to his office, and once we get there, he calls for Leslie from HR to come down. They talk at me for a while, but I don't really listen. Maybe this was fate. Maybe I wanted to get caught.

"You've left us no choice," Jim states, his frown a flat line underneath his tan eyes. "You are on unpaid leave indefinitely, effective immediately."

The words register, but I can't seem to form any sort of emotional response. "Okay," I tell them. "I understand."

"Do you have any questions?" Leslie asks, almost apologetically.

"Can I go now?"

"Please do," Jim answers. "Leslie will walk you out."

Driving home, I feel numb. I just ruined the only career I've ever known—three years of effort, drive, and dreams, thousands of dollars for a degree and a permanent riff with my family, and for what? All so I could self-destruct.

I wonder what Dr. Dengel will say about this.

It doesn't matter. At least, that's what I tell myself. In a few hours, I'm supposed to meet Febe at the Perkins close to school, and if Jim and HR don't like it, well, they'll have to take out a restraining order to keep me away.

I spend the time before I'm supposed to meet Febe on my computer, looking at the housing market, trying to figure out how much my home would go for. I also research grad programs in playwriting, even though I know I'd just create more debt without the promise of any income. Yet I fantasize, imagining myself on a college campus, writing full time, staging productions, working with undergrads . . . and who knows? Perhaps I could become a professor. It's probably all a pipe dream, but so what if it is?

Finally, it's time to go to Perkins. I get there five minutes early just to be sure I don't miss Febe. When I walk in, the first thing I see is the bakery counter, with all its mammoth muffins and pies behind glass and the giant cookies resting in a basket on top. My stomach growls.

"Ms. Ford! Hi!" The hostess greets me with a smile, and I realize she's an ex-student. Problem is, I'm terrible at remembering the names of most of my students once they've graduated; it's like they melt from my memory. I figure it's a necessary measure my brain must take to clear the space for the approximately two hundred students I currently have—or had. I guess I don't have any students anymore.

Luckily, this ex-student wears a nametag. I try to glance at it without being obvious. "Rochelle!" I exclaim, raising my voice an octave. "It's so good to see you! How have you been?"

"I've been good. Just working, you know?"

I nod. I'm starting to place her. Rochelle was in my Creative Writing class two years ago, and she excelled at poetry. She'd asked me to write her a letter of recommendation to get into college, which I did, but I'd never heard if she'd been accepted.

"Good for you," I say, understanding that she must not currently be in school and sensing she might be embarrassed about it. "I hope you still find time to write, though. Your poetry was so impressive!"

She laughs but seems pleased. "Actually, I do still write from time to time. I've even published some stuff on poetry websites. Should I send you the links?"

"I'd love that!"

"Great. Is your email address still the same?"

"Uh-huh," I respond, wondering how long it will be before my school email address will be deactivated. It should take a while; they're going to have to go through some major steps before they can actually fire me.

"Cool. Thank you for all the encouragement you gave me in high school." Rochelle smiles. "I doubt I'd still be writing if it wasn't for you and your class."

"Well, that means a lot. Thank *you* for telling me that."

"Of course." Rochelle shifts her weight from foot to foot. "So, did you want a table for one?"

"Oh." I breathe in, feeling heat beneath my cheeks. "No—I mean yes, I want a table, but I'm meeting someone. She should be here any minute. I'll just wait to be seated until she gets here, okay?"

"Of course," Rochelle says again, but this time her tone is a little unsure. "Just let me know when you're ready." She moves behind the counter and starts arranging the baked goods that already look perfect on their display. I take my phone out from my purse and start playing solitaire, hoping it looks like I'm busy writing or reading texts.

Where are you, Febe?

The minutes creep by at the rate of sap dripping from a tree. I lose game after game of solitaire, telling myself each time that if I win this one, Febe will show up seconds later. But I'm not a winner, and Febe is obviously a no-show. Finally, I put my phone in my purse and look at Rochelle. "I guess my friend can't meet me. Take care, Rochelle."

"You too, Ms. Ford."

I push out of Perkins, torn between concern and anger, all toward Febe. Now what do I do?

"Ms. Ford!"

The voice comes from behind a stone pillar lamp used to light the parking lot at night. I see a figure emerge.

"Febe! What are you doing out here? Why didn't you come inside?"

She rolls her eyes at me like I'm crazy. "Everybody at school was talking, saying that you're in major trouble for coming in when you weren't supposed to. I don't want you to get fired for real, and if someone saw us together at Perkins, I bet you would be."

"Oh." I look at Febe, shivering in the coat she always wears to class. Indoors, the coat probably makes her way too hot, but out here, she's like a kitten without enough fur to protect her from the cold. "It's sweet of you to worry, but I don't care if they fire me. Let's go in, warm you up, and I'll buy you some pancakes. You look hungry, and I know I am."

"No, Ms. Ford. You may not care if you're fired, but I do. So do lots of other students. We even started a petition."

"Seriously?"

"Yeah." She smiles, but her eyes pool like tears might fall. "You can't leave Dixon Heights."

"Okay." I press my lips together, thinking. "I mean I might have to leave, but we won't go into Perkins. I can drive you home, though, and maybe we can stop somewhere on the way and get you something to eat."

"That's alright. You don't need to do that."

"I want to."

"Ms. Ford, please don't worry so much. I've got plenty at home to eat."

"And where is that?"

"Huh?"

"I saw that your house was boarded up, so where have you been staying?"

Febe's face twists first into shock and then into annoyance. "Are you stalking me?"

"Please! I'm worried about you; that's all. You're lucky I'm not calling child protective services, with what I've heard."

"I'm almost eighteen. I can take care of myself."

"Great. I'm glad to hear it. Now, tell me where you've been staying."

"At this group home. It's totally chill."

"At a group home?" I scrutinize her and see her chin tremble a bit. "Like for homeless teens?"

"You make it sound bad. But it isn't."

I walk toward my car and open the passenger side. "Get in." Thank heaven Febe does as I say and climbs into my car. I get into the driver's side and pull out of the parking lot, turning left.

"You should have turned right," Febe says.

"Nope," I respond. "I'm not taking you back to a homeless shelter."

"Then where are you taking me?" Febe's voice is soft like she regrets the question even as she's asking it.

"I'm taking you home with me."

CHAPTER 49

For the rest of the ride home, Febe quietly stares out the window. That's okay; so much has passed between us, and when we talk again, I'll need to see her face, have my eyes meet hers, and hear what she has to say without needing to divide my attention between her words and the road.

I pull up in front of my house, and Febe tilts up her head, taking in my bungalow. "You live here by yourself?" she asks.

"Now I do," I state. "Before he took off, Mr. Valby lived here with me."

"Oh yeah. Still, this is so big for just one or two people. And it's such a pretty neighborhood."

"I like it a lot." I unlatch my door. "Come on; let's go inside."

She climbs out, and I lead her in through the front door. "Wow, Ms. Ford. This is beautiful." She looks around, and I see my living room, as if for the first time, through her eyes. The red walls, repurposed wood shelving, and colorful paintings skillfully hung that accent the bohemian furniture and oriental rug—it's all very striking.

"The paint job and artwork, none of that was me. Mr. Valby spent a lot of time decorating and turning this into an 'artist's space'." I take a sharp inhale. "It makes me wonder how he could leave so easily."

"Huh?"

I shake my head, tossing away the thought. "Nothing. Are you hungry? Or tired? What do you need?"

"I don't need anything, Ms. Ford. You're the one who insisted on taking me here."

"Oh, cut the crap, Febe."

Her mouth drops open in shock.

"Seriously," I continue. "You've been living at a shelter, so you've got to be hungry and exhausted. And you must be totally stressed from what's been going on; anyone would be. So, I will forget that you lashed out at me, and I won't take it personally since you've got way too much to deal with. But please, level with me and tell me the truth, about everything."

Febe crosses her arms over her chest, defiant, and tilts her chin like she's about to put up a fight. But I meet her gaze, and I won't look away. After a moment, she slumps and lets out a sigh. "Fine," she utters, her voice soft. "The truth is, I haven't eaten or showered for over a day."

"You don't get lunch at school?"

She shakes her head. "I can't go near the lunchroom, Ms. Ford. People at school hate me, and it's not safe."

"Okay. Come on."

She follows me upstairs where I grab a towel, some sweatpants, and a sweatshirt for her to change into, and I lead her to the bathroom. "You can shower here. After you're done, you can either take a nap in the spare bedroom or you can come down to the kitchen, and I'll make you something to eat. Then we'll chat."

Febe nods. "Okay. Thank you."

I head downstairs, not knowing if she'll choose to nap or eat when she's done showering. Either way, she'll surely want to eat at some point this evening, so I rummage through my refrigerator, looking for ingredients that would compile a meal. I pull out a box of chicken stock, a couple of frozen chicken breasts, carrots, and noodles from my pantry. Chicken soup will be a good start, but as hungry as Febe must be, she'll need more than that. Remembering the bakery counter at Perkins, I find some frozen cinnamon rolls at the back of my freezer. I don't even know how long they've been sitting back there, forgotten about, but I preheat the oven and take the packaging off the heat-and-serve pan they came in.

By the time Febe wanders downstairs, my soup is simmering on the stove, the rolls are bubbling in the oven, I'm loading the dishwasher, and the scent of cinnamon combines with the savory soup, filling the air. "Something smells amazing," Febe says.

I almost do a double take when I look at her. It's the first time I've seen Febe without her hijab, and her dark glossy hair hanging in loose waves down her back is stunning. *The dark hair on Vance's scarf* . . . No. It doesn't matter, not right now. I need to uncover one messy truth at a time.

"Have a seat," I say, pointing to my kitchen table. "I'll serve you some food."

After I've placed a steaming bowl of soup and a gooey cinnamon roll in front of her, I sit in the chair opposite her.

"Aren't you going to eat, too, Ms. Ford?"

"Yeah, I will. First, and you don't need to tell me everything all at once, but just tell me this—did you write the story about Brady Burns? And is it true?"

Febe's huge brown meet mine, unafraid yet weary. "Yes, I wrote the piece that everyone assumed was about Brady Burns. As for it being true, well, that's complicated."

"No. Either it's true, or it's not."

Febe stirs her soup, looking like she'd dive into it and hide if she could. "All of it is true, but some details were altered for artistic purposes."

I scowl at her. "You can't 'alter details' and still maintain that something is true."

"I disagree, Ms. Ford. But I'll explain so you can understand what I mean. Get ready, though, because it's a long story."

I lean toward her. "I was born ready, Febe. Lay it on me."

So, she does.

CHAPTER 50

First, there are so many things that people get wrong about her, so many assumptions they make and so many things they don't know. Febe realizes she could share more, she could let people in on her secrets, but would they be overwhelmed or scared away? If she told someone the truth about her life, they might pity her or even flee.

Or maybe they would hate her.

Her father was a faculty member at the university in Tehran, the one where that dormitory was raided in 1999, and it sparked student protests. He protested along with his students, and things got pretty intense. He was arrested more than once, and Febe's mother worried that his actions were endangering their family. So, when Febe's aunt and uncle moved to the U.S., Febe's mother begged them to take Febe along so she could have a better life and a chance for opportunity and growth. Febe's parents would join them in Minnesota soon, her mother promised. But Febe could tell it was the sort of promise that wouldn't be kept.

Her aunt and uncle had agreed but only if Febe's parents sent money every month to help support her. Nobody asked Febe what she wanted, but she was just a kid. She cried and screamed and clung to her mother, and once she was in the U.S., she'd pleaded to be sent back. "Don't you realize how lucky you are?" her aunt demanded. "Here you are, living in a peaceful place, with a large Muslim community. Few have it as good as you."

While her aunt and uncle weren't exactly kind, they at least tolerated her. But after 9/11, they got really stressed out, with everyone assuming they were terrorists, so they were in a bad mood most of the time. Then came the heart-heavy, devastating news from home: Febe's mother had breast cancer. By the time the doctors detected it, it was already stage four, and although Febe begged to go back to Iran to say goodbye, her aunt and uncle said it wasn't possible. Travel to the Middle East wasn't safe, especially for Middle Easterners.

Febe spoke the last words she would ever say to her mother over the telephone, and her mother's last words to her, "I love you; be good," were broken up and staticky, coming from thousands of miles away and sifted through guilt and tears. Febe tried to mourn her mother from afar and to live up to the request of "being good," but every day, she was at a loss, not even knowing where to start. Mean-while, after her mother's passing, her father went off the grid. He'd always been erratic, but now, who knew? Maybe he was fighting in some rebel army, or maybe he'd remar-ried and started a new family, but he had forgotten about Febe.

And that meant her aunt and uncle received no money to help support her.

They didn't exactly take it out on Febe and at least tried to do well for her. Sometimes, life wasn't so bad. Junior year started off promising. Her workload seemed manage-able even though she'd enrolled in three AP classes, she was active in Key Club, and her best friend, Najah, had the same lunch hour as she did. September was hopeful; the leaves turned bright colors, yet the air was still warm, and she'd stay after school to help decorate for homecom-ing or to organize the canned food drive for refugees.

But then October came, and two bad things happened. First, Najah begged Febe to go to a post-football game party with her, but Febe had an essay due for AP History that she hadn't yet found the time to work on; so she devoted her entire weekend to getting the essay done. It was increasingly hard to devote herself to her studies, mostly because her home life was so chaotic. Her aunt and uncle had five boys, and as the older female cousin, she was expected to babysit. She was told that family came first, and they also told her she wouldn't be going away to college anyway. The best that she could hope for was a two-year program where she would commute from home, so there was no point in getting a 4.0 and taking honors courses.

Yet, Febe wasn't one to give up easily. She figured that, if she got a full ride somewhere, anywhere, to college, her aunt and uncle couldn't stop her from going. So, she regretfully told Najah that she'd be studying on the Saturday night of the party, and Najah wasn't exactly cool about it. "You're so lame," Najah had told her. "I wish I had a real friend to hang with outside of school."

The thing was, there were lots of Muslim students at Dixon Heights. It wasn't like they got stared at for wearing a hijab. There were always going to be racist comments, people accusing them of belonging to the Taliban or telling them that, if they hate America, then they should just go back, but it wasn't all bad at Heights where the Muslim population was stronger than in other places.

Yet, going to school with a lot of other Muslims meant they were divided into two camps: strict Muslims and "chill" Muslims. The chill Muslims went to parties, broke the rules, and drank; sometimes, they even did drugs or messed around, when clearly, the Quran is against all mind-altering activity, especially anything that could lead to premarital sex.

But Najah had a rebellious streak, and she questioned stuff all the time, like why should she have to wear a hijab?

"One day, I'm just going to stop wearing it altogether," she kept promising.

Najah wanted people to see her as a "chill" Muslim, but she wasn't quite brave enough to make all the required moves independently. She'd wanted Febe to be her side-kick, but Febe wasn't so sure. "Be good." Her mother's last words kept ringing in her ears.

The Monday after the party, Najah would barely look at her, and when Febe asked her how the party went, Najah shrugged and clamped her mouth shut. At lunch, Najah sat with a different group of girls and shunned Febe when she approached their table.

For two weeks, Najah snubbed her, but then one morning, Febe found Najah at her locker, tears silently falling down her face. Nearby, Brady Burns stood laughing and making crude jokes with his friends. "What's wrong, Najah?"

"He's pretending like I don't even exist," Najah said.

Febe walked Najah to a quiet spot in the pool hallway where nobody could eavesdrop on their conversation, and Najah confessed to Febe what had happened.

"He flirted with me at that party," Najah told her, "and he kept bringing me beer and acting like I was all that. I had more to drink than I'd ever had, and the world started spinning, and then it's like, suddenly we're alone, and Brady is all over me, grabbing at me and touching me everywhere, and I had to push him off me."

She'd been able to get away, but as she ran from Brady, she heard his friends taunting him, saying he'd lost the bet. "They bet Brady that he couldn't get me drunk enough to have sex with me." Najah started sobbing. "And the worst part is that Brady laughed it off and said he'd rather pay up than bump uglies with me."

Turns out, Brady and his friends played this game where they would try to get Muslim girls to cut loose, take off their hijab, drink, smoke, and mess around—all the forbidden stuff. But the boys maintained it was just a game; none of them actually wanted to have sex with a Muslim girl because they stank and were dirty. Everybody knew that, according to Brady and his friends.

Febe had been aware of their cruel game and their hateful attitude, but she hadn't let it bother her until now. It was just a small portion of the boys in her class, and they were stupid. But after Najah had been a victim, it all hit close to home. And she'd been trying to figure out how to help Najah when her own world, her own home, got yanked out from under her. It was the second bad thing that happened in October.

"Your uncle got laid off," Febe's aunt told her. "We need to move."

Her uncle did some boring job that had to do with billing and hospitals. Febe paid no attention, but they had her attention now when they told her he was going to work for the Mayo Clinic.

"But that's in Rochester! And everyone knows that town is super white and stuck up. No way!" Febe argued, refusing to leave school and everything she'd been working for.

Her aunt and uncle said she was being bratty, that she was lucky they will keep supporting her, that she should stop complaining. The only thing Febe could do was beg Najah to ask her parents if she could stay with them. After a lot of pressing, Najah agreed, and she could convince her mom and dad to let Febe stay, but Febe's aunt and uncle still did not approve.

"If you do not come with us to Rochester, never come to us for anything again. You will be on your own."

Febe didn't care. She was sure her aunt and uncle were bluffing, and anyway, now Febe would finally have some peace and quiet. Najah's house was like a haven. Najah's only sibling was away at college, and her parents understood girls deserved a chance at higher education and gave them the time and space to study.

At first, it was great. Najah and Febe went to school together every day, studied and hung out, and got along well. But then Najah became moody like she never really got over what happened with Brady Burns. Febe decided Najah felt things more deeply than most; she was one of those people who took stuff extra personally and lashed out when she was hurt.

"It's your fault," Najah repeatedly said to Febe. "If you'd just gone with me to that party, none of it would have happened."

But there was always going to be another party. When the next one Najah wanted to go to came, Febe felt she had no choice but to tag along. That meant sneaking out and defying the rules Najah's parents had laid out, and the rules they'd been born with, to be modest and obedient and comply. "Don't worry about it," Najah had insisted. "It will be fine."

But Febe was worried, and her anxiety didn't ease when they got to the party, and Najah started making the same mistakes all over again. She accepted hits of pot and flirted back when one of Brady's friends came onto her. Febe yanked on Najah's arm, pulling her away from the party's action. "Are you crazy? Don't let them mess with you like that!"

"I'll do what I want," Najah replied; she was already clearly out of it. "I came here to have a good time. It's not my problem that you're no fun."

Febe wanted to leave the party, but she stayed so she could keep an eye on Najah. That was her worst mistake. If only she'd insisted that they leave, if only she'd dragged Najah out of there and home to safety, where they could have watched a movie or even just gone to bed, then the rest of it wouldn't have happened. But she didn't drag Najah home, so they were still there an hour later when the police busted the party because neighbors had complained about the noise and suspected underage drinking and drug use.

When the police barged in, Febe had been sitting with a group of kids she knew from band, and they were immersed in a cloud of pot smoke. Febe pretended to take a hit but didn't inhale, praying for forgiveness as she did; she just didn't want to stick out so blatantly. But try explaining that to the police. Try explaining that to Najah's parents who believed Najah when she told them that going to the party had been Febe's idea, that Febe was the bad influence, that it was all Febe's fault.

"We just don't think this is working out," Najah's parents told Febe two days later, sounding regretful and unable to look her in the eye. "Najah hasn't been the same lately, and we need to give her our undivided attention and help her. Do you have somewhere else you can go?"

Febe lied and said she could stay with another friend, but really, she googled "Minneapolis Teen Shelter" and found the one nearest school, hoping the people who ran it wouldn't ask too many questions once she arrived. They gave her a bed, meals, and bus tokens but required her to partake in group activities and counseling sessions, and they also required her to contact her aunt and uncle. "We warned you," her uncle said. "Now you are in trouble, but you must find your way out."

The people who ran the shelter agreed to let her stay for a while. The adults were nice and well meaning, but they knew little about what went on when they weren't in the room, at night when the lights were out. Other kids who stayed there had all been through a lot, and they weren't about to let some new girl take over. Not that Febe wanted to take over. She just wanted to stay out of the way and keep her head down. But that wasn't possible.

They called her terrible names. They blamed her and her family for 9/11. They messed with her stuff, stealing her books and homework just to be mean. That was the girls. The boys were nicer, or they pretended to be. One boy, Karl, always had his eyes on her, always wanted her to sit with him at meals, always seemed to be right behind Febe wherever she went. At first, it was okay; at least he was friendly. But then it became overbearing, and she couldn't get rid of him. If she tried to keep away, he'd accuse her of being a stuck-up bitch.

And that's how it happened. She had been trying to avoid him, and she didn't go downstairs one evening for game night, claiming she had to study, which was the truth. But Karl found her alone in the room she shared with three other girls and forced himself on her just the way she had described in that piece she wrote about the girl at the party and Brady Burns. He grabbed at her breasts, he smacked her bottom, he ripped at her hijab and sucked her neck.

He would have gone further, except Febe managed to simultaneously bite his hand and knee him in the balls. He pulled away, his rage more vivid and concrete than any of the mundane details of the room, like the hospital green walls or the brown shag carpet. "You'll pay for that," he charged, holding up his bloody palm. "I have physical proof you attacked me."

On one level, Febe knew they would question him. If he accused Febe of attacking him, then they'd have to wonder what he'd done to spur her on. Still, she didn't even know what it was like to be given the benefit of the doubt, and if Karl told the adults at the shelter that she was some rabid man-hating terrorist who bites people for fun, they probably would believe him. So, she took off. Febe didn't want to ever see Karl's face again, nor did she want to get blamed for violence that was simply self-defense.

"So, you see, Ms. Ford, everything I wrote was true. It all really happened. Only the details have been changed, but the details aren't what's important."

CHAPTER 51

"Let me get this straight," I say to Febe. "You wrote that piece about Najah and Brady Burns as if it was you and this Karl guy?"

"Yes," Febe states with a simple strength, yet she won't look at me.

"But what happened between you and Karl . . ." I sigh, trying to find the strength to say the words. "Karl tried to rape you, right?" Febe nods yes. "But Brady only grabbed at Najah, right? He didn't go as far with Najah as Karl did with you."

"*So?*" Febe sits up straight, tilting her chin and raising her voice. "It's still terrible. Brady Burns is still an asshole, and he deserves what's coming to him."

"I'm not saying that he doesn't. But there are distinctions here. You can't just say that details don't matter and expect the world to agree."

She hangs her head, and I go cold and hot at once, a peculiar mix of regret and anger washing over me.

"Febe, I'm sorry. I should have started by saying how awful it is that all this happened to you. It's not fair, and you've had to be so strong, and I'm going to try and make things right for you, okay? More than anything, I want you to feel safe."

She sniffs back tears, vulnerability seeping out of her in waves. I've never seen this side of her before. "Hey." I keep my voice soft, trying to be soothing. "Since you left the shelter, where have you been staying?"

"At this hotel on Central Avenue. My friend Salma—she graduated last year—her family owns it. Whenever I can, I clean rooms for free. In return, Salma lets me sleep in a vacant room if they have one. Most nights, I have a place to stay. In the afternoons, I usually go to the library, or sometimes the McDonalds, if I have enough money to buy food."

"What if you don't have enough money for food?"

She shrugs. "I brave the cafeteria and eat at school."

"And if there isn't a vacant room at Salma's family's hotel? Where do you sleep? And where do you keep your stuff?"

Febe shakes her head. "I keep my stuff, like my hijabs and toiletries, in my locker at school. As for the rest, you don't want to know, Ms. Ford. I mean I could tell you, but it will sound bad, worse than it really is."

My heart breaks a little. Febe is trying to protect me from her truth. Still, there is more I need to know.

"Okay," I tell her, "you don't have to tell me. But I need to know . . . *Why* did you do it? Why did you write that article and invite even more trouble? I don't get it."

Febe rubs her eyes and answers in a choked voice. "I wanted to make people uncomfortable. Everybody goes about their day assuming they won't be challenged or that they won't have to believe something they don't want to believe, and I'm sick of it. People worship Brady like he's this god, and meanwhile, nobody cares when girls are attacked, especially if the girls aren't white and if they don't make a fuss. It's bullshit, Ms. Ford; all of it is. And if that's how it's going to be, at least I can benefit and cause a stir. I can say, 'Yeah, I published this magazine. I edited it. And look how big it became', and then maybe I'll get a scholarship so I can escape the situation I'm in." She shrugs defeatedly. "I figured it was worth a shot."

"Except, you've been vilified at school and bullied to where you can't go down to the cafeteria, and you miss your only meal of the day. And now, even teachers believe you are lying, so how do you think you'll get any of them to write you recommendation letters so you can get a scholarship?"

"Ms. Ford, you're only making me feel worse!"

"That's not my goal. But you to understand what must be done."

Febe gives me a sideways glance, sucking on her bottom lip. "Oh yeah? What's that?"

"We need to publish a new edition of *Burnt Moon* where you come clean and tell the same story you just told me. And you need to attach your name to it."

"No!" Febe's eyes widen with panic. "I can't do that. Najah would never forgive me."

"Najah is not your friend, Febe. And with the way she's been treating you, I'm surprised you care about her forgiveness."

"It's not just her. If I tell that story, everyone will hate me. I won't be able to show my face at school ever again."

I pause, rubbing my face, wishing tears weren't so close to the surface. Truth is, I have no answers for Febe or any idea how to help her. I can't even fix my own life; how can I possibly fix hers?

"Febe . . ." I begin. "I understand, or at least I think I do. And I'll tell you something. It's a secret, okay?"

She nods, her eyes wide and solemn.

"I've started seeing a therapist because I can't remember what happened, not just with the accident, but before, with my relationship with Mr. Valby. And it's causing me literal physical pain. I have to deal with the truth, or else the headaches I'm experiencing will only get worse, and I'll pass out more often."

"I'm sorry, Ms. Ford."

I wave my hand dismissively. "No, no. Don't feel sorry. I'm only telling you this so you'll understand why I want you to write your story. My therapist told me to write something to help me remember so I can deal with what happened. I think that's what you need to do as well."

Febe swallows hard, the color draining from her face. I study her. "What is it?" I ask. "Is there something else you're not telling me?" Like about the MySpace page? I silently will her to come clean without me having to press her. That would be too much all at once.

"No," she murmurs.

"Alright," I say, letting it go for now. "How about this? Write the story, the *real* story of what happened to you, as if it's going to be published in *Burnt Moon*. But we won't publish it until you're ready."

"And if I'm never ready?"

I push out a heavy exhale. "I don't know," I tell her. "Let's just focus on writing it first."

Febe and I get to work right away, and I lose track of time, helping her commit her story to the page. Hours go by before I think to check my cell phone, which I'd set on vibrate earlier so I could give Febe my undivided attention. Turns out I have six texts. One is from Anton, the union rep, demanding that I contact him ASAP. One is from Cyrus, checking in to say hi and to see how I'm doing. The other four are from Olivia.

Are you crazy? Can't believe the stunt you pulled today. Call me!

That was sent at four-thirty. The next text came through at six-fifteen. *Hazy, I truly believe today was a cry for help. We need to talk!*

Then, at six forty-five, she sent this: *Avoiding me will not work.*

A little before eight, she calls me but doesn't leave a voicemail. Moments later, she sends this text: *I'm seriously worried. On my way over to your house.*

I look at the clock. It's eight twenty-two. "Crap!" I yell, rushing around, locking the doors, and turning off the lights.

Febe looks up from my laptop, which she'd been using to work on her story. "What's wrong?"

"Olivia—I mean Ms. Davis is on her way over to check up on me. She can't come in and find you. I'd never hear the end of it."

"Okay, so what's the plan? Are you trying to make her think you've gone to bed?"

"I guess."

"Wouldn't you leave a light on downstairs? Isn't that what people do to deter burglars?"

"I suppose."

Febe stands, closing the laptop and hugging it to her chest. She flips on the kitchen light and then heads toward my stairs. "Come on, Ms. Ford. Hurry before she gets here!"

We make it up to my bedroom and sit on the floor, and it feels exactly like doing an active shooter drill at school— we're in the dark, out of sight, waiting for someone to come bang on the door.

"Wow," Febe whispers. "I thought girlfriend drama went away once you're an adult. Guess I was wrong."

"Trust me; it never goes away." I laugh. "Sorry to put you through this, though."

"No worries."

We hear an engine running outside of my house, and then it turns off. A car door slams. Febe creeps over to the window and peers outside, keeping most of herself hidden. "I think it's her, Ms. Ford!"

After a second or two, I hear the lock turn, and the door opens, only to get caught on the security chain. Thank God I'd thought to put it in place. But Olivia is undeterred. There's more banging on my door. "Hazy! You've got to be home. You need to let me in."

I sigh. "God, I wish she'd leave me alone."

"Why don't you tell her that?"

"It's complicated. She took care of me after the accident. I owe her a lot, and I don't want to hurt her feelings. She's my friend."

Olivia's banging gets louder, and so does her voice, imploring me to answer the door.

"Ms. Ford, remember what you said earlier tonight, that Najah isn't really my friend?"

"This is different, Febe."

"Okay. But it's bad, Ms. Ford. Don't get angry, okay? It's just . . . That picture that was posted on MySpace? The one of Mr. Valby in his classroom having, you know . . .?"

I stare at Febe. She and I have been whispering, and the silence after her words is smothering. "What are you saying?"

Febe takes a deep breath, and on her exhale comes her breathy, frenzied confession. "She was supposed to be your friend, Ms. Ford. And I saw the way Mr. Valby was treating you. Then, when I needed to ask him a question about the digital camera I'd checked out, I accidentally walked in on them having sex in his classroom. It was like, *ick*, but I was also furious, and I didn't think. I just snapped a picture, and I planned a way to get them both to treat you better."

My heart goes cold like an icy anchor has dropped to the bottom of my chest. Vance and Olivia? No. I can't think about that now; I can only respond to the other part of what Febe just said. "Seriously? It *was* you who posted that photo?"

"No! I didn't post it. I just used a fake account, and I emailed it to Ms. Davis and Mr. Valby to scare them, you know?" Febe gives a dejected nod. "Please don't tell anyone. And I'm sorry if it hurt you in any way. I hope you'll believe me, though, that I was trying to help."

"Hazy!" Olivia booms from downstairs, outside my front door. "If you don't let me in, I'm calling the police. I need to know that you're okay."

"Dammit," I mutter, standing up. "She'd do it, too. Stay up here, Febe. I won't let her upstairs, but if she finds out you're here, we could both be in big trouble."

"Okay. But don't let her know you know!" Febe whispers loudly.

I respond by pretending to zip my lips shut, and then I make my way downstairs to open the door and let Olivia in.

CHAPTER 52

"Hazy, thank God! Are you okay? I was worried about you." Olivia seems a little dazed after all her frenzied knocking. She peers around my living room like she can't quite find her bearings.

"What did you think, Olivia? That I'd hurt myself? That's not my style."

"I know, but you haven't been yourself lately, what with passing out at school and your angry outbursts and unstable behavior."

I keep my response brief and emotionless. "I'm fine, except I'm exhausted. Let's talk tomorrow. I want to go back to bed."

Olivia puts her hands on her hips. "I came all the way over here. Let's talk now."

"I didn't ask you to come over."

"Maybe not directly, but your behavior lately has been a cry for help."

"Not to you!"

"Excuse me?" Olivia narrows her eyes. "I am your best friend, and I'm the only one who understands what you're going through. Didn't you say you'd stop taking me for granted?"

I sigh and rub my forehead. "I know. But I just want to go back to bed."

"Okay." She feigns patience like she's speaking to an unruly child. "But first, tell me two things. One, why didn't you change into your pajamas before 'going to bed'? Is it because you were actually still up when I got here?"

"Good God, Olivia. I put my clothes back on when you started banging on my door. That's why it took me a minute to answer."

"Right." She narrows her eyes and looks past me, a few feet away. I follow her gaze, turning around to spot Febe's backpack sitting innocently on my living room floor. "So, the second thing is, when did you get a new backpack?"

I huff out my response. "What difference does it make?"

Olivia raises an eyebrow. "It doesn't. It's just that with that patch of some Persian emblem sewn on the front pocket, it looks like Febe's backpack."

It's actually a patch of the University of Tehran's coat of arms. I'd once asked Febe what the lettering meant. She'd said, "It's their motto, Ms. Ford. *Rest not a moment from learning.*" But I just shrug, nonplussed and determined to betray nothing. At that moment, Baby Girl saunters into the room, rubs against my legs, and, surely sensing that our focus is on the backpack, goes over and starts sniffing it.

"Huh." Olivia crosses her arms over her chest. "I'd be careful, Hazy. It's awful when bad things happen to someone you care about."

My anger boils over. "Is that a threat?"

"I'm talking about Baby Girl sniffing that backpack. Who knows where it's been and what might be inside it! Vance would be horrified that you're putting her at risk."

"That's it! Give me back my house key and get out!"

Olivia squints at me and lowers her voice. "You're making a big mistake, Hazy. You've aligned yourself with the wrong people."

"Seriously? Jeez, Olivia, why do you have to make it sound like we're at war?"

Her face reddens. "Because sometimes, we *are* war. Don't you get that?"

"No. No, I don't, and I don't understand what you want from me."

"I want us to be on the same side!" Olivia throws out her hands, gesturing wildly. "I want you to trust me and rely on me how you used to! Why is that so hard?" She shakes her head. "I don't even recognize you lately. And if Vance were here, he wouldn't recognize you, either."

"Yeah, but Vance left. The bastard took off while I was in the hospital, and I hope I never see him again."

Olivia's eyes instantly fill with tears. "How can you be so cold? Aren't you worried about him?"

My entire body twitches, like it desperately wants to lunge toward Olivia and shake her until her teeth rattle. "*I'm* being cold? *I* should worry about *him*? He *abandoned* me!"

Olivia puts her hands on her hips and plants both feet firmly against my hardwood floor. "Get a grip, Hazy! Vance was hurt in the accident, too! He's staying with his parents so they can care for him! He isn't answering you because he's strung out on painkillers!"

"What?" Olivia's words echo in my ears, giving me a sense of vertigo. "No. That's not right. He said in an email that he was fine. You said he was fine."

"No. I said he was okay, that he didn't have any life-threatening injuries, and he doesn't. But his face was burned and scarred, and his nose was shattered. He needed two separate plastic surgeries, and he'll still never look how he used to."

I back up, knowing my legs are about to give, and collapse onto my couch. "Why didn't you tell me?"

"He didn't want you to know or to see him like that. He felt vulnerable. You broke up with him, after all."

"What? Do you mean at the Christmas party, right before the accident? Because you know I don't remember–"

"God, Hazy, you really are a mess. I'm not talking about that. You'd broken up with him two weeks before. Totally out of the blue, breaking his heart for no reason when he'd just been trying to make you happy. You never deserved him, you know."

I stare at my hands, suddenly remembering.

CHAPTER 53

"I think you should come for Christmas this year."

We were in our living room when Vance dropped that statement on me like a casual bomb, without warning, and with some effort, I hid the detonation inside me and remained calm. Sure, I had been waiting two years for such an invitation, but now that it had finally come, I couldn't believe its authenticity.

"Really?" My voice sounded squeaky to my own ears, so I attempted to speak in a lower register. "Have you mentioned it yet to your mom?"

"No, but she'll be fine with it." He stretched, his shirt riding up and revealing a fuzzy patch of belly that bordered on his crotch area. It was another Sunday, a week after we'd agreed to do cross-curriculum projects on the American Dream. Vance and I had spent the morning lounging around, and now I was settled on the couch with a stack of essays to grade while Vance gathered his paints and supplies for some "studio time."

Okay. He hadn't cleared inviting me with his mother. "Great," I said, "but I won't consider my invitation official until after you've talked to her."

"She's not the boss of me," Vance stated. "If I want you to come, then you're coming."

I laughed, unconcerned if I sounded sour. "Oh, come on, Vance. Why can't you admit that you're scared of her?"

"Because I'm not scared of her!" Vance's nostrils flared. "And I resent the accusation."

I sighed. Vance's relationship with his mother was a sore subject, one that I didn't like to poke at too much. I knew Vance worried he'd disappointed her by becoming a teacher rather than pursuing a more glamorous career as an independent artist. And while he never said so, I figured his relationship with me only compounded his insecurities; everyone in his family was sophisticated and gifted and there I was, an average Kansas girl who bored them.

"I'm sorry, Vance. But you admit your mom is a control freak. I just think you should talk to her first. She might not want someone as ordinary as me sitting at her table."

"Come on, Hazel. That's not fair. And you know you're not ordinary."

"Yes, I know that. But do you? Does your mom?"

Vance shrugged. "We can't all be extraordinary, Hazel, and we can't all be gifted. If we were, then 'gifted' wouldn't even be a thing. But you have lots of good qualities, and I know my mom will accept you coming for Christmas."

The smile he tossed was one he kept in his arsenal, meant to cajole and charm. It showed a hint of his gleaming white teeth, and his eyes crinkled at the corners, almost like he was winking. Then he started off as if the subject were settled.

And maybe it should have been settled. It was only last year that I'd been so angry over summer plans that I'd dumped an entire pot of soup into the sink. I should have been thrilled that he wanted me to come for Christmas, except I wasn't. Suddenly, all my festering resentment toward Vance threatened to overpower me.

I stood from the couch and followed him down to our three-season porch where Vance set up his easel, some paints, and a space heater.

"Wait a sec," I said, and Vance turned around in surprise. He hadn't realized, until then, that I'd followed him out to the porch. "I just want to make sure I'm clear on this." Taking a deep breath, I count off on my fingers. "I don't even know how we got onto the subject of being gifted, but since we are, let's delve deep. You're obviously gifted. Your mother is gifted. Your father, again, obviously gifted. Same for your sister." By then, I was holding up four fingers, with only my thumb still folded against my palm. But I raised it up and curled the rest of my fingers into my palm. "Me? Not so much." And I made a broad sweeping thumbs-down gesture to punctuate my statement.

"You're missing my point," Vance countered, somewhat peeved.

"No, I get your point. You're saying your mom and the rest of your family will 'accept' me because I bring something else to the table. I'm steady, right? I ground you. I make you a better man."

"Yeah. So? What's wrong with that?"

I sighed, and the truth hit me not hard and painfully but like a seeping fevered chill, one that left me tired and resigned. "I can't live my life feeling like everything that's good about me is really something that's good about you. It's like that at work, and at home, and . . ." I took a deep inhale. "It just can't always be about you, Vance."

Vance let his mouth drop open, shocked. "I don't know what to say to that."

It was such a terrible, weak, safe response. I took stock, letting my eyes roam up and down Vance. I took in his beauty, which now seemed like a form of anemia, making him forever vulnerable to self-importance. The unfortunate truth reverberated in my mind, demanding to be heard: Vance was incapable of being the man I needed him to be. "Okay," I said calmly. "How about you admit the truth? We were never meant to last, were we?"

"I don't know."

"Well, I do." I stared at the easel Vance had set up so I didn't have to look at him. "I think you should move out."

"What?"

I kept my voice steady. "I get that during the holidays it might be hard to find a place, so you can take your time. But you should start looking."

"You've gone crazy."

"No. Perhaps I was crazy, believing that one day you'd be as into me as I've always been into you. I let you play me for two and a half years, Vance. Now, I'm finally going sane."

He shook his head. "You'll change your mind. I know you will. Whatever I did wrong, I can fix it, okay?"

I suppose it was sweet that he was trying, however lackadaisically, to save our relationship, nevertheless, I suspected he was more upset about losing his address than he was about losing me.

"I won't," I replied. "You can stay on the couch until you figure out where you'll go. But I mean it, Vance. We're done."

He gasped. "What about Baby Girl?"

"She stays here, in the only home she knows."

Vance's response comes out in a growl. "We'll see about that."

Then, he turned his back to me. I let him walk away.

CHAPTER 54

I feel Olivia's eyes staring into mine, and I'm sure my revelations broadcast clearly across my face.

"What do you want from me, Olivia?"

I ask her this, yet I already know, and I also know she won't give me an honest answer. She wants to make sure I won't reveal that it was her in that photograph. She wants me to give up whatever hold I might have on Vance so she can have him for herself. She wants to keep me under her thumb so I can't hurt her with what I may or may not know.

Olivia sighs. "I want you to not destroy your life in the process of 'figuring things out'."

"I'm not."

"You are! Lately, you're like a suicide bomber, charging forward and not caring about the wreckage you've left behind."

"I think that's a little hyperbolic."

Olivia wrinkles her brow. "I teach math, remember? Spare me the ACT vocab words."

"You're being overly dramatic."

"Then why couldn't you just say that?"

My head hurts, and I press my palm to my forehead. "Olivia, it's time for you to go." I walk to my door, open it, and turn to her. "Good night."

She rolls her eyes and lets out a huff. "Fine, I'll go, but this isn't over. And I'm not giving you back your key."

"I realize that." I also realize it might be easier to get my lock changed than to have her fork my key over.

Olivia heads out, and I sigh in relief as she gets into her car and drives away. I bolt my door and turn off the porch light. Then, I climb upstairs and find Febe.

"Wow," Febe says. "She's vicious. I can't believe what she said about Baby Girl and my backpack."

"You were eavesdropping?"

"It was impossible not to! You were both yelling at each other."

"Right." I flop down on my bed. Febe had been sitting cross-legged on the floor. She rises and sits next to me on the edge of the bed like she's unsure if she's allowed to do such a thing. I look at her. "So, you must have heard that she suspects you're here. I have no idea if she'll tell on us."

"Oh, I bet she will. Are you sure I should stay?"

"Completely." I smile and pat her knee. "You can stay for as long as you want. But I really am exhausted. Can we work more on your story tomorrow night?"

"Of course." Febe rises. "I'll just head back to your guest room. Do you know if there's a bus stop nearby so I can get to school tomorrow?"

"I'll give you a ride."

"No, Ms. Ford. It's too risky."

"I'll drop you off several feet away before we're actually on school grounds. It will be fine."

"Are you sure?"

"Yes."

"Okay." She moves like she's heading out but then turns. "Thank you, Ms. Ford, for everything."

"You're welcome."

"Umm, so . . . are you mad at me about the photo?"

Febe stands, hovering in the doorframe, looking tiny, except for her saucer-like eyes, which are pooled with anxiety.

"No, of course not. I'm still on your side."

"Then, you believe I didn't post that MySpace page?"

I do. Right now, I trust Febe more than I trust anyone. "Yes."

I almost add that she helped me remember what it's like to live for someone other than myself and that witnessing her strength and hearing her story reminds me of how little I really know about struggle. But if I tried to express all that, I'd probably mess it up.

Sometimes, it's better to keep things simple.

CHAPTER 55

It was Vance's birthday, and she wanted to make it special. She texted him, telling him to meet her at 4:00 p.m. at "their bar," a little place about fifteen minutes from school but in the opposite direction of where most people would go.

She got there first and ordered a margarita. Normally she didn't partake in happy hour until Friday, but Vance's birthday was cause for celebration. Sitting in the darkened bar, she sipped her drink and sucked on the salt crystals that landed on her tongue. The more she thought about it, the more convinced she became that she was doing the right thing, that she was about to do the right thing.

Just when she began to wonder if Vance stood her up, he walked in, all smoldering energy and sex appeal. Why did just looking at him still make her feel this way after everything that happened between the two of them?

"Hey, *you*." He said it softly, sweetly, with an emphasis on *you*, like he'd been waiting a long time to meet her eyes, like she was the one who mattered to him, above everyone else. And she knew she was reading too much into such a simple greeting, yet her heart fluttered and she felt that gravitational pull toward him.

"Hi," she responded. "Happy birthday. What do you want to drink?"

"A Guinness."

"Ick. Okay." She'd never understood the appeal of that dark, dense beer, but whatever. He'll drink it, not her. That day was long past when his likes affected hers so drastically. "I'll get it for you. Sit and relax; you're the birthday boy, after all!" She got up, went to the bar, and ordered it for him. It wasn't busy, so she got quick service and returned moments later with his black hole of a beverage. "Here you go, sir."

He laughed at being called "sir," which she threw out there because it was like she was waiting on him, but maybe he thought she was going for some subservient dynamic? Hopefully not, because that was the opposite of what was about to happen.

The candlelight showed her his eyes, and they were smiling at her. She smiled back and felt herself relax into the scene before her, knowing that it would all go down as she had planned and wanting every step to be as romantic as possible. Why had she ever thought that he was like other men? Gazing at him made it all make sense.

She hated to mention it, but she had to. "I think we're out of the woods with that photo. Whoever took it would have done something by now if they were going to."

Vance sipped his beer, and a thin layer of foam lingered on his scruffy upper lip. He avoided her stare, as if doing so could make the awkward silence go away. "I hope you're right," he said.

She wished for something else to talk about, something that wouldn't force them to face the reality of the photo situation. She wanted to ease the tension in the air.

"Hey," she started hesitantly, "tell me about that cloud painting you've been working on."

They chitchatted for a few minutes and some of the tension slipped away, though it was there in the air between them like a nagging reminder of what had yet to be discussed.

"So," she finally said, "I've been thinking about you and me."

He raised an eyebrow and smiled slightly. "Oh yeah?"

"Yes, and I've made some decisions." She took a deep breath and prepared herself.

Vance leaned in slightly and his smirk-like grin turned into anticipation. "Tell me more."

"I've decided we should leave Dixon Heights together. Let's go somewhere new and start all over." She could feel her heart beating faster as she continued, "It would be great for both of us—no family or friends meddling, no judgmental attitudes hanging over us—just me and you, together, like we should be."

"Yeah," Vance responded tonelessly, his frown deepening. He sat there, rooted to his chair, and crossed his arms defensively. She watched him, her gaze steady and unyielding. She could almost feel their connection, like a wire stretched so tight that it threatened to snap. He glanced away, a muscle twitching in his jaw as he processed her words.

"The thing is, I like teaching at Dixon Heights, and I like being close to my family. I don't want to leave."

She took a drink from her melting margarita, buying time. This required delicacy, and she adopted her most patient tone. "Vance, you need to face the truth. We could be forced out at any moment, and if that photo gets seen, we're done for. You're used to getting your way, and your sense of entitlement is part of your charm. But I can't put up with it anymore." She took a deep steadying breath. "After a lot of thought, I've decided that I still want you in my life, but there's no way we can stay here. So you have to quit your job and come with me to a new place."

"C'mon; you can't expect me to give up my job and go into the unknown with you!" He laughed, his tone sharp, unpleasant, and super annoying.

"Yes, actually I do expect that, Vance. If you don't come with me, I won't hesitate to get you out of Dixon Heights by any means necessary. Got it?"

"What are you talking about?"

"Do I really have to spell it out for you? Having an affair with your student teacher, someone who is barely legal? That's grounds for firing right there. All I have to do is go to HR and give them the scoop. Whether or not it's true doesn't matter."

He leaned forward and hissed, "I told you nothing happened between Annabelle and me!"

"I don't care if it's true; what matters is what I can make people believe. Vance, let me make this as clear as possible so there's no confusion: quit your job and move out of state with me, or I'll drag your reputation through the mud by making sure everyone knows about you and Annabelle. You decide which option is better for you."

His face twisted in rage. "You're *blackmailing* me?"

She smirked. "Well, you can call it whatever you want. All I care about is the future, and I won't let anyone stand in the way of that."

Horror seemed to wash over his entire body, and he spoke through gritted teeth. "I won't let you do this, Olivia. It's twisted, and wrong, and I swear to God you won't get away with it."

She leaned in close, eyes sparkling. "You sure you want to take that risk?"

He didn't respond, and his heavy silence was enough for her.

She went home, placed her laptop on top of the Formica table that Vance so generously helped her move into her apartment, and got to work. Olivia knew enough about photoshop to make the picture of her and Vance look like one of him and Annabelle. They both had long dark hair, so all she really needed to do was darken her skin since her face was hidden. Getting into the MySpace account Vance created for school was too easy since he used the same password for everything, the idiot. And shame on Hazel for thinking she's just a simple uncreative math teacher because the anarchist rhetoric that Olivia spewed about the "American Dream" was pure gold.

Satisfied, she posted it and then settled on her couch to watch a scary movie.

CHAPTER 56

The weekend comes, and when Cyrus suggests we get together, I agree because I already miss him. However, for his sake more than mine, I plan to put things on pause. I suggest that we meet at a restaurant. He can choose the place, and once we're there, I'll explain that, while my feelings for him are graphene-level strong, I need to step back so I can figure things out. I don't want to be a total basket case while starting a new relationship.

Cyrus chooses a Thai restaurant known for their bright red décor and amazingly delicious spicy shrimp soup.

"Just one taste, and it's like you're in paradise," he promises.

It's only been a few days since I've seen Cyrus, but it seems longer. I suck in a deep breath, wishing it was easier to play it cool.

"How have you been?" I ask, sitting across from him at the small table he's already nabbed for us. We're in the front room of the restaurant, closer to the outside door. There's another room behind me, and I sit with my back to it.

He laughs. "You ask that like it's been forever since we've seen each other."

"I know. It's only been a couple of days, but so much has happened. It feels longer."

We order the shrimp soup, fried spring rolls, and cocktails, and Cyrus tells me all about what went down at school this last week, like the fallout of the protests and all the different factions who are at odds with each other. "That one piece in *Burnt Moon* has really opened a can of worms," Cyrus says. "Did you ever talk to Febe about it? I'd love to know her side of the story."

"Yeah." I sip from my soup, stalling for time so I can form my response. "Actually, I've talked to Febe several times. We're in close contact."

Cyrus raises an eyebrow. "Really? I can't believe you didn't lead with that. Tell me everything."

I shake my head and reach across the table for his hand. "Here's the thing—and you'll probably be mad—but I can't tell you about what's going on with Febe. And for your own good, we should maybe take a break for a little while. I'm fine jeopardizing my own career, but I don't want to jeopardize yours too."

"What?" He frowns. "Come on, Hazel. We've had this conversation already, like several times. You keep warning me against you, and I keep telling you it's fine. And it is. I want to spend time with you." He brings my hand to his mouth and kisses my fingertips. "I don't care about the risk."

I could melt into him if I let myself. Sighing, I offer him a sad smile. "But I care about the risk, because, honestly, I'm crazy about you."

I sense a presence above me, so I look up and a jolt of electricity surges through my veins. There stands Vance, his face distorted with nearly graphic scarring, his nose swollen and flat, his jaw tight with anger. His parents stand behind him.

"Vance," I whisper in shock. His eyes blaze with hot fury as he steps closer to me. Cyrus drops my hand as we both sit up straight in our chairs. "What are you doing here?" I ask, my voice tight.

"My dad has an opening at a gallery in Northeast," he replies gruffly. "They told me it would be good for me to get out."

"Oh," I reply helplessly.

Cyrus looks like he wants to run, but he takes control of the moment and speaks to Vance's parents first. "Hello! Patricia, it's good to see you again. Do you like Thai food? Isn't this place amazing?" He turns to Daniel, Vance's father. "I don't believe we've met. I'm Cyrus."

"He's Vance's replacement at Dixon Heights," Patricia says to her husband. "Cyrus helped me pack the stuff Vance left behind in his classroom."

Vance barks out a laugh. "And now, here we are." He talks to Cyrus. "Clearly, you're still lapping up my sloppy seconds."

Cyrus tugs on his collar as if it's choking him, his lips pressed tight, his nostrils flared. Is this what a superhero looks like when he's about to transform from a regular guy to something angry and powerful?

I stand abruptly, and my chair scrapes loudly against the floor. "You all were on your way out? I'll walk you to your car."

"That's okay," says Vance.

"No, no, I insist." I turn to Cyrus. "I'll be right back." My cheeks are burning, but the heat doesn't isolate itself to my face. My body temperature has spiked, and it's like I'm on fire from the inside.

"Please don't, Hazel. You've already done enough." Patricia glares at me but looks at Cyrus before she speaks, directing her words to him. "Have a good evening," she says. They all stride off through the restaurant and out the door.

My mouth drops open, and it takes me a moment to become unparalyzed and rush out the door. They are half-way down the block by the time I get out there, probably going toward their car.

"Wait!" I shout, taking off after Vance. His parents continue walking, not looking back. I catch up to him and almost stumble in my haste. "I'm sorry," I gasp. "I know it looks like I'm replacing you too fast and that I'm just trying to fill the gap you left, but it's not that simple."

Vance raises an eyebrow. "Explain then, Hazel."

"No one told me about the accident. You said you were fine but . . . I was still recovering, too. And all those emails I sent you that you barely answered . . ." my voice trails off as I remember the loneliness of being ignored.

"We were already broken up by then, Hazel! What did you want me to do? Respond and keep things going?" He scowls, his eyes darkening at the memory.

A chill wind whips past us, reminding me that I rushed out without my coat. I wrap my arms around myself and continue. "Vance, we don't have to rehash this now, but you were cheating on me with Olivia. And yeah, I made mistakes, too, but you made more. At least now you can be honest with me about it all. You owe me that much."

He looks away, and I can't tell if it's the cold that's making him sniff or if he's sniffing back tears. "I loved you in my way, you know. And now everything is ruined. My career, my relationship with you, my appearance . . ."

I place a gentle hand on his shoulder. "It's not so bad," I say. "I bet after your face heals, you'll look almost the same, just more rugged. And your eyes and your mouth . . . I mean come on. You'll always be gorgeous."

His lips quiver, any attempt at a smile quickly fading away. "I'm sorry for everything, Hazel," he says softly.

"Me too," I reply, my arms crossed tightly over my chest as I shake slightly from the cold.

Vance looks like he's about to offer me his coat but thinks better of it. "Look, you're right. We can talk about all this later when we've both had a chance to recover. But there was something I wanted to talk to you about, and I've been putting off saying anything because it's just so difficult."

"Baby Girl? Because she's staying with me, Vance."

"No, I know. But I get visiting rights."

I hug myself, shaking now from the cold and uncertainty of the situation. "Okay then, what is it?"

Vance sighs and speaks slowly. "You said you don't remember what happened surrounding the accident—"

Guilt surges through me, and I cut him off. "Was it all my fault? You can tell me if it was. I can handle it."

His face twists in surprise. "No, of course it wasn't your fault."

"Really?"

His mouth opens, seemingly unsure of what it will say next. "Hazel, come on. Look, you clearly know about Olivia and me . . ."

My heart races at his words. "Yes," I reply.

He continues, unable to meet my eyes. "Olivia isn't someone who is easy to say no to. I want you to be careful around her, Hazel. She was the one who posted that MySpace page; she had access to the photo and she was trying to hurt me by doing that. Who knows what else she might do if she decides she wants to hurt you?"

It's hard to make sense of what he's saying, and my mind flails. "Wait. Why would she want to hurt me? You and I have already broken up, so why would she care?

Does it have something to do with Jim? Is it because I might tell him it was her in the photo?"

Vance nods his head slowly, his lips pressing into a tight line of worry. "Maybe, yes, but there's more than that . . . She's scared you might remember the accident, scared that you'll remember it was her who caused it in the first place."

The truth hits me like a freight train: Olivia caused the accident. How could I have been so blind? Then again, she was gaslighting me while I had a brain injury, so maybe I shouldn't be too hard on myself. But I wish I had trusted my gut that something wasn't right. Now, all I want is to say goodbye to Vance and put this entire nightmare behind me.

I need to go home.

The rest of my conversation with Vance feels jumbled, with a stiff goodbye as his parents watch us from their parked car, probably within earshot. Woodenly, I make my way back into the restaurant. "Are you alright?" Cyrus asks when I approach the table.

"I have to go," I answer.

"No, Hazel, please stay. Whatever you and Vance talked about, you can tell me."

"I'm so sorry, Cyrus." Taking my coat from the back of my chair, I put it on, and pick up my purse, putting the strap around my shoulder. I'm swallowing back tears. "What I was saying before, about taking some space, I mean it. If you're smart, you'll stay away from me."

Before he can protest, I rush off, praying he doesn't follow and feeling both sad and relieved when he doesn't.

CHAPTER 57

I must look deathly pale when I walk in after getting back from dinner because Febe clasps my wrist like she's checking to see that I still have a pulse. "Are you okay, Ms. Ford?" She leads me over to the couch.

I nod slowly. It's all I can do as my thoughts and my heart both race. I press my thumbs against my temples as if that could slow the train wreck inside my mind. "First of all, we're way past you calling me Ms. Ford. To you, I'm Hazel. Okay?"

"Okay," she whispers.

"And second, I want you to know that I trust what you say more than anyone else. For whatever reason, you're the person most likely to tell me the truth, like when you told me that Vance—I mean Mr. Valby—and I were broken up. Nobody else had the guts to say it to me. And nobody but you are brave enough to talk about Vance and Olivia—I mean Mr. Valby and Ms. Davis." I yell up at the ceiling, beyond frustrated, "Oh, goddamit!"

"What?" she responds, clearly scared.

"Nothing. I can't talk about such personal stuff using their surnames. It's just too weird and more difficult than getting through a Russian novel. We're going by first names for all teachers, okay?"

"Sure."

I breathe in. "I'm sorry to put you in this position, Febe. Truly, I am. But I need you to go to Principal Thomas and tell him about the photo you took. I think our safety is at stake if you don't."

"Okay."

"Really?"

She nods. "Yeah. I mean I sort of figured you'd say that." There's a pause. "Hey, guess what? I finished my confession."

I sit up. "Seriously? That was quick."

She shrugs. "It wasn't hard once I got going."

"I want to read it."

Febe hesitates, scowling.

"Come on; please?"

"Fine." She reaches for my laptop, calls up the document she'd been writing, and hands it to me. Then, she stands. "But I can't be in the same room while you're reading it."

"Okay."

Febe walks off, and I brace myself for a truth more brutal than what I've already been given tonight.

CHAPTER 58

What Really Happened
By Febe Rashidi

For weeks after it happened, my stomach would ache in random cutting stretches as though my body was scolding me, saying that I did not deserve to feel well. On one level, I knew the attack was not my fault. But I also knew the world would not agree. Many people would think I'd been too immodest, that I'd invited his attention to reassure myself I was an object of desire.

Others would say that, by wearing my hijab, I'd placed a target on my head, that I was marginalizing myself and buying into some messed-up idea about patriarchy and culture; my headscarf screamed, "Yes, I am already a victim! So please, attack me some more."

Neither version was the truth. I wear my hijab because I like it. To me, it seems as if Western women are often only valued for their appearance, as sex objects, or to sell a product or an idea or a lifestyle. They don't even realize it, but it's true! Daisy Buchanan from *The Great Gatsby* nails it when, speaking about her daughter, she says, "I hope she'll be a fool—that's the best thing a girl can be in this world, a beautiful little fool." Daisy herself is no fool, but she acts like one because she understands that, in her society, women aren't valued for their intelligence, so she decides it's best to be a fool if you're going to be treated like one because, that way, you won't miss the respect you're not getting.

But I didn't want to follow Daisy's plan. I wanted my own plan, one of discipline, devotion—one that would help people see me and respect me for who I am. It has not been an easy plan to follow. I've lost friends and made enemies. But throughout it all, I could not look in the mirror without seeing the eyes of my mother gazing back at me; she'd known pain and oppression, and she'd loved me so much that she'd given me up, sending me across oceans to find a better life, where I would have the opportunity and the chance to find my voice. My mother died alone, and I could not hold her hand as she passed, or thank her for her sacrifice, or whisper in her ear that I love her.

So, I've made it my goal to remember her, to live up to her memory, and, above all else, create the life she'd dreamt for me. Yet, I've made so many mistakes, and now, I wonder if it's too late to start over.

After he attacked me, I could only see myself the way he must have seen me. I was an empty vessel, forgettable warm flesh for him to press his crotch into. I was there to grope, to insult, to pull into, and then violently push away. I was a cheap throwaway, a forgettable whore.

I despised the girl he'd created—the girl I was sure I'd become. *You are that girl,* my stomach would tell me with its every rugged throb. I couldn't eat. I could rarely sleep. And I didn't think I deserved kindness or help. I didn't want to tell my story, so instead, I told someone else's story.

The general idea was the same. Both are about abuse and prejudice and what happens when girls are used for their bodies and how we're taught that we don't matter. I told this story because I thought people might care more if it wasn't about me.

At first, it worked. People did care, lots of people read it, and everyone talked about it. I felt I had a purpose. My stomach stopped hurting, and I could sleep for more than a couple of hours at a time. But then, people got angry and blamed me. That school board member said vile things about all Muslim girls, and I felt responsible, like I'd invited criticism that should have been specific to me rather than an entire group that was about way more than my personal problems.

And then everybody was so upset about Brady Burns, saying he was innocent, saying he's the victim here, saying it was all lies.

I'm not going to apologize. Brady Burns and his friends get away with mistreating and marginalizing not just Muslim girls, but all girls. They get away with it because people let them.

I had a choice: I could go after a guy whom society had also forgotten about, a shelter kid who has his own issues, or I could go after the basketball star, the guy who everyone worships because he can throw a ball through a hoop and he will live his whole life feeling entitled because of it.

Brady Burns is not innocent. I'm not innocent, either. None of us are. And now, my hope is that we can all start working on being part of the solution instead of part of the problem.

***

It doesn't take me long to finish reading Febe's piece. There aren't a lot of details. I'd thought she'd write an explanation of everything that had happened and why. Instead, this intense personal account of her choices and motives cuts right through me way more than a laundry list of past events would have.

I go upstairs to find Febe. She's in the guest room, reading a magazine. "Hi," I say as if I hadn't seen her just a few minutes ago.

"Did you read it?" She curls the edges of her magazine as if she's wringing her hands.

"Yes."

There's a heavy pause. "Well," she says, "don't keep me in suspense, Ms. Ford—I mean Hazel. What did you think?"

Taking a deep breath, I know I can't take back what I'm about to say. Just uttering these words is like signing my name in blood. "I think you should stay here, with me, for as long as you need, even if that means through graduation or even beyond. I think we need to figure out how to make things better for you. I think that, personally, I'm tired of being part of the problem. Let's you and me, together, find a solution."

Then, I don't know why I break into tears.

Febe stands and approaches me. "What's wrong?"

I shake my head, smiling and shrugging at once. "Everything. Nothing. Who knows?"

Febe laughs softly. "Okay . . ."

"Febe, would you like to stay here with me?"

"Yeah, I mean if you're sure that's okay."

"I'm sure."

I reach for her, and we hug as if we're both the last solid thing that the other has to hold on to.

CHAPTER 59

The next day, I make waffles, and over breakfast, Febe and I talk specifics. "I can apply to be your legal guardian," I say. "That will make it easier for us to make changes for you."

"What sort of changes?" Febe asks.

"Well . . ." I pour a bit more syrup onto my already soggy waffle. "I was thinking—how would you feel about switching schools?"

Febe frowns, but I continue, speaking quickly. "I live in the Minneapolis district. Patrick Henry is only a few blocks away, and it has a great reputation. Plus, it's really big, so it's not like you'd be living under a microscope the way you've been at Heights. It could be a way to start over."

"Wouldn't I be running away?"

"I wouldn't put it that way."

"How would you put it?" Febe asks, right as I pop a bite of waffle into my mouth.

I chew and contemplate my answer. "I'd say you're walking away, not running. There's a big difference. Besides, as you pointed out in class one time, it takes courage to reinvent yourself. It also takes courage to be strong and find your power. Luckily, you're the strongest, most courageous person I know."

She smiles. "I am?"

"You really, really are."

Febe taps her fork against the rim of her plate, studying my face. "What about you, Ms. Ford—or, jeez, I mean

Hazel?" Laughing, she shakes her head. "I need to get used to calling you by your first name. Anyway, what about you? Are you going to run away from Heights, or are you going to walk?"

"Neither," I tell her. "I'm not saying I'll stay teaching there, but I'll not let them force me out. Last night, after reading your piece, I felt inspired to do some writing, and I finished my own play about the Furies. It helped me remember some things I'd blocked out or forgotten, and I realized that everything that's happened since the accident is connected to the trauma and the lies people told me and the lies I told myself. I'm ready for the truth."

Febe knits her brows together. "Good for you. But . . . what if certain people aren't ready to give you the truth?"

I square my shoulders and straighten my spine. "Certain people won't have the choice."

As if on cue, my phone buzzes with a text from Olivia. *We need to talk. I'm coming over.*

A deep resigned sigh erupts from the pit of my stomach. "You should probably go up to the guest room," I tell her. "Olivia is on her way."

"Alright . . ." Febe draws out her syllables, emphasizing her doubt and hesitation. "Will you be okay?"

"Of course. I'm more worried about protecting you," I respond.

She smiles sadly. "Thank you." She sounds teary, and I realize it's been way too long since anyone has worried more about Febe than they have about themselves. This poor girl, forced to grow up way too soon, deserves a little looking after. And I'm going to be the one to do it.

"Don't worry about it. Just go upstairs, put in your earphones, listen to music, and get some homework done. I'll be fine."

332 BEAUTIFUL LITTLE FURIES

"Okay. Thanks, Ms. Ford—I mean thanks, Hazel."

She goes upstairs, and I wait for Olivia to arrive. It doesn't take long.

"Hazy!" she exclaims as soon as she walks through my door. "Are you alone?"

"Of course," I reply. "Unless you count Baby Girl." My beloved kitty is nestled nearby, sleeping in a spot near the window where the sun warms the carpet.

Olivia glances briefly at my cat, but her eyes don't linger long. "Good. I think it's time we come clean." Her long brown hair swings in its ponytail, and suddenly, it occurs to me that the hair I'd found on Vance's scarf could easily have belonged to Olivia.

Duh.

I take a deep breath. "I know you and Vance were sleeping together."

Olivia doesn't flinch. Instead, she sits opposite me on the couch where, for countless evenings, Vance and I had snuggled, me grading essays and him sketching.

"This will be hard for you to hear, Hazy, but Vance and I became involved almost as soon as you and he did. I think he chose you as his like," she uses air quotes, "'primary' relationship because you were a better fit with what his family wanted. You're artsy and erudite, and you have this pseudo-European look going with your pixie haircut and vintage chic. But Vance always felt torn between us."

Her words sting, but I pretend they don't. "I'm sure he did," I say. "So, why didn't you two just come clean, like months ago? You could have been together, and none of this would have happened."

Olivia presses her lips together. "I was waiting for Vance to be ready. But he's just so weak."

"True," I state.

She huffs like I've just condescended to her. "You have no idea, Hazy. You never knew him as well as I do."

I look at my hands folded in my lap. I want to know how she could pretend to be my friend while she was lying to me and sleeping with Vance and how both of them could so carelessly betray me. But if I get emotional and make accusations, there's no way I'll find the missing pieces to the puzzle. There's a fine balance between assertion and aggression, and I can't push her to her breaking point. The gray area in between is tenuous, and I must tread lightly.

"Please tell me what happened on the night of the accident and how everything fell apart."

"Why do you care?" Olivia throws out her hands like she could whip them across the room and smack me in the face. "You'd broken up with him by then."

My mouth drops open, stunned. "That's not the point!"

"It's completely the point. You didn't want Vance anymore, and you begrudged me for having him!"

"No." I roll back my shoulders, trying to stay grounded. "That's not true."

"Yes, it is! You've never been stupid, Hazy. Some part of you must have known about Vance and me, even if you didn't want to admit it to yourself. And then there was Annabelle." She shakes her head in disgust. "It's not my fault you started arguing about it all at the Christmas party."

"Well, it's at least partly your fault. You stirred the pot by posting that MySpace page. I saw Vance last night, and he told me that the photo is of the two of you and that you're the one who posted it."

Olivia leans back, making herself comfortable against the couch. "You can't prove that."

"Perhaps. But I can tell Jim what I think. And he'll believe me because of what happened at the party."

I'm sort of bluffing here. After talking to Vance last night, more bits and pieces are coming back, but they haven't fully crystallized. Still, I'd bet my lunch that Olivia was arguing with us as we left and that she followed us out.

Olivia's face betrays nothing, but her voice has a hard edge. "You mean how you guys sucked me into the argument? That was Vance's fault. You know Vance only stayed with you so he could keep living here with Baby Girl, right? It's that cat he wanted, not you."

I struggle but manage not to respond to that. "So, what happened after that?"

"You seriously don't remember?"

I pause, letting my mind reach for the truth. And suddenly, it's able to grasp something. "Vance and I were yelling, making a scene at the party until, finally, I insisted that we leave. I tried to get the keys from Vance because he'd had a lot to drink, but he wouldn't give them to me, and you . . ." I look at her, remembering clearly now. "You said, 'Just get in the car with him, Hazel. Let him drive. I'll follow closely behind and make sure you're okay. Then we can talk about all this somewhere private.' You acted like you were my friend, like you really cared, but actually . . ."

Olivia rolls her eyes and crosses her arms over her chest. "It's always about you, isn't it?"

"What?"

"I loved Vance, too! Why can't you grasp that?"

I train my eyes on her and use my most intimidating teacher voice. "You need to tell me exactly what happened."

CHAPTER 60

For years, Hazel took her for granted, and Vance lied to them both. At first, she tried to be a good friend to both Vance and Hazel, but neither ever really valued her or took the time to get to know the *real* Olivia. They got all the attention at school, and their "love for each other" was so pretentious and annoying, and she knew all their secrets and all their failings. Vance would confide in her, promising that, when the time was right, he would leave Hazel and then they would be together. When he refused, that was the last straw.

She didn't mean to cause the accident. She was just following them, thinking she could keep them safe on the ride home, and then once they all got to Hazel's house, they could have it out and she could convince Vance that she was the one for him. Hazel could finally be honest and admit that her relationship with Vance was over. Maybe she would even give Olivia and Vance her blessing, and the three of them could go back to being friends, like the way they used to be, only different.

She was fantasizing about the possibilities when her car slid on a patch of ice, rammed into them, and sent them spinning into an intersection.

Of course she pulled over to see if they were still alive. She's not a monster. Vance's face was all bloody and burnt, and Hazel was passed out. Olivia called an ambulance. Then she took off, hoping that neither Vance nor

336 BEAUTIFUL LITTLE FURIES

Hazel would know what happened, that they wouldn't rat her out.

The next day she showed up at the hospital to check on them, and nobody seemed to question how she knew to be there. Vance was coherent, his parents by his side, saying they were taking him home, that they'd hire their own plastic surgeon to fix his face. He asked his parents to give them a moment alone.

"I know it was you," he mumbled through swollen lips. "Not just the MySpace page, but the accident, all of it."

"You should thank me, Vance. Now everyone is going to feel bad for you, and you'll have a much better chance of getting hired back next year."

His eyes grew cold. "You can't be serious, Olivia."

"I'm totally serious. Let the dust settle, and don't cause any more drama. If you want any chance of getting your old life back, you'll stay quiet."

He thought for a moment, his brain synapses obviously slow from pain medication. "What about Hazel?"

"She hasn't woken up yet. When she does, I'll tell her you had to go. Give me your house key, and I'll check in on her and take care and make sure she never figures out what really happened."

Vance was too out of it not to comply, and that was it. Somehow, Vance escaped without really confronting either of them. So, she told everyone at school that she'd driven home that night in the opposite direction, but she'd been called to the hospital since she was listed as Hazel's second emergency contact after Vance. Olivia took over, taking care of Hazel, taking care of *things*, and not challenging her delusions because the doctors said it was better to let her remember stuff on her own.

She told the staff at school, out of consideration for Hazel, not to mention the fight at the Christmas party. It would just add more stress to an already awful situation. She called Annabelle, told her about the accident, and advised, in a firm but non-threatening tone, for her to stay away from Hazel and Vance. No need to gum up the works.

Olivia realized her situation was precarious. If the police put two and two together, or if any of her coworkers filled Hazel in, she could be toast. Thank God there were no traffic cameras at that fateful intersection and that all the staff at school was so Minnesota nice.

Now, Olivia's only mission was to keep Vance quiet and to keep Hazel in the dark. It had been easy for a while to gaslight Hazel, to convince her not to let her parents come, or that she was even more forgetful than she already was, or that, laughably, the accident was Hazel's fault. Lending her that gun was a stroke of genius; as long as Hazel felt vulnerable, as long as she remained freaked out, Hazel would rely on Olivia and would trust whatever she said to be true.

But then Febe started to get in the way, and no matter what disparaging things Olivia said about her, none of it mattered to Hazel. Everything was thrown into a lurch. It became a situation that Olivia could not control, and she really hated not being in control.

CHAPTER 61

I wait anxiously for Olivia to speak, my patience evaporating with every second she remains silent. Her lips are a thin line of anger and betrayal, and she finally hisses her words out of her mouth like venom. "I'm going to leave now."

"That's it? You're not going to give me an explanation?" I demand.

"I don't owe you one. I don't owe you anything."

My fists are clenching tight as I spit my words back at her. "I disagree. Seeing as how it's public knowledge that you and Vance had sex in his classroom, I think you owe me that and much more. Don't think I won't talk to Jim about it."

Olivia is a caged animal, her limbs spastically jerking out here and there as she paces the room in fear. "You want to know what happened? Fine. I'm sick of all the lies, Hazy, so here it is. I left the party at the same time as you and Vance, okay? I followed you to make sure you were okay. It's not my fault it was icy. And yes, it was me who rammed into you from behind with my car, leaving the both of you there while I drove off. But before that I called an ambulance! Vance had just dumped me; I was so upset. God! Don't you *get it?*"

Rage floods my head, making it buzz until I can barely think straight. "Why did you lie about it? Why didn't you just admit it?"

She looks at me like I'm the biggest idiot in the world. "Why the hell would I admit to something like this? I'm not suicidal! You don't understand what kind of trouble I could get into if anyone found out what happened!"

My mouth drops open, and I'm stunned into silence. Then, Olivia marches into my kitchen. I hear rattling and banging, and when I follow her, I see she's found the gun she lent me. My heart stops. Olivia whips it around and the barrel points at me, and I'm gasping for air.

"What . . . are you . . . doing?" I stutter, my stomach lurching to my throat.

"You never cared! You never even saw how much you hurt me!" she screams, her eyes wild and cheeks flushed. "This is for everything you took from me!"

It feels like a scene from a movie, but no, it's reality, and I swallow hard. I could argue with her, but she has a gun in her hand. "Olivia, I'm sorry," is all I can say.

"Right." Her voice drips with sarcasm. "Come on. We both know that you're not sorry and that you'll throw me under the bus the minute you can."

She strides closer and thrusts the gun at me, her eyes fierce with contempt. "This is the way it's going to be: you will go upstairs, and email Jim your *confession*, that Febe manipulated the photos, created the MySpace page, and that it was you driving on the night of the accident. You will take full responsibility, claiming you pulled a Daisy Buchanan, that *you* were behind the wheel on the night of the accident, and Vance was covering for you. This way Vance won't be blamed for anything, and I will be out of your life for good."

None of this is funny but panic and disbelief create a potent cocktail, and I laugh. "Wow, Olivia. A *Gatsby* reference? I'm impressed."

"Do not underestimate me! You always think you're so intellectually superior, but you're not." She arches her eyebrows, and for a moment, it's like she's the old Olivia, my funny friend who likes to give me a hard time. "Can you even explain what a postulate is?"

"Umm . . ." If I'd known back in high school that my life could depend on paying attention in geometry, I'd have put in more effort. I chuckle nervously, my mind racing for an escape plan. "No. Okay, you got me. But can you please lower the gun? There's no way I'm going to follow your instructions, and come on, Olivia, you're not seriously going to kill me."

She jabs the gun in my face, and her tone drips with malice. "You're probably right. But do what I say, or else I'll make it look like Febe broke in here and did all this. Everyone already knows she's unstable . . . You know how it works."

I'm startled by the creaking of the floorboards and, from the corner of my eyes, see a flash of a hijab. "Stop!" I yell, my voice bellowing through the chaotic air, trying to scare Febe away. But it's too late.

"I'm not the unstable one, bitch!" Febe screams. She runs into the kitchen and launches herself onto Olivia's back.

"Febe!" I let out a shriek of terror. They continue to tussle, and in an act of desperation, I lunge for them, only to find Olivia's arm still gripped tightly around the gun. A deafening boom resonates through the room as my ears ring with an intensity so great I think I'm going deaf. Miraculously, I'm still standing.

It's not until my eyes flicker to the corner of the kitchen that I realize someone has been shot.

"No!" Febe yells. I see her hunched over, crying, a small pool of blood at her feet.

Olivia sits up, stunned and probably in shock. "Give me the gun!" I demand, and Olivia looks at it in her hand like she doesn't know how it got there. She gives it to me without protest. Then I move quickly to Febe, to the corner of the kitchen that houses Baby Girl's food dish and litter box. "Febe, are you okay?"

"Your cat!" she cries in anguish.

I look down and see my poor sweet Baby Girl in distress.

She's been shot, but she's still alive. In fact, while she's losing blood, it looks like it's coming from her tail, like the bullet hit her right in the middle of the narrowest part of her body. I rush and get some towels and wrap her in them. "We need to get her to the emergency vet!"

For one moment, Febe and I turn our attention back to Olivia who can barely move. I say, "It's over, Olivia. Febe and I are going to get Baby Girl medical help, and you need to leave and never come back. We want nothing to do with you anymore."

Olivia says nothing but simply nods her head in acknowledgement of my words. Relief washes over me; she knows she's done something horrible and now she'll back off. Febe and I grab our shoes and coats and my car keys. "Wait," Olivia says hoarsely. "You can't just leave. What are you going to tell Jim? What are you going to tell Vance?"

I shake my head at Olivia, feeling nothing but pity toward her. "You should be more worried about what I'm going to tell the police."

"You'd tell the police? But then, what will happen to me?"

Wow. She really lives in denial. "Olivia, I don't care what happens to you. Just get the fuck out of my life."

We exit my house with Baby Girl and with the gun hidden in my purse, leaving Olivia behind.

Hours later, when we return home, Olivia has left, having locked the doors on her way out. She left my spare key on the kitchen counter, along with a note. *Sorry about Baby Girl. I hope she's okay. If you don't call the police, I won't bother you again. But can I please have my gun back?*

Febe reads the note over my shoulder. "Don't give her back her gun. She's way too crazy to be armed."

"I agree. But what do we do with it?"

"Keep it. There's nothing wrong with protecting yourself. But Ms. Ford—I mean Hazel—no offense: you need a better hiding spot."

EPILOGUE

Months go by. Olivia and I never spoke again after that fateful day when she shot Baby Girl. While our friendship is definitely dead, Baby Girl is still alive, though her tail is reduced by several inches. Still, I expect that cat will survive us all.

Meanwhile, Jim and I mended our professional relationship, especially after I confided in him about everything that happened with Febe and all that I went through after the accident. He gave me tenure and agreed to let me work part time after I received a grant from the Minnesota Playwrights' Center to have my play, *Beautiful Little Furies*, produced. I would have left Dixon Heights altogether, but he convinced me otherwise.

"You should stay," Jim tells me. "You're meant to have a long career at Dixon Heights."

Olivia and Vance did not receive the same treatment. After our tussle, Olivia never returned to Dixon Heights. Jim didn't give me any real details about her resignation, but later, Vance gave me the lowdown. He said that after he and I spoke outside that restaurant, he decided to do the right thing. So Vance called Jim and confessed to everything about the MySpace page, implicating himself and Olivia, but protecting Annabelle and clearing her name.

So, I stay at Dixon Heights, as does Cyrus. We keep our relationship relatively private, but we see each other all the time. Febe approves, which, I'll admit, is important to me. Now that I'm her legal guardian and she's doing so well at Patrick Henry High School, I only want her to be happy, safe, and secure.

"That's why I'm so nervous," I now say to Cyrus as we sit in the audience at the coffee shop where Febe is about to perform some spoken word. It's not even an open mic night; she's been invited to perform. "I'm afraid of Febe being rejected more than I fear rejection for myself. I'd rather stand up there naked, wrapped only in pages of my own writing, than see Febe disappointed."

Cyrus laughs and puts his arm around my shoulders. "The idea of you naked and wrapped in your own writing is super hot, but you worry too much. She's going to do great."

"Promise?"

He kisses my cheek. "Hazel, I'll promise whatever you want."

The MC for tonight's event comes up and introduces Febe, and almost instantly, she's on stage, standing before us, clearly nervous but clearly strong. "Hello," she says. "This is from a piece I wrote last winter, and it's dedicated to my mom."

"Look at me," she states, her voice confident, like a bell. "I am your girl. But I am nobody's cause. My grace came from you and the generations before you. When I was born, you didn't condemn me to be a beautiful little fool. I see through eyes that fight for clarity, I feel with a wounded heart, and I speak with a voice woven from strength. I come from grit, I earned my backbone, vertebrae by vertebrae, and I stand up tall, ready to take a tiny corner of the world to call my own."

I squeeze Cyrus's hand, knowing Febe speaks the truth, and yet, there's so much she still doesn't know. She will always be my family, there will always be more I'll want to teach her, and I'll forever hope that she continues to teach me.

Most importantly, I know that, together, we will continue to grow.

AUTHOR'S NOTE & ACKNOWLEDGEMENTS:

In the fall of 2000, I began teaching at Columbia Heights High School. I had no idea at the time what a profound impact teaching there would have on my life. The friends I made became my family. They celebrated with me in times of joy, grieved with me during times of loss, and allowed me to do the same for them. They mentored me, laughed with me, occasionally got angry on my behalf, and kept me sane every day, because teaching high school truly can be crazy. There are too many of you to list by name, and I know I'd accidentally leave someone out anyway. But if we ever laughed together in the copy room, shared gossip in the stairwell, if we ever cried together, went for happy hour after a long week, if we ever leaned on each other when we needed support, or if we ever shared outrageous stories during lunch, then this book is for you. Thank you, with all my heart.

And then there are my students. If I had you in class, and you read this book and stuck with it all the way to the acknowledgments, then I am deeply flattered, privileged, and grateful. However—I must include a disclaimer. It would be natural for you to assume that I modeled Hazel after myself, but I only wish I had Hazel's dedication and courage. Also, some of you might wonder if you were the inspiration for Febe. The answer is yes. Febe's strength of character, talent, bravery, and precocious wisdom were qualities that I saw in so many of you, and I never stopped being in awe. Thank you for the opportunity to be your teacher, and thank you for all that you taught me.

Finally, additional thankyous to Black Rose Writing for publishing this novel that isn't quite a thriller but is edgier than straight-up drama or women's fiction. Thank you to Shauna, Matt, Allan, and Mom for reading and/or proof-reading for me. And of course, thank you to Rich, Eli, and Pauline. I love you so much.

About the Author

Laurel Osterkamp is from Minneapolis, where she teaches and runs her blog, laurellit.com. Her novels have received awards and rave reviews. Her novel, *The Standout*, was a 2015 Kindle Scout Winner and was published by Kindle Press. In August 2022, Black Rose Writing published *Favorite Daughters*, which was inspired by the friendship between Chelsea Clinton and Ivanka Trump. Recently, her short fiction has been featured in Abandon Literary Journal, The Metaworker, Tangled Locks Journal, Idle Ink, and Bright Flash Literary Review. When she's not writing, she enjoys family time, running while listening to audiobooks, and reliving her twenties while watching shows like *Friends* or *Freaks and Geeks* with her teenage children.

Other Titles by Laurel Osterkamp

Note from Laurel Osterkamp

Word-of-mouth is crucial for any author to succeed. If you enjoyed *Beautiful Little Furies*, please leave a review online—anywhere you are able. Even if it's just a sentence or two. It would make all the difference and would be very much appreciated.

Thanks!
Laurel Osterkamp

We hope you enjoyed reading this title from:

www.blackrosewriting.com

Subscribe to our mailing list – *The Rosevine* – and receive **FREE** books, daily deals, and stay current with news about upcoming releases and our hottest authors.
Scan the QR code below to sign up.

Already a subscriber? Please accept a sincere thank you for being a fan of Black Rose Writing authors.

View other Black Rose Writing titles at
www.blackrosewriting.com/books and use promo code
PRINT to receive a **20% discount** when purchasing.

Printed in the USA
CPSIA information can be obtained
at www.ICGtesting.com
JSHW080003021023
49224JS00001B/2

9 781685 133399